OPEN SEASON

OPEN
SEASON

James Magnuson

DOUBLEDAY & COMPANY, INC., GARDEN CITY, NEW YORK
1982

ISBN: 0-385-17778-X
Library of Congress Catalog Card Number 81-43295
Copyright © 1982 by James Magnuson
All Rights Reserved
Printed in the United States of America
First Edition

To Hester

CHAPTER ONE

Mark came reeling down the mountain, letting momentum carry him, leaping deadfall timber like a broadjumper, crashing through thickets of willow and chokecherry, across the jumble of boulder fields. He was moving faster than he should have been, but it felt too good to stop.

Above him the slopes of the Tetons were still white, but around him everywhere were signs of spring. The creek was full now, the racing water carving fragile caverns beneath the banks of dirty snow. Shafts of sunlight filtered through the soft green of the aspen, burned his face with an intensity they had lacked a month before. Coming across an open meadow, his eye could pick up the first bits of color, gentian, Indian paintbrush, harebells and columbine.

Making a cut back in the trail, down into a stand of pine, Mark scared up a cow elk and her calf, the animals crashing through the timber below him. Mark was almost running now, the pack on his back felt like nothing. He caught at the branch of a spruce, swung himself halfway around, breaking his descent for a second. A flock of ravens flew up in alarm.

He didn't know quite where he was but it didn't matter. Delirious with the sense of his own liberty, he had avoided the familiar trails, left trails altogether to plunge down rock slides. He was somewhere in the jigsaw puzzle of national park, national forest and private land that made up the Teton range. Heading down, he would find the valley at one point or another. He would know where he was soon enough.

Coming back was always hard. Weekends in the mountains, Mark could imagine himself as free as a mountain man or a Blackfoot warrior a hundred years ago. But coming down with the reminders of civilization multiplying around him—plastic rings from a six-pack decorating a tree, a glimpse of flashing lights, far below, lights from the airport's new landing strip—the old feelings of strangulation came back. He was no Blackfoot warrior. He was a high-school teacher who put up with a lot more crap than he should have from a bunch of petty administrators just so he could have the chance to be out here. He was a guy with a halfway to nowhere relationship with a woman, a relationship he never knew if he wanted or not. Ellen was a good person, a gentle one, and yet there was some barrier they couldn't seem to cross, some difference that left them both, again and again, mystified and hurt. It was just too damn typical and there was nothing that Mark hated more than being typical.

Mark kept on, headlong, swatting away the branches of trees, splashing through spring mud. A marmot sat up suddenly, stared for a second, then flipped over the side and disappeared.

Mark came into a clearing and then onto the grassed-over ruts of tire tracks. He followed the old roadbed, moving more quickly, striding easily until he made a turn, and there across his path was a buck-rail fence and a gate with a chain across. On the gatepost was a metal sign. Someone had shot up the sign pretty good and the holes were rusting out, but it was still easy enough to read: NO TRESPASSING PRIVATE PROPERTY: VIOLATORS WILL BE PROSECUTED.

Mark stopped, shifted the pack on his back, considered. The buck-rail fence ran down into the weeds in both directions. He sure wasn't going to walk all the way around. The notion of private property could always get a rise out of Mark. He could never accept the idea that a piece of the mountains belonged more to somebody else than it did to him. Mark swung his leg over the chain and moved on down the road.

It wasn't quite the same as before. Mark was a little wary now. When a woodpecker started drilling into a nearby tree, the sudden staccato made Mark stop in his tracks. This was somebody's land, he didn't know whose, but private property was a serious matter to a lot of people out here. What privately owned land there was, still tucked in among national park and national forest, was immensely valuable, coveted, and zealously protected. To get hold of property like this you had to have gotten in a long time ago. Nobody had that kind of money anymore. The new money could come out and buy condominiums and ski chalets, but it was the old money and a few diehard ranchers who had a lock on the big places, the last corners of the real wilderness.

As Mark moved on down the road he heard the whirring of a helicopter. The sound grew and then he saw the blades cutting through the tops of the trees. He tensed, but kept up his pace. He decided against running. The copter was overhead now. They must see me, Mark thought. He stopped, watched it pass, and then as he turned he saw it rise, shining in the sunlight, tilting as if it were swinging back to get another look at him.

Reaching back with both hands to grab hold of the metal frame of his pack, Mark trotted into the woods. He pushed through the underbrush, glancing up, his heart beating quickly. He saw the gleaming blades flash above the trees and then disappear. He stayed stock-still, listening to the sound fade. When it was gone he noticed that his hands were sweating.

He felt a little foolish. They weren't interested in him; probably he'd made the whole thing up. It probably was the park rangers. That was what the sound of helicopters almost always meant in the mountains: a child lost, a fallen climber in one of the canyons, someone in trouble.

There were one or two ranchers in the valley Mark had heard of who used helicopters to herd cattle, spot strays and downed fences, survey their domain, pick up poachers and guys like him. Rumors were always going around town about unwary people getting shot back in here for cutting across somebody's land or fishing the wrong side of the river without asking, but Mark had never known anybody it had actually happened to. The truth was, most of those hard-ass Western types, the guys who would blow away your dog for running their cattle, were gone. Still, there were enough stories floating around to keep your paranoia alive.

Mark made his way more carefully now, almost stealthily, staying under the cover of trees, alert to every sound. Off to his left he heard the rushing of a stream. He moved toward it. The stream was full. The sound was louder below. There must be a falls down there, he thought. He picked his way along the rocks. The constant rushing of water soothed him, calmed him. He had almost gotten free of his wariness when he heard, somewhere below, the whinny of a horse.

Mark stopped in his tracks, but he did not hear the sound again.

He moved cautiously forward, staying close to the stream, climbing among huge, glistening wet boulders.

The water dropped away suddenly and Mark came out onto a ledge of rock. Across the stream, a horse grazed in a small clearing. It was saddled, reins loose and dragging. Set at the back of the clearing was a line cabin that looked as if it hadn't been used for years.

Mark stiffened, suddenly on edge again. He didn't move. He wasn't going to move until he figured out where the rider of that horse was.

The only thing that made sense was that the horse belonged to one of the cowboys up from the ranch, a hand riding fence maybe. But what cowboy would leave a horse loose like that? It was too careless, too slack.

Mark scanned the trees around the clearing. He saw nothing. As he moved forward a step on the ledge, he accidentally kicked loose some shale that tumbled down to the water below. The horse looked up for a second, ears perked, then went back to grazing. Mark stared down at the stream and then felt a chill spread along his back like a web. He'd been looking too far. What he'd been looking for was there, beneath him, sitting, back turned, straddling a boulder, right in the middle of the roaring stream, not more than thirty yards away. It was a woman.

Mark froze.

The stream raged around her. There was no easy way to get out to where she was. She'd had to climb from rock to rock, some of them slick and wet from the high water, and at one point she must have had to balance her way along a fallen, half-submerged tree. Mark wouldn't have done it. He didn't think of himself as a cautious person, but he had more sense than that. He knew what a fall could do to a person alone out here, how powerful that roaring water was, how dangerous a slip into that freezing stream could be.

She never looked back. The steady roar of the stream could drown out almost anything. Still, Mark had heard the whinny of the horse, she must have heard it too. Why hadn't it alerted her?

She was bent forward, she looked almost as if she was cradling something. Mark saw that she kept glancing up at the clearing and the line shack, as if she were afraid that if she took her eye off it for one second it would change or disappear. When she moved her arm slightly, Mark could make out the corner of a white pad; only then did he realize that she was sketching.

She was in an expensive green and blue down vest, the soft leather hiking boots, the well-fitted jeans, auburn hair nicely cut at just the right length. She straddled the boulder like a man. He couldn't see her face but it didn't matter. She was probably attractive, they all were. They had to be, to be here. The way Mark figured it, she was either the wife or the daughter of the man who owned the place, just the way she sat there, she looked like she belonged. Men who had land like this, very expensive land, had no reason not to be with attractive women. They could afford to make sure that their daughters turned out to be attractive women.

Mark felt the inevitable rise of antagonism. The problem was that she belonged here, he didn't. She was probably from New York or Main Line Philadelphia, she probably only came out for the summer, had money, thought she was an artist, they all did. People like that thought that the West was their own private preserve, latter-day versions of Teddy Roosevelt. She was out there doing her artwork while she left her ranch foreman to punch out the block letters on the NO TRESPASSING signs. *They* were the trespassers, he wanted to shout out at her, not him.

All the same, he didn't go away. He stayed and watched her. She kept on. She would sketch, look again, sketch, erase, look yet again. She gazed out at the horse, the clearing, the woods beyond, he couldn't be sure at what, but she was perfectly still, intent. It made Mark curious.

Mark shifted his pack slightly. It seemed odd to him that she couldn't at least sense his presence. He began to feel uncomfortable, a little like a spy.

The movement of her hand as she sketched was small, exact, forceful. Her almost perfect concentration worked on Mark like a lure. Without being quite aware of it, he took a step or two further out on the ledge, moving closer. The sound of the water racing through rock walls seemed to grow louder, more focused. She shifted slightly as if she was restless, drawing up a knee, wedging her foot against a rock. Her jeans stretched taut along the thrust of her extended leg. Mark pulled on the shoulder straps of his pack. He was uncomfortably aware now of the arching of her slender body. The churning water parted around her, the glittering rush of it grew more trancelike. Poised above her, his keeping watch like this was a violation, a threat that needed to be dissolved.

He bent down and picked up a rock. All he needed to do was roll it down the bank, she would turn and see him, it would be all right.

She suddenly stopped sketching and stared at what she had done. After several seconds she tore the page from her sketch pad. When she stood up, Mark instinctively stepped back.

She stared again toward the clearing, the line cabin, the horse, then folded the piece of paper, tore it, folded it again, tore it a second time. Whatever it was that she'd been after, she'd gotten it wrong.

She methodically tore the paper into smaller and smaller bits, then opened her hand and let the tiny pieces slip through her fingers, flutter into the stream that bore them swiftly down, over the falls. The paper was gone in a second. She bent to the stream to wash her hands.

The water roared past, but slowly Mark became aware of a second sound behind the sound of rushing water, the second sound growing stronger, then recognizable, the dull thudding of the helicopter. The woman heard it too.

She turned quickly, looking up, and it was then that she saw him. Mark stood exposed on the open rock.

Her gaze did not waver.

She rose slowly from her kneeling position to face him. Mark was too taken aback to even judge whether she was attractive or unattractive, but her look was extraordinary. The most extraordinary thing about it was that she gave no indication of surprise, as if she had known all along that he was there. She had caught him spying, yet she gave no sign of anger.

There was neither invitation nor rejection in her gaze, but there was a kind of penetration, strength. For a second it was so confusing that Mark thought that he'd been mistaken, she hadn't seen him.

The beating of the helicopter grew louder, closer, more alarming. His hand was still closed tight around the rock. He should speak to her.

The roar of the water enveloped them both. He felt his throat tighten. She wouldn't hear him even if he shouted.

He stepped back without a word or sign, his hand clenched around the small, now warm stone, and then, for motives at that moment obscure to him, he turned and fled, plunging down through the spring forest, blindly breaking a path where there had been none before.

Chapter Two

The mountains sat up there, ringing the town, razor-edged against the sky, cool and taunting and out of reach. There was no way Mark was going to get to them, not today. He strode quickly through the meandering, gawking tourists, brushing some of the sawdust from his jeans, clenched his fists over fresh blisters. His face was grim.

The town of Jackson, Wyoming, had its swagger back. After a winter of heavy snows, a late runoff, the battle with mud and black flies, the slow retreat of the elk off the refuge back into the high country, summer had finally come. It was Jackson's time to make it.

All winter long, sitting in the coffee shop at the Wort Hotel, Mark had listened to the refrain of his friends: "If only I had a nickel for every tourist that comes through this place in the summer . . ." To get that nickel they peddled soft-focus wildlife photomurals, buffalo burgers, silver pins in the shape of the Tetons, organized Western writers conferences, led tours of the high country by helicopter, on horseback, in jeeps. All winter long, Mark had laughed at them, made fun. Not everybody appreciated the laughter. Who do you think you are anyway? A high-school teacher taking home ten grand a year, acting like you're too pure to make a buck? Let's see where your moral indignation gets you.

June came and Mark had his comeuppance. He had refused, as usual, to make plans, and so he had ended up making furniture for Patrick Murray, ex-communard and small-time capitalist, ended up in a Rocky Mountain sweatshop banging together rustic cabinets for four dollars an hour. Half a day's work and he'd already mashed a fingernail on his left hand.

Mark sidestepped a freckly-faced eight-year-old in Indian headdress and red Converse sneakers, then slipped between two slouch-shouldered, long-haired backpackers. Mark spied Jack Wescott leaning in the door of the Cowboy Bar, all duded up in fancy chaps and black ten-gallon hat. Jack was there to collect the cover charge, now that the season had started. The sound of Willie Nelson drifted out into the street. Mark didn't feel like talking to Jack. The summer comes, Mark thought, and we all turn into a bunch of clowns. It made him sad.

Mark stepped off the boardwalk. Across the street, in front of
Fitzpatrick's Whitewater and Scenic Float Trips, sat the first cara-
van of the season. The giant rubber rafts ballooned out behind
their vans. A stack of orange life preservers sat next to one of the
rafts. A couple dozen tourists stood by, some sitting patiently on the
curb, faces lifted to the Wyoming sun, others leaning against
nearby cars, chatting, trading stories, all of them looking a little
aimless and good-humored, waiting to be led.

Set among them, Tommy O'Donnell looked like all the hero anybody could ever want. He was standing up on one of the rafts,
yanking straps tight, and talking over his shoulder to two blond
twenty-year-old women. He had them laughing. He scowled at
them, pretending to be offended at something they said. They
laughed some more. He pulled down on his form-fitting black
rubber vest and sprang easily to the ground. What a honcho, Mark
thought, laughing to himself, what a show-off.

Mark cut across the street, loping quickly in front of a slow-moving Winnebago camper with Minnesota plates.

Tommy saw him coming and raised a hand in greeting.

"Hey, man, how you doin'?" Tommy leaned out and clasped
Mark's hand.

Mark eyed the two women, saying nothing. Tommy's gaze faltered, but only for a second.

"You know where they're from, Mark? Take a guess." Mark
didn't want to. "California. Tarzana, is that what you girls said?
You ever heard of a place called Tarzana, Mark? They drove the
whole way, that's one hell of a trip. You've got to admire somebody
that drove all the way from Tarzana. I know *I* do." One of the
women laughed. Tommy winked at her. "I'm going to show them a
little Snake River whitewater this afternoon." Tommy picked up an
armful of orange life preservers and tossed them into the back of
the nearest van. "What can I do for you, man?"

"Judy asked me to come by," Mark said.

Tommy froze for a second, his smile suddenly became a little
hard.

An elderly white-haired woman with a grandson in hand tugged
at Tommy's elbow. "Excuse me, sir, but could you tell me how
rough the water's going to be?"

"Ma'am, I've got no way of knowing that."

"Is this the scenic trip?"

"No, ma'am. This is the whitewater. Excuse me for a second,

won't you?" Tommy took Mark by the arm and drew him aside. "So what does she want?"

"She doesn't want anything. She was having trouble with her car, so she had to take yours."

"Well, hell . . ." Tommy pulled at his nose, put his hands on his hips and squinted down the street in exasperation. "I don't know what it is that she keeps doing to that car, man. It's like pouring money down a hole. Really, Mark."

"It's not her fault, Tommy. That car's ten years old. Come by later, I'll give you a ride home."

Tommy glanced back over his shoulder at the two women from Tarzana. One of them cocked her head, smiled brilliantly, and Tommy raised his eyebrows back at her, grinning. "Oh, God," Tommy said under his breath, "summer's incredible, isn't it? Really incredible. Who can resist it?"

"A person can try," Mark said. He said it gently enough, but Tommy picked up the reproach. He had a sure instinct for when he was being judged.

"You're sounding more like a high-school teacher all the time, you know? I had a coach once who sounded just like you."

"Sometimes, man, you are impossible to talk to," Mark said.

There was a silence between the two men. It was always like this between them, a rough joking that wasn't really joking, that could hurt. There was always an edge to things, an edge that could be either affection or anger, or both. Tommy patted Mark on the shoulder.

"All the same, I appreciate your trying. Just that I've got to get back to work. And don't worry about me. I'll find a ride on my own."

Tommy turned back to the anxious grandmother, put a reassuring hand on her shoulder. Mark waited a second, watching his friend, till he saw that there was nothing more to say, then headed on.

Mark broke out into a jog. He was late, Ellen would be waiting for him.

Mark turned in at St. Michael's Episcopal, the old stone church hidden from the street by a row of spruce trees. Set off a hundred yards from the church was the Teton School of the Arts, which, despite the brightly painted sign, still looked more like the parsonage it had originally been.

Mark flung open the door and stepped inside. It took his eyes a second to adjust to the darkness. The place smelled alternately of old moldy carpets and fresh paint. There was the sound of a piano playing a slightly off-key Debussy.

The swinging glass doors to the rehearsal hall were still shut. A mother sat on a bench, reading a book. Mark didn't bother to look at her, went instead to the glass doors and peered inside.

A dozen girls, seven to twelve, all in leotards, twirled uncertainly across the waxed floor like fledgling swans, their arms raised above their heads. Ellen moved back and forth among them, talking quietly to one, straightening the back of another.

Mark stood watching her. He tried to imagine what it would be like if he were seeing her for the first time. Her face was lovely right now, flushed with exercise, her light-blue eyes, her blond hair cut short and framing her clean, open features. Everything about her spoke of strength and patience—the squared shoulders, the tapering waist, the knotted bare feet of the dancer. She never looked up from her work, her gentle hands shaping a child's arm into position, lowering a child's shoulder. All those things Mark knew well, and yet today he found that patience put him on edge. The class was running over. Her patience was making him late.

He turned back and there she was, watching him. The woman sitting on the bench was the woman he had seen on the mountain, sketching by the stream. She put her book down on her lap. Mark thought he saw a trace of amusement on her lips.

He stared. He was too taken aback to do anything else. She had a slender, boyish figure in blue jeans and a simple green sweater. Mark guessed that she was in her mid-thirties, but there was something very young about her face, something very open. On her left wrist was a silver bracelet, a single curved strand that didn't quite make it all the way around, but ended instead in two elegant droplets.

"Are you waiting for a child?" she asked.

"A teacher," he said.

"Aren't we all?" she said.

Mark laughed and she smiled back at him. He wondered if she recognized him. Her face came alive when it was animated, it was nice. His first impression of her, on the mountain, had been wrong, Mark could see that now.

The outside door opened and a large, middle-aged woman in a bulky white sweater poked her head in. Once she saw the class was still in session, she looked curiously at Mark and the woman sitting on the bench, shrugged and let the door slam shut again.

The piano stopped for a second. Mark turned, thinking the class was over, but when he glanced inside he saw that Ellen was illustrating a tendu for the class, showing how the foot should be placed. The girls obediently tried to follow. Ellen nodded to the pianist and the music began again.

Mark turned back to the woman on the bench. She waited for him to speak. Attractive women can do that, Mark thought, they're that sure, they know they can wait.

"One of these kids is yours?" he asked.

"Yes."

"Which one?"

The woman stood and came to the glass doors. "There. The very straight-backed one on the end. With the ponytail."

"And the New York City Ballet t-shirt," Mark said.

"Her name's Sarah," the woman said.

"She's good."

"We think so."

"We do?"

"Her father and I." She glanced up at him, something still light and playful in her voice. Mark wondered why he was amusing her. Maybe she did recognize him . . . but, no, it didn't make sense, she wouldn't be this at ease.

"Are you from here?" he asked.

"In a way."

There was something impudent in her voice that Mark picked up and gave right back to her. "What way is that?"

"We have a place we come to in the summer."

"That must be nice."

"It is."

Her gaze was more curious now. Mark began to feel scrutinized, as if she were on the verge of uncovering him. He didn't like the feeling. He looked back at the hall of young dancers.

"They're running late, aren't they?" he said.

"That's fine with me," the woman said.

"Not with me," Mark said. He'd told Patrick he'd be back from lunch by one. It was almost twelve-thirty now.

"No?" she asked.

"No," Mark said. The woman waited for him to explain, but he wasn't going to. "Where's your place?" he asked.

"North of town. Past the airport turnoff. The Red Willow Ranch."

"It's beautiful up there."

"You know it?" she asked. She remembers, Mark thought, she's just playing with me.

"I know the area."

"And what do you do?"

"At the moment I'm making cabinets."

"But what do you really do?"

"Really do? Does everybody have to have something they really do?" Mark was starting to enjoy sparring with her, he found himself rising to the challenge.

"I think so, yes."

"And I suppose you have something you really do?"

"Yes."

"Well, good for you." She smiled, quizzically. She wasn't sure quite how to take him. "I'm perfectly serious. I'm Mark Erickson."

"I'm Barbara Campbell." She extended her hand. Mark took it.

Mark decided to take a chance. "I think I've seen you before," he said.

"I know you did," she said.

Mark felt his face warm quickly, but he was saved by the door bursting open. The young dancers stampeded out, Sarah in the lead. The pretty, ponytailed girl leaped up into her mother's arms, whirling the two of them around.

"Mom, we're going to have a concert!"

"Who says?" Taking her daughter's face in both hands, the woman's face filled with sweet, totally unironic pleasure.

"Ellen says! And I get to be an Indian, Ellen said so, and you have to make me a costume. Is that all right? With eagle feathers!"

Sarah tugged at her mother and her mother looked at Mark in supplication. Mark laughed.

"Mark?"

Mark turned his head when he heard his name and saw Ellen standing in the doorway of the rehearsal hall.

"I'm sorry we ran late," Ellen said. "We didn't get started until almost eleven-thirty."

"It doesn't matter," Mark said. Little girls swirled around them, searching for shoes and sweaters and blue jeans, chattering and laughing and going up on point to try their pliés one more time.

"How was your morning?" Ellen asked.

"I managed to mash my thumb, but that was about all. How was your morning?"

"Fine." There was something cool, suspicious in Ellen's voice. She glanced at Barbara Campbell.

Unfair, he thought. He was being unjustly accused. Whatever Ellen had picked up, it wasn't true. That was part of the problem between him and Ellen, she was too alert, too sensitive to the smallest change in him, and once she picked something up, she didn't know what to do with it.

Barbara stood back, her daughter climbing all over her, smiling at them.

"We were watching all of you from out here," Barbara said. "You looked wonderful."

"Tell her, Ellen, about my costume," Sarah pleaded. "She has to make it for me, doesn't she?"

"That's between you and your mother," Ellen said.

Mark reached up and wiped the sweat from Ellen's forehead. "You've been working hard," he said.

"We should get some lunch," Ellen said. "I know you don't have much time."

Mark saw Barbara's eyes registering it all. She took her daughter's hand. "Come on, Sarah, we should go too. We promised your brother that we'd go riding this afternoon."

The pianist, a slight young man with a worried look and sheet music in hand, wagged a beckoning finger to Ellen. She went over to speak to him.

"We could buy some feathers, Mommy, we could do it now. . . ." Mark turned back to Barbara and her daughter. "It would only take a few minutes and it wouldn't be so hard to sew them. I could help . . ."

"We'll see, Sarah."

"That's what you always say, Mommy. If Daddy were here, he'd get them for me."

"I know he would, darling. Don't worry. He's coming, sweetheart, he's coming."

Mark looked down, smiling, and then, almost as if there had been some signal, his eyes rose silently to meet hers. Neither of them spoke or smiled. It was a look so grave, so inappropriate, it needed to be broken, deflected.

A little girl in a leotard hopped uncertainly on one foot, trying to yank on her cowboy boot. Mark put out a hand to steady her.

"It was nice meeting you," Barbara said.

"Nice meeting you," Mark said.

She moved Sarah to the door. Her light, bemused smile was back again. Mark looked across the hallway of milling children. Laying on the bench was her paperback book, a copy of *The Banquet Years*. Mark stepped across and picked it up.

"Hey," he shouted. "Your book."

Barbara Campbell stopped in the doorway and looked back. Mark handed the book to her.

"Thank you," she said. This time her voice wasn't so playful. There was the unmistakable note of upset, of something wrong. She looked down at the book, holding it with both hands, and, without another word, stepped out into the sunlight and let the door shut behind her. Mark turned back to Ellen, who was patiently explaining a piece of music to the pianist.

CHAPTER THREE

One of the reasons Mark liked Wyoming was that in Wyoming you usually didn't get asked certain kinds of questions, the kind Barbara Campbell had asked him. In the West, people didn't push for explanations. They didn't press to find out where you were from, where you went to school, what you really did. Mark knew all about those kinds of questions, questions of rank, position, money, family. He knew how to field them, how to deflect them, and, to an extraordinary degree for a guy who pretended not to give a damn, he knew all about what the answers meant.

How might he have answered? Quickly, without a second breath —he was a kid from Jersey, whose parents ran a motel and had invested all their hopes in his education, Mark had gone to Princeton and fallen in love with a girl named Kendra, no description necessary, the two of them had gone off to Yale graduate school, where Mark had floundered, screwed-up, ceased to believe, she didn't like the idea of living with a failure so she had an affair, he discovered it, moved out. There. All in one breath, over with.

The university had given him a leave of absence. He told his parents as little as possible, just that he was taking time off to work on his thesis. It was more than three years later, after a succession of bad jobs and false starts and stretches of lost time, that Mark headed West, to New Mexico where his friend Richard had a job with an engineering firm. Mark left with no plan, only a desperate need to change his life.

He stayed with Richard for a month, until Richard's girlfriend started to feel crowded, and then he headed north, found a job as a cook's assistant at the Taos ski valley. He stayed there through the winter, living in a tent. Even by Taos standards it was a little extreme, and that appealed to him. At times it hit fifteen below zero and there he was in his tent, reading Balzac. His parents wrote him worried letters. They still clung to the pathetic hope that he would go back and finish his thesis and they didn't see how anyone could finish a thesis while they were living in a tent. If he went back to Yale they offered to help him financially.

He had no intention of going back. The mountains had taken hold of him. He had never seen anything as beautiful as these mountains, had never felt beauty this intensely. The endless foldings of canyon and shadow, the desert stretching away, the cold delicate mornings, all filled him with a sense of the holy. In his exhilaration it was as if what happened between him and Kendra, the lost years afterwards, were small, dwarfish, confined and drab, they weren't even interesting.

Yet no exhilaration is perfect. There were nights alone when the wounds opened up again. He would think of Kendra and his parents and their expectations of him. Two or three times he called Kendra in New Haven, called her collect from the pay phone in the lobby of the ski lodge. He would tell her how wonderful his life was. She would be mildly skeptical. He would come back at her.

"O.K., maybe I'm not explaining it very well to you, but there's something real out here. It's not like anyplace else. I feel free out here and I never felt that before. I'm where I want to be finally."

Mark had a way of stating things that made them sound more solid than they sometimes were. He worked for a while in the kitchen chopping vegetables alongside the half-Hungarian, half-Cuban cook who cursed in three languages and threw food when things began to go wrong. It was not a liberating experience. He was not making very much money. Mark began to see how full of hype the Taos scene was. Everybody had a hustle, nobody was normal. The place was all ex-novelists running motels, video visionaries living off of older wealthy women, widows of Los Alamos physicists, every waiter was a would-be producer. Beginning with the ever-present turquoise jewelry, everyone kept insisting on overly ornamenting their lives.

By spring he knew it was time for him to move. He began looking at lists for teaching jobs in the West. There was one available in Jackson, he applied for it, drove a thousand miles in a day and a half to get to the interview, and was hired.

He turned out to be a very good teacher. He taught English and coached the junior-high basketball team. The principal, an ex-coach, was impressed by the fact that Mark had gone to an Ivy League school and could still be a regular guy and an athlete to boot. Mark threw himself into his teaching and developed a reputation of being outrageous and effective. Mark became a hero of sorts and he thrived on it.

Best of all, he was still in the mountains. Fall weekends he spent exploring, making long, hard climbs up into the Tetons, the Gros Ventre, the Absarokas, discovering canyons and rushing streams. He would sit motionless up on high ledges at dusk and watch elk drift out of the timber to feed in open meadows. The mountains here were different than those in New Mexico, the peaks higher, colder, more spectacular. It was music in a new key, but it was still music. The old exhilaration returned.

Mark stood one afternoon on top of Signal Mountain. All morning it had looked as if the valley was in for a blizzard, but now, unexpectedly, the weather was breaking. He could see it all happening from where he stood. He could see the mighty row of peaks clearing, see great white clouds come pouring down the canyons like steam under heaven's door. Everywhere light and dark were in motion. Far to the north purple blankets of storm still swept over Jackson Lake, yet he stood in the sun, around him fresh snow thudded down out of the trees in the sudden warmth, and below, on the aspen slopes, there were elk bugling, the sound eerie and wild, like panpipes, and at that moment it seemed to him that beauty could not be more extreme, that until now all his responses had been muted, his life somehow abridged. Mark had read radical theologians who talked of Christ coming to abolish authority, to shake the foundations, to set men free, but it was here, standing on Signal Mountain, that Mark felt authority fall away. Here he was above authority, what people wanted or expected of him was all down there. No one had hold of him here.

Jackson was not a place where people talked about their quasi-religious experiences. In Taos everybody did, and maybe that was

one of the reasons why Mark found Jackson so much easier a place
to live. In comparison, Jackson seemed almost down home. A lot of
people complained that it was looking more like a Colorado ski
resort every month, but there was still a mix of cowboys and
hunters and rock climbers and rangers, people who, for one reason
or another, loved mountains.

On weekends Mark would go to the bars and drink and listen to
country music, dance a few times with the local women, who gen-
erally paid attention to the real cowboys who kept their hats on
when they danced, wiry hard-stomping old guys.

In Jackson there were women who liked cowboys and women
who liked skiers and women who liked floaters. There was not
much crossover. Those who liked skiers wouldn't have anything to
do with cowboys, and vice versa. A cowboy who walked into a ski
bar by accident wouldn't find a woman who would talk to him unless he went home, took off his cowboy boots and his hat and put
on a turtleneck and clumpy ski boots, came back and pawned himself off as a new member of the ski patrol. As far as Mark could see,
there was not a category of women whose passion was teachers. It
didn't bother him much, not at first. He enjoyed himself, listening
to the stories of hunting guides and fire-jumpers and poachers and
old guys who had cooked up at the Rockefellers' ranch. It seemed
like a perfectly good way to spend Saturday nights.

It was on one of those Saturday nights that Mark first ran into
Tommy. Mark was standing at the bar when he became aware of a
large, muscular and somewhat drunk man in a flannel shirt staring
at him.

"Hey," Mark said, "how you doin'?"

Tommy glowered at him. "Hey. Hey, man, are you one of them
'cologists?"

"Cologist? What do you mean, cologist?"

"You know. One of them guys that don't believe in cuttin' down
trees."

"No, I think it's great to cut down trees. In the right places. At
the right time."

Tommy wasn't satisfied by the answer. "You ever rode a horse?"

"Yeah, I've ridden a horse."

"You ever shot an elk?"

Mark stared at the flushed, inebriated face. "Sure," Mark said.
"I'm the guy that shot Bambi's mother."

Tommy stared glassily, uncomprehending for just a second, and

then a slow grin crept across his face. Then it totally cracked him
up. It was the funniest damn thing, Tommy claimed, that anyone
had ever said to him. He put his arm around Mark's shoulders and
took him around, introducing him as the guy who'd killed Bambi's
mother. He bought Mark a beer, Mark bought him one. Within an
hour they were fast friends.

Tommy turned out not to be the redneck he had seemed on their
first beery meeting, but he and Mark were still an odd pair to be
friends. Tommy was a lot smarter than he let on, he knew a lot
about rivers and mountains and wildlife, he could be serious and
thoughtful, at other times boyish and charming, and yet Mark always felt in him a submerged and dangerous streak of meanness.
Whatever reservations Mark had, they finally didn't matter, because Tommy had decided that they were going to be friends, and
that was that.

One bonus was that Tommy's wife became as good or better a
friend than Tommy. The first time Mark went over to their house
Judy scarcely spoke. Tall, with long, dark hair, very pretty, dressed
almost always in jeans, sweatshirts and hiking boots, Judy could be
strangely passive at times, the sort of person who let people interrupt her when she was talking. She taught private music lessons,
and had more students than anyone in the valley. There was no
self-pity in her. If she knew about Tommy's compulsive womaniz-
ing she didn't let on, but she could be very inward and there were
times later, once Mark had gotten to know her a little better, when
she would speak softly of her feelings for up to half an hour without Mark having the slightest notion what she was talking about.
Over a couple of months Mark found himself warming to her more
and more. She was grateful for the simple fact that he listened to
her. She worried about his eating right, gave him vitamin pills
when he was sick. It was Judy, not Tommy, to whom Mark first
confided the story of his relationship with Kendra.

Tommy liked the idea of Judy and Mark talking. The way
Tommy thought about it was that they were better at talking than
he was, but eventually Mark became aware of a mild jealousy beginning. Judy and Mark continued to have their talks, but Mark
was a little more careful. All along, Judy had said that Mark should
let her introduce him to some nice women.

He met Ellen at a dance concert. It was something that Judy
dragged him to—dance concerts were not something that Mark
sought out on his own. Ellen was one of the dancers, yet it was ap-

parent from the moment Mark saw her onstage that she lacked the soul of a performer. Her technique was fine, even superior to the others, but she seemed so vulnerable out there, shy even. Mark felt the blood rise in his face watching her. There was a reserve about her, the suggestion of things not to be revealed to audiences.

Judy introduced them after the performance. They were surrounded by dancers hugging and kissing, flushed with exertion and excitement. The air was filled with extravagant praise. Ellen extended her hand to him, her face radiant, meeting his eyes with a level gaze. It was only a moment. She turned back to ask Judy a question. She was a woman who didn't fish for compliments. Two days later Mark called her up and invited her to dinner.

Their first evening together Mark would remember as being marred by awkwardness, odd silences. Ellen wouldn't remember it that way at all. Her most vivid impression was how easy he was to talk to, how he let women in. She was used to men who went on endlessly about themselves.

She was from a small town in Illinois, along the river, and she loved her family. She had married an up-and-coming St. Louis lawyer, a hostile and ambitious young man who did a hundred push-ups every night before he went to bed and made little lists every morning of what his goals were for the day. She was angry at him a lot, a little bit afraid, and yet he represented everything that she thought she should want. He was substantial, it was undeniable, his substance became clearer every day she lived with him. When he left her for another woman she was shattered. She took it as a judgment. She went into therapy, used it to punish herself. She wanted to learn all the worst things about herself.

She had come to Jackson to be healed. She and her husband had taken a vacation in Jackson once, she remembered it as being the loveliest place she had ever seen, and so, a year after her divorce, knowing that she had to leave her old life, yet without a compelling scheme for starting a new one, the idea of the loveliest place she had ever seen had a lot going for it.

She hadn't come to Jackson to be a dancer. Dancing was just something that she cared about. Teaching classes brought in some money, she liked it more than she let on, but she didn't know if she wanted to do it forever. What she wanted to do forever, she had no clue.

Mark was very attracted to the Puritan strain in her. She gained enormously by comparison to the California divorcees who came pouring into Jackson with fat alimony checks and top-flight ski equipment. In the beginning Ellen didn't know how fast she wanted to go with Mark. They hadn't read the same books, they disagreed about a lot of things. The way she used the things her therapist had told her to interpret the whole world irritated him. She didn't like him attacking her therapist. She was a person of utter integrity. She was also slow to trust him. There was a period, when they first became lovers, when she wouldn't let him stay the whole night.

All through the winter Mark wavered. He didn't know whether he wanted the relationship or not, yet they went on seeing one another. She seemed so different than him, yet she was the best person he knew. As she began to trust him more and, inevitably, to rely on him, her language changed. She ceased talking about the things her therapist had convinced her she should care about—expressing anger, freeing one's self from guilt, making demands, not being a victim—and started to talk more openly of the things she actually cared about—her love for her family, her sister's children, of the bonds of love and honor, care and obligation that weave people together. She was more concerned about doing her duty than she was about making sure that she wasn't victimized. Mark found that very impressive. It also scared the hell out of him.

He felt that she assumed things about where love should lead people; to marriage, to a home, to children. Mark wasn't sure those assumptions were unreasonable, but they made him clutch. At times she would have real depressions about never getting what she wanted, and he would talk her out of those depressions by inferring that he could change, even when in his heart he didn't know if he could change or not. It was dishonesty, and later Mark would resent her for making him lie. He lied because he couldn't stand her being without hope. When they talked of families, what he thought of was a motel near the Delaware Bridge, his father's motel, and of being jammed into an old car for claustrophobic Sunday drives. He thought of trapped people.

He was secretly very critical of her. Her angers and depressions were too much. She didn't know what she wanted. She didn't think things through. She was too conventional. Worse, she would come to demand a conventionality from him. Yet, there were times when he clung to her like life itself, like a buoy in high seas.

Halfway through winter, he was feeling as if something was wrong with him. He was wrong for not wanting the right things.

He found himself withdrawing from her, wanting to spend more time alone. He began to think of himself as being screwed up. He felt some part of him drifting out like ice breaking from the shore. He was haunted by the thought of having to move again, before he had taken hold. He had made the mountains into the answer, and now he feared that he was losing his grip on that answer, he feared that it was all going to come round to nothing once again.

Mark was a person who didn't like the idea of divided loyalties, what he wanted was to be an all-or-nothing kind of guy, and it was just that notion of all or nothing that worked like a wedge, driving deeper, splintering his soul.

One cold afternoon in March he stood motionless on a low bluff along Oxbow Bend, watching a band of coyotes battle a pair of trumpeter swans over a nest of eggs on the banks of the frozen river. The swans were overmatched. The birds squawked and wheeled overhead, swooping to attack with furiously beating wings the advancing coyotes. The coyotes trotted back and forth across the ice, never in a hurry, but always persisting. One coyote would advance and the swans would drive him back, but even as they did another was creeping forward from the far side. Coyote tracks were laced in intricate patterns across the snow, as if in some winter game of children. They were wearing the protectors down. The cries of circling birds were both mournful and frantic. Mark knew that all he had to do was step forward and the coyotes would melt back into the woods, but there was no point to it, as soon as he turned they would be back again, the thieves with their dainty steps. There was no way to ward off the inevitable.

Chapter Four

The bicyclists strung out in front of the truck, bending low to beat the wind. Mark edged the truck out to the left as he came up, giving them a wide berth. Lumber rattled in the truckbed behind.

"Base to thirty-two, base to thirty-two . . ." Patrick's voice crackled over the radio.

Mark yanked up the receiver. "Thirty-two to base, come in, Patrick."

"Where the hell are you, man? Over."

The last cyclist in the line looked over his shoulder, saw Mark coming, veered to the far edge of the highway.

"I'm on my way, Patrick. I'm on the highway, I'm almost there. I'm a mile north of Blacktail Butte. I'll be at the Campbells' in five minutes . . ."

"Step it up, man. We told them eleven o'clock. They're waiting for us."

The truck was even with the cyclists now, he could look down on their lean, t-shirted backs, the pumping brown legs, the long hair flowing out of their plastic helmets, the slender frames of their bikes, the bedrolls tucked snug behind the seats. It was what you called traveling light.

One by one the cyclists looked up at him as he passed. They all seemed a little bit wary.

"I'm moving, Patrick, so just relax, man."

"I'll bring the good Skilsaw when I come up . . . You got the metal brackets? Mark? Hey, Mark . . ."

Mark reached over and snapped off the radio. He roared past the cyclists, making sure he was well past before he cut back into the right lane. He saw them turn their heads to the side, their lightweight bikes buffetted by the sudden blast of air.

He honked and waved in his sideview mirror. They waved back quickly, almost in unison.

He watched them recede in the square of glass. They were probably heading up to Yellowstone, maybe up to Glacier after that. They were pumping hard now. They looked like they were in dynamite shape. He envied them their freedom.

Patrick wouldn't like the fact of Mark's snapping the radio off on him. He was probably steaming now.

Mark hit a bump in the road and heard the lumber bounce behind him. He glanced once more in the sideview mirror. The red warning flag fluttered out behind the truck. The string of bicyclists had drifted out to the center of the highway, fluid as a line of migrating birds.

The evening before, he and Ellen had floated a section of the Snake with Tommy and Judy. Tommy had, in his words, sprung them a raft.

Tommy had been running trips down the river all day and was muscle-sore, he thought maybe he'd sprained something in his back, but he was in top form nonetheless. With the four of them, when Tommy was up, they all had fun.

They had brought fishing rods, and though none of them were very good at it, Tommy pointed out the good holes, working hard against the current to get them to a hot spot, showed them how to lay a soft cast in under a bank without getting hung up. They lost more than they caught, but they still ended up with a half-dozen good-sized fish.

Ellen was in a great mood. She teased Tommy about his oarsmanship, he teased her back. Mark didn't know exactly the cause of it, but she was wonderful when the clown came out in her.

They floated on down, Tommy guiding them, effortlessly it seemed, in and out of channels as the river divided and regathered around sandbars and gravel islands. They glided past groves of aspen, past ranches set back off the river, past beaver dams and willow thickets. They only saw one of the huge orange float boats full of tourists. Tommy had great eyes and they were able to spot a blue heron stalking back through a stand of cottonwood, an otter swimming out in front of the boat. Periodically they frightened up mergansers, the ducks spanking low along the surface of the water.

Mark watched Ellen trailing her hand in the cold, glittering water. She wasn't aware of his looking at her. How graceful she could be when she thought there was no one looking. He felt himself fill with emotion for her. He only wanted her to be happy. She wanted peace, Ellen, that was what she always talked about, and for that moment, that was all he wanted too.

Tommy oared them into a sandbar. Tasks were divided. Mark went to gather wood, Judy and Ellen got a fire going at the base of the bleached trunk of a downed cottonwood, Tommy went off a discreet distance to bang the fish against the stones, skillfully gut them out. A gray jay flitted through the dark trees.

They gathered around the fire. Mark balanced on his heels, tending the frying fish. They all got up close for warmth; it still got real cold when the sun went down. An owl hooted on the far side of the river.

Everybody was hungry. They ate quickly, washing the fish down with beer, sharing a pie that Ellen had brought. Tommy leaned back against the cottonwood, looking tired suddenly. Mark lay down on his side, listening to the river whispering around them, the rustling of animals back in the woods.

Judy and Ellen talked quietly, Mark only half-aware of the conversation at first, staring at the dying fire. Judy talked about her piano students and how things always picked up with all the summer people and then, oh, yes, she knew she had something to tell Ellen, Barbara Campbell had called her, wanted her to teach Sarah music. It had happened often enough before, Judy and Ellen teaching the same students, it had ceased being that much of a coincidence. She sounded quite nice on the phone, Barbara Campbell.

Mark pulled up to a sitting position, holding his knees. "She called Patrick too."

"Patrick?" Tommy said. "What the hell can Patrick do for her?"

"She wants us to do some shelving and cabinet work, I don't know what all. They're building a sculpture studio. We go out there tomorrow."

"Sculpture studio? Well, la-dee-da," Tommy said.

"What do you mean by that?"

"Nothing. Just la-dee-da."

"She's an artist then?" Judy said.

"I guess so," Mark said. He leaned forward and poked at the fire with a stick.

"You'll probably enjoy that then, won't you?" Tommy said.

"I don't know what you're talking about."

"You get along with people like that," Tommy said. "People you can talk to." Mark didn't miss the reference. Tommy hadn't forgotten the conversation two days before in front of the float-trip office. Tommy looked across at Ellen. "He's not like us, not really. You know that, don't you?" Tommy flopped back on his elbows. "Hey, Princeton, hey, Tiger."

"Jesus, Tommy, what's wrong with you?"

"I'm just tired, that's all. I'm tired of these people who come out every summer."

"You better not be tired yet," Mark said. "The summer's just started." Mark looked across the fire, at the shadows flickering over their faces.

Judy, as always, was the one to try and smooth things over. She asked Mark something about Patrick, if Patrick was getting along with his new woman. She tried to get the conversation back on line, but the barb was in. They could be so close, the four of them, and then Tommy would say just one wounding thing. It made it hard to get close again. Mark imagined the animals in the dark woods, listening, waiting for them to leave, imagined them in another hour, nosing through the dead coals.

He and Ellen drove through the back streets of Jackson, on the way to her house. He'd been quiet all the way in.

"There's nothing wrong, is there?" Ellen said.

"No, not really."

"It's not that remark Tommy made, is it? That was just ridiculous."

"I know. I just worry," Mark said. "I just want us all to be all right. I want this to be a good summer. I worry when Tommy starts bullying people. I want Tommy to treat her right."

"He loves her. He'd never leave her, you know that."

"I know. I just don't want him screwing up."

Ellen reached out and covered his hand with her own. "I got a letter from my mother today. I want you to read it when we get back. Will you read it?"

"If you want me to."

The letter was there on her writing desk, in a light-pink envelope. Mark picked it up and opened it. Besides the letter there were a couple of snapshots of some straight-looking cousins of Ellen who must have just graduated from high school, to judge from the voluminous gowns they were wallowing in. Ellen went into the kitchen. Mark examined the pictures. Corny-looking guys. Didn't know they still gave haircuts like that. Mark heard the refrigerator door slam.

"Ellen?"

"Yes?"

"Are you all right?"

"I'm fine."

Somehow the edge was off the loveliness of the hour before. He would make it all right again, but later. He was just too damn tired and cold, his feet were numb from sitting in the freezing water at the bottom of the boat. He set the letter back on the desk.

"I think I'm going to take a bath," he said.

Five minutes later, she stood in the bathroom door. Mark looked up from the tub. She was waiting for something.

"Hey," he said.

"Did you read the letter?" she said.

"I glanced at it," he said. She gazed at him, expecting more. "I saw the pictures. . . . Those are some cousins you've got . . ." She turned away, upset. "Hey, what's wrong?"

"Nothing's wrong."

"Look, I'll read it later."

"You don't have to read it at all."

"I know I don't have to read it." He stared at her, utterly frustrated. God knows what he'd done now. "Look, would you get me the letter?"

"There's no rush."

"I know there's no rush. Would you please get me the letter, or do you want me to track water all over the living room?"

She left, returned with the letter, handed it to him without a word. Mark glanced up at her, but she didn't acknowledge him. This was going to have to be one step at a time. She opened a cabinet, took down fresh towels, put them on the rack, left the bathroom again.

Mark skimmed down the letter, holding the pages at the edges to keep them from getting wet, aware the whole time of the oceans of silence Ellen was creating in the other room.

He skimmed until he came to the part that mattered.

I'm coming on the 18th and can stay about five days. I hope that will be all right. I'm very excited about your concert and have told everyone in town about it. I know you're working hard, so much effort has to go into something like that. Tell Mark I'm looking forward to meeting him. I've heard so many wonderful things about him and I'm sure he's as fine a young man as you say.

Love,

Mother

Mark folded the letter carefully, tapped it against the side of the tub.

"Hey, Ellen?"

"Yes?"

"Come in here." She reappeared at the door. "You should have told me your mother was coming."

"It was in the letter." She reached down and took the letter from him. "I thought you would like to read all those nice things she has to say about you."

"I did, sure." He sat up in the tub. "All she knows is what you've written her."

"Is there anything wrong with that?"

"No."

"Maybe I shouldn't have told her anything."

"Hey, come on, Ellen."

"Maybe it puts too much pressure on you. You'll go into one of your declines."

She had hit the note upon which they usually started one of their fights. This was the kind of dance they did; no one's fault, exactly, just two people out of step. He knew what she was saying. He objected to the phrasing. He pushed himself up to his feet, reached for a towel.

"Come on," he said. "Let's not fight. We don't need to."

"You resent what my mother said, don't you? You feel it as a kind of pressure."

"Come on, stop it! I don't resent it. I'm glad your mother's coming, we'll have a great time. I should have read the letter when I came in, but I didn't . . . it still doesn't have to be such a big deal!"

"I was excited about my mother coming to visit, I wanted you to be excited too."

"I know." He rubbed his wet hair with the towel, staring distrustfully at her. She didn't look as if she was through yet.

"You know I'm not scintillating enough for you. I'm not intellectual enough."

"Oh, come on. You think I need to live with Will Durant? That's not true."

"It is true. You can deny it, but I know it's true. You're dripping on the floor."

"Oh, Christ, fuck the floor!" He threw his towel against the wall.

She looked down, folded the letter. "Sometimes I think I don't understand how you work at all."

Again he stared at her. It was odd that actually she understood exactly how he worked, and yet she would back away from that understanding. Anxiety could erupt in her at any time, but never without reason. She operated on instinct, premonition, and she knew when he wasn't fully present to her. Tommy's words haunted him: "You're not like us, not really."

"What are you thinking?" she asked.

"Nothing," he lied. "I was thinking we should go to bed."

In the morning sleep had done its work. Mark reached over, slipped an arm under her arm, snuggling close, kissing the back of her neck. She woke, rolled over to face him. She looked lovely, trusting.

"What time is it?" she asked.

"Eight-thirty." His fingers rested lightly at the top of her collarbone.

"You'll be late. Patrick will be upset."

"Patrick never gets upset."

They made love. He wanted everything to be all right again. He didn't want to be like Tommy and Judy, he had a kind of pride that wouldn't let him see himself getting caught up in the bickering and jealousy that other couples got involved in. He saw himself as being above that.

He wanted one intense act of love to restore everything, to stroke away the quarrel he still felt in her limbs, to get them back to the river, to that moment of grace on the sandbar. He felt her watching him as they made love, as if she didn't trust him quite, for a time there was a wary resistance in her, before they were taken, the way the fast-flowing currents had taken them.

Afterwards he ran his fingers over her flushed, serious face.

"I love you very much," she said. "Do you know that?"

He nodded. "We'll make it really nice for your mother when she comes," he said.

"I'm sorry," she said.

"Sorry for what?"

"Sorry for the way I was."

"Yeah? But I think I was the one who started it," he said. She smiled, took his hand away from her face.

"You'd better get up and get going," she said. "I don't want Patrick to be shouting at you."

Mark eased his foot onto the brake as he saw the gravel road that led to the Campbells just ahead. He didn't want to come into the turn too fast or he'd be slinging two hundred board feet of one-by-twelves all over the highway.

The truck bumped over a cattle gap. It was a brilliantly clear day. The house was set back on an impossibly green lawn with cattle grazing in pastures to the right and the left, and the peaks floating up behind the house took on a sharp-edged unreality. A light cool breeze coming down from the mountain carried the oddly magnified barking of a dog. Mark felt himself tense, he didn't know why. The sun brought up the smell of new pasture grass. A lark warbled on a fencepost just ahead of him, and then, as he drove closer, took flight.

When he drove into the yard a red setter raced out of the trees to bark and bite at his tires. Barbara came down from the house to greet him.

Patrick had called her to say he would be out within the half hour.

"I can get started unloading this stuff," Mark said.

"There's no big rush," she said. "You can do that later. Why don't you come out back and have a sandwich with Rob and me?"

"I'm not really hungry," Mark said. "Really, I'm fine."

"You're probably just being polite."

Mark smiled, put his hand on her arm. "Then you should let me be polite," he said.

"Really, come on. We're getting bored reading the Denver *Post*."

He let himself be led by her up across the lawn, past five or six pieces of sculpture, cool, curving bronze surfaces. The sculpture was well-done, it reminded him of Henry Moore and it occurred to Mark that of course it was hers, but she passed them without comment. When they came around the corner of the house, a handsome, athletic-looking man glanced up from his chair, rose to greet them. Rob was in worn jeans, a flannel shirt, scuffed cowboy boots, and there were dirt smudges on his face. He looked as if he'd been working. He greeted Mark as if he'd heard about him before. Barbara went inside to get Mark some iced tea.

The two men sat down in the lawn chairs. Rob asked the questions at first, nice, intelligent, polite questions, but Mark didn't feel like being pressed, even politely, and he started turning the questions back on Rob.

Rob didn't seem to mind. He was happy enough to talk, about what his favorite books were, about his childhood in New York, about seeing Joe DiMaggio in his last year as a Yankee, about his sense of place, here in the mountains and in the city, how each had nurtured a different side of him. Mark thought it was interesting to hear a man use the word "nurture." He sort of liked it.

Bees flitted around the sandwiches on the platter before them. The second time the sandwiches were offered, Mark accepted.

They had just started in on the sense of place in American literature when the screen door banged shut behind them. The two men turned to watch Barbara come down the steps and across the lawn, carrying Mark's iced tea. Rob watched dimly. He intended to go on with their conversation.

Rob talked on, switching easily from subject to subject. He talked about why European writing on finance and business was better than American, because of Marxism, because of the sense of class, and how, even from an adversary position, this added bite and analysis. At first Barbara interrupted with hard questions, quizzing him, then became quiet. Rob went back to discussing the West, writing, Perry Miller's class at Harvard. Mark began to warm up, to talk. He was interested.

Barbara sat without speaking now, smiling at Mark from time to time, then staring down toward the river. Mark leaned forward on his lawn chair, asked Rob a question about what he thought of Wallace Stegner. In the middle of Rob's answer, Barbara got up and went across the lawn to feed the dog scraps from her plate, making the dog leap for the bits of meat. Rob paid no attention to her, but there was a faltering of energy, a drop in the temperature of the conversation. Rob was not a man who liked to go unattended.

Finally he stood up, staring across at Barbara. He looked down at Mark, put a friendly hand on his shoulder.

"I should be going," he said. "Barbara, I've got to take off. Ike says he's seen that pack of wild dogs up in the north pasture. They've been getting some of the calves. I told Ike I'd go take a look."

Barbara came back across the lawn, the red setter prancing at her side, hopeful of more scraps.

Rob smiled steadily at her. "So," he said.

"I'll walk you to the car," she said.

Barbara accompanied her husband, Mark stayed put. Looking down at his glass, Mark listened to them talking about arrangements: who was picking up the children, a doctor's appointment, the garage that was supposed to deliver some parts. Watching the light playing in his glass, Mark waited for her to come back.

When she did come back, Mark was aware of the immense stillness pressing around them, interrupted only by a crow calling in the trees down by the river. He stood up as she came toward him.

"I don't know where Patrick is," Mark said.

She smiled. "You don't have to worry," she said. "Patrick will show up, sooner or later."

When she bent to pick up some of the plates, Mark did the same.

"So polite!" she said, mocking him. "It's nice. Why don't we go inside? I can make us some more tea."

Mark sat on a stool while she made tea. She asked him questions about his family. His answers were a bit abrupt and short. He watched her slender body stretching up to put some plates back in the cupboard.

"You don't like your family?"

"I love my family," he said.

She looked back at him. "Such assurance," she said.

"You don't? Love your family?"

"I suppose I do. I just lack the assurance."

It was easy for her to begin to talk. It had been easy for her husband too, but that had been different, that had been, nice as it was, a performance. This was more open and urgent than that.

She had grown up in Chicago, where her father had been a young lawyer. According to the stories Barbara would hear later, at the start of the forties her father had been the rising star in Illinois politics, one of fortune's darlings, making every step a correct one as he moved into the bright and inevitable future.

A year after the birth of Barbara he joined the Navy, another perfect step, Barbara spent her early years in a houseful of women, being raised by her mother, her grandmother and her aunt. The first stories Barbara remembered hearing were stories of her father's accomplishments. He died when his plane crashed into a mountainside in the fog on one of the Pacific islands.

Mark sat and listened, his hands wrapped around a glass of iced tea that he never drank. The kitchen was full of expensive, cunningly designed appliances. There was a huge crock of freshly cut flowers and, against the wall, a corkboard with notes and pictures and schedules secured with pushpins. There were snapshots of them as a family, eleven-year-old Jeffrey pitching hay, Sarah taking a bow in her ballet tights, her brother posing uncomfortably beside her, a shot of the four of them on horseback, all mugging, pulling out their cheeks with their fingers. In the pictures they looked happy and funny, yet the voice that Mark listened to now was a voice that, however stiffened by irony, was driven by sadness and a barely suppressed anger.

He looked up at her, met her eyes fully, held them. All the self-consciousness, the abruptness he had felt before, was gone, dissolved in the sympathy he felt for her and her story.

"What did you do?" he asked. "When your father died?"

Her gaze faltered and she walked across the sunlit room, stared out the window. She began to speak again.

Her mother remarried, almost too quickly, "suspiciously soon" as her aunt would whisper to Barbara years later. She married a very wealthy man who owned a lot of real estate on the North Shore.

They moved into a mansion in Lake Forest, where Barbara had a huge room that looked out on Lake Michigan. There were riding lessons, servants, and a stepsister to contend with. A year later, Barbara's mother gave birth to the first of two daughters she would bear her new husband.

Barbara had a miserable time in her new home. She hated her stepfather, who ignored her, and she hated her stepsister and two half sisters, who feared her violent rages. Her mother was totally at a loss as to how to handle her.

Barbara began shoplifting in the third grade and, after six months of remarkable success, was caught. The policeman drove her up to the huge house and was asked to stay by her stepfather, asked to stay and witness the most humiliating dressing-down that Barbara would ever receive.

Finally her mother, confused and weary of the constant battling, sent Barbara at the age of eleven off to an eastern boarding school, where she became, to the shock of everyone, a model student, the way she found to honor her dead father.

"And was your mother pleased?"

"I don't know that she paid that much attention. She had troubles of her own." Barbara touched the handle of the tea pitcher. "Do you want any more?"

"No, thanks. I'd float away."

"She and my stepfather were divorced on my fourteenth birthday . . . or at least that's how I perversely chose to remember it. He married his secretary." Barbara let a spoonful of sugar slide into her iced tea. "Indecently soon." She looked up at Mark and laughed. "The secretary was finally able to bear him a male heir. I understand it made him very happy. My mother has had a very difficult life. I always thought a lot of it was my fault."

The stillness of the room was shattered by the heavy clomping of feet overhead. Startled, Mark stood up.

"Bar-ba-ra!" came a loud, insistent male voice.

Barbara set down her glass and pushed herself away from the counter. "Oh dear," she said, smiling wryly. "Yes, Michael?" she shouted back.

Her only answer was a great rumble, as if someone was falling down the stairs.

"You were supposed to wake me . . . you broke your promise, sweetheart."

Bursting into the room, tucking in his shirt as he came, rushed a tall, willowy man in tennis whites. Seeing Mark, he stopped short and stared. "Oh. Hello," he said. He glanced back at Barbara. "I hope I'm not interrupting anything."

"How could you ever interrupt anything, Michael?" Barbara said. "Michael, this is Mark. Maybe you've met."

"I don't think so." Michael tugged at the bottom of his shorts, his eyes seeming to twinkle and expand as he sized up Mark. "Just because she knows everybody she expects the same from us."

"Mark's going to help us with the addition on the studio."

Michael raised an eyebrow, reached across Barbara and took a sip of her iced tea. "Where's Rob?"

"He's gone off to see about the wild dogs that have been getting into the cattle."

"Oh, God, the Wild West, I keep forgetting . . ." Michael opened the refrigerator door and peered inside.

"I can fix you something," Barbara said.

"That's sweet, darling, but I'm late. I was supposed to meet a young lady at the Racquet Club at noon and I'm late because you didn't wake me."

"After your performance last night, we thought you could use the extra hour or two. We only let you sleep for your own good."

"Darling, my own good has never been achieved by sleep. . . . However, working up a good sweat with a sweet young thing . . ." He smiled at Barbara. He was ignoring Mark, whether intentionally or not.

"You're sure you don't want to sit out in the sun and visit with us?"

Michael leaned over and kissed her lightly on the cheek. "Dear Barbara, you already have your entertainment for the afternoon, you shouldn't get greedy. Did Rob tell you that Kate called?"

"He did."

"So you know she's coming?" Barbara nodded. For the first time Michael seemed uncertain. "Just checking, dear. Always trying to be the responsible guest." He headed for the door and then stopped. "Damn! The squash racquets! Did Rob . . ."

"They're in the car," Barbara said.

He looked at Mark and shrugged. "Where would any of us be without her? Nice to meet you," he said. He rushed out the door and disappeared, letting the screen door bang shut behind him.

Mark looked up slowly at Barbara.

"He's an old friend of Rob's," she said. She went over and pulled the screen door all the way shut. "They met at Oxford the year Rob was there. He's a film producer . . . or, rather, he's trying to be."

"He's got the right style," Mark said.

"Oh, he's never without that. He usually manages to come out at least once a summer to add his own manic touch to things. A bit of a mooch, but he can be very charming, very funny."

"Mmm."

"Well, sometimes it's more apparent than others," Barbara said.

They were both quiet. They were in a different place than they had been before and they didn't know how to get back.

"Maybe I should try and call Patrick," Mark said. "See what's holding him up."

"You don't need to," she said. "Unless . . ."

"No, I'm fine," he said.

"You know what I have?"

"What?"

"I have a whole album of pictures. Of my family." He looked at her, a little surprised. "Only if you'd like to see them."

He smiled easily. "It would be great," he said.

They went into the living room and sat together on the couch, the picture album between them. There were pictures of her father, a handsome young man, standing next to Adlai Stevenson, then kneeling in a canoe, proudly holding his eight-month-old daughter aloft, then again, in his Navy uniform, waving from the prow of a gigantic ship.

There were pictures of great rambling houses, always set back from the road, often with a brook winding lazily through the grounds, porches where handsome young men in white suits posed casually, pretending to read their papers.

Barbara told stories to go with the pictures, and while the stories were fine, deeply felt, almost innocently told, it seemed to Mark now that there was something odd about it, some taint of illegitimacy that hung over them. Maybe it was Michael's slighting reference to Mark as an "afternoon's entertainment." When Barbara leaned across to point out a stepsister, a schoolfriend, her aunt, she seemed almost childlike in her trust, but now Mark wasn't sure that he had earned this intimacy. There was something being assumed that he did not understand. He was grateful for it, he was flattered, and yet, at the same time, he was suspicious. The more she told him, the more mysterious she became.

As they bent over the album, turning the heavy yellowing pages, he became aware of her leg brushing his. He wondered for a second if he was the only one conscious of it. It made him uneasy, doubtful, but no, he finally decided, she had to be aware of it too. Eventually he moved his leg away, even though part of him didn't want to. The only other sound in the room beside her voice was the ticking of the grandfather clock. He became aware of the scent of her freshly washed hair. They were alone, yet at any minute Patrick could come in, or the children, or Michael coming back, having forgotten something else . . . It alarmed him that he was even calculating this way. Christ, stop it, he thought.

He tried to focus in on her stories again, he asked her a question. When she didn't answer, he looked at her and saw that she was crying.

He sat there stunned, overcome with a confusion of desires, wanting to give consolation, wanting to make everything all right again, wanting to seize her, comfort, hold her, she wouldn't stop him, he knew that she wouldn't, she wouldn't have gone through this ritual if she hadn't known where it might lead . . . Yet he wasn't sure enough. He needed to understand more. When he finally reached across and put his hand on her arm, she turned for just a moment to face him, a sharp, deep look of warning in her eyes, and then she stood up and put the album away.

Now there was only the ticking of the clock. He sat on the couch, not moving, not turning to look at her as she moved behind him. Then came the distant sound of an automobile, moving closer, then the sound of the dog barking as it ran out to meet the sound.

Mark stood and went to the front window. He watched through the thin curtains as Patrick slid his long frame out of his car, then fend off the leaping dog. Mark felt Barbara's eyes on him as she stood at the bookcase.

"It's Patrick," he said.

"I know," she said. Her voice was husky with emotion. "I'm sorry."

Mark only glanced at her. He raised his hand to the curtain. Patrick stood in the yard, puzzled, staring at the lumber still piled in the back of Mark's truck, then, shielding his eyes from the bright sun, looking from building to building. The dog bounded around him.

"I'm sorry too," Mark said.

Patrick strode up toward the house, his long arms flapping at his

side, taking a quick swipe at one of the bronze sculptures that
gleamed in the midday sun.

CHAPTER FIVE

Mark didn't see how she could have fooled him that badly. He
fingered the small clay figurine of an animal. He turned it over
and over in his hand, slowly, like an amulet. Sunlight poured
through the windows of the studio.

The work was done. It had taken longer than Patrick had
planned. Mark and Patrick had come back for a second day, set up
a table saw in the yard outside the studio. It quickly became apparent to Mark what a novice carpenter he was. It was exacting work,
measuring, fitting and cutting, and Mark was new to it, everything
took twice as long as it should have. He got used to the whine of
the electric saw, the taste of sawdust in his mouth, the feel of a
shirt wet with sweat sticking to his back.

Working in the studio and the yard outside, Mark found his eyes
wandering up toward the house, almost against his will. It was impossible not to notice the comings and goings of Rob and Michael
and Ike Watkins, the ranch manager, impossible not to notice Barbara sunning herself on the front porch, laughing with her children,
impossible not to be drawn in by the playfulness of the slender
woman racing her children across the wide green lawn. Anyone
would have found a kind of beauty in it. She never once looked
down toward the studio. It was as if she and Mark had never
spoken, as if nothing had ever passed between them. For a morning
it didn't bother him too much.

It wasn't hard to envy their life. Rob and Barbara were attractive
people. There was a sense of constant movement and energy, and
with the pastures and cattle and horses and the dazzling mountains
behind it seemed like some dream of freedom and ease and abun-
dance.

Mark just didn't know how to read it. He hadn't forgotten the
talk with Barbara, the tears that had come out of nowhere it
seemed, mysterious, tears over that family long ago that hadn't
been a family at all for her. Remembering that talk changed what
Mark saw, made him skeptical. It seemed to him that something

was off, like a film running at the wrong speed, the words and the moving lips not quite matching. If Barbara noticed him watching her she gave no sign.

At noon, seven or eight people showed up for lunch. They were business types, the cars angled about the yard included two BMWs and a Mercedes. Mark saw a couple of the men walking toward the house in expensive suits, cowboy hats and boots, swinging hand-tooled leather briefcases at their sides. Patrick and Mark had no time to watch. They were working hard to finish up, Patrick was angry that the job had taken as long as it had.

Mark was out at Patrick's truck, looking for a new drill in the toolbox when the men came out of the house. They were well-fed and boisterous after their three-hour lunch. Michael and Rob were with them. The men ambled across the lawn toward the cars, toward Mark.

Michael, waving his arms as if he'd had a little too much to drink, held court. A couple of the men seemed almost dizzy with merriment. Others shook their heads, exchanged furtive glances the way men do when someone is willing to go totally out of bounds.

Mark watched them come down the hill toward him. He was in plain view, but they weren't really aware that Mark was there. Behind Mark was the sporadic sound of Patrick's electric drill.

The men stopped at the door of the Mercedes. Michael glanced over the top of his tortoiseshell glasses with the impatience of a man who knows he's got a good story going and wants to get on with it.

"So then Kate comes up to Garrett's wife and said, 'I've always wanted to meet you, I hear you're a wonderful wife and mother.' And Garrett's wife said, 'I'm so glad to meet you too, I understand you're a great lay.'"

Michael's audience convulsed with laughter, all but Rob. Mark stood motionless with four or five drill bits in his hand. A man wiped tears of laughter from the corners of his eyes, reached out and opened the door of the Mercedes.

Michael looked across at Rob in silent appeal. Rob said nothing, unamused, his face tinged with red.

"That's not really fair," Rob said. "You know that, Michael. You like Kate as much as anyone."

Michael paused for a beat, rankling at being betrayed mid-performance, not liking to be made to appear small.

"No, no, not as much as anyone," Michael said, his voice touched with acid. Then, appealing to the others, he said, "So forgiving, you see? He's always been so forgiving to these crazy, doomed ladies." Michael reached out and threw a series of jabs at Rob's stomach. "Soft, soft, soft."

The lid of the toolbox fell on its own. The sharp metallic clang made Rob turn, see Mark for the first time. It wasn't a welcome surprise. Mark could see the disturbance in Rob's face, the anger, as if Rob thought he'd been spied on. Mark's first impulse was to apologize, even though he'd done nothing. It didn't matter, there was nothing he could say. The sharp whine of Patrick's drill rose behind them.

The next morning Barbara called Patrick to say that one of the cabinets needed to be rehung and that there was still some sanding and finishing they'd missed, could one of them come out and do it?

When Patrick mentioned the call to Mark, Mark quickly volunteered for the job. He assumed that he would see her. His intuition was that her purpose for calling had to be more than just to get some sanding done; yet, when he arrived she wasn't there. No one was there. There was a page of instructions, very specific, addressed to no one in particular, stuck inside the door of the studio. That was all.

He tried to be calm about it, tried not to treat it as a deliberate affront, but what choice did he have? It could scarcely be a mistake. She must have guessed that he would be the one coming out, it required no great leap of imagination to figure that he would want to see her after the conversation they had had. What had gone on between them had not been ordinary, not something you forget from one day to the next. He was hurt and angry.

He was through now, there was nothing left to do except sweep up sawdust and wood chips from the floor. Mark was in no big hurry. Alone in the studio for the first time, it was his chance to explore.

At first glance no one would have identified that room as feminine, as a place where a woman worked. There was a sandpit in the center of the floor, a sunken furnace, welding tanks leaning against one wall, graphite crucibles, odd metal tongs and instruments. Set back at one end were the new cabinets, wooden racks and shelving.

Then there were her materials, scattered here and there, a block of smooth white stone, not a mark on it, bits of wood and wire, rock and metal, a wasp's nest, a series of animals in clay, different sizes,

pen-and-ink sketches strewn like leaves across a battered desk.
There must have been the beginnings of forty different projects.

Anger colored everything he saw. Another time he would have
been more sympathetic; this time all that stuff seemed like toying
around, most of it, anyway, mere dabbling. His critique was interrupted by the sound of a truck bouncing down the road outside.
Mark set the tiny clay animal back on the shelf, bent to the
window.

A red pickup pulled in behind Mark's truck and Ike Watkins, the
Campbells' ranch foreman, got out.

Mark knew Ike Watkins only by sight, had seen him around
Jackson some during the winter. Ike was close to a legend. He'd
been around Jackson as long as anybody could remember. He was
lean, tough, didn't talk any more than he had to, and the story was
that he could do anything, from delivering calves at twenty below
to jerry-rigging busted tractors with an eight-inch length of wire
and a piece of tape.

He stared at Mark's truck for several seconds, not looking puzzled exactly, just sort of taking it all in. He walked down to the
shed next to the barn, disappeared inside for a minute, then came
back out with a rifle in his hand. Mark watched Ike trudge back up
the hill. Mark wasn't sure what to do. He waited until Ike was pulling himself back up in his truck before he stepped out of the
studio.

"Hey," Mark said.

Ike looked back quickly, his eyes widening with surprise as he
saw Mark. The rifle was still in his hand. "Hey," he said.

Mark walked slowly toward the truck, feeling the need to explain. "I'm Mark Erickson," he said. "I'm working on the studio for
Mrs. Campbell."

"I know that," Ike said. "I've seen you in town." Ike reached out
and took a box of shells off the dashboard of the truck.

"You haven't seen the Campbells, have you?" Mark said.

"They went into town this morning. I don't know when they're
coming back. I gave up trying to keep track of them." Ike opened
the chamber of the rifle, started feeding the shells into the gun.
Long pauses didn't bother him. "You just about done in there?"

"I'm done now, actually," Mark said. He nodded at the rifle.
"You goin' huntin'?"

"Not exactly," Ike said. He closed the chamber and threw the
rifle across the front seat, looked back at Mark like he was consider-

ing something. "I got a call on the radio. We've been havin' trouble
with a pack of wild dogs."

"I heard that," Mark said.

"Oh, yeah? Somebody up the road says the dogs had one of our
calves down. I'm going up there to take a look. You want to come
along?"

"Sure," Mark said. "Let's go."

They drove back out to the main road, then north on the highway. Mark made a couple of stabs at conversation, but Ike didn't
seem to be in the mood. Mark rested the rifle against his shoulder.
It seemed a little strange, sitting in a truck with this man he didn't
know. It was nice too, riding with somebody like Ike, it made Mark
feel honored, like a kid who's been lucky enough to be included
with the grown-ups. The only thing was, Mark wasn't sure why he
was being honored.

They turned off the highway and Mark got down to open the
pasture gate. Mark let the pickup through, locked the gate behind
it, pulled himself back up in the truck.

"Thanks," Ike said.

"I hope I didn't surprise you too much."

"When was that?"

"Coming out of the studio like that. I thought maybe I surprised
you."

The truck bumped across the pasture, tools rattling behind. "Surprise me? Hell, no, nothing surprises me up here anymore."

"No?"

Ike's eyes moved all the time, scanning the wide field. "Hell, no.
They've got so many people comin' and goin' all the time, the
surprise kind of goes right out of it."

Cattle lay directly in the path of the truck. They got slowly to
their feet, faced the oncoming pickup warily, waiting till the last
second before bucking and kicking up their heels, giving way.

"Some of 'em, like you and me, are workin', most of 'em, just
playin' . . . some they invite, some just come."

Mark's feet were wedged in a corner of the floor, next to the toolbox, loose wrenches, oily rags. He put his hand on the dashboard
for balance as the truck bounced through a gully.

"You know this guy Michael?" Mark asked.

"He's one of the ones who just comes."

Suddenly Mark spied a spot of black down in the grass a couple of hundred yards off to the right. "There," Mark said. "I think I see something."

"Buzzard," Ike said. "There's a dead cow down there . . . Dogs got it last week. Might as well go take a look, see if there's any sign of 'em."

As the truck approached, the huge black bird flopped awkwardly into flight. Ike stopped the truck, surveyed the meadow. There wasn't much left of the cow, just a pile of hide and dark old meat in the tan grass.

Ike started the truck again without a word, veered off to the left, toward a high ridge. They scared up a bunch of young calves that had been nestled down in the tall grass. The young animals, tails flying, ran alongside the truck. The mothers that had left them to graze came trotting back from all directions, their heads high with alarm, bawling like foghorns, to protect their young.

Mark remembered Michael's story, the story he wasn't supposed to have overheard. "You ever met someone named Kate?" Mark said.

Mark saw the muscles in Ike's jaw working as his eyes moved up and down along the ridge. Mark held the barrel of the rifle tight to his shoulder so it didn't bounce.

"You know her?" was all Ike said.

"No. I guess I just heard somebody mention the name."

"No, I've never met anyone named Kate," Ike said. "I see the same kinds of stuff goin' on, summer after summer, I keep my eyes closed, I do my work . . . I figure it's not my place to say anything."

"But if it was your place, what would you say?"

"What would I say?" Ike considered. "Oh, I guess about all I could say would be, 'You poor bastards . . .'" Ike rolled down the window, spit, eyes squinting, still focused on the ridge. "They said the calf was down somewhere up in here. Hold on."

Ike gunned it, the engine whining as they lurched up the incline, Mark grabbing the dashboard with one hand, holding the rifle even tighter with the other, his feet pressed to the floor.

At the top of the ridge under a tree was a cow. As they drove closer, Mark could see the calf, sheltered among the roots of the tree.

They got out of the truck. The mother trotted off a few feet, then stopped to watch them. Half of one of the mother's ears was gone, all that was left was a bloody stump.

The calf just lay there, curled up, head down on the ground, the soft young eyes following Mark and Ike as they approached. Its black and white head was flecked with blood and there were traces of blood on the flanks, but no real signs of a wound. Ike stood over the animal, nudged the calf's belly with his foot. The calf still wouldn't get up.

"She'll be all right," Ike said.

"What about the mother?" Mark said. "Look at that ear."

The cow still eyed them suspiciously, switching its tail.

"Yeah, the dogs do that," Ike said. "The mother tries to keep them off her calf, tries to butt them and they get hold of the ears and gnaw the damn things off. Nothing we can do for 'em. Let's go."

They got back in the truck, drove slowly along the ridge, looking down into the wooded ravine for dogs. Ike was silent. Mark wondered if Ike intended to tell him anything more. He felt as if Ike, in his way, had been trying to let him know something. That was the problem with these old-time Westerners, nicest people in the world, but they were just too damn cryptic.

"I didn't know that dogs were such a big problem," Mark said.

"Oh, yeah. More and more."

"Why is that?"

"Ain't the dogs' fault. The thing of it is, people don't think about the consequences of things. They don't think ahead. All they think about is how nice it would be to have a dog out here for the summer. Fall comes, the idea of bringing this dog back to their apartment, it doesn't seem so great. So they just turn the dog loose . . . Take any animal, you stop feedin' it, it goes wild . . . They start killing calves . . . get the mother when she's down in the field delivering, and the calf too, just as it's being born . . . these dogs get together in packs, they'll go right through a herd of cattle. You take that little calf back there, one of them dogs will get at each end, they'll shake the hell out of that calf, they'll tear it in two . . . And I'm the bad guy who gets to go out and shoot the sweet little animals."

"I don't see how you'd ever find 'em."

"It ain't as hard as you'd think. Hunger makes any animal go a little simpleminded."

They drove on in silence. Mark stared down through the trees, the light trunks of the aspens flitted by. It seemed like an impossible task, spotting anything out here, there was too much territory to cover, the dogs could be in the next county by now. Then suddenly Mark saw something white at the bottom of the ravine, his heart leaped for a second, but then he thought no, it must just be a trick of the light, it's probably just a stump, Ike's probably seen it already, no point in embarrassing myself. Then, as they drove slowly on, Mark saw the white shape move.

"Hey, this time I do see something," Mark said. Ike put on the brakes. "Back up. I think I saw a dog." Without a word, Ike jammed the pickup in reverse.

"Damn right it's a dog," Ike said. "Ain't just one of them down there, either. Hell, there's one, two . . . four of 'em down there. See 'em? Up five, ten yards from the white dog, behind the tree there."

Ike was right. There was a little black-and-white slick-haired dog, the one Mark had spotted, and then further up the hill, resting against a tree, was a collie, a big tan mongrel, and another dog that looked part shepherd. They were all alert now, head and ears up, aware that the truck had stopped.

Ike reached slowly for the rifle. The tan mongrel got up and trotted over the top of the hill with tiny coyote-like steps. Ike raised the rifle to the open window, balanced it on the glass. The shepherd got slowly to its feet and followed the mongrel back into the trees.

The little black-and-white dog was on its feet too, but came forward a few steps, then stopped, confused, tail wagging, looked back toward the other dog. The collie hadn't moved.

The shot rang out. There was a pinging sound as the ejected cartridge ricocheted off the inside of the truck's windshield.

The black-and-white dog yelped and did a complete three-sixty flip in the air.

The collie was up and running. Ike fired again, the shot going high, plowing into the side of the hill. The dog darted down toward the bottom of the ravine, its tail low like a running fox, and Ike fired again. The dog fell, howling, got up and ran again, leaped a log, Ike fired a fourth time, the bullet rattling through a thicket. There was no more sound.

Ike and Mark worked their way down into the ravine, sliding on the steep slope. A jay was calling in a nearby tree. They found the blood spot where the collie had been hit. They followed the spattered trail of blood and then Mark saw the pile of intestines, just on the far side of the log. They were bright pink on the forest floor.

"Gut shot," Ike said somberly. "He can't be far." Ike walked on, pushing the brambles out of the way with his rifle barrel. "There he is."

Mark looked where Ike pointed. The collie lay on its side, dead. There was a huge wound where the bullet had torn the intestines out of it, and yet the animal had staggered up for one more desperate leap. The eyes were still moist, they still looked alive. Mark reached down and touched the warm body, instinctively gave it a pat.

He stood up, gave Ike a strained smile. He could see the body of the little black-and-white dog fifty yards away, further up the hill. Ike stared at the ridge line, searching for some sign of the other two dogs. Mark looked down at his hands. There was blood on them. He reached up and wiped his fingers on the long needles of a pine. Ike looked back at him, then turned the body of the dead collie over with his rifle barrel.

"That's it. That's the sad part, the ones that always catch it are the ones that aren't quite wild enough yet."

Chapter Six

Barbara no longer held the same charged position in Mark's mind that she had before. Part of the reason was circumstance. Ellen's mother arrived, a small woman of immense energy and evident confidence, and both Mark and Ellen were busy entertaining her.

Mark hit it off with Mrs. Hargreaves, despite the fact that he was inevitably being viewed with certain assumptions in mind: here was someone to make her daughter happy, a possible son-in-law, a father to grandchildren. Mark was afraid of being falsely advertised.

As the week went on, Ellen became totally taken up with rehearsals for the dance concert and Mark tried to be of whatever help he could, from running the tape recorder and quieting the eight-year-old dancers as they waited their turns onstage to driving around town tacking up posters.

The main reason for his changed attitude toward Barbara, however, was that he felt snubbed. The solitary morning of work in her studio, her failure to appear, the odd and slightly ominous conversation with Ike Watkins had thrown a new cast on things. Whatever had been vibrant, intriguing before had been reduced to the cold familiarity of a cliché: an upper-class married woman, intelligent, attractive, privileged, of wandering attention, spending some of her time fooling around with younger men, adding some diversion to an otherwise too easy life. It was the kind of thing Mark had heard of before. Mostly he had heard it from his roommates at Princeton, talking about their mothers' affairs, confessing late at night, usually after a bit too much to drink, speaking cynically about the way the world was.

Mark disliked the idea of participating in any such tawdry archetype. He felt a little depressed, a little taken in, but mostly he felt turned off. He had thought he had achieved a kind of intimacy with her. In fact, he realized bitterly now, all that had happened was that he had been charmed. It had been nothing more than an afternoon's flirtation. A dent had been put in his erotic imagination.

There was still enough of a charge there, however, that during the dance rehearsals Mark found himself intently watching Sarah. She was one of Ellen's best dancers, moving with energy and almost total abandon. To Mark she seemed so innocent and eager, so sure of her world. Watching the small graceful girl leap and run, Mark was filled with sadness. He imagined her in ten years, telling her college roommates stories, cynical and self-pitying, about the way the world was. Yet even as he imagined that, he knew that his imagining was a kind of cruelty, a kind of revenge that he was taking on her mother, a revenge for what her mother had awakened in him. Mark turned his eyes from her, ashamed, stared down at the spinning reels of the tape recorder. Outlaw music, outlaw thoughts.

On Friday night, the night before the dance concert, Mark and Ellen and her mother went to the rodeo.

Everything was in full swing by the time they arrived. Mark led Ellen and Mrs. Hargreaves through the tough young guys in their tractor hats and down vests, past the three old cowboys huddled over their cooler, past the knot of teen-agers sharing a bottle of wine with their dates. Ellen and her mother were absorbed in their own conversation and didn't seem to notice any of it. It was just as well, because as they passed the beer tent Mark saw Tommy lounging up against the bar, talking to some blonde in tight green pants and a Farrah Fawcett hairdo. He didn't see Judy.

Maybe it was nothing, but there was something in Tommy's stance, the way he leaned in when he talked, something in the way she laughed at him, that indicated a guy on the make. Mark had never said anything to Tommy about Tommy and women; Ellen thought Mark should say something, and the two of them had argued about it. He had ceased even to feel really angry about it. It just depressed Mark, and when he saw evidence of it, it just made Mark feel like there was a little less hope available for everybody.

Mark put his hand on Ellen's shoulder, moved them away, toward the bleachers.

In the center of the arena a pair of rodeo clowns fussed over what was supposed to look like a fire engine. The pitiful machine backfired, its wheels wobbled, the siren erupted erratically. The two clowns pulled women's underwear out of their first-aid kit, took turns shooting each other in the pants with a shotgun and hollering at the public-address announcer. When the clowns finally wheeled their fire engine off to make way for the bull riders, they turned and waved gamely to the smattering of applause.

Mark leaned forward on his hard bleacher seat, watched the cowboys clustered on the fences surrounding the chutes. He could hear the bulls rattling against the boards. Somewhere in the back of his head he heard Ellen and her mother talking. A dozen hands lowered the rider down on the bull like a deep-sea diver being lowered into the ocean. The buzzer sounded.

The bull exploded out of the chute, his rider flopping and jerking like a rag doll. As the tormented animal bucked and kicked its way across the ring, Mark could hear the angry snorting, feel the force that lay behind it. The cowboy held on desperately, one hand twisted in the short rope, the other free and waving above his head, but he started to lose his balance. He tried to right himself, but there was no chance to stay atop the enraged, cork-screwing animal. The rider fell, hands outstretched, rolled in the dirt, trying to stay free of the kicking hooves even as the rodeo clowns raced out, arms waving, to distract the bull.

Mark looked over quickly at Ellen and her mother. They were still talking and laughing, oblivious to the action in the ring. Mark hunched forward on his seat.

He watched the bulls and riders, one after the other. It totally absorbed him. The second rider was thrown almost immediately, he scarcely made it out of the chute before he went right over the horns, but scrambled away unhurt. The third and fourth rode through to the final buzzer, but the fifth rider was thrown hard against the fence, then kicked as he lay there defenseless. He tried to walk off, holding his ribs, but fell, then rose again. Four or five cowboys came out, hands extended to meet him. People rose from their bleacher seats to applaud him.

It was the presence of danger that held them all. Even the clowns were transformed. They rushed out as soon as a man was thrown, whistling, flapping their arms like barnyard geese, harrying the animal, working as a team, turning the bull from the downed man. In the presence of danger their clowning took on a kind of brilliance. One stood five feet from the bull's nose and snorted, pawing the ground with his hands when the bull pawed the ground, lowering his head when the bull lowered his head. His partner crept in from behind, snatching the bull's tail. When the bull charged the clowns ran hard, throwing themselves high against the boards, clinging to the top rail as the bull ran beneath and the audience oohed and ahhed. The presence of danger chastened Mark, excited him. He caught Ellen's eye, smiled. She took his hand.

The last rider made it all the way, a terrific ride, stayed on top of the humping, leaping, infuriated bull through to the buzzer, then leaped off onto the fence, swung himself over to the other side and ran, fist held high, into the arms of his buddy. They were right below Mark and he could hear the exultant rider. "Skeeter! Damn, I tol' you I could do it, Skeeter!" Even after his buddy let him down, the rider still paced up and down, shot full of adrenalin, while his bull trotted around and around the ring. Mark felt a twinge of envy; he knew why a person would do this.

A little boy in front of them had started to cry. His father, bearded, full-bellied, wearing a hand-tooled leather hat, shook the kid's arm. "Hey, now, hoss, cowboys don't cry. I'll have to take your hat away from you if you're gonna cry."

Mark smiled and then looked up, saw them standing near the gate: he saw Barbara first. She was wearing a blue down vest. Rob and Michael stood behind her, laughing with the two children.

Agitated, Mark looked away, across the corral at the mountains that loomed above them like dark, hunched beasts. He didn't want to see her.

The public-address announcer's voice echoed through the stadium. "Riding Timber Topper out of Idaho Falls, will be Slim Marshall . . ."

"Ellen! Ellen!" It was a child's voice, Sarah's voice calling up to them. The little girl raced halfway up the bleachers toward Mark and Ellen, then stopped and looked back at her parents. She held herself like a dancer, poised, graceful, a little prim. She motioned impatiently for them to follow her.

Barbara waved up at Mark, smiling. She pointed, questioning: Were there seats? Jeffrey was already following his sister, jumping the bleacher steps two at a time.

Sarah made the introductions. She was proud of her dance teacher and made a proper production of it. Ellen's mother beamed approvingly at the little girl.

"I'll bet she makes you work very hard, doesn't she, Sarah?" Mrs. Hargreaves asked.

"Pretty hard." The little girl had wedged herself between Ellen and Mrs. Hargreaves. Barbara edged past and sat down on the far side of Mark, patting him playfully on the shoulder. Rob grabbed Mark's arm, smiling.

"Hey, Mark, how you doin'? I didn't know you were such a cowboy."

"Who's a cowboy? I come out to root for the animals."

"You must be excited, Sarah," Mrs. Hargreaves said. "You have your big concert tomorrow night."

"I guess so," Sarah said.

"You guess so? You're not nervous, are you, Sarah?" Mrs. Hargreaves said.

"She shouldn't be," Ellen said. "Sarah is a wonderful dancer. She's got nothing to be afraid of."

Sarah stared straight ahead, smiling, basking in the compliments, but not quite sure how to handle it.

Barbara leaned across, her hand on Mark's arm, to speak to Ellen. "I meant to speak to you before, Ellen. We're having some people out to the house after the concert. You're all invited. Children, parents, dance-groupies like Mark here, whatever . . ." Her voice was light, whimsical. "It will be a celebration."

Rob and Michael stood up, cheering for one of the bronc riders.

"You don't have to do that," Ellen said. Mark picked up the note of reserve in her voice. "I've been telling people that we were going to have coffee and cookies afterwards, there in the hall . . . nothing very elaborate . . ."

"I don't want to disrupt anybody's plans. Whoever can make it should come, whoever can't can't. But everyone's invited."

Michael looked down the row at her, his eyes bright, inquisitive. "Really, dear, you're the one who should be the producer. You've got the instincts for it."

Unperturbed, Barbara patted Mark's arm. "You come if you can. It will be fun." Mark's glance apparently wasn't reassuring enough. She suddenly looked like a child who's been unjustly reproached. "I haven't done anything wrong, have I?"

"No," Mark said softly.

He was utterly confounded by her. She was presenting herself so blithely, as if nothing had gone on between them. Had it been a total fabrication, his fabrication, a piece of fantasy-work? Was she so oblivious to conflict? Maybe the problem was that she didn't understand the simplest convention, simple stuff like, "You're with your husband, I'm with my girlfriend, so let's not squeeze each other's arm." No damn decorum. But she was too smart for that. It was all deliberate, he decided. It's all theater for her.

He was very uncomfortable. He looked down the row, saw Ellen leaning forward, talking with Sarah. Ellen was gesturing, illustrating a hand position. Mark could see the shy pleasure in Sarah's face. That was the only thing that could keep this bunch together, the innocence of a child, a child's admiration for her teacher.

Ellen lifted her head, saw Mark watching her. She held his gaze for a second before going back to Sarah. Mark turned his attention back to the arena.

After the bronc-riding winners were announced, Jeffrey stood up. "Mom."

"Yes, Jeffrey?"

The next contest was being announced in mellifluous tones. "This will be the calf scramble, ladies and gentlemen, and every little cowboy and cowgirl between the ages of eight and fourteen is invited to come down and try their luck with one of our little doggies . . ."

"Jeffrey, you know what I think," Barbara said. "You know that I think it's dangerous . . ."

"But you promised, you said that I could . . ."

"I didn't promise, Jeffrey, I said we'd discuss it."

"Mom, I handle calves bigger'n that on our place every day . . ."

Rob stood up and put a hand on his son's shoulder. "Barbara, he'll be all right."

"That's what fathers always say."

Rob looked at her for a second without speaking, in mute appeal. "He's a big kid. Nobody gets hurt in these things."

Barbara still looked skeptical. "O.K.," she said.

"Thanks, Mom," Jeffrey said. With trembling, excited hands, he emptied his pockets. "Mom, could you keep these . . . my wallet and my army knife . . ."

"Go on," she said. "Just be careful."

The boy bounded down the steps, narrowly missing the hand of a drunken cowboy who lay spread-eagled across several yards of bleachers.

There were forty kids edging up to the chalk starting line, and when the dozen skittish calves were let out of their pens there was a stampede. The frightened calves kicked their heels and wove back and forth through the milling children, leaving kids sprawling in the dirt. The object was to tear a blue ribbon off the horns or tail, but the calves were brilliant broken-field runners, bucking out of corners, spurting through gang tackles: for the first ten minutes the kids didn't stand a chance. The announcer exhorted them onward, playing to the audience. A little boy in cowboy boots stood bewildered in the center of the ring as calves and children raced past him. Jeff ran well, utterly determined, sprinting alongside a frisking calf.

Barbara stood up to watch her son, her arms held tight to her body. Mark could feel the tension in her.

"Come on, Jeffrey!" Sarah shouted.

Jeff threw himself at the calf, but it twisted away, and the boy fell in the dirt. Mark felt Barbara's fingers clutch involuntarily at his shoulder for just a second.

Jeff picked himself up, wiped the dirt off his face. Mark looked up at Barbara. She took her hand away.

"Really," she said. "I know he does it just to terrify me." The remark was ironic, but the look on her face wasn't; she was afraid for her child.

A couple of boys hobbled, dusty but victorious, toward the announcer's booth, waving their prize ribbons aloft.

Jeff continued his pursuit doggedly, leading a pack of kids. The gang of them finally cornered one of the tiring calves and Jeff leaped at it, throwing a hold around the neck, pulling the ribbon free. The calf bucked his way out of the hold and Jeff rolled triumphantly on the ground. As he did, a bigger boy in a denim jacket stumbled on top of him, ripping the ribbon away.

The two boys leaped to their feet, facing one another. Jeff moved on his adversary, but the bigger boy shoved him away with a straight arm. Jeff tried to grab the boy's jacket but the boy pulled free.

Rob stood, his hands cupped to his mouth, shouting something down to the ring.

"Let's not fight now, boys!" came the booming but good-natured voice of the announcer, but that was all; nothing was to be done to correct the injustice.

Jeff followed the boy across the ring, arguing, but the boy only veered away from him, not answering, the ribbon clutched in his fist. The chase after the remaining calves went on around them.

Barbara stood silent, her face taut and upset.

Jeff turned away, defeated, and began walking back across the ring alone, past a ribbonless calf that stood there, stock-still, confused by the sudden lack of harassment.

"Sarah," Barbara said, touching her daughter's shoulder, "you stay here with your father and Michael."

"I'm coming with you," Rob said.

The two parents picked their way down the bleachers to meet their son; Barbara let Rob go first, using a hand on his shoulder for balance. The boy looked up and saw them, his face covered with dirt and contorted now as he tried to fight back tears. The rest of them—Mark, Ellen, Ellen's mother, Sarah, Michael—watched silently.

The winners were announced, along with their hometowns and special congratulations to their proud moms and dads out there in the audience. Mark watched Rob and Barbara leaning over the fence, comforting their son. Rob lifted Jeffrey over the barrier. Barbara tried to wipe some of the dirt from the boy's face, but he quickly turned his face away. Michael was pushing his way down the bleachers to join them.

Sarah, craning to see, had unconsciously taken Mark's hand. He looked down at her. "He's just fine, Sarah. There's nothing to worry about," he said.

"That poor little boy," Mrs. Hargreaves murmured.

Sarah looked angrily at Mrs. Hargreaves. "He's not *little*," she said.

"I know," Mrs. Hargreaves said. "I'm sorry."

Watching Barbara care for her son, Mark knew that he had been wrong about her, or at least unfair. There was more to this woman, he was sure of it, and he would find out what it was, he set himself to it, as he stood there in the bleachers holding her daughter's hand.

Rob and Michael led the boy slowly through the crowd, heading toward the gate, while Barbara made her way back up to retrieve Sarah.

"I'm sorry," Barbara said. "But I'm afraid we've got to regroup and head home."

"Oh, I hope he'll be all right," Mrs. Hargreaves said.

"He'll be fine. It was his pride that was hurt more than anything else. It's the injustice of it, that's what seems to hurt the most at that age."

"Oh, I know," Mrs. Hargreaves said.

The two mothers looked at one another, smiled, at their common knowledge of what hurt children. Mark and Ellen stood on either side of them, preempted.

Barbara took her daughter's hand. "Come on, Sarah." She smiled at Ellen. "Good luck tomorrow. We'll all be there with bells on. And tell everyone you see to come over to our place afterwards. We'll make a real bash out of it."

Mark, admiring her, abandoned his caution. "We'll go down with you," he said. "The rodeo's pretty much over anyway."

"I think so," Mrs. Hargreaves said. "We've had all the excitement we need for one night."

They walked out together, Mark leading the way, escorting the two pairs of mothers and daughters. He felt so full of solicitude for all of them, it was like a state of inspiration. They seemed so extraordinary to him, these four; he wanted to hug them all, to protect them from lurching drunks and careening teen-agers, he wanted them never to be hurt, by anything.

Outside the gate, someone called Ellen's name. It was the anxious mother of one of Ellen's dance students and she had a barrage of questions about the concert.

Mark was caught, not knowing whether to walk on ahead with Barbara or stay behind with Ellen and her mother.

"Is your car very far?" Mark asked.

"No, it's just up ahead," Barbara said. Then she saw why he was asking. "Oh, no, don't," she said. "We're fine."

"It's O.K.," Mark said, but there was a note of quietness in his voice, of worry, of too much weight. Barbara's look questioned him. He walked on with her, saying nothing.

Sarah was a few steps ahead of them, looking for the car. There were a lot of people trying to leave at once, jeeps and vans jockeying for position, bumping over the grass, blocking one another, laying on their horns. Beams of car lights washed back and forth across the lot.

"I was out at your place the other day," Mark said.

"I know," she said. "You did a good job. Everything looks great."

"I thought you'd be there. I thought I'd see you."

She stared straight ahead, not looking at him, resisting him. "We had to go into town. Sarah, be careful!" she shouted ahead to her daughter.

"I was looking forward to seeing you again," Mark said. "To tell you the truth, I was kind of surprised that you weren't there. I guess it's hard sometimes, when you meet someone you like . . . it's hard to understand things correctly."

She looked at him sharply. "What do you mean?"

Already he had gotten into deeper water than he'd intended. He felt his face flush.

"I liked talking to you."

"And I liked talking to you."

"I've thought about it a lot since."

A jeep spun its wheels as it careened past and someone yelled out the window at them. Barbara stared at him, and in the flickering car lights he saw the anger in her face.

"I usually don't talk the way we did that day," she said. "Don't misunderstand me. It was nice. But it was a luxury, an indulgence. I have my family, my work. I have a great deal to tend to."

"I know that," he said.

"Some people like to court danger," she said. "Maybe I did too, once. But not anymore. Thank you for walking us. Good night."

"Good night," Mark said.

He watched her go, the slender, auburn-haired woman putting her head down, running to catch her daughter. Mark turned. A van backed up, nearly hitting two quarreling drunks. One of them thumped the side of the van.

"You son of a bitch, look where you're goin'!"

Dark figures raced through the fan of lights, hooting. Mark looked for Ellen but didn't see her. He walked faster, the knot of panic rose in his stomach and then he did see her, still talking to the anxious mother.

Mark came up behind her. "Aren't you cold?" he said.

She glanced at him with a dark look. A Chevy van five feet away from them sounded its horn.

"Hey," he said. "We should get out of here before we get run over."

Chapter Seven

Mark sat alone behind the desk, fingering the list of reservations. He could hear the young dancers talking and laughing backstage, their voices coin-bright with expectancy. Every few minutes someone would try to shush them, but it only worked temporarily; curbing their excitement was like trying to hold back a full spring stream. From time to time one girl or the other would poke her head out from the side of the curtain to see if her parents had come in yet. If Mark spied them the head would disappear abruptly, the edge of heavy velvet trembling only for a second.

The first parent to arrive had been Ellen's mother. She kept Mark company for a while, but once people began to gather she took her seat in the front row center, dutifully reading and rereading the program. From time to time she looked over to smile at Mark.

Ellen was on automatic pilot. Mark caught only glimpses of her, rushing past to tend to a misplaced costume, or to set up an extra row of folding chairs. Mark knew that the best policy was to stay out of her way when she was like this. Anxiety made her tight-lipped and remote, and attempts to reassure her were useless.

It was an old pattern between the two of them; she would become anxious and distanced, he would try to calm her and fail, then become angry because he couldn't reach her. She kept telling him not to take it so personally, that there were just times when the only remedy for her was to get things done.

It was hard not to take personally and particularly hard now. For the past week, since his encounters with Barbara, it seemed as if every detail of his emotional life was magnified, the smallest tremors demanded scrutiny. Was Ellen's remoteness from him before a dance concert perfectly normal, or was it some mirror of his own change of focus?

It was too hard to figure out. The only thing to do was to sell tickets, to be a decent guy, and trust to things getting better. Mark chatted up the parents as they came in. A lot of them he already knew and one or two seemed to enjoy giving him a hard time. Mark enjoyed it too. All these years, he thought, I've had the soul of a Rotarian struggling to get out. Barbara hadn't arrived. He wondered once or twice about it, but it didn't bother him, he was too busy. People began arriving in bunches.

Barbara and Rob and Michael and Jeff ended up being the last four people to arrive. They came in a rush, Rob with his face flushed and hands up in a gesture of exasperation and apology.

Barbara, in comparison, was a model of composure. She was in a long print dress, her bare arms tanned, her auburn hair shining. She seemed to be in a wonderful mood, straightening her son's collar, laughing at a remark of Michael's.

When she saw Mark behind the desk she opened her mouth in mock surprise.

"You look awfully dressed up," she said.

"You're seeing my other side," Mark said.

Barbara burrowed her hand under her husband's arm. Rob reached for his wallet. "I think we should go in, Barbara. It's starting any minute."

Barbara looked at the people already seated, smiled and waved at a friend. Rob put a twenty down on the table. Mark started to make change, but Rob stopped him. "Just keep it," he said. "Consider it a contribution to the general cultural scene."

"We'll put it toward the Wyoming toe-shoe fund," Mark said. Rob laughed, putting his wallet away.

Barbara had moved off a few feet. "Rob, there are four seats over here." There was a note of impatience in her voice. She glanced back at Mark for a second, her smile thinner, a fraction tauter now.

They found their seats just as Ellen came out. Ellen walked past Mark into the outer hall, turned off the hall lights. Mark flipped the top down on the cashbox and stood up. It was time to begin. He caught Ellen's hand as she was coming back.

"It's going to be great," he said.

"Thanks," she said.

She wasn't paying attention. He held her hand, insisting. "I mean it."

She smiled, not giving very much, not saying anything.

Mark walked across in front of the audience, took his spot next to the tape recorder. The lights dimmed.

Ellen came out to open the program. She stood on the bare floor, only a dozen feet from Mark, her face flushed. She gave a general welcome, thanks for everyone who'd helped with the concert, spoke of the goals of the summer children's dance program, but Mark couldn't focus on what she said. He was too keenly aware of her, too attuned to her vulnerability.

She spoke softly, spoke well, the audience listened attentively, but Mark knew her discomfort, the terrors she felt about speaking in public. She was shy: more than once she and Mark had discussed it, how she always felt as if words would fail her, fly from her at the crucial moment.

He watched her as she stood talking, her poised dancer's body betraying nothing, the stage light behind her shining in her hair. She looked lovely. Beyond her Mark could see the faces in the audience, see the parents, Mrs. Hargreaves, Michael rolling up his program, Barbara whispering something in Rob's ear, but for now they scarcely mattered; what mattered was Ellen, that she do well, that she get through it.

The concert began. The music for the first dance was a medley of Indian songs and folk and Western ballads. It was a clever piece, the young performers cavorting their way through Western history. There was nobody missing; there were Indians and trappers and cowboys who galloped across the stage on invisible steeds. There were sodbusters and outlaws, all small-bodied and quick, bowing to one another with a sweet courtesy and then leaping off like young antelopes. There were mess-ups: one little boy with a load of beaver traps, who clutched at his entrance and had to be gently pushed out onto the stage by Ellen, and there was a little girl who kept losing her place and looking around, puzzled and mad, as if she had just missed her school bus. But if it was the spirit of the West they were after, of bravery in the face of adversity, they succeeded. There was no way the terrors of the wilderness could be any worse than the terrors an eight-year-old girl faces going out in front of an audience that includes her mother, her father and a brother who might, no matter how much his mother had warned him ahead of time, make a face to make her laugh.

There was great applause at the end of the piece and Mark felt a wave of relief. It was going to be just fine.

The second piece was real ballet, music by Mozart. The young dancers tottered as they went up on their toes, arms curved above them, stretched upward like uncertain young birds. Sarah's face was set with rocklike concentration. It was as if the audience didn't exist for her at all; all that mattered was remembering every step, making no mistake. She needn't have worried. The music was so tender that it softened any error, forgave weak ankles, sudden waverings, missed turns.

Sitting in the dark beyond the performing area, Mark could look through the young dancers into the audience. He watched Barbara sitting upright between her son and her husband. Her attention was totally on the performance. As the dancers flitted across his field of vision, Mark found himself held by her gaze, a gaze meant for her daughter. He examined her face with all the care of a thief, in it he found all kinds of treasures; generosity and pride, amusement and intelligence, love and solemnity. Her gaze struck him the way a gong might be struck unintentionally, brushed by someone's elbow as they passed in a dark corridor.

It was a look that he wanted for himself, what he wanted was for her to care for him. The dancers spun past. The music set his mind on fire. The music forgave him for what he was thinking. There was nothing wrong in wanting her. It was not crazy to want her, she was desirable, anyone could understand wanting a woman like that. Maybe it was even all right to admit that, at least to yourself. It was just that he couldn't have her. From the darkness he stared out, across at her, sitting in darkness too. Between them lay a band of light filled with the soft, twirling bodies of children.

The final piece of the concert was simple fun. Ellen came out in a clown outfit, baggy pants, white face, her hair tucked under a floppy hat. The music was a tape of an old drummer named Baby Dobbs and Ellen did a dance of pratfalls and flops, struts and unexpected collapses. There was no trace of her earlier shyness; Ellen had become a herky-jerky Emmett Kelly, a one-woman parade, limber and free. After five minutes of invention, she swaggered to the back curtain, lifted its corner, and out strutted all the young dancers, all clowns now, elbows swinging, some jive city, others country trucking, forming a real parade, following Ellen around the stage, each of them showing off a turn or flourish of their own.

It was a wonderful way to end. The audience of mothers and fathers and brothers and aunts all rose to applaud them, and Mark rose too. Ellen stood hand in hand with her young dancers, and when she took her bow she glanced over at Mark, her face shining.

Afterwards Mark wended his way through the knots of parents and children. He pulled Ellen to him, gave her a kiss on the cheek. She gave him a quick, appreciative look; her body was still tense with the excitement of performing. He rubbed her back; beneath her baggy overalls her leotard was drenched with sweat.

"You were working out there," he said.

"What did you think?" she said.

"Dynamite," Mark said.

"Really? You're not just saying that?"

Mark smiled, smoothed a tangle in her wet hair. "I'm just saying it, but it's also true," he said.

Mark stood by as people came up to congratulate her. They hugged her, they kissed her, they asked her to sign their programs. The father of one of the young dancers, a rancher with a string tie and battered cowboy boots, said he didn't know what you were supposed to say after a dance, but if he knew he'd be saying it, because he sure did think it had been great. He held Ellen's hands, shaking them with enthusiasm, his string tie swaying, and he didn't let go until his wife, muttering apologies, pulled him away.

Any doubts Ellen might have had about the evening being less than a triumph were being quickly dispelled. As Ellen loosened up, she became radiant with charm. Ellen's mother stood alongside Mark, beaming in solidarity, drinking it all in. Nine-year-olds in leotards dashed past, looking for their lost coats.

Rob came up, leading Sarah, who had a rose in her hand. Mark watched as the little girl presented it to Ellen. Ellen bent down and kissed her. Rob took Ellen's hand, thanking her. He asked her and Sarah questions about the dance, listened attentively to their answers. Ellen laughed at something he said. Rob seemed like a person who knew exactly what to say after a dance, Mark thought. Ellen, flustered by all the appreciation, smiled, stuck for anything to say, holding the rose and her floppy hat before her with all the unconscious grace of the trained dancer. Rob patted her elbow, stepped back. He was not oblivious to her charms. Mark felt the quick seizure of possessiveness.

"If you need a ride out, we've got room," Rob said.

"Ride out?" Ellen said.

"To the party." Rob's voice was impatient; she was supposed to have remembered. "You *are* coming, aren't you?" Rob looked sharply over at Mark. "You must!"

"I guess so," Mark said.

On the ride out, Ellen's mother wanted to know everything about the concert, and Ellen, happy and relaxed, was delighted to oblige her. They went over each child, their parents, the troubles in rehearsal, the unexpected delights at the performance.

Mark listened, saying nothing. His eyes were on the road, the white stripes of the highway swept beneath them. He was in too much turmoil to join their conversation.

He was proud of Ellen, pleased for her. There had always been these moments in their relationship, when Ellen was confident and up, when she seemed to be lit with serenity, but she had never been as attractive to him as she was now. Attractive enough, desirable enough, for him to feel the pricklings of jealousy when Rob had been talking to her.

Mark was aware enough of the contradictions. How could he dare to feel the ugly contractions of mistrust when he, only a half hour before, had been swept up with desire for this same man's wife? It was ridiculous. Perhaps one had caused the other, perhaps it was precisely his wanting Barbara that had attuned him to jealousy. It was repellent. How could he want one woman, then the other? He had no core. To want this and this too, it was like a child, a not very nice child, and yet there he was, without defense.

Eventually his silence had to be noticed. As they turned off the main road, Ellen touched his shoulder.

"Mark, are you all right?"

"I'm fine," he said. "I'm just a little tired."

The lights from the Campbells' house shone ahead of them. Mark eased his car in at the end of the line of cars parked at the side of the dirt road. They walked toward the house, Mark a step or two ahead of Ellen and her mother; this was familiar territory to him now. As they came closer Mark could see a fire burning on the front lawn. Ghostly balloons bobbed lazily in the night air. The excited voices of children carried clearly, as if over water. There was a brief sputter of firecrackers. The dark silhouetted figures of the adults surrounded the fire. Already the June evening was turning cold.

A tall, familiar figure, with a sparkler in hand, came down the lawn to meet them.

"Hey, man, how you doin'? Hey, Ellen, congratulations." Patrick leaned down and gave Ellen a kiss. "Word is the concert was outta sight. I woulda been there too but the phone just kept ringing. Seems like every condo in the valley's just decided it wants rustic redwood cabinets. I'm not knockin' it, I gotta keep this boyfriend of yours in spending money . . . Hi, Mrs. Hargreaves, how you doin'?"

"What are you doing at this party, Patrick?" Mark asked.

"Hey, an event like this, word gets around . . ." Patrick suddenly tossed his sparkler away. "Wow, you can burn your hand with these things, don't believe what they tell ya." It sounded to Mark as if Patrick was stoned. "Hey, man, come on up, they've got a load of hot dogs and marshmallows . . . like we're all back in camp, you can dig on that, can't you?"

They followed Patrick up to the circle around the fire. As soon as people realized that Ellen had arrived, a cry of delight went up and a couple of the men applauded and whistled. The children flocked around her, tugging at her arms. One of the mothers offered her a stick with its freshly toasted marshmallow.

Barbara came across the lawn to meet them.

"Well, here we are!" she said. "We were starting to get worried." She leaned forward and kissed Ellen. Patrick stood over them, beaming happily and patting Ellen on the back.

"All the kids have been asking when you were coming," Barbara said. "Why don't we all go inside? It's too cold out here and, anyway, I want to introduce you to some people."

Barbara ushered them all indoors. Mark and Patrick were gradually eased out as one person after the other came over to greet Ellen. The two men stood together next to the liquor table, watching Barbara introduce Ellen to her friends.

Mark poured hmself a gin and tonic, never taking his eyes off Barbara, not quite trusting her. Mark felt very protective of Ellen, but everything seemed to be all right. Barbara seemed to be making a special effort with her, taking care of her, being particularly gracious, particularly warm. He heard Ellen laugh at something Barbara said as they came up to a white-haired woman decked out in turquoise jewelry.

Patrick saw Mark staring at Barbara. "Yeah, she's really got it down, doesn't she?" Patrick said. "I mean you talk about *control*. I mean you know that woman comes right out of the gene pool that creates diplomats and shit. Am I right?"

"You're right," Mark said.

Patrick sipped at his drink. Barbara had her arm around Ellen's waist as she leaned over the white-haired woman, telling some animated story about Ellen.

"I mean, this is great, man, you've got to get into this. Look at this guy Kramer over there." Patrick nodded toward the rancher in the string tie, drink in hand and dimly ill at ease, who was waiting to talk with Ellen. "Now, that's one intimidated cowboy. That character runs a five-thousand-acre spread up north of Moran, he's got skin so thick you couldn't put a buzz saw through it. I've seen him face down a half-ton bull when the bull was mad at him, man. But look at him, Mark, he's squinting at the paintings on the wall and you know he doesn't know what that's all about and he tries to listen to these people talking about pliés and somebody's dance teacher at Wellesley and real old money and he realizes he ain't nothing but a shit-kicker."

Mark saw Ellen reach out to touch Barbara's arm, objecting to the extravagance of something Barbara had said, saw Barbara catch Ellen's hand with her own, saw the play between them and Ellen's quick appreciative smile.

"The man is subdued, Mark. There's a lesson in this, that's what I'm sayin'."

"What lesson is that?" Mark asked.

Patrick was taken aback by Mark's question. "You want me to spell it out?"

"Sure, spell it out, Patrick."

"Lesson is that you can't escape it, man, it's like the air . . ."

"You're happy enough drinking their liquor, aren't you, Patrick?"

Patrick frowned, looking betrayed. Usually he could count on Mark pitching right in with antiestablishment views, it was taken for granted that they understood one another.

Patrick sighed. "Tell you what I'm going to do. See that preppie little girl over there by the fireplace?" Mark took a look. There was an attractive-looking brunette in topsiders, jeans, pink dress shirt, string of pearls and tweed jacket, standing alone, nursing a drink.

"What do you think?" Patrick said. "Does she look like the type who would be interested in a man of my social views? A sympathetic face? What do you say?" Patrick squeezed Mark's arm and angled across the room, happy to escape.

Mark stood alone, watching, as a circle formed around Barbara and Ellen. Rob came up with Sarah, put his arm around his wife. The sounds of glasses tinkling, people talking and laughing rose around Mark, indistinguishable from the sounds of any good party. Mark, drink held tight to his chest, picked his way through the knots of guests, avoiding conversation, and slipped through the door onto the porch. Three glum nine-year-olds dangled their legs off the edge of the porch.

"What are you kids doing?" Mark asked.

"We're prisoners," one of the boys said.

"Uh-huh."

There was a fierce shout from somewhere out on the lawn. Mark stared out into the darkness. Children came dashing out of the night, past the bonfire, into the eerie yellow light cast by the porch light, skittered and dashed off again when sighted by other children. One or two flashlights flickered on and off in the trees, there were childish cries of warning. Jeff rushed up onto the porch, alert and wild-eyed as a warrior.

"Hi," Mark said.

"Hi," Jeff said. His eyes darted, searching the darkness for enemies.

"What are you playing?"

"Capture the Flag. I'm guarding the prisoners." Jeff stopped talking, alert again, then dashed down the steps onto the lawn. A figure had emerged from the lilac bushes. "There he is! It's Kevin! There he is!" he shouted in warning.

Three of Jeff's teammates dashed back to help. Kevin held up his hands, sauntering across the lawn. "Aw, Jeff, come on, I'm already caught."

"Then why aren't you in jail?"

"I had to get a drink of water."

One of Jeff's teammates grabbed at Kevin's wrist, but Kevin pulled away.

"Don't pay any attention to him, he's already caught." Jeff backed toward the porch. "They're such cheaters," Jeff said.

He observed Mark thoughtfully for a second. "Want to play?"

"No, thanks. I probably should be going back in."

"I don't like parties so much. All people ever do is talk."

"I know what you mean," Mark said.

Mark looked back through the window at the party. Someone had put on music, and dancing had started. Barbara was in the middle of the floor with Michael, clowning, beckoning him with a roll of the fingers. They were both laughing. Patrick lurched storklike across the floor, elbows swinging, freaky and free. Rob, gallant and attentive, stood talking with Ellen. Barbara stopped for a second to try and pull Ellen into the dance, but Rob protested, pulling her back.

There was a shout. Mark turned in time to see Kevin and the three prisoners race across the lawn. Jeff ran after them, screaming in protest.

"You were caught, Kevin, you can't, you're a prisoner!"

A second band of children came running out of the darkness, surrounding Kevin and the escapees. Kevin threw up his arms.

"I just said that, I wasn't really a prisoner . . ."

"Kevin, that's not fair. We could have caught you before, but we didn't . . ."

"So? That's your tough luck."

"Cheater, Kevin, cheater!"

The argument escalated in the cool night air. Mark stood up and went back inside. The sounds of Smokey Robinson and the Miracles filled the house. Patrick huddled on the couch with the girl in the tweed coat. She was explaining something to him, gesturing frantically with her hands. Ellen was talking with a group of mothers. Mark put a hand on her shoulder.

"Hey," he said.

"Hi," she said. She seemed surprised. "We missed you."

"I was outside. Watching the kids play."

"Are you all right?"

"I'm great." He put his arm around her, looked out at the dancers. Michael was bent low, shaking his rear and shouting, "Heard it on the grapevine, oh-oh-oh." Rob, dancing with a tall, tanned, middle-aged woman in a silk shirt, laughed and took a swipe at Michael's head.

"Why don't we show 'em how it's done?" Mark said.

He led her out into the middle of the floor and they began to dance. He was proud of the way they danced together, he knew that people watched them. She was an extraordinarily responsive dancer, turning whatever he tried into something graceful and inventive; they made things up as they went along. He spun her away from him, holding her at arm's length, gave her a mock sultry look. She smiled, she was happy to have him back. He pulled her in again, spun her around, held her.

"I'm proud of you," he whispered.

"I'm glad," she said.

He felt clearer now. He could feel people's eyes on them, but he focused only on her, on her glowing face. She was lovely, the loveliest person there. He swung her out, turning her free and catching her again.

Then, somewhere through the steady beat of the music, came the dull, insistent ringing of the phone. Mark looked across the room, saw Barbara leap toward the kitchen, snatch the receiver off the hook.

As Ellen slipped under his upraised arm, Mark saw Barbara put a hand over one ear, as if she was having difficulty hearing. Barbara turned, winding herself in the cord, and as she turned back Mark saw the stinging brightness in her face.

Mark pulled Ellen back toward him; her dark glance told him that she had noticed the sudden faltering of his attention.

When the dance ended, the rancher with the string tie, a little red-faced from alcohol now, came up, wanting to dance with Ellen. Mark gave way. He watched Ellen and the rancher for a second, then moved toward the kitchen. Barbara sat on a green stool, fingering the telephone cord.

"Yes . . . yes . . . it will be wonderful, Kate . . . The children will be so excited. I'm sorry, I can't hear . . . yes. As soon as you can. Just hold on." She held the receiver to her side, came out from the kitchen, as if she didn't even see Mark, standing only a few feet away. "Rob? Rob!" Rob looked up from a conversation. "It's Kate."

Rob's face was utterly blank, as if he hadn't understood.

"Hey!" Michael shouted. "Let me talk to her!" Michael abandoned his dance partner to rush to the phone. He grabbed the receiver from Barbara. "Hey, Katie, darlin', how you doin'? Michael! Michael! Who did you think? Smashed, absolutementé. Rock-and-roll in the Rockies, that's right."

Rob waited patiently, but saw that he was not going to get the phone from Michael. Michael glanced at him, then waved him away. Rob smiled at Barbara, she attempted a smile back, wiped a strand of hair from her forehead.

"I'll get the phone upstairs," Rob said. He set down his drink and headed up the stairs; halfway up, he began to leap them three at a time.

"Fishin', that's right, you bitch," Michael said, "we're going to take you fishin', let you gut them yourself, cutthroat trout, honey, real Americana, just like you."

Barbara was suddenly standing alone. She turned, saw Mark watching her, the muscles around her mouth tightened, angry that he had caught her so unmistakably at a loss. Mark did the only polite thing. He left.

He walked back out onto the porch. Children still raced like warriors across the lawn. Sarah had joined her brother's side and was running and leaping like a fawn, shouting warnings to her team-mates. Mark sat down on the porch swing.

The game had taken on a new level of intensity. Children dashed up to the porch, breathless and sweating, eyes wide with excitement, pausing only for a second before dashing off again on a yet more daring foray into the darkness. The beams of a flashlight glimmered for a second down by the barn and then went out. A boy darted from tree to tree, then ran for the corner of the house. Cries and taunts went back and forth, then a quick shout of alarm that someone had been spotted.

Mark closed his eyes, leaned back in the swing. He heard the porch door open. He looked up. It was Barbara.

"Hi," she said. He smiled at her. "It's cold out here, isn't it?" she said.

"That's June in Wyoming for you," he said.

She sat down next to him, close to him. "They look so wild," she said.

"They *are* wild."

"What are they playing?"

"Capture the Flag."

He felt the warmth of her body against his own, felt himself flooded with confusion.

"It's a nice party," he said.

"Not *that* nice."

"You don't like it?"

A big lumbering boy chased a smaller boy past the porch, just below them. The smaller boy darted to the left, doubled back, then leaped across the bonfire, sending a spray of sparks into the air.

"Not particularly," she said.

"Well, I suppose if you don't like the way things are you can always change them."

"Some things you can never change," she said. He looked quickly at her. She sounded deadly serious. When she spoke again, her tone was lighter. "You're nice and warm. A nice, warm fellow." She squeezed his arm. "I'll go in in a minute. I just wanted to see how the children were doing."

"That was a friend of yours that called?"

She let a beat go past before she answered. "Yes. A good friend."

"Really?"

"Really. Best friends," Barbara said. "She's coming out. You'll meet her. You'll probably like her. Everyone does. She's an actress.

Quite something, you'll see." She patted Mark's arm and was about to get up when the screen door banged open behind them. Michael stood, arms outstretched like Ahab on the *Pequod,* and let out a whoop.

"Whaa-hee!" He plunged down the steps and out across the lawn, scooping a stunned Sarah up in his arms.

"Put me down, Michael!"

"How come?"

"Cuz I'm guarding the prisoners!"

Sarah squirmed out of his grasp, but Michael wasn't done yet. He stumbled across the lawn, hooting and grabbing up protesting children until he finally tripped and went sprawling on his back.

Michael lay gasping and laughing as children buzzed around him like angry wasps. They screamed their outrage at him; he had ruined their game, someone had snuck off with the flag during all the commotion, it wasn't fair, it was all his fault. One little boy was crying.

Michael, amiable and drunk, didn't understand what he'd done.

"Hey, I was only playing!"

"But *we* weren't, Michael, we weren't!"

Two little girls sat cross-legged and dispirited on the damp lawn. More sullen children began to drift in and out of the darkness. Barbara took a girl inside to find a Band-Aid for her skinned elbow.

Mark found himself suddenly in the middle, trying to appease the unappeasable children. He grabbed at Jeffrey as he came running past.

"Hey, Jeffrey, come on, man, slow down."

"He spoiled our game! He did!"

"Jeffrey, take it easy, he didn't mean to, he was only fooling around."

"It doesn't matter!"

"Mark."

Mark turned at the sound of Ellen's voice. She and her mother stood at the foot of the stairs. Mrs. Hargreaves had her sweater on.

"Mother's tired, Mark. I'm going to take her home."

Jeffrey pulled free of Mark's grip. Mark let him go. Several slightly tipsy fathers stood on the porch, their hands on their hips, looking mystified by the ferocity of their children.

"Are you going to come back?" Mark asked.

"No, I don't think so."

"I don't understand . . ." A mother brushed past them, leading away her angry eight-year-old son. Around them the air was filled with a chorus of childish complaints about the game gone wrong. "I'll go with you, then," Mark said.

"You don't have to. You can stay if you want. You can always get a ride back later with Patrick." Stumped, Mark stared across the lawn at the now risen and apologetic Michael. "You do what you want to do," Ellen said.

"It's awfully early, isn't it?"

"Stay, then," she said.

He knew her tone. She was feeling ignored, disappointed, hurt, she would say later, not angry. She was being even-handed now. It was an even-handedness he would pay for. She was testing him: what he was supposed to do was disagree with her, insist that they leave together, and then, even if they did leave together, it wouldn't be over, she would be silent in the car and when they were alone finally she would say there was nothing wrong so he would have to pull it out of her, go at her to make her come out with it . . . He looked back keenly at her.

"O.K., I'll stay," he said. "I'll get a ride with Patrick."

Mark walked Ellen and her mother back to the car. Mark took Mrs. Hargreaves' arm to help her on the dark, rutted road. Ellen walked slightly ahead carrying the flowers that one of the dancers' mothers had given her. Mrs. Hargreaves was silent and seemed a bit stiff, hard-mouthed.

Mark was not clear yet about what he'd done. The lights of the party still glowed at their backs. When they got to the car Ellen gave Mark a light kiss on the cheek, a quick cool touch in the night wind that gusted across their faces.

"I can still go with you now," he said. He fingered the car keys in his hand. "It really doesn't matter."

"No, you do what you want. Everyone should do what they want." She took the keys from him and slipped into the car.

"I won't be long," he said.

She pulled the door shut. Mark stepped away and watched as Ellen turned the car around. The headlights flashed over him. He waved. He couldn't see if they waved back. He watched the car lurch down the dirt road and onto the highway, then accelerate and disappear.

Looking back, Mark could make out the figures in the circle of yellow light on the lawn, hear the angry, tired voices of the children. He started back down the road, drawn toward the amber light. He felt the cold wind through his thin shirt.

Maybe it was just that he'd had a little too much to drink, but he felt as cunning as a hunter. He was starting to see these people for what they were. He felt cleverer than any of them, these people who prided themselves on their cleverness, he felt as if he was starting to see through them now, and that feeling of clarity, whether true or false, excited him.

The party wasn't going to last much longer. Even as Mark reached the lawn, children were being collected and bundled on shoulders. Rob walked the white-haired woman with the turquoise jewelry across the lawn, his arm around her shoulder, as she told him what a wonderful time she'd had.

Mark stood alone, watching for several minutes as people began to drift toward the cars, then walked up the steps and into the house.

The only people in the living room were Patrick and his new girlfriend. The two of them sat cross-legged in front of the hi-fi, going through the Campbells' record collection with the numbed concentration of dope smokers.

"Hey, man, how you doin'?" Patrick said, his smile dreamy, his tone affable. "We were trying to find some music to sort of cool things out a bit, you know what I mean?"

"I know what you mean."

The girl held up a record jacket by one corner and a record slid out, landed in her lap.

"This is Janey," Patrick said.

"Hi."

"Hi."

Mark scanned the other rooms. A middle-aged woman dashed out with her child's sweater in hand, the door banged behind her.

"How about John Coltrane?" the girl said.

"Too heavy," Patrick said.

Mark made a stack of empty plastic glasses and brought them into the kitchen. He waited, unsure. Overhead he heard the toilet flush, the quick thudding of children's feet. He looked back into the living room where Janey was trying to slip a record back in its paper sleeve, where Patrick reached over to put his hand on the back of her neck. Both operations took place with the same syrupy slow motion. It wouldn't do to interfere.

Mark stood again on the front porch, alone. The party was over. All the cars except for Patrick's were gone. Out on the lawn the fire was down. Two dark forms lay beside it. Mark listened to their voices, so clear in the still night air, the voices of Rob and Michael.

Mark came down the steps. Michael raised up on an elbow, lifted a hand.

"Hey, chappie, come on over."

Mark walked evenly across the lawn.

"I'm supposed to be getting a ride with Patrick," Mark said, sitting down. "And Patrick seems to be occupied."

"Oh, don't apologize!" Michael said. "Nice to know that not everybody's gone to put children in bed. Barbara will be down in a minute." Rob looked up, saying nothing. He seemed tired and a little subdued. He did not seem surprised at Mark's being there.

The light from the dying fire played unevenly over the men's faces. Rob poked and prodded with a stick and one of the logs burst briefly into flame. Mark was uncomfortable. He knew he'd made a mistake, the situation was too exposed. He shouldn't have stayed, he thought. When the screen door banged, all of them turned to see Barbara coming out of the house. She took long skips across the lawn.

"Well, look at you all!" she said. She rumpled Mark's hair. "What a nice surprise. Move over, Michael, don't be such a hog." Without looking at Mark, she squatted cross-legged next to Michael, making him scramble over.

"The children went to sleep all right?" Rob asked.

"Oh, they were fine. Sarah was just exhausted. She'd been so keyed-up about the concert, and then, of course, Michael and his great brouhaha just did her in."

"Come now, Barbara," Michael said.

"Really, Michael, you did provoke them. It's surprising, someone like yourself, a professional guest, we don't expect such lapses."

"Hear this?" Michael appealed to Rob. "Now she's calling me a leech."

Rob smiled and said nothing.

"Not a leech, Michael," Barbara said, "just someone who trades on other people's assets."

Michael groaned. "I don't know why you're always so hard on me, dear. Just let up, let up."

Barbara had no intention of letting up. She had a series of stories, all of them at Michael's expense: stories of Michael breaking his bed at Yale during a vigorous coupling with one of Andy Warhol's Super Stars, Michael's insulting a senator in a New York elevator, Michael's liaison with an Eastern European princess in a London town house. Rob drifted toward sleep, staring into the fire, not seeming to listen. Slender tongues of flame slithered in and out of the blackened logs. The stories seemed to be for Mark's benefit, yet Barbara scarcely glanced at him.

Michael protested that she was exaggerating. The two of them sparred. The talk was clever, quick, cruel, giving full play to bitter pleasures. Barbara jabbed absently at the fire with a charred stick.

"Look what we've done to your poor husband," Michael said. "We've bored him right to sleep. Rob? Hey, Rob." There was no response. Michael got to his knees and rubbed his fingers in the dead ashes. "Here. We can decorate him up a bit." Michael reached across and daubed a bit of the ash in the center of Rob's forehead. "How does he look?"

"Don't," Barbara said.

"Why not? Rob's an open-minded sort of fellow, if he woke up looking like a New Guinea mudman I'm sure he'd take it all in stride . . . What's that?" Michael swiveled his head back toward the house.

"I suppose that Patrick must have finally found the right record," Mark said. It was the sweet, formal music of Mozart, the violins slow-paced and grave, the music the children had danced to, hours before.

"Ahh," Michael said. The three of them listened silently to the music for a minute. Barbara tossed the charred stick into the flickering embers.

"When did Kate say she was coming?" Barbara asked.

"Two weeks. Her show's closing. God knows how it lasted as long as it did. She's coming out right after."

Barbara thought for a second, wet her fingers, leaned forward and rubbed the spot of ash from her sleeping husband's forehead. "Will you still be here?" she asked.

"Could be," Michael said. "I'm going to L.A. next week for a meeting, see if the moguls will trust young Michael with their millions. Keep your fingers crossed. I could come back, I suppose. If I'm welcome. If I'm not lapsed . . ."

"Don't be ridiculous."

"I wasn't being ridiculous. Just checking." Michael looked quickly across at Mark. "Oh, Kate will love him, won't she? Just her type, tall, athletic, sincere . . . She goes for the Gentle Ben types. What do you think, Barbara?"

"Mark's got someone."

"Well, I just didn't know how open-minded he was." Mark stared into the bright embers. He should shut Michael up. He glanced at Michael, saying nothing. "He'd better look out, all the same. A classic heartbreaker, our Kate. A little bit of the Saint Francis in that woman, she'll charm anything that moves, birds in the trees, movie directors, college boys on trains . . . In a game of Capture the Flag you'd definitely want her on your side." Leaning back on his elbows, Michael looked lazily back at Barbara to check her reactions. "A charmer, don't you think, Barbara?" Barbara said nothing. "Or do you think she's losing it?"

"Oh, Christ, Michael, stop it!"

"I'm sorry, darling, I just can't help myself. I always thought Jennifer was more beautiful than Kate, I know it's a minority view. And I told you what's happened to our sweet little Jennifer . . ."

The talk went on. The fire was gone except for a glow of coals, and the voices kept on, disembodied now. Mark couldn't listen anymore. He lay back, stared up at the dark mountains, at the wisp of cloud forming at the top of the Grand. The Mozart ended, Mark heard an owl call somewhere deep in the woods, and then the Mozart began again. Mark listened more closely to the music now.

There was a clarinet tossing out brief, swirling fragments and then the fragments were picked up, passed from instrument to instrument. The sweet, forgiving music could not blot out the unforgiving talk, the casual and nasty talk going on beside him, but what it did do was to bring the whole evening back to him, the innocent young bodies spinning across a bright floor. Suddenly Mark was angry. This was to have been Ellen's evening, not these people's, he saw clearly now he'd let them steal her time, and he was sickened by what he'd done.

He pushed himself to his feet. "I'm going to go look for Patrick," he said. "I think it's time for me to cash in on my ride home." His voice didn't hide his anger.

Barbara's eyes widened in the darkness. Michael stirred.

"O.K., chappie, if you insist," Michael said. "Just be careful you don't step on those two. God knows where you'll find them."

Mark moved up the lawn toward the music, across the long, sharp shadows cast by the house lights, up the porch steps and inside. Patrick was not there. Of course. The door to the back was wide open, a cold breeze blew through. The Mozart rang through the empty living room, phrases rolling out like matched pearls, one after the other. The house still smelled of smoke from the party. There was a spidery blotch of white on the Navajo rug where someone had sprinkled salt to soak up spilled wine. Record jackets lay scattered about the floor. Mark leaned over the stereo and clicked it off.

"Mark." His name was spoken softly, a few feet behind him.

He turned. It was Barbara.

"Are you all right?" she asked.

"I'm fine," he said. His eyes filled with tears, like a boy's.

"Did we disgust you?"

"No," he said. "I just thought it was time that I left."

"Sometimes we even disgust ourselves." She put her hand against his chest, "I'm glad that you stayed. I was glad, when I came out of the house, that you were there, by the fire." She kissed him lightly. "You shouldn't torture yourself about things. It's never worth it, you know."

"No?"

"No."

She stared at Mark, her eyes seeming to widen and deepen, at the same moment wakening fear and quelling it. She leaned into him, her head and hands against his chest, seeking comfort. He could feel the trembling in her body. He gently raised his arms around her.

It was then that they heard Patrick's hoarse singing somewhere out on the back lawn.

CHAPTER EIGHT

Her fingertips trailed across Tommy's bare back. It felt good, especially when she stopped fooling and dug deep into the shoulder muscles, the muscles that never quite lost their soreness once the whitewater season started.

"San Diego, right?" he said.

She squinted back at him. She was one of those women who are always having trouble with their contacts.

"San Diego," she said.

"Well, Cheryl, you thank San Diego for me. I'm going to miss you," he said.

She smiled. It meant a lot to Tommy, knowing that he could make women smile. Probably it meant too much.

Their clothes lay in a pile on the floor, her digital watch nestled in the folds of her embroidered jeans. Tommy reached out, picked up the watch, punched the button for the time. One-thirty. He had to get going. He was scheduled to take another raft of tourists down the river at two.

She shouldn't have come to his house. He had warned her before, never to come to his house. Always before they had met at the condo she was sharing for the month with her girlfriend. Once or twice they had met at the Big Sky Motel. Her coming to the house was taking too big a chance, but somehow they'd gotten away with it.

He'd been annoyed when he saw her coming up the walk. He'd yelled at her. "But it's my vacation," she'd yelled back, "it's the last of my vacation, I'm leaving."

"Yeah, it's your vacation, but it's my goddamned life," he'd shouted back.

In the end he'd let her stay. He said at first that he wouldn't sleep with her, it was too dangerous, and besides there was no time, he was due back at his next raft trip in an hour. He'd changed his mind somehow. She was going back to California in a couple of days and secretly it flattered him that she'd come, that she'd wanted him that much. Danger was part of it anyway, from the beginning.

He rolled over on his back, pulled her down to him, kissed her. She tried to pull away, but she was only playing. He held her with one hand, ran his other hand across her bare breasts, staring into her eyes. She looked at him dimly, wondering.

"Don't you have to go?" she asked.

"Yes, I have to go," he said.

Her face, above him, was round, soft, pretty, a hovering plum. He didn't think she was very smart. She and her friend, both elementary school teachers from San Diego, had come out to the Tetons for a month of fun; to ride horses, play tennis, get healthy, meet men. She'd come out to have a good time, that was all, nothing serious or dangerous, just indulge herself and forget a frustrating year with bratty eight-year-olds.

She was ready and willing and seemed to have no idea what the

word "consequences" even meant. Tommy both liked that and
didn't like it. Only once or twice had they talked about his wife,
and she didn't seem that interested in what he'd had to say. She
didn't realize the danger because there was no danger to her, and
he sure as hell wasn't going to tell her; just that once in a while he
wished she'd catch on by herself.

She hadn't so far. He was just part of her vacation, a nice piece
of scenery, like the elk and the rodeo and the sunsets over the
mountains. She was still beaming at him, waiting to see what he
wanted. She reached across to the bedside table and scooped up a
pair of Judy's earrings. Teasing, she pressed them to her bare
breasts, let them dangle down, shaking them in his face.

"Hey, come on," he said.

He grabbed the earrings away from her. He didn't think it was
funny. He put the earrings back on the table, next to the bottle of
hand lotion, the pile of Judy's unanswered mail. A blouse that Judy
had washed that morning hung drying on the closet door.

He started to feel real bad. It made him feel spooky, having this
woman in their bed. Only politeness kept him lying there.

It wasn't all his fault. He hadn't started any fight. He had been in
a good mood that morning. It was all so stupid. The phone had
rung while they were having breakfast, and Judy had jumped up to
answer it. When she came back to the table she was glowing. A
friend of theirs, a Mrs. Richardson who ran the café across from the
elk refuge, had called to confide in Judy that she was pregnant
again—for a fourth time. Tommy made a remark about her being a
baby machine. It was a dumb remark, maybe, a grumpy remark, he
wasn't even awake really, and that set Judy off. Was it so horrible
having a child? Was it any less worthy an activity than floating
tourists down a river in a rubber raft?

"So you want to be like her," he'd said.

"No, but I want to have a child," she'd said.

They were back into it, the old argument, the familiar pain. So
how are we going to have a child, how are we going to afford it? If
you'd get a real job . . . Real job! What the hell is a real job? A real
job is not playing make-believe cowboy. Tommy'd ended up shouting at her: I make more money than you do, why don't you make
some goddamned money, real money for a change, if you want a
kid so bad, carry your weight, I'll carry mine, what am I supposed
to be?

It wasn't going to get any better, he knew it. He wasn't going to give up what he had. Give it up for what? For a child, for some crummy job selling auto parts, working in a filling station, he couldn't think of what it would mean, he couldn't think his way through it.

What he had was the river. He was a good boatman, the best they had, at least up here in Wyoming. Every day he could go out and prove to himself that he was good, that there was nobody better at finding the tongue of the rapids, that smooth V of water that would rush a raft safely through, past the rocks and the boiling water.

Working the river, things came his way. How could people blame him for noticing. These girls from California threw themselves at him. He didn't take them up on it that often, just once in a while, when things started to close in on him.

He knew how glad he would be to see Judy when she came home tonight. That was how it always seemed to work. He would realize that it was Judy, his wife, that he loved, nobody else, the rest was just crap. This woman rubbing his back could think what she wanted, could think that what he and she had was real, but Tommy knew it wasn't. It would be over, he would treat Judy better, the equilibrium would return for a few days at least. The only real change would be the little rise in self-contempt Tommy felt with each repetition of betrayal.

He rolled himself up into a sitting position. "I've got to go," he said. Her hands fell away from his back. He stared out the second-story window down onto the street. Later he would wonder what odd perception or instinct for self-preservation made him look out that window just then, because it nearly saved him. Judy was walking down the street toward the house.

"She's coming!" he said. For a second Cheryl didn't get it, just stared at him in wonderment. "My wife! Jesus! Get your clothes, get into the bathroom! Move it!"

Cheryl squinted out the window and didn't see anyone. "Are you sure?"

"Goddamn it, just do what I tell you!" Tommy was on his feet. He grabbed up the pile of clothes and thrust it at her. The digital watch fell to the floor. He bent down to retrieve it, jammed it into the pocket of her jeans. "Get going!"

"What are you going to do?"

"Just let me take care of that!" Tommy flung open his closet door, belts fell to the floor, buckles clattering. He plucked his bathrobe off the hook.

"But what if she comes upstairs?"

"She won't. I'll take care of it. Get going!" He pushed her toward the door and she finally went, tiptoeing down the hallway. Tommy leaped down the stairs, pulling his bathrobe on as he went.

He made it to his big chair just as he heard the screen door opening. He scooped up an old *Newsweek* off the floor and opened it. Heart pounding, he tried to focus on the picture of the Osmond family.

"Tommy?" he heard her call from the porch.

"Yeah," he said, pulling his bathrobe tighter around him.

When she came in he closed the magazine and looked up at her. She seemed bewildered. He felt weak, giddy, not sure of himself yet.

"What are you doing home?"

"I didn't have another trip until two. My back was hurting like hell." He tossed the magazine aside. "I came home to soak it."

"I'm sorry," she said. She reached out, put her fingers on the back of his neck. Her lips were tight. She wasn't ready to smile yet; their fight from the morning still left its traces.

"I'm sorry about this morning," he said. "It was my fault."

"I don't know if it was or not," she said. "I wish I did."

"I thought you had classes all day," he said.

"I do. I just forgot that I was supposed to bring a new music book to the Harrison girl. She's going into Intermediate."

He stood up, flexed his sore shoulder. "Oh, yeah? I thought she wasn't that good. It must be that you're teaching up a storm out there." He felt an almost irresistible urge to laugh. He was so happy to have pulled the whole thing off, it just seemed hilarious.

Judy walked across the room, opened the piano bench.

"You know, Judy, I was thinking about this morning . . ." She looked back at him suspiciously. "I was thinking that maybe we're just seeing these things wrong."

"What things?"

A board creaked in the ceiling overhead. His face reddened but he tried to show no alarm, tried to keep talking.

"I don't know exactly," he said. "Just that we always end up getting so hung up. If we could find another way to talk . . . It's my fault, too, I'm not saying that it's your fault . . . but it's like we forget that we're on the same side."

Again there was a creak in the ceiling. What the hell was she doing up there? What did she need to go walking around for?

Judy stood over the piano bench, waiting to see if he had anything more to say. "Do you know where the music books went?" she said finally.

He walked toward the piano. "I thought I saw them up here this morning. Let's see . . ." He leafed through the piles of sheet music on the piano top, setting aside the little salt busts of Beethoven and Brahms that Judy passed out to her students as prizes. "What about these?"

"No, Tommy, new books."

The third time Judy heard it too. She glanced swiftly at Tommy. "Who's upstairs?"

"Nobody."

"Somebody's upstairs, Tommy!"

He said nothing and she ran past him, heading for the stairs. He grabbed her by the arm. The sheet music he'd been holding sailed to the floor. Judy pulled away.

"Don't go up there!"

She ran up the stairs, avoiding his lunge for her, and he ran after her.

"Oh, Christ, Tommy, oh, Christ!" Standing in the bathroom door, Judy turned away, covering her mouth with the back of her hand. Tommy stared in, over her shoulder. Cheryl was down on all fours on the floor, dressed only in her underpants and her bra. She squinted up at the two of them, her round face trembling with humiliation.

"I can't find my contact," she said.

Judy laughed, terribly, and then a sound came from her like a moan.

"Get up, goddamn it!" Tommy shouted. He turned to Judy, put his hand lightly on her shoulder, "I'm sorry . . ." She pulled away, taking a couple of steps down the hall.

Tommy stepped quickly into the bathroom, grabbed Cheryl by the wrist, tried to pull her up. "Hell, get off the floor at least," he whispered hoarsely.

"Leave her alone!" Judy shouted.

Cheryl was on her knees, steadying herself with one hand on the sink. "I'm sorry . . . I'm sorry . . . please . . . I can't find my contact . . . please don't step on it . . . I'm so sorry . . ." she whimpered.

Tommy spun around, crazed. Judy stood in the hallway, both hands on the wall, her head back as if she'd just had the wind knocked out of her.

"Judy, look, I'm sorry . . ." The word "sorry" tasted like poison in his mouth. That was just what the whining Cheryl kept saying, sorry, sorry, sorry. Everybody was sorry. "We'll talk about it," Tommy said, "all of it, anything you want, just let me get her out of here."

"Why here, Tommy? Why did you have to bring her here? In our house? On our bed."

"I didn't bring her here, Judy. I told her not to come here. I did." Judy was silent. Tommy didn't know what to expect. He'd never been in anything that came even close to this. He thought he had a chance. She wasn't coming back at him. She was hurt, but as long as she wasn't coming back at him, there was a chance. They would talk, he'd face up to it like a man, but then they'd get through it, he'd stop acting like an asshole. The thing was to just keep talking.

"It's the first time I ever, Judy . . ."

"The first time!" Judy was incredulous. "Tommy, no, don't." She suddenly began to laugh.

"My first time here," he said, correcting himself. "I never before . . . had anyone . . . in the house."

"You don't have to tell me where, Tommy. You don't have to tell me how many. I know. I know. I've always known . . ."

Judy had come a step closer. Tommy was in the bathroom door. Cheryl had risen slowly to her feet behind him. He was wedged in.

"You think I can't tell . . . these little numbers of yours? The way they look at me when I pass them on the street, little blond California girls giving me that little curious look. Why should it matter how many?" she said. Judy stared past him at Cheryl, who had hurriedly pulled on her blouse. "Does it matter to her?"

"I don't think of myself as a little number," Cheryl said.

"You don't?" Judy said. "Well, you'd better. As a matter of fact, you'd better get used to the idea of thinking of yourself as a rather high little number." Cheryl wasn't looking at her now, but concentrating on buttoning her blouse. Judy kept on. "You probably think that you're unique, that this is something special . . ."

Cheryl looked up. "I think that Tommy and I have a relationship."

Judy laughed, put a trembling hand to her forehead. Cheryl blushed with anger.

"You can laugh at me all you want. Go ahead. But don't think I don't know all about you. About all your bitching and complaining that the house isn't neat enough and why doesn't he get a real job."

"Cheryl, shut up!" Tommy said.

"And you never want to have sex because you're too tired or too worried because you don't have your little suburban house with a carport . . . How you never enjoy it, just lay there and wait for it to be over . . . and then think that you've done him a favor. That's why he turns to other women and always will. You don't appreciate him for what he is. I do."

Judy, white-faced now, looked up at Tommy, who was squeezed between the two of them. "You told her this?"

"I didn't. I didn't. She's fuckin' making it up out of her head."

"Is she? Are you sure? Because it sounds to me like it's pretty much true. It's all so simple and stupid anybody can see it. Even her. It doesn't take a genius."

"I'm not going to stand here and be insulted," Cheryl said. "I happen to be a teacher. I'm going now. This is just between the two of you . . . Excuse me, but I'm going now . . ."

"Don't listen to her, Judy, she's nuts. Who the hell is she, anyway? I don't know where she got this stuff, I didn't say anything. Maybe this is the way they talk in California, shit."

"I'm leaving, Tommy," Judy said. "I'm leaving, do you hear me?"

"She's nuts, Judy, just let me get her out of here."

"It's so simple and stupid," Judy said. "All along . . ." It looked as if her face was caving in. She pushed past Tommy, past the terrified Cheryl, swinging around, grabbing wildly at the shower curtain, tearing it free. The pipe pulled loose and a spray of plaster showered onto the floor. Cheryl pressed herself against the bathroom wall. Judy spun around, her arms outstretched, knocking bottles off the top of the toilet, sending them flying.

"Judy, stop it!" Tommy shouted. He grabbed her and she struggled against him, twisting free, pounding on the mirror of the medicine cabinet with her fists, shattering the glass.

"Judy! Judy!" he shouted, but she didn't seem to be able to hear him. He felt himself losing control, it was like the boat hitting fast water, when the oars are touching nothing, flailing air. He reached up and slapped her across the face. It was the first time he had ever hit her. They stared at one another. The only sound now was Cheryl's sobbing as she sat on the edge of the bathtub, clutching her shoes.

CHAPTER NINE

It was Barbara who took Judy in. When Judy ran out of her house that afternoon she knew she wasn't going back to Tommy. It was over, she knew that absolutely, yet she had no idea what she was going to do or what steps had to be taken. She had afternoon music lessons to be taught. She would teach them. There was nothing else at hand.

The lesson with the Harrison girl went well. They worked hard, the little girl had improved immensely, and was delighted when she was presented with her new music books. After leaving the Harrisons, Judy drove to the Campbells, and it was there in the middle of the lesson, with Sarah repeating some of the simplest finger exercises, that Judy began to cry.

Barbara came in and saw that something was terribly wrong. She took Judy into the kitchen, telling Sarah to keep working on her lesson by herself for a while. Judy told Barbara everything, told her that she was never going back, not that night, not ever. When she couldn't talk anymore she wept again, Barbara holding her, a woman she scarcely knew, the only sound in the big house the repetitive rising and falling of scales as Sarah obediently worked on alone.

Barbara said that Judy could stay with them. Judy resisted at first, but Barbara insisted. There was a lot of room, there would be a lot of privacy, and it would be no trouble for them. Judy could stay as long as she wanted, she needn't pay them anything, and in any case Sarah could stand a few extra music lessons.

That evening after Judy had gone up to her room, Barbara told Rob and the children a version of what had happened. Later, when the children had been sent to bed, she filled Rob in on the details. When he heard that Tommy had slapped her, he was enraged.

"The man should be arrested," Rob said.

"Rob, come on."

"I'm serious. If he beat her up something should be done."

"He didn't beat her up, Rob," Barbara said. "He slapped her. Once. It's something that happens."

"I've never slapped you."

"No, you never have," Barbara said.

"And I never would," Rob said. "I know the people out here. I've dealt with guys like Tommy all my life. I know how they treat women."

Barbara stared at him across the table for several seconds. "O.K.," she said. "Maybe you know. But just don't do anything, all right? Just leave it alone."

In the morning Judy decided that she was going back to the house and move out all her stuff. Both Rob and Barbara thought it was a crazy idea. If Judy needed anything, let them go collect it. That way there would be no danger of another confrontation.

"I'm not afraid of him," Judy said. "Why should I be afraid?" She was going to get her things, that morning, and by herself.

When she drove up to the house, Tommy was gone. There was a note for her on the kitchen table that she tore up without reading. She worked quickly; she had almost everything in boxes before Tommy's car came up the driveway.

Their fight was terrible, worse in its way than the fight the afternoon before. Tommy was crazy with fear and need. He demanded to know where she'd spent the night, accused her of spending it with some man. She tried to take the boxes out to the car, but he physically blocked her way. He began to pull things out of the boxes and throw them on the floor. They began to scream at one another.

"Go ahead, clean me out, take everything!"

"I'm just taking what's mine, Tommy. I'm taking these boxes, and tomorrow I'm coming back with a truck and I'm going to take the piano, and then that's it, the rest is yours."

"Hell if you are! Hell if you are going to take that piano! I paid for that piano!"

"You did not, Tommy, you did not! I paid for that piano, two hundred dollars, I got it from those friends of the Harrisons, you know that's not true! There's no question about it."

"I think there is a question. You take your boxes and you get out of here, but that goddamned piano is staying right where it is."

Judy stared at him. What a fool he seemed, how totally farcical in his lying, a bully and an ape. All she felt for him was disgust. She couldn't imagine how she had ever been married to him.

"Maybe I'll start playin' it," he said. "You don't know. You just don't know." He picked up the salt busts of Beethoven and Brahms and Wagner and calmly winged them against the wall.

Judy turned and ran out of the house, got into her car and roared off, without having taken a single box of anything. She drove back to the Campbells' and collapsed.

Mark heard all of this not from Judy, but from Barbara, who called him at work. Judy was going to call you herself, Barbara said, but she was so exhausted and sometimes telling your friends is the hardest thing of all. It was pretty confusing on the first telling—something about Tommy and a girl, Judy getting hit, Tommy not letting Judy move out—but the favor Barbara was asking was clear enough: would Mark go by Tommy's and pick up Judy's things? They were all packed in boxes, probably all still right there by the front door. It sounded crazy to Mark. It sounded like meddling, but Barbara made it seem both urgent and essential, her voice edged with the hysteria that was infecting everyone.

Somehow he agreed to do it. It was the first time she had ever asked anything of him. Vulnerable as he was to her now, there was almost nothing he wouldn't have agreed to, yet it made him profoundly uneasy.

Mark told Patrick that he had to leave and didn't offer any explanation other than it was something personal, something he had to do, and he couldn't say when he would be back. Mark was out of the shop before Patrick's shock had a chance to register.

Mark drove by the float-trip office, hoping to check it all out with Tommy, but Tommy wasn't there. The woman at the desk said he hadn't been in all day.

Mark drove to their house. He stood outside, knocked, there was no answer. The door was open. Mark opened it and stepped inside. Someone had slid the piano halfway across the floor where it now sat on a diagonal, blocking the stairs. The half-dozen boxes were all there, just where Barbara said they'd be, and it took no more than five minutes to load them all in the car.

Mark spent the half hour it took to drive out to the Campbells' trying to figure how Barbara had gotten involved in all this and why. Hearing about the explosion between Tommy and Judy was like hearing about something Mark knew would happen, sooner or later, it was the recitation of the inevitable, but why was Barbara the one doing the reciting? She didn't even know them. Mark wasn't sure if it was an act of kindness or an act of intrusion.

When he got out to the ranch Barbara helped him carry the boxes into the house. Jeff and Sarah were making sandwiches in the kitchen, working with the somber look of children laboring under parental orders. Barbara seemed tired and drawn, yet there was an air of authority about her, the air of someone who'd taken charge.

"We'll just leave the boxes down here for now," she said. "I think Judy's finally asleep upstairs." Barbara set down the box she was carrying. Mark set his on top of it. She dusted off her hands.

"Is there anything else I can do?" Mark said, feeling strained and oddly formal all of a sudden.

"Not really," she said. "I told the children we might take a hike this afternoon. If it was quiet around here maybe Judy could get some real sleep. You could come with us if you wanted. But you probably have to get back."

It took Mark only a second to answer. "At this point, hell, Patrick can get along without me. Let's do it."

The children set out up the mountain at a fast clip. Barbara and Mark tried to keep up, without speaking at first, except to point out some yellow buttercups, some red Indian paintbrush in a meadow, a blue grouse waddling stupidly under a nearby spruce. There were a million questions hanging in the air, but this was not the time to ask them. The total focus now was on keeping pace.

As they moved higher, they could see down through the trees to a corner of the ranch. Sarah delighted in pointing it out. At each turn in the trail she would turn and look back. "There it is, Mom, there's our place," she would say.

The clouds started to move off the mountains and it became beautifully clear. Finally Mark left Barbara and raced ahead to play with the children, leaving the trail to crash through the woods and across the stream. They played a kind of hide-and-seek, Mark concealing himself in the cliffs along the stream, only to reemerge to let the children pelt him with snowballs that they had gathered from the white patches that still lay in the most sheltered part of the forest.

As he made his way along the rocks, from handhold to handhold, watching the children's shapes flickering through the trees on the far side of the stream, Mark's heart beat fast with the game of it, listening to the echoing children's voices shouting back and forth, searching for him.

Playing was a release from the darkness of the morning, a way to shake the dread that had clung to him from the moment he'd walked into Tommy's empty house, moved out the boxes of his friend's wife. He wanted to be good with these children. Up ahead he heard the roaring of a waterfall.

They found a wide, flat rock just above the falls where they could lay out their picnic. The kids weren't much interested in eating, they were too wound up from their hiking and playing, full of energy and ready to go on. There were beaver ponds in the meadows up ahead, Jeffrey said, he remembered them from last year when their dad had taken them.

"It's not that far," Jeffrey said. "It's probably not even a half-hour walk, easy."

"You and Sarah can go," Barbara said. "Mark and I are going to stay here and finish our lunch like civilized beings. We'll come up later. Here. You take a couple of apples with you."

"Mom, it'll be fun."

"I'm sure it will be. So you better get going. Sarah, come on now, finish your sandwich."

The children ran off, up the trail, with Sarah shouting to Jeff to wait for her.

Barbara and Mark were alone now. They said nothing at first, listening to the voices of the children grow fainter and then disappear as they moved up the trail. Mark stared into the rushing water that sparkled with afternoon light. The steady explosions of the falls were mesmerizing.

"You were wonderful with the children," Barbara said. "They loved you."

"I'm not sure that they loved me, but they sure liked to hit me with snowballs."

"You're a nice man. You were nice to help out."

"I've known Tommy and Judy a long time. They're my friends. Both of them," Mark said. Barbara was silent. "Do you think Judy will go back to him?"

"I don't know. You know them better than I do." Barbara picked up the remains of one of the children's sandwiches and wrapped it in cellophane. "Do you think that she could?"

"They've been together a long time."

"And so?"

"So I think it would be real hard to make a break."

"It can be real hard to stay. After something like that," she said.

"It was nice of you to take her in the way you have. Someone you don't even know."

"I like her. I liked her the first time I met her."

"But it's a little odd, isn't it, that she would come to you . . ."

"No, not really. Sometimes it's easier to turn to a stranger at a time like that," Barbara said, her eyes rising to meet his. Mark looked at her quickly, but she turned away as if it was nothing, when it was a long way from nothing. Mark saw then that she had been affected by what had happened to Judy, her taking her in was more than just upper-class graciousness, she had identified in some way that Mark didn't fully understand.

Mark stared down at the tiny magenta monkey flowers at the water's edge. "What will she do then?" Mark said. "If she doesn't go back to Tommy?"

"She can stay with us. For as long as she wants."

"Rob agrees?"

"Oh, absolutely. Rob sees himself as a great protector of the innocent."

"Are you serious?"

"Why wouldn't I be?"

"Well, I don't know. Just that sometimes I have a hard time telling. Maybe it's my problem. I know you like to talk. But a lot of the time I don't know what you're telling me."

"Maybe sometimes I'm being ironic."

"Maybe. But the way you play with words, it seems to me that a lot of the time you hide behind them." The remark was too harsh. Mark didn't know why he'd said it.

"What is it that you want to know?"

"I'm not sure. Maybe nothing at all. It's just that every time that we're together, that we get close to saying something, we get cut off, one way or the other."

"No one's cutting us off now."

"No."

"You want to know about Rob as a protector of the innocent? Well, maybe it's time I told you."

Mark lay back on the flat rock while Barbara talked almost without interruption. She told Mark first about Rob's father, who had been not only a hugely successful businessman, but an educated and cultured one as well. He sat on the boards of museums as well as those of banks. He was a man of inexhaustible energy. He was a

Roosevelt Democrat who reared his children never to act as if they were any better than anyone else and, at the same time, to secretly demand perfection from themselves.

Rob's father was a hard act to follow.

In the summers Rob and his family spent a month at the ranch in Wyoming, where they worked at being ranchers in the same way they worked at business or science or education; with the assurance and tenacity of those who know they are born to conquer things. The ranch meant more than Rob's father's other achievements. For all his culture, education and breeding, Barbara had always suspected that Rob's father secretly saw himself as the Virginian, brave, hard, competent, just. That piece of Wyoming land, those mountains were to be his true measure; he worked hard at winning the respect of the old-time ranchers and settlers.

During those summers Rob learned to ride, dig postholes, handle livestock, hunt elk, and yet he was an imperfect heir of his father's passion. He often yearned to be back in New York, hitting the Long Island beaches, or traveling in Europe like his schoolmates. Rob remembered going in search of stray cattle with a transistor radio playing Johnny Mathis stuck in his saddlebag.

Rob went to Harvard, where he was involved in student government his first two years, then was gradually drawn into the civil rights movement and joined the march to Selma. When he returned to Cambridge, there was a brief period when he considered dropping out of school to do voter registration work in Mississippi. After a long, earnest conversation with his father, he didn't. In his senior year he worked with a student-faculty committee on civil rights, serving on the committee with faculty members who remembered what an outstanding student Rob's father had been.

Barbara met Rob late in his sophomore year. He didn't pay much attention to her at first; she was at Holyoke and there were plenty of Radcliffe women willing to give him all the attention he might want. Barbara, however, persisted. He seemed to her the most desirable man she had ever met; he was charming, he was gentle, both authoritative and curiously innocent.

When he went to England on a Rhodes she followed him, studying art in London. When they returned together in June, the announcement of their marriage had already been made.

He went to Wharton Business School while she worked and took sculpture classes at night, but the art didn't matter much then, what mattered and absorbed all her energy was the romance of his family. Having won Rob, she couldn't stop there, she had to win his parents as well. Rob's father had been reserved with her at first; he found her a little too flippant, too acidic. Gradually she began to see signs of approval, and then when she gave birth to Jeffrey, delivered the family's first grandson, she knew that she had won, won something back that she had lost years before, a father's love.

Six months after Jeffrey was born, Rob's father died. It was as if the rules of the universe had all been changed once again. For about six months Rob was troubled by bouts of depression, of sadness, and then things began to happen.

He'd been working at his father's bank and very quietly he began to take a few chances. He started putting money into the kind of entrepreneurial ventures that his father had always frowned on: offshore hedge funds, new inventions, smaller, off-beat operations. He turned out to be very good at it.

Rob had always enjoyed being around people much more radical and daring than he was. He was the perfect foil for them; he laughed at their stories, argued cunningly without offending. Now, suddenly, he had a greater freedom to devote to these friendships. For a while it seemed as if they were having someone over to dinner every other night; someone who'd just returned from smuggling dope out of Turkey or working with Chavez in California or marrying a Soviet dissident to help them escape Russia. Rob loved these people. Barbara began to see that he needed them.

Then one night a new couple came over. She was a writer, with long dark hair, very beautiful, very tough and profane, a historian at Columbia. He was a novelist, older than she was and a bit desiccated, sardonic and witty. They had been married once, then divorced, but they had remained close. They were each other's best friends, they said. The remark made Barbara very depressed later. Rob had argued with her that it shouldn't have. He was intrigued with them.

The woman's name was Margo. A week later, Rob mentioned that he was having lunch with her. Then, a week after that, he mentioned that he'd run into her again.

"Were you jealous?" Mark asked.

"A little," Barbara said. A red squirrel had crept out onto the rock, sniffing for food. Sunlight slanted through the trees, played across the rush of water. "I was afraid. I would tease him, wanting him to reassure me. Then one night he came home and asked me what I would think if he and Margo slept together. It was an incredible question, an unfair question, and he put it to me with such innocence, like a little boy, as if it were all up to me and whatever I decided he would abide by. He was very tender. He said he'd been thinking about it for a long time and had been afraid to talk about it, and yet why shouldn't we be able to talk about it? He said it made him feel better just to be able to utter the words. I was outraged and I was frightened. Flabbergasted, that's the word, isn't it? That's what I was." The word made Barbara smile, for just a second. "At first I couldn't say anything. I felt as if there should be some rule for me to apply, some common-sense rule, but I didn't know what it was. I got up and went into Jeffrey's room. I remember looking at him asleep in his crib, all the stuffed animals on the shelves and the bright paintings on the walls, and then I remember looking out into the back garden with all the lights from the town houses behind. All I could think of was how protected I'd thought I'd been, when I hadn't been protected at all. That there was no protection. That I kept trying to make order, a neat little picket fence around my life, and people kept knocking it down. It was ludicrous. Rob asking permission! I sat there in Jeffrey's room for a long time, feeling quite sorry for myself, watching the lights go out across the garden, and then Rob came in to see if I was O.K. and I said I was. Did I want to come to bed? In a minute, I said. And he was so very tender toward me for the next few days. More tender than ever."

"And did they have an affair?"

"No. Of course not. I didn't say anything, I couldn't, and after about a week he came home early from work one day and told me he couldn't do it. That the most important thing in his life was our marriage, that things would be just like before."

"Were they?"

"No. At first I thought there was a chance. We tried, I think, both of us. But something had changed, or maybe we just let it change. I felt I couldn't invest everything, not in the same way. I needed a hedge. I wasn't going to rely on the fixed order of things. I started to take sculpture classes again. My teacher at Cooper Union was a man named Salvatore, stocky, barrel-chested, with a beard that came almost up to his eyes, short, powerful arms, and very bad English. Very charming.

"The other students were all young, urban, poor and hip, and frankly I felt condescended to. I was square, but one thing about us squares is that we're reared for competition. I was determined to prove to them that I was not just another upper-middle-class matron fooling around with art. They were all pretty scornful at first. One of the nicest things about Salvatore was that he didn't seem to notice certain things, maybe it was just that he didn't know the signs—the way you brushed your hair, the kind of bag you carried, it really didn't matter to him. He liked my work. He liked the fact that I worked hard.

"I knew that he was flirting with me, but then he flirted with everyone. I liked it, but I didn't think very much about it. At times I thought it was just his idea of courtesy, that if he didn't flirt with women they might be offended.

"My work got better and better. I proved that I was better than anyone else and I even started getting some respect from those hip girls who grew up on Eleventh Street. My work was chosen to be exhibited in a show, and Salvatore was very excited about that. Work was something that he was terribly serious about, and he became more and more exacting about what I should be doing. It was exhilarating.

"At the end of the year Salvatore threw a party for all his students at his loft. I went by myself. Rob was working and I admit I was just as glad. There were a lot of Salvatore's friends there, faintly scandalous-looking people; a Swedish flag-maker in a silk jumpsuit, a man who ran a pornographic jewelry shop, some young, very attractive Italians claiming to be out-of-work film directors.

"Salvatore made a palenta for all of us, and afterwards he got out his banjo and we all sang songs in Italian and Spanish and French, whatever we knew. Salvatore kept laughing all the time.

"Someone put records on and dancing started. There was nothing very subtle about Salvatore's dancing. At first I was embarrassed. We were dancing in front of the other students, all of whom knew that I was married. Part of me liked it, of course, it was just another way of showing them. Everything about Salvatore was very strong, very strong hands, he was hard to pull away from, but there was nothing mean about him.

"After we danced he took me around his loft to look at his sculpture. There were pieces everywhere, finished and unfinished, models and casts, bits of machinery and junk that he hadn't found a use for yet. He was asking me things about myself in his soft Italian voice and I scarcely heard him, I was burning up. Then he asked me if I would stay with him. I said no, I had to go back to my husband. All he said was 'Why?'

"A perfectly stupid question. I would have laughed, except I thought maybe he hadn't understood, the old language barrier. I think I said something, something ironic probably, like, 'It's an old American tradition, going home to your husband,' something like that. He just looked at me and then he asked me, 'Is that what you want to do?' And I said yes, it was.

"I left then. I got my coat and said goodbye to the other students as best I could and walked out on the street. There I was on Houston Street at one in the morning trying to find a cab and there were no cabs and I was trying to figure out why I'd left, when I hadn't wanted to leave . . .

"Salvatore had made it sound so simple. All I had to do was figure out what I wanted. As if that was a simple matter. It's really funny, isn't it? For someone like me, who, as you say, likes to talk . . . and this man with his thousand-word English vocabulary." She spoke to Mark as if their experiences had somehow been the same. Mark picked a pebble from the rock surface, pitched it into the water below.

"I stood there on Houston Street with some part of me just crying out like a child. I thought about Rob coming to me and asking whether or not he could sleep with Margo, I thought about . . . oh, God, I don't know. One thing for sure, I wasn't going to go uptown and ask Rob's permission. If there was anything I'd learned, it was that there was no one to rely on, no order to rest on. I had waited for my father to come home and he hadn't, tried to be a good wife and mother and then had my husband come asking for rule changes . . . I know, it sounds like special pleading, doesn't it? Well, maybe it is. But it suddenly all seemed like a great comedy.

"I must have walked around for at least another hour. Then I went into a pay phone at the Esso station. Salvatore didn't sound surprised to hear from me. He was quite good-natured on the phone. I asked him if he was alone and he said he was. Salvatore was the sort of person who would not be held to telling the truth if lying was the more gallant thing to do, he probably cleared his loft out five minutes after I called. I asked him if I could come up. Said that I was ready to take a chance . . ."

"And you made love to him?" Mark asked.

"Yes."

Mark tossed a stick down into the water, watched the stream swirl it down over the falls. He felt a wave of sadness come over him. What she was telling him made sense to him, but he felt that she was not like him, that she had experienced things that he had little access to. It never occurred to him to condemn her for what she was saying, it seemed too inevitable, but it made him sad.

"How long did that go on?" Mark asked.

"A year and a half."

"Did Rob know?"

"He discovered it. Eventually."

"How?"

"It was perfectly awful. It was carelessness . . . I don't know. We took more and more chances, and then one January day in Central Park the photographer for the *Daily News* was out looking for a nice wintry picture and he got one, of me and Salvatore sliding down the hill on a tray."

"And Rob saw it?"

She nodded. "A lot of people saw it. I was purportedly downtown buying a birthday present for Sarah. God, did that make it worse. Everything made it worse."

"Did you try to lie your way out of it?"

"No. It didn't occur to me. For a while I didn't think we were going to survive it."

"But you did survive it."

"We're still here, aren't we?"

"Do you still love him? Rob, I mean?"

She hesitated for a second. Jeffrey's Swiss army knife was on the rock beside her and she picked it up, closed the blade with the flat of her hand. "I don't know. We've shaped each other. We've had children together, wonderful children. We've gotten through so much . . . that means more than you think . . ." She looked sharply at him.

"What was it like? Seeing that guy . . ."

"Salvatore," she said.

"Salvatore. Seeing him like that. A year and a half is a long time. No one knew?"

"No one. One or two people suspected, maybe. It's very hard, remembering exactly what it was like now. Most of the time it was good, I thought it was good, and some of the time it was very, very painful. It was intense and sensual and I was willing to rearrange everything to be with him . . ."

"I can't imagine," Mark said.

"It was a totally double life," Barbara said. "The transitions were the hardest. Trying to rearrange myself as I took the cab uptown, checking my face in the rearview mirror, trying to hide every sign, erase any slip of paper, making foolproof excuses . . ."

Mark stared at her. Did she want him to judge her? Why was she telling him this? Why was she risking herself with him?

"Then it ended after Rob found out."

"That's right."

"How long ago was that?"

"It doesn't matter."

"Do you ever see him anymore?"

"I go to his exhibitions when I see them listed in the paper. I don't go on opening, or when I think he might be there. That's all."

"But then, since then . . ."

She smiled wryly. "I don't make it a practice of mine." She looked away, pained suddenly. "But it wasn't the only time, no." Neither of them spoke for what seemed like a long time. "I wonder what you're thinking," she said. "You think I'm terrible, don't you?"

"No."

"You think I'm a rapacious, hungry, spoiled upper-class bitch who just won't grow up."

"No, I'm just confused."

"Why?"

"That wasn't what I was expecting you to tell me."

"What were you expecting?"

"I don't know. I thought you were going to tell me about Kate," Mark said. Barbara looked down, smiling. "Is that funny? Everybody keeps talking about this Kate, Kate's coming . . . you didn't mention her once."

"And?"

"I thought you were going to tell me that Kate and Rob were lovers."

"They were," Barbara said. She stood up, dusting off her jeans. "I wonder where the children are? Do you think they're all right?" She stared up toward the trail and then she began to cry.

They didn't go look for the children. Barbara cried for not very long, Mark standing there, numbed, unable to go to her, to touch or comfort her, and then they sat down on the rocks again, not speaking, watching the rush of water. Mark felt as if he couldn't focus or think, too stunned by what he had heard already.

Barbara began to talk again.

She and Rob had known Kate for years. Kate was beautiful, as beautiful as anyone at Radcliffe, many thought, and without doubt the best actress. She had immense talents, both intellectual and dramatic. Everyone who saw her onstage at the Loeb during those years predicted instant stardom.

It didn't happen. She certainly hadn't failed. She had worked more or less steadily in either films or onstage, but somehow, after a dozen years, her career had mysteriously stalled. Some said it was just bad luck; films that were shot but not released, the lead in a musical version of *Heartbreak House* that turned out to be the fiasco of the decade. Some said she'd had bad advice. Others claimed that she was difficult to work with, that she sabotaged productions, that she was too cerebral or not hungry enough. Many felt she saved her truest performing instincts for her private life.

There had never been a shortage of men in Kate's life. Kate laid out a rich table, someone had said of her once. She was charming, talented, beautiful, intelligent, and no one was more skillful at arranging for men to fall in love with her. Kate herself admitted that she needed it; having men fall in love with her was a way of avoiding scrutiny, avoiding detection. The men she chose were usually intelligent, kind, rather gentle, and their relationship with her ordinarily ended up being the one high drama of their lives—which was the way that Kate insisted that it be. These affairs never lasted more than a year and were always conducted in public.

The initial raptures and declamations of hope were quickly followed by darker insights, small hurts escalating into fearsome battles. These once passive men were inspired and goaded into previously unimaginable paroxysms. The pattern was fixed: rejection and reconciliation, new outrages, flurries of notes and phone calls, hysterical confrontations in front of friends, stage managers and waiters and, after all this, massive recriminations, the trauma of ending always softened by the presence of the next man, always gentler and kinder than any of the others. Precisely because she offered such dazzling possibilities to men, it seemed that there would always be other men, that she could feed her romantic addiction indefinitely, continue what she knew to be evasions. It seemed that she could go on forever.

After two years on the West Coast doing work on films that went nowhere, Kate came back to New York to make another assault on the legitimate stage. It was then that she began to see more and more of Rob and Barbara.

It was her relationships with women that Kate prided herself on,

despite the fact that the vast majority of women feared her, instinctively fled her. Barbara liked her. She enjoyed Kate's intelligence,
her malicious wit, her charm, and a generosity that seemed to blos-
som when Kate became genuinely close to someone. In part they
grew close because they became fellow conspirators.

Barbara admired the candor with which Kate conducted her
affairs. Barbara envied that apparent forthrightness that contrasted
so sharply with the secret double life that Barbara had led for so
long, that life of deception that could be maintained only by an
endless act of will, of attention to detail.

As the two women grew closer, they inevitably began to exchange confidences. It was fun: they laughed over the absurdities
of men, of themselves, forgave each other their shortcomings, dug
deeper, began to invent theories of why they fell from grace as
often as they did. Barbara relaxed with Kate and over a period of
time confessed most everything. Those accumulated confessions
were something Barbara came to regret; Kate's reputation, after all,
was built on candor, not discretion, and it's always been true that
the easiest people to tell secrets to aren't necessarily the best people to keep them.

It was in New York that Kate finally became involved with a man
who was as strong as she was. Philippe Chinard was a powerfully
built man of fifty who had won many awards for his documentary
films on Algeria, Cuba and Mozambique. He was a man of immense presence, a well-educated man of private income who
courted danger, a man with left-wing, even revolutionary, sympathies who still managed to enjoy drinking with the best people
in the best places. Philippe lived his life every bit as dramatically as
Kate did hers.

Philippe and Kate battled and raged at one another, stormed out
of restaurants, wrote vicious letters, took cabs crosstown at four in
the morning to make up. Philippe never backed down. When Kate,
exhausted, wanted to end it, he wouldn't let her. None of her escalating, hysterical attacks would make him back off.

At the start of the affair Rob had considered himself a friend of
both of them. He would go over to Kate's apartment to deliver mes-
sages for Philippe when Philippe and Kate weren't talking. He
would meet Philippe for a late drink when Philippe needed consoling, take a cab to the theater district during his lunch hour to
calm a distraught Kate.

Rob looked up to Philippe; because the older man was an artist,

an intellectual, a fearless man of action, because Philippe was fa-
mous and Rob was impressed with fame. Most important of all,
from Rob's point of view, was the fact that, even if Philippe was
something of a bastard, he also seemed to have led an uncom-
promising life.

Rob was fascinated by the battle between Philippe and Kate.
Barbara was drawn into it too, but she quickly saw the dangers involved and tried to pull away. Rob's willingness to be sucked in
began to frighten Barbara and she tried to talk to him about it, but
he claimed not to understand. Philippe and Kate were their friends.
When your friends are in trouble you help them out, it was as simple as that.

In the last stages of their relationship, Philippe and Kate turned
everything at hand into a weapon. They began to compete over
who was closest to Rob, who had his true sympathy. Kate was in
terrible shape, suffering killing headaches, unable to sleep without
pills. She had to drop out of the play she was rehearsing. Again
and again she tried to break it off with Philippe, but Philippe
wouldn't hear of it. She would cave in, spend a night with him, and
that would only make it worse. Kate's doctor told Rob that she was
near collapse.

On the crucial afternoon Rob was at Kate's apartment. Rob, the
protector of the innocent, was tending her. She was in the bedroom,
trying to get some sleep. Rob sat in the living room, intercepting
phone calls. Philippe called and was furious when Rob told him he
couldn't speak with Kate. Philippe demanded. Rob refused. A half
hour later, Philippe was pounding on the apartment door. Rob and
Philippe fought in the open doorway. Rob was inspired; he was
Shane, defending the beleaguered; it was the first time in his life
he had dared to take anyone on of that size, with that authority. It
was an extraordinary moment.

Rob and Kate became lovers. To the two of them, at that moment, it seemed inevitable. He was her savior, she had come to rely
on him totally. He nursed her, he was tender with her, the way
Philippe never could have been. Barbara was told, they were
quite out in the open with it. Kate had insisted. Perhaps inadver-
tently, perhaps not, Kate let Rob know that she knew about Barbara's falls from grace, knew more than Rob did, as it turned out. It
wasn't that Rob was merely having a retaliatory affair, or trying to
get back at her. On the contrary, that would have demeaned what

he thought he had with Kate. What he thought he had was the great love of his life.

Barbara watched in horror, not able to stop them. It was no consolation to watch Kate revert to her old patterns of manipulations and vacillation. It's never much of a consolation to watch your husband make a fool of himself.

It was a nightmare time. Philippe was not a man to bow out quietly. He came to take Barbara out to lunch, to sympathize with her situation, to apologize, and then later, over a second cup of coffee, to suggest that Barbara might find other consolations with him. He tried to put it gracefully, but it was not the kind of thing that lent itself to grace: Philippe had inferred from things that Kate had said that Barbara was no innocent herself, after all, what adult was? Barbara began to cry. No, she said, no. He called a week later, to apologize for the way he put it, not for what he'd said. The offer was still open. She hung up on him. He sent her flowers. It was horrid.

Barbara sat up, put her arms around her knees. Mark did the same, unconsciously imitating each of her gestures. She was not at all like him, really, but if anyone had come down the trail just then and seen them sitting side by side on the rock they might have thought they were seeing double, twins, brother and sister.

Barbara paused for a second. A kingfisher glided silently above the rushing falls and disappeared into the dark woods on the far side.

Mark felt as if the wind had been knocked out of him by the brutal recitation. What was the point of it? The telling was so cool, so well-contained, with no attempt at evoking sympathy, sparing no one, not even really making judgments; all her effort was focused on being perfectly clear.

Barbara began to speak again.

Suddenly it was over. Rob couldn't meet Kate's demands. He didn't have the same kind of psychic energy; he just wasn't in her league. Even while he was claiming that Kate was the great love of his life, that what they had was unique and special, he couldn't forget that he was a father and husband. He couldn't be clear and decisive about what they should do; this was confirmation of what Kate had always known about men. One afternoon when Rob rushed over to see her, there was a young actor there having tea. Kate asked the young actor to leave and he did; he was very polite, very earnest with Rob.

Then Kate told Rob that they couldn't be lovers anymore. They would be friends again. You already have the best part of me, Kate said, I'm a better friend than a lover, you know that. Sex was never the essential part of their relationship, Kate could see that now.

This all happened early in the spring. For the next two months Rob was himself near the breaking point, victimized by depression and black rages. Barbara was the one to try and hold him together, patch him up, console him for the loss of what he thought had been the great love of his life. Having to do that, having to nurse her hurt, betraying husband, filled her with fury that she couldn't express, not if there was to be a chance of their family staying together.

She needed desperately to be away from it all. She told Rob that she was taking the children out to the ranch as soon as their school was over. He could come or not come, as he wished.

Mark had not interrupted her. There was something in her telling, or perhaps in Mark, that had made questioning impossible. Now he looked over at her.

"But Kate's coming here," Mark said, his voice unaccountably down to a hoarse whisper. "Why?"

"Ask her. For her it's just one more part of the drama."

"But they're no longer lovers."

"No. But Kate's one of those people who after they break all the dishes in the house need to stay around to help clean up."

"But why are you letting her come?"

"How can I stop her? How can I? Rob knows what I feel."

"I don't understand. If there's something out there in the dark that wants to maul you, why the hell would you want to open the door and let it in? Call her and tell her you don't want her here."

"I don't care if she's here or not. Really. Let them muddle through it themselves. I know what's going to happen. Nothing. It will be just more waste, and after she goes Rob will be furious. Not as furious as before, probably. Let him go through it one more time. Then maybe he'll see that it's over. Really over." She frowned. "I wish you wouldn't look at me like I'm the offended innocent. I had it coming."

"No one has it coming," Mark said.

"I'm not sure," she said. She smiled thinly. "I just hope you've understood."

"I have. From beginning to end."

Mark said nothing more, because he didn't know what to say. He

didn't even know what he thought. It seemed such a tangle of
lovers and deceivers, it was tawdry and banal, bad stuff, a
confirmation of the stupidity and vanity and self-indulgence of the
upper classes; but no, that was not what he thought, that was just
an attitude that part of him thought he should have. What he felt
was sympathy. What he felt was how hurt she was. How simple
and crude Tommy's deception of Judy seemed after this catalogue
of betrayal! Yet it was sympathy he felt for Barbara, he didn't
blame her, he hadn't an ounce of scorn for her, and, admit it, he
was glad.

She had told him exactly what he wanted to hear. He was blind
to everything now except the sense that he could rescue this
woman and, in that rescuing, have her.

A water ouzel darted from rock to rock, the quick small bird
disappearing in the water for a second, then reappearing. The
water shone with the afternoon sun.

They had talked for an hour, maybe more, Mark had lost track of
time. Mark felt a sudden pang of anxiety about the children, but
Barbara lay back on the rock.

Mark leaned back on his elbows. He wondered what she wanted
him to do. He looked over at her. Her eyes were closed, face to the
sun. Her hand was not far away. He reached over and covered her
hand. She did not pull away. She didn't look at him, but turned her
face away, staring down at the stream. A streak of red flushed
across her face. He worked his fingers into her hand.

He felt as if everything he was thinking and feeling had been
suspended. The steady roar of the water lulled them. Mark had no
sense of danger.

He ran his fingertips slowly up and down her arm. She lay still,
then turned her face to him. His hand was still. He thought of
Philippe. He was worse than Philippe, taking advantage of her
pain.

"Hi," he said.

"Hi," she said softly. Her eyes were wide, as clear and trusting as
a child's. He ran the back of his hand along her leg. He felt her
waiting for him. With a single finger he traced a line along the
seam of her jeans, not meeting her eyes. He rolled toward her. His
hand was between her thighs, he felt the warmth there, felt his own
excitement. She sat up suddenly, looking scared and wild-eyed.

He moved to her quickly, sorry instantly, cradling her in his
arms, running his hand over her hair again and again, soothing her.

He couldn't quite believe what he was doing, he didn't know what he was doing, he had surrendered knowing.

They sat like that, her head buried in his arms, him stroking her hair for several minutes without speaking. Once, and then twice, Mark felt her tremble in his arms. He stared at the water exploding below them. He felt as if he could slip into that water and that it would carry him away. He looked up and saw a hawk circling above the trees, borne effortlessly on air, felt the weight of her head against his chest.

The stillness was broken by a crash in the woods on the far side of the stream. They separated quickly. A marmot flopped his way across fallen timber. They both laughed in relief.

Barbara stood up. "We should go look for the children," she said.

Mark stood up too, unconsciously taking his cues from her. He would do whatever she said. It was all in her hands now.

Silently they began to gather the picnic things. Mark didn't feel the need to say anything more. There didn't need to be a name for what they were doing. When he looked up he saw that she had a grave smile on her face.

"Do I look funny?" he said.

"No."

"Then, what are you smiling about?"

"It's just a nice moment," she said. "The moment that says that there's another chance."

Mark didn't say anything for a second. "Here's Jeff's army knife," he said finally. He dropped the squat heavy knife into the wicker basket.

As they climbed up the rocks away from the falls they heard the children coming down the trail. Jeff and Sarah were full of their adventures. They had seen a small herd of elk in the meadow and they'd been able to sneak up on them, get within a hundred yards, according to Jeffrey.

"You should have been there, Mom, you would have liked it. We thought you were coming. We were waiting for you."

"Mark and I got talking," Barbara said.

Sarah reached up and took her mother's hand.

"But that's all you ever do," Jeffrey said. "You should have seen them, Mom, we saw this little calf nursing, it was so beautiful."

"I'm sure it was, Jeffrey. I'm sorry we didn't come."

As the four of them came back down through the timber, through glens of lupine and blue harebells and foxtail barley, they could again see the valley below, make out the corner of the ranch, where Mark imagined that Judy must have awakened from her sleep by now. He imagined her, waking in that strange room, not knowing if it was day or night, but knowing that everything in her life had changed. How odd it must seem to her, he thought, and then, when he thought again, he realized that it was himself he was thinking of, not her.

<h2 style="text-align:center">CHAPTER TEN</h2>

It was the insistent ringing of the phone that woke him, but as he rolled toward the sound, Ellen had already picked it up.

He lay there, perfectly still, as he always did when they were in her bed and someone called. He could tell right away from Ellen's tone that it was her mother calling long-distance.

"He's fine. I will. I'm sorry? No, the connection's not real good. It was a wonderful visit. Yes, I'll tell him, Mother."

Their legs were touching beneath the covers. He turned and stared out the window at the morning light. He listened to Ellen talk, knowing that he was going to betray her, turn her life around and that she had no clue . . . He reached out and ran his fingers down Ellen's arm. Ellen reached back and took his hand away.

He lay quiet as she hung up the phone, then rolled over to face him.

"Good morning," she said.

"Good morning."

She touched his face. "You look so sad."

"Me? No. Just a little sleepy."

"Tell me what you're thinking," she said.

"Nothing."

"I know you were."

"Nothing, really."

Ellen said nothing more. She leaned over and turned off the alarm clock, then got out of bed, went to her dresser. Mark watched her run a comb quickly through her hair.

"How was your mother?" he said.

"She was fine. She sends you lots of love." Something was wrong. Though her back was turned to him, he could see her reflection in the dresser mirror, see her face in a pout as if she were about to cry.

"What's wrong?" he said.

"I don't know," she said. He swung his feet down onto the floor. She turned to face him, her eyes filled with tears. For a second he felt as if he was going crazy. She was reading his mind, she knew everything.

"Sure you know," he said. "Come on."

"I just feel as if my life is so small and selfish."

"Selfish! What are you talking about?"

She tossed her comb back on the dresser. "It's as if we haven't grown up or something. We don't live in the real world."

Mark found it a relief to be able to get angry. "Oh, come on, Ellen! How many times do we have to go through this? Where's the real world? Tell me. Decatur, Iowa? L.A.?" Mark heard the badgering quality in his voice and hated it. "You're just thinking like this because you've just talked to your mother, you miss your family, I can understand that."

"No, it's not that," she said stubbornly. "We're leading a cloistered life, Mark."

"Oh, God," he muttered. They stared at one another. "I don't think that's the word you're looking for," he said.

"Isn't it?"

"You just spent a month getting these kids ready for a dance concert. You knocked yourself out. That didn't seem selfish to me. Or cloistered. And it was terrific. What you did was terrific. Do you know that?"

"That's not what I'm talking about."

"Then what *are* you talking about?"

"I don't know. You're angry at me."

"Maybe I am a little. I feel like when you're saying all this, it's me you're talking about. That there's some judgment involved."

"What kind of judgment?"

"About what I'm not giving you. That I'm the one that's selfish. That I'm not the right sort of person."

"I'm sorry if you think that," she said. "I don't know what's wrong. Maybe I'm just tired."

"It's O.K.," he said. "I'm sorry too. Why don't we go out for our run?"

"You're not angry anymore?"

"No," he said, knowing that he was lying.

They dressed silently, pulling on sweat pants and shirt, heavy socks and running shoes.

Mark was sullen, he couldn't help it. He knew perfectly well what she was talking about. Maybe selfish wasn't quite the right word for what Ellen objected to in their lives, but it was close enough. They weren't the only ones. Virtually everyone under thirty-five who'd come to Jackson—the runners, the skiers, the climbers, the divorcees who worked behind the desks at the big hotels—all had adopted therapeutic attitudes toward their lives. They were all trying to get well, get in shape—"the most beautiful hospital ward in the world," was what one of Mark's friends called the valley—and the constant topic of conversation was how happy they were to have escaped, whether it was a bad marriage, polluted city air, or the general rat race.

Ellen's instinct was right; there were times when all that cheerful self-absorption was too much, Mark had felt it too, he and Ellen had talked about it a million times.

He knew that what Ellen missed was the connection to family, the sense of being committed to people over the long haul. It made sense, wanting what she wanted, but that kind of sense seemed so remote from him now, as if it was a land from which he was exiled.

He jerked tight the laces on his running shoes. He glanced over at her, pulling an extra t-shirt over her head. He was angry not because she was wrong, but because he was being judged, judged more acutely than she could know.

When Mark and Ellen spent the night together their routine was to run together in the morning. Their route was fixed: south along the highway out of town, then the gravel road through South Park and back again. It was a little over four miles.

This morning they ran silently. When they were on the highway, Mark ran behind her. Ellen kept up a good pace, with her elbows high and pumping, head up. She had a jaunty running style that almost always put Mark in a good mood. Today it didn't. He felt heavy and sluggish and couldn't quite get his breath.

When they made the turn onto the gravel road Ellen glanced up at him. "I'm sorry," she said, her face soft and glowing from the exertion of running.

"It's O.K.," he said, but it wasn't O.K. There was a demon in him that wouldn't let his anger die. They were running side by side now, matching strides. As they came around the corner of the butte

he could see the mountains, cool and blue, snow-topped. He had
lain in those mountains, only a day ago, lain by a waterfall listening
to Barbara telling him everything. There had been no anger in him
then.

Mark reached up and wiped the sweat off his face. A dog came
bouncing down a driveway, barking fiercely, the same nasty dog
that seemed to wait for them every morning. Without breaking
stride Mark reached down and scooped a rock up from the road.
Let him come, Mark thought, I'll kick the shit out of him. The dog,
sensing Mark's mood, stopped at the head of the driveway and
satisfied himself with barking until they were a hundred yards past,
then trotted smugly back toward the house.

Once range land, South Park had been divided into one-acre resi-
dential plots. The houses were virtually identical, small ranch-style
homes with log exteriors and picture windows, rail fences, skis
leaning against the door, yards filled with trikes, swing sets, jeeps
and snowmobiles. A few people kept horses in small corrals, but the
feel was markedly suburban.

The houses were not cheap, but South Park was one of the few
places where a family without big money could live. The place
smelled of compromise. It had always depressed Mark, thinking of
these people who, just like him, had come West to be free and then
ended up here. They were here because they had families, because
there were necessities to be met, usually in monthly payments, and
in the end there was not much more left of their freedom than a
view of snow-covered mountains out of a medium-sized picture
window.

It was all part of Mark's quarrel with Ellen. Was it so selfish of
him to want to stay out of places like this? To want to preserve
some zone of freedom? Because, God knows, if she got what she
wanted, marriage, a family, this was exactly where they'd end up,
hell, on two teachers' salaries they'd be lucky to end up here. He
knew how angry it would make her if she heard him say it, how ar-
rogant she would think him, but the thought of living the way these
people lived seemed so dismal, mediocre, crushing.

Mark moved to the shoulder of the road as a pickup barreled
past.

Ellen looked back at Mark. "There he is," she said.

Ahead of them an old man worked on his buck-rail fence. He was
out there almost every morning that Mark and Ellen ran, and

though he always looked bustling and industrious, hauling rails back and forth, signs of real progress were minimal.

The old man raised a hand to greet them. Early in the spring, when Mark and Ellen had first started running, the old man had ignored them, but he'd gotten friendly over the last few weeks; they'd learned that his name was Rey, that he used to work for the County, that he was retired and lived alone and that he thought running was the craziest damn thing they'd come up with yet. All the same, he was out there to greet them almost every morning and Mark suspected that he came out so early partly so he could exchange a few words; they were part of his routine now.

"How you doin', Rey?" Mark shouted ahead.

"O.K." The old man leaned on his axe.

"How's that fence comin'?"

"Lookin' beautiful, ain't she? Hey, Ellen." They swerved over to his side of the road, slowing to a jog. "Haven't seen you out here for a few days." There was a note of reproach in the old man's voice.

"No, not for a while," Ellen said.

Rey laughed. "That's a bad sign, now, when your man starts to go lazy on you."

"I know, I know," Ellen said, jogging in place.

Mark was back-pedaling down the road. "We'll see you later, Rey," he shouted. He didn't say tomorrow. "Want to see you finish that fence up now."

Rey shouted something that Mark couldn't make out, but Mark laughed anyway and the old man waved him on.

Mark felt the quick stab of guilt. To the old man, he and Ellen were a couple. The old man didn't know what arrangement they had worked out, what promises they'd made or hadn't made, he just saw that they ran together each morning, it was proof enough for him.

Mark suddenly felt how blind he'd been. Hadn't he seen where all this was going to lead, into what terror? It was because of him that Ellen was always on the edge of tears, he knew it even if she wouldn't acknowledge it, it was because they were in perpetual limbo, always in some emotional holding pattern. From the first night that he'd met her Mark had known that she was a good person, an exceptional one, yet he'd withheld himself. Out of fear. Fear of what? Fear of ending up with a bourgeois life. Fear of not fulfilling some vague sense of special destiny that he'd always carried around with him.

But he hadn't lied to her. He hadn't. All along he had been careful not to make promises he didn't think he could keep, but honesty was beginning to seem like the thinnest of virtues. The point was that he wanted to be with someone else.

Mark felt himself bursting with undirected anger. The last half mile of their run he went into a kick, leaving Ellen well behind. He leaned against the front gate, getting his breath back, slowly shaking out one leg and then the other. He lifted a hand as Ellen came around the corner. She slowed to a walk, not even bothering to make a real finish of it.

"That was quite a sprint you put on," she said. She reached up and took off her sweatband, not quite meeting his gaze.

"It was O.K.," he said.

"I guess that just goes to show you what anger can do," she said. "A little adrenalin in the system."

Mark didn't bother denying it. He reached out and wiped the sweat from her temple. "I'll tell you what I'm going to do. You go in and shower and I'll go down to the store and get some bread and eggs, and when I come back I'll make you my super-duper French toast. O.K.? Bacon too, maybe."

On the way to the store and on the way back, he made up his mind that he was going to make everything all right. They'd have a good time, he'd be calmer, more patient, just for now. Who knew what was going to happen, at least he could be decent. But when he came back he saw that she'd been crying and he felt the old rage rising up in him again.

He put down his bag of groceries, went to her, held her. She looked up, her eyes red with crying. He saw the need there that he couldn't meet and he couldn't stand it.

"What's wrong with me, Mark? What's wrong with me?"

"I don't know. Maybe nothing's wrong with you. Maybe it's me. Maybe what you want is for a strong man to come in and give you everything. And maybe I'm not him."

"You think so?"

"I don't know."

"That's pretty awful if it's true." She had stepped back from him now. Mark gathered up the groceries and took them into the kitchen.

"Maybe it's not true then," Mark said.

"It's a pretty awful thing to say."

"I'm sorry," Mark said. He began to lift the groceries out of the bag, place them methodically down on the kitchen table.

"You're still angry, aren't you?" she asked. He stared at her mutely, without a pose, without a condolence. "What if I believed what you tell me? What would that mean?"

Mark turned away from her, took a bowl down from the cupboard, then lifted two eggs from the egg carton.

"I don't think I want anything to eat," she said.

Mark held the eggs in the palm of his hand for a second, then set them down carefully. "O.K.," he said. "What do you want?"

"I think I want to be by myself for a while," she said.

"All right." He reached for her arm, but she pulled away. As he walked past her he put his hand on the back of her bowed neck, gave her a gentle squeeze. He went to the closet, lifted out his jacket. Sitting on the floor of the closet were his hiking boots. At the back was his heavy coat he'd left hanging there since the winter, an extra sweatshirt was draped on the same hook with one of Ellen's shawls—all the signs of how their lives had grown close, even without their having made real decisions about it. It was killing him. He heard her crying in the kitchen, but he did not turn around. What I'm about to do is unforgivable, he thought. Hurt her and get out, don't stay and hurt her more. She was not going to stop him.

He opened the door, stepped outside, and pulled the door quietly shut behind him.

He drove the ten miles home to Wilson to shower and change clothes for work. In the mailbox was an envelope with no return address, but he recognized Barbara's handwriting. He tore it open even before he got inside. It was a drawing, a series of caricatures, with a Pied Piper figure, tall and skinny, obviously intended to be Mark, whistling and leading a parade over the mountain. In the parade were Barbara, Jeffrey and Sarah, several elk, a marmot, a bear and a number of blissful-looking birds. It was very cleverly done; it made Mark smile.

He put it on his desk and then, after he'd showered and dressed and was on his way out the door, stopped, came back, looked at the drawing again. He folded it and jammed it in his shirt pocket next to his heart.

When he came back from work, he thought of calling Barbara, but decided no, it was crazy. He tried to call Ellen but there was no answer. It was not a night he wanted to stay home, he was too restless. Changing his shirt, the drawing fell out of his shirt pocket. He picked it up, unfolded it, stared at it, flicked it across his desk and walked to the phone.

He stood there for five minutes without doing anything. It wasn't quite six yet. They were probably all getting ready for dinner. If he called there was no guarantee that he would get Barbara—Rob was no doubt the kind of person who made it a point to be the one to answer the phone if he was anywhere near.

Mark tried to tell himself there was no reason to be nervous. He hadn't done anything. Not yet.

It took three tries. Twice he dialed and hung up before it had a chance to ring. The third time he let it go through, his heart pounding, weirdly matching the dull, insistent throb of the ringing phone. Twice, three times it rang. What a fool he was, he had no idea what he was doing. But that wasn't true. Part of him was perfectly cool and calculating; if Rob answered, he would be utterly calm, invite them to dinner, that would be fine. He noted how quickly he was picking up the necessary skills of deception.

"Hello?" It was Barbara. Her tone was oddly tentative and subdued; for a second Mark didn't recognize her.

"Hi," Mark said.

"Hi," she said, sounding just a little alarmed or puzzled, Mark couldn't tell which. He'd hoped for more. "How are you?" she said.

"I'm just fine," he said. "I got your drawing in the mail today. It was great." She was silent. He felt the beginning of panic. He thought he heard her children arguing in the background. "I just wanted to call and thank you," he said. "Maybe this isn't a good time to talk."

"No, no, it's fine. The kids just chased the dog out of the house and Rob's out tinkering with the pickup. Don't worry." She laughed, more relaxed suddenly.

"I'd like to see you," he said. "I've thought a lot about our talk and . . . well . . . it would just be nice to see you."

"Yes, it would be," she said. "I'm coming into town tomorrow to pick up some things. Maybe we could meet for lunch."

"That would be great," Mark said.

"The local artists are supposed to be displaying their wares on the square. We could go take a look at that. I know how much you love art."

"Anything," he said. "Sure."

"You know the delicatessen just south of the square?"

"The Sweetwater."

"I'll meet you there. Oh, God, here they come again . . . Jeffrey,
I do not want that dog in the house!" Mark heard the sounds of
muffled protest. "That's right!" Barbara shouted at her children,
then came back to Mark: "One o'clock, O.K.?"

He came without a plan, none, at least, that he was willing to
admit to himself. She was in a bright, playful mood. They spent a
half hour wandering around the square looking at paintings. The
artists, lined up and dispirited as birds in the rain, slouched in folding chairs across from their artwork. It was standard Western stuff:
dusty roundups, broken-down Indian chieftains, a herd of elk
trudging through a snowy meadow, a trumpeter swan beating
across a pond to protect her young. Nothing great, but nothing
worth making fun of either, the way Mark saw it, yet Barbara had a
look of barely suppressed amusement on her face. There was no
sign of sorrow in her, or of the memory of what had passed between them on the mountain. It was a sign that he needed from
her, that he had come for. They ended up arguing.

"You don't really think it's nice," Barbara said as they stood in
front of a flawed painting of moose feeding at a mountain lake.

"I don't think it's so awful. Really. It's conventional. Nothing
wrong with conventions."

"But it takes no chances, none of it."

"Does it have to?"

"For me to like it, it does," she said.

A motorcyclist wove slowly through the backed-up traffic, his leg
extended for balance, heavy black boots scuffing against concrete.
Mark knew he shouldn't say anything more, yet he did.

"If someone likes mountains and wild animals and wants to hang
a picture of them on their wall, terrific."

"You don't think that," she said. She was still being playful. He
wasn't. She didn't pick that up right away.

"I do think it. People do the best they can."

She looked sharply back at him. "I wasn't criticizing the people
who paint these things."

"I know you weren't." This wasn't what he'd intended, but he
went on, a little too urgently. "If being in the mountains makes
people happy, and it does, lots of people, why not have pictures . . ."

"As proof? Or so you don't forget? It's a rather exhausted idea of happiness."

"Not for everybody," he said. She stared straight ahead, her face suddenly a mask. "People yearn for things, people desire things, and mostly they express it imperfectly." He tried to smile. "Even me." He reached out and put a hand on the back of her neck, gently brushing back her hair, trying to make it better. "Forget it. It doesn't matter. Why don't we go eat, O.K.?"

The Sweetwater was rustic, but classy, a place where people went if they wanted to talk. Harnesses and yokes decorated the walls, and drinks came in mason jars. There was a touch too much of Colorado chic, but it was a nice place. Their hamburgers came with little slices of fruit on the side.

Barbara's playfulness had disappeared. During the meal they edged around one another with a wary formality, staying on safe topics: how Judy was doing out at the ranch, the adventures of the children. Whatever the reason, all the closeness and sympathy and desire they had felt on the mountain was gone now, he could scarcely conjure it up. Whenever anyone came in, Barbara noticed. Mark noticed her noticing.

Inside the restaurant everything was shadows, while outside the summer sun was dazzling, muting all colors. Over coffee Barbara said, "The children like you so much. You'll have to come out again. Maybe on the weekend. We could all go riding."

"I don't really ride," Mark said, a bit flatly. It wasn't a family friend he wanted to be. He didn't see how, at this point, she could still mistake him for one. Maybe she was pretending. Or maybe she was backing off.

A middle-aged woman in a tan vest sat at a nearby table watching them. She looked vaguely familiar, but maybe it was only Mark's anxiety that made her look that way. He couldn't place her. Mark stared back, bullying her, and she quickly turned away, blushing, and reached for her purse.

"You could learn," Barbara said.

"I've ridden a few times," Mark said. "Horses scare me."

She smiled. "Really? I'm surprised. Horses scare me too," she said. She picked at her salad with her fork. "I remember the first time I came out here and I had to ride with Rob and his father. I was determined not to let them know how terrified I was . . ."

She went on with her story. There were plenty of empty tables around them now, it was getting late. Mark leaned back in his chair, stared at his folded hands. He knew that he did not want things to just run on, he wanted to be close to her, he wanted what they had had on the mountain and he wanted more.

It was up to him. If he wanted he could do nothing, just let her talk. She loved to talk, she wasn't going to run out of words, he knew her well enough by now. The story would go on until she looked at her watch and saw how late it was, she would have to go then, he would walk her sullenly to her car and they would say goodbye yet another time and he would be left with the same dissatisfactions, the same questions. He could spend the afternoon going around half-provoked, half-depressed. Or he could do something.

"And they never knew how terrified you were?" he said suddenly, interrupting.

"No," she said. "Some people show it when they're scared, others don't. I'm real good at not letting on."

Mark pushed his plate to one side, reached across and cupped Barbara's elbow in his hand. It was not the world's most graceful gesture. She was taken by surprise.

"Well? What would you like?" she said, as if it was a joke.

"What I'd like," he said, "would be for you to come to my house for a while." There was more emotion in his voice than he thought there'd be.

For a second she looked scared, startled as an animal caught in the flare of headlights in the night. Mark took his hand away, folded the remains of his paper napkin. He looked at her without flinching, saw a darkness sway in her.

"I guess it would be all right," she said. "I have to be back before too long."

"O.K.," he said. "I wasn't intending on keeping you forever."

They drove in her car. She did all the talking, Mark silent except when he gave directions. Mark's arm lay across the back of the seat, his fingers resting lightly on her shoulder. She drove fearlessly, a little recklessly, swerving the Datsun across two lanes of traffic to make the right turn off the highway. Mark felt disconnected, a bit dazed, the way you do right after a fever has broken. He felt as if he was being carried into something that didn't have to do with him anymore.

On either side of them were pastures, cattle grazing in the afternoon light. They crossed the Snake River bridge. The water was low now, the glinting channels rippling through gravel banks that rose up like ancient half-submerged beasts.

"I don't know quite why I'm doing this," she said. "Maybe it's just that you're such a popular fellow and I'm trying to win you away from everyone."

Her remark hurt, joke or not, but he let it pass. "The turn's right up here," he said. He didn't like the idea of her not knowing why she had come with him.

They drove up the familiar dirt road, passed the bar, then the rodeo grounds. Mark pointed to the house set back behind the stand of aspen.

"There," he said. "You can pull into the driveway."

Barbara ran her fingers over the owl wings sitting on the bookcase. Mark stood waiting behind her.

"Terrific," she said. "Where did you get them?"

"Ellen found them," Mark said.

"Found them? How do you find owl wings?"

"On the highway. It had been killed by a car, but it was still intact . . ."

Barbara moved across the room, her fingers brushing the fronds of the hanging ferns. "The plants. They're Ellen's idea too?"

"Uh-huh."

He didn't like the idea of her exploring his place, it made him nervous. She went to his desk, lifted the page sitting in the typewriter so she could read it.

"Hey, come on," he said.

"I didn't know you were a writer."

"I'm not."

"What's this then?"

"Just something I'm working on. I don't think you'd be interested. An article about why the government should designate the Gros Ventre as a wilderness area."

She lifted the already typed pages off the desk. "Is this the rest of it?"

"You don't want to read that. Come on. It's not art, it's a piece of straight-out propaganda. About mountains, about one of your exhausted ideas of happiness."

She ignored him. She sat down at the desk and began to read. At first Mark sat on the couch, watching her, but that was too distracting for both of them, so he went around behind her, picking off the pages as she finished them, reading them over again himself.

"This is good," she said.

"I didn't think you'd like it. I didn't think you'd like the ideas."

"I like the writing. It all fits, it flows, it does more work than it seems to . . . it's all leaves from the same tree."

"Thanks," he said. "It's nice to hear. That's what I was aiming at. It's not finished yet, you can tell that."

"But you're a writer."

"I'm not a writer. I haven't done anything."

"You've done this," she said. "No, come on, it's exciting. You sly dog, you, hiding in the weeds like that." Mark felt as if he was blushing, a child glowing with the simplest praise. "Let me finish," she said. "I have only a couple more pages."

He stood behind her now, watching her read. Her kindness, her excitement had broken through the wall that had separated them. She was a smart woman, a sympathetic one, she was real to him again. He had his hands on her shoulders. Standing over her, he read too, the end of the article in which he had described a winter camping trip he'd taken with Tommy in the Gros Ventre. The last two pages told of the terrifying ski journey he and Tommy had taken back down the mountain, a blind, wild, ill-advised run, zig-zagging down an avalanche slope, cutting back again and again, always just ahead of cascading snow. He still wasn't sure whether the description worked or not, whether it fit with the rest of the piece, maybe it was too personal, but the way he wanted it to work was as an evocation of the danger and the beauty of the wilderness and of the freedom he had found there.

One of Barbara's hands reached up and took his; her hand was glowing warm. He moved close to the chair, pressed himself against her. Everything in him was racing now. She turned and looked up at him, her face flushed. She put her hands in his, lifted herself out of the chair. They put their arms around one another's waists. She kissed him softly, quickly.

"It doesn't have to be heavy, does it?" she said. "It can be whatever we want it to be, can't it?"

"Sure," Mark said, "it doesn't have to be heavy."

They sat on the edge of the bed in the half-dark room, the shades drawn and glowing amber from the outside afternoon light. Neither of them spoke. He held her, ran his hands slowly up and down her back, inside her blouse. Her eyes were wide open, dilated pupils huge and dark as a fawn's in the shadowed room. He began to unbutton her, not meeting her gaze. When she lay back naked on the bed, her hair fanned out behind her on the white pillow, she was beautiful to him. He lay on her, swimming in warmth, in pleasure, kissing her a hundred times lightly, lightly, on the face and shoulders and breasts, how soft she felt, and then kissed her deeply on the mouth, surrendering to the gentle darkness; but when he tried to enter her, it was awkward, strange, he fumbled, tried again and lost it.

He looked at her, distressed with himself, his eyes clouded. He pulled her on top of him, looking very grave, then rolled over again, burying his face in her neck and hair, hiding his panic. He couldn't get it back. He shook his head from side to side, almost laughing, ready to scorn himself.

"Christ, Christ . . ."

She caught his head in her hands, made him be still and look at her.

"What?" she said.

"I'm sorry," he said. "I don't know what happened."

"No, don't," she said, "don't." Her fingers brushed a soft circle around his face. "Sex is a serious business. We have to treat it with respect. Give it the time it wants." She smiled at him.

Mark was silent, again impressed by kindness in a place where somehow he hadn't expected kindness, in a strange terrain. They held each other for a long time, talking softly, and then they made love. He felt her caring for him, it was gentle, not passionate, and yet when he came he whispered her name again and again.

Afterwards he walked her down through the trees to her car. Through the trees they could see the horses in the rodeo corral, lined up at the fence, swishing away flies, staring back curiously at them. Outside in the sun Mark felt free, his spirits soared. He kept looking at her and smiling, struggling to find things to say; he wanted to tell her everything, tell every hope and fear.

"You're lovely, you know," he said.

She looked at him and laughed.

"You were so nice to me," he said.

She laughed. "You sound surprised."

"It's a funny thing to say, isn't it? But I guess I was feeling . . . I don't know. . . ."

"We're pretty fragile. All of us," she said. "I think that's what you find out."

"You're amazing, you know that?" he said. "You're even much more amazing than I thought."

They stood at her car. He embraced her, kissed her, wanted to kiss her more, not to give her up, he was excited all over again, but she pulled away. Her face suddenly was grave.

"Why do you look so sad?" he asked.

"I don't know. Maybe because you've turned from an honest pleasure into a dishonest one." She smiled slowly. "You're a nice man," she said. "I feel safe with you."

She got into the car. He wanted to tell her that he loved her, but then he remembered that he had promised that it wouldn't be heavy.

He stood in the driveway and watched her turn the car around. She leaned forward and waved and he waved back. He had turned toward the house when he heard her hit the horn two or three times lightly, but when he looked, he couldn't see the car through the trees.

Chapter Eleven

He was running alone now, on a different course, and he was panting like a dog. Even in the first mile down the Gros Ventre Road it felt as if his legs were bound by steel bands. It was just punishment. That was the thing about running, it was concrete. If you laid off running for three, four days you knew you were going to hurt like hell the next time out, even if you didn't know what it meant that you'd just slept with a married woman.

He had awakened early that morning, more than an hour before dawn. He lay in bed, turning all that had happened the day before over and over in his head. Each time he started to drift toward sleep a fresh eddying of anxiety turned him back toward wakefulness. Finally it just seemed pointless. He pushed himself out of bed and got into his running clothes.

He didn't know if he would call her right away or not. He would wait. Let her call him. He didn't want to think about it. Why should he? She had said that she didn't want it to be heavy, neither did he. So let it ride for a while.

It was a strange game, guessing at what you feel, what you will feel. There was something not quite real yet about what had happened between him and Barbara. It seemed insubstantial, like the strands of morning mist lifting off the trees on the mountainside.

It would be so easy to end it now, not so easy later. To go on, to squander emotion and feeling when nothing could come of it, when it had nowhere to go . . . But that was why he'd wanted it, exactly because it could go nowhere, that was the appeal, the fact that it was safe, a nicely defined emotional cul-de-sac. If he was going to get hung up he'd better just break it off now.

As he came through a grove of aspen, birds flew up suddenly out of the brush, startling him, sailed through the trees, through the filtered light. For no reason he could discern, it all came back to him, with an aching vividness, the two of them standing by her car, of his holding her, her telling him how safe she felt with him. He thought of how kind she'd been, how open he'd felt with her.

It was time to change focus. The hill seemed to stretch up and up forever. He wasn't going to make it unless he started playing some new games, count his breaths till the top of the hill, he could make it in fifty, easy. Just one foot in front of the other, keep going, he'd get there. There was always the point in running when the pain drops away and you start to fly, you count on it. Twenty more breaths. Fifteen. Pick it up.

Pushing hard, he made it to the top of the hill. He threw his head back, sucking for air, shook his legs out. His legs felt like putty. He was disgusted with his pain. He was in lousy shape, he had made this hill with no trouble before. He heard water roaring through the cliffs far below him.

He started to feel better. He began to stretch out a little bit, lengthening his stride, feeling his own power. He started to see things: the aspen groves wet and clean in the morning mist, horses grazing on pastureland far below. Things were getting clear again. He passed the four-mile mark, then the five. His sweatshirt was soaked through, the only sound the steady slap of his running shoes and the distant call of ravens. He felt as if he could go on forever.

It wasn't until he started up the next long incline that he heard the car behind him. At first the sound was far off and above him, then rumbling down and closer. The car was right behind him. Mark moved over to the shoulder, but the car didn't pass.

Mark kept up his pace, growing irritated; he didn't like to be
fooled with. Then came a flash of fear. Some of the rednecks out
here hated runners, didn't like them much better than long-haired
hippies. There were stories of runners being shot at, run off the
road.

The car horn sounded. Mark was angry now. Without looking
back he waved an arm for the car to pass. Then came the paranoid
leap: someone knew, someone had seen Barbara coming out of his
house yesterday and had been following him.

Mark looked back over his shoulder and saw the familiar battered, blue Volkswagen. He stopped running. The car crunched
slowly across the gravel, pulling alongside. Tommy leaned across
the seat and rolled down the window.

"Hey, buddy, you wanna race?" Tommy said.

"What the hell you doing out here?" Mark said.

Tommy shrugged. His face looked real bad, puffy and white.

"I went by your house and saw that you were gone," Tommy
said. "I figured you were running."

Mark stared down the empty winding road. It was eerie being
tracked down like this.

"Get in, I'll give you a ride back to your car." A ride back wasn't
what Mark wanted, but Tommy had already pushed open the door
on Mark's side. "Come on."

Mark folded himself into the car, his knees jammed painfully
against the dashboard. The car smelled of gas. There was a leak
somewhere that Tommy was always saying he was going to get
fixed and he never did. It was the story of Tommy's life. Oil cans
and tools and maps littered the floor.

Tommy swung the car around.

"You're up awfully early, aren't you, Tommy?"

"I guess so."

"What time do you start floating? Ten? Eleven?"

"I'll have to check. It's different every day," Tommy said. "I
haven't been sleeping so good lately."

"Yeah," Mark said, more softly. "I guess I can understand that."

Tommy looked over quickly at him, his glance suspicious, bellig-
erent. "Why should you be able to understand that?"

"No reason. But it would make sense, wouldn't it?"

Tommy said nothing for several seconds, staring down the road,
both hands knotted to the steering wheel. The same pair of ravens

Mark had passed earlier flapped up heavily once more from their feeding.

"I feel like shit, Mark!" Tommy banged the heel of his hand on the steering wheel, looking back at Mark, his eyes rimmed with tears. "I want her back."

"Sure," Mark said. "Sure."

"You think that's ridiculous, man?"

"No, Tommy, I don't think that's ridiculous." Mark pulled his wet sweatshirt away from his stomach. He was still sweating from his run.

"No, come on, admit it, I don't care, really . . . I'm fuckin' ridiculous, right? I don't deserve her back, is that what you're thinking? Well, maybe you're right. But there can be a difference between what I deserve and what I want." The car crawled along the mountain road. Tommy stared straight ahead as he spoke, as if too ashamed to look directly at Mark. "I treated her like shit a lot of the time, I'm not denying that. I ran around on her, I didn't give her enough, I know that. But being without her is driving me crazy . . . Can you believe that, Mark?" The car stank of Tommy's misery.

"Sure, I can believe it."

"Certain things don't hit you till it's too late, isn't that what they say? It takes a while for certain ideas to sink in . . . but, damn it, Mark, I don't want to be the way I've been, I want to be different . . ." He swept his hand suddenly across in front of him, his fingers taut and clutching at air, the gesture powerful, confounded.

"You should call her up then," Mark said.

"I tried."

"What do you mean, you tried?"

"This guy Campbell answered the phone. He said Judy wasn't there."

"Maybe she wasn't there. Maybe she was out teaching lessons."

"Maybe," Tommy said.

"And then what did you say?"

"I asked him to have her call me back. He said he'd give her my message."

"And she didn't call you back."

"Of course she didn't call me back! I'll bet she was standing right there while I was talking to him, man."

"Tommy, Tommy . . ."

"He's got no right to mess with my marriage, Mark. Marriage is a holy thing, man. He's got no business interfering between a man and his wife."

"Nobody's interfered, Tommy. They took Judy in because she had nowhere to go."

"They don't even know her!"

"No, but they knew it was the decent thing to do. They took her in because she came home and found her husband crawling around with some naked lady on the bathroom floor. Nobody interfered."

Tommy blinked several times, wrinkled his nose in a frown. When he spoke his voice was perfectly even. "You don't have to tell me what I did, man. I don't blame them for helping her out. All I'm saying is that there is a fine line."

"I know," Mark said. They had come to the base of the hill.

"You came and took the boxes out of our house," Tommy said.

"Yeah."

"Well, I'm not sore about that. I can understand that. You're her friend too, right? Friend to both of us. It's a hard position to be in. But I want you to do me a favor now. I want you to talk to her, Mark, I want you to tell her that I'm sorry, that I was wrong, and that I want her to come back."

Mark rolled down the window, saying nothing. The smell of gasoline was suffocating. Mark's car was parked a hundred yards on down the road.

"Can you do that, Mark?"

"I don't know," he said. It was wrong that he should sit there, unreproached, being asked to be a messenger of reconciliation. It was wrong and it was spooky.

"Mark, please, she won't listen to me."

"My car's right up here," Mark said.

"She won't even answer my phone calls. She'll listen to you, Mark, she knows you're a person she can trust. I can change, Mark, I know I can. I need her back. Just tell her that, that I need her. If I can't make this work I don't see how I'll ever be able to make anything work . . . Help me, Mark, just tell me that you'll help me."

They were at Mark's car. Tommy leaned forward, his fingers dug into Mark's shoulder. It hurt. Tommy had strong boatman's hands, hands used to oars and battling currents. Mark reached up and took Tommy's arm away. He glanced into Tommy's pleading eyes, but the intensity of the need he saw there made him look away. So this is what betrayal is about, he thought, being placed in false positions. Still, there was only one answer to give. He opened the door of the car, looked back again at Tommy.

"I'll do what I can, man."

CHAPTER TWELVE

The oddest thing about it was that nothing seemed changed. Mark waited for some sign of retribution, or at least some intimation of suspicion, and instead there was nothing. It was as if sleeping with Barbara was an act without consequences. He didn't feel as if anything terrible had happened to him. He didn't feel as if he was hurting anybody. He felt, much of the time, as if he had a wonderful secret. If anything, he felt freer, looser.

Ordinary life reasserted itself. The next day Ellen came by his work. To see how he was, she said, to see if he wanted to have dinner with her. Of course, he said. She wanted to make up, he knew that. It was the sort of thing that had happened before. That was one of the great things about Ellen. After a fight, she was always honorable.

They met for dinner at the Silver Spur. At first they were both subdued and careful. She wore a cream-colored blouse of unbleached heavy muslin. It was the same blouse she'd worn the first time they had gone out. Mark did not miss the allusion to better times. Mark told her a long story about Patrick and work, trying to get her to laugh. Then, even before Mark had quite reached the punch line of his story, Ellen apologized for attacking him the other morning.

"You don't have to apologize," Mark said. "Everything you said was right."

"But you're still angry at me."

"I'm not." Mark was acutely uncomfortable, poking at his plate of chicken with a fork.

"But something has changed. Hasn't it?"

"Everything's changing. All the time. Come on, Ellen." Mark looked up at her, aware suddenly of how much he would hurt her, no matter how careful he was.

There had been other times in their relationship when they had gone three or four days, even a week, without seeing one another.

Those other times they had always come back together, talked things out, Mark talking more than Ellen, because the way it worked was that she counted on Mark's innate optimism, on his need to be positive. Most of the time it was a strength, Mark's being unwilling to endure people being down too long. He worked to get them up, wheedled around to somehow give them hope.

Mark took a package from the seat beside him and handed it to her. "I brought you a present," he said.

There was a look of surprise on her face. "A present? It's not my birthday."

"No."

"And no one's going away."

"No one's going away," he said. "I just felt like giving you something." She tore open the wrapping, lifted out the new paperback biography of Nijinsky. "I guess I always give books, don't I? Not too imaginative."

"No, it's nice," she said. On the cover was a picture of the reclining dancer with his intense, staring eyes. Ellen opened the book, found the inscription. She read it out loud, turning it into a question. "With all my affection?" she said.

"That's right," he said.

She reached across and squeezed his hand. She leafed through the book, looking at the pictures. "He went mad, didn't he? You can see it in the eyes."

"It was all that energy, all that excess . . . demonic too, I suppose . . ." Mark smiled. "But attractive too."

"I suppose some people find madness seductive," Ellen said. "It scares me."

Mark pushed his plate away. "Hey," he said. "You know what we should do? They're playing some music out on the square. They're going to have some old-time fiddlers, that's what I heard this afternoon . . ." The strained cheerfulness in his voice didn't get past either of them.

Out on the square people were having a wonderful time. The fiddlers were going great guns and there was a crowd. Mark ushered Ellen into the middle of the onlookers, his hand on her elbow. People clapped and stomped their feet and finally an old couple, swept away, started clog-dancing, feet going a mile a minute, arms hanging loose, torsos perfectly rigid, faces dead sober.

A cheer went up for them, and then a seven-year-old boy broke away from his parents to dance too, scuffling his feet as fast as he could, not much technique but a lot of soul.

A very large woman with a beehive hairdo and nurses' shoes, evidently one of the fiddlers' wives, cut through the musicians and pulled a paddle-puppet out of a large paper bag. The doll-like figure was almost a foot long, suspended on strings between two boards. The woman sat down on a folding chair and pinned the top board beneath her ample thighs, then started batting the bottom board with her hand, making the puppet dance.

The puppet pranced just the way the clog-dancers did, all fast-moving feet, loose-jointed arms, expressionless face. Mark found the imitation disturbing, the too tiny doll in hillbilly clothes jerkily keeping pace, mechanical, witch-like, possessed. The clacking of the board against the puppet's twitching feet kept time with the fiddlers, the dancing old couple, the happy young boy.

Mark's hand was on Ellen's shoulder. She held her present close to her chest. She reached up and took his hand, then turned around, her face flushed with pleasure. Her eyes were bright; she loved the dancing.

"It's wonderful, isn't it?" she said.

"It is," he said. His smile felt stiff, forced.

She squeezed his hand wordlessly. He gave her fingers an answering squeeze, then let her hand drop, their fingers trailing apart.

"What do you say I walk you home?" he said.

She knew he was evading her. She knew that they weren't going to spend the night together and she didn't make it hard for him. They stood together on her porch. Mark fingered the drawstrings on her blouse, she took his hand away. She kissed him lightly on the cheek and said good night.

Mark walked back toward the street, then stopped and turned back. She still stood on the porch, her face in shadows. He couldn't care for Barbara any more than he cared for the woman standing there. He tried to smile reassuringly; the misery that awaited them could be put off for another time.

"I'll talk to you soon," he said.

The next morning he called Barbara. She seemed pleased to hear from him, yet kept the conversation skimming from surface to surface until he interrupted her.

"I've thought a lot about you."

"You're nice," she said, as if what he'd just said was nothing more than a compliment. "You're a nice man." Then she said, "I've thought a lot about you too."

"It was lovely for me," he said, then stopped, afraid of applying too much pressure, not wanting to bully. "I'd like to see you again," he said.

"I'd like to see you too," she said. It worried him a little, the fact that she was making him say everything first.

They agreed to have lunch on Saturday. Saturday turned out to be the warmest day of the summer. In the morning Mark went shopping, bought wine and soft St. Andre cheese, fresh peasant bread and ham for their lunch. There was a knot in his stomach and he felt dazed. Suddenly he wasn't feeling so loose anymore.

When her car finally turned in the driveway he was there at the open door, leaning against the frame, making a joke of nonchalance, not even attempting to disguise the fact that he had been waiting.

They were shy with one another. They kissed lightly in the doorway, but when they were inside and the door closed behind them, Mark tried to hold her and he could feel that she didn't want to be held.

She slipped away from him, still holding his hand, not wanting to be too abrupt about it. She scanned the room, saw that he'd put away his typewriter.

"Have you finished your article?"

"No," he said.

"You should finish it," she said. "That's my problem, I don't finish things. It's a terrible habit to get into."

It was a very awkward beginning. She finally sat on the couch and he sat on the chair opposite, they could have been in a doctor's waiting room. She looked lovely, in white pants and a soft green blouse, but she was tense and distracted. There was something wrong, something locked in, frozen. Mark found himself becoming irritated. She knew he wanted to be there next to her, holding her. She wasn't dumb. It was as if she didn't trust him, as if they were two tongue-tied teen-agers. She looked so trapped. He didn't see how everything could have changed that fast.

In the middle of a story about Michael and his forever-impending movie deal, Mark stood up.

"Would you like something to eat?" he asked.

"No," she said. "I'm not really hungry. It's so hot. It's amazing, isn't it? When I left, the kids were spraying each other with the hose. I don't ever remember it being this hot this early in the summer."

Mark considered her for a second before speaking. "What would you like to do?"

"I don't know." She smiled up at him. "It's so nice outside. Could we go somewhere? It just seems like a crime to be inside on a day like this, doesn't it?" She didn't miss his quick, ironic smile. "Anyway . . . I guess I feel a little uncomfortable. I'm sorry."

"Don't be sorry," he said. "It's fine. I know just where we'll go."

"You're not angry?"

"How could I be? Let's go."

Mark drove up toward the pass, his car straining at the steep grades. Every so often they'd pass a second-rate motel, a mock-chalet, then a beer garden, a pair of motel guests out walking on the road, looking a little blitzed and intimidated by the mountain air. Several trucks wheezed past them going the other direction, gearing down and praying for their brakes to hold. As they moved steadily upward, Mark could see the valley slipping away in the rearview mirror. Cars were parked at each of the turnouts. They drove over a couple of full mountain streams, the sound of them rushing, urgent, musical. Looking back, Mark could see hikers picking their way along the rocks, following the tumbling water up toward its source.

They scarcely spoke at all. Barbara had her window down, her face angled toward the sun. Mark's mind juggled all the possible hurts. Didn't she remember what it was like? Maybe it hadn't been the same for her. Maybe she didn't want to make love to him again, it hadn't been good enough for her, she was only being kind . . . Was it going to end here? No, he wasn't ready to believe that.

He tried to imagine what she'd told Rob, what excuses she'd had to give him. The first time could be something that just happened, but from the second time on it had to be set up, it took some cold-blooded calculation. All for what? A quick hour here, a quick hour there.

It wasn't a quick hour that Mark was looking for. What was it then? He didn't know how this was supposed to work. Maybe that was the point, the cumulative point of a few thousand years of experimentation; it wasn't supposed to work. Cheaters never win.

He thought resentfully of the food sitting in his refrigerator. What a waste. Peasant bread and soft French cheese, hell, he'd never eat that kind of stuff on his own. Maybe she'd decided that it was wrong and was waiting for the right time to tell him. She had a husband, children, she'd been through this before and she wasn't very proud of it, she knew how dangerous it was. That made it different for her.

He looked over at her. She had her arm trailing out the window, letting the wind push through her fingers. Her averted face seemed so quiet, so trusting; she didn't know he was looking at her. He felt a rush of emotion. He would not push her, whatever she wanted would be all right, it was her life, he did not want to hurt her. If she wanted him to wait, he would wait, for as long as necessary, it was his place. How odd it seemed that even here, in the most illicit of situations, that the proprieties were as important as ever.

At the top of the pass Mark pulled the car over into the turnout and parked. Barbara glanced at him in surprise.

"Here?" she said.

"No, not here. This is just the start."

"You're taking me to Idaho, I can't believe it."

There were a half-dozen cars parked. People with cameras and binoculars ambled back and forth, a little wobbly as if drunk on the wind, checking the view, stretching their legs. Some climbed the embankment to get an even higher angle on the panorama of the valley and the silver winding of the Snake River far below. A mother sat in the open door of her car, handing out sandwiches to her children.

Barbara stood beside the car, smiling uncertainly, wiping away a strand of hair that blew across her face.

Mark looked back and saw her hesitation. Even harmless tourists weren't so harmless anymore, not for her. All it would take to collapse her world would be for one person to recognize them.

"Let's go," he said. "I'm going to show you something."

Mark led her across the highway and up the steep bank, giving her a hand up, then along a trail that went through deep forest, away from the road. A grouse drummed somewhere deep in the woods. They moved higher, came out into a meadow of low alder bushes and flowers, Indian paintbrush, mountain gentian, columbine. Marmots sat upright on boulders, whistling their warnings, then disappearing. Mark pushed the pace, walking ahead. He had something he wanted her to see and it was a good ways. Neither of them spoke. The boulders seemed to get bigger around them. They were walking on a sponge of tundra now.

If it was going to end, Mark thought, let's do it decently. It was too nuts imagining where they could go with this.

Across the meadow was a sharp talus slope, a couple of hundred yards high, crisscrossed with dirty banks of snow. Mark looked back at Barbara.

"We're going up there?" she said. Mark nodded. "You've got to be kidding."

"You can make it."

"If I'd known we were going hiking I would have worn different shoes."

"So would I," Mark said. "It's not much further. Trust me."

"What other choice do I have?"

It took them another fifteen minutes to reach the top of the ridge. At the top the wind was blowing hard; Barbara reached for Mark's hand to steady herself.

"Incredible!" she said.

They were high up and yet the peaks around them seemed to have suddenly shot up even higher. To the north was the towering string of peaks of the Tetons, to the south they could see forever, down to the valley and across to still more mountains. Directly at their feet was a sharp drop of at least five hundred feet, down to a small, impossibly blue lake. The slope, shielded from the sun, was still deep with snow.

There was no sign of life, just rock, snow, wind and sky. Mark had been here a dozen times before. He had always found its fiercely alien beauty exalting, its vastness a kind of medicine.

They stood without speaking. At first there seemed to be no sound except the wind, but then they could make out the sound of water running, somewhere deep beneath the boulders, and then, a hawk's cry. Mark's eyes searched the basin and finally he saw it, floating high in the wind over the lake, yet still hundreds of feet below them. Mark pointed out the hawk.

"That bird's out of its mind," she said.

She walked on out along the ridge and Mark followed, staying a dozen paces behind. She moved slowly, careful to keep her balance on the high spine of rock, sober as a tightrope walker. Her shoes and the bottom of her pants were wet from the snow. She looked so lonely out there, framed only by the distant walls of granite. She was pondering something, he could tell. Mark reached down and picked up a handful of melting snow, packed it into a ball, flipped it over Barbara's head so that it landed right in front of her, a strictly junior-high move.

She turned back and smiled. She pointed ahead.

"What's that?" she said.

"Where?"

"There."

It took Mark a second to see what she was talking about, so well concealed among the huge boulders was the delapidated line shack. Mark had never seen it before.

"I don't know. Let's go see."

It really was only the skeleton of a building. It must have been years since anyone had used it. One wall was gone, the roof had been crushed by the weight of winter snows. The remains were scattered; window frames, the innards of a stove, a broken-legged table. Barbara was fascinated, rummaging through the moldering debris, picking up for examination a rusted hinge, a decaying coffeepot.

"Who in the world could have ever lived up here?"

"No one, I'm sure," Mark said. "It's just a line shack. Rangers maybe used it, or the power company when they were putting lines through."

"Oh, I'm sure it's something more exotic than that. Look at this."

It took her a series of yanks to pull an old sled out from under a wreckage of boards. She held it on end like a prize. The runners were brown with rust and one of the slender boards was missing. She beamed.

"Now, why would this be up here?"

"I don't know. Maybe they pulled supplies up on it."

She brushed some of the snow away, rubbed the runners with her hand. She gave the sled a shove with her foot.

"What are you doing?" he said.

"I just want to see." Her sense of whimsy had been engaged. She gave the sled another, harder shove. It slid about four feet on its own.

"You're not going down on that thing."

"Why not?" Her face shone with pleasure.

"There are boulders down there. You'll break a leg. Look, there's no way to steer the thing, it's busted."

She sat down on the battered sled, inched it down the steep slope with her heels and hands.

"You'll break a leg and we'll have to get a ranger up here to get you out. It will be humiliating. Then we've got a scandal."

"Are you going to give me a push?"

"No, you're going to kill yourself."

"You always take the dire view," she said. "Just watch."

She leaned forward, trying to lurch the sled into motion in the wet snow. Slowly she began to slide. She waved back at him, pulled her knees up. She started to pick up speed. There was no way to keep the sled on a direct course and it started to veer left. Mark saw her lean to the right, trying to correct it, but it did no good, the sled was flying now, out of control, and thirty yards ahead of her was a massive boulder, the sled hurtled right at it. Mark shouted at her to fall off, but she didn't, hanging on. He thought for a moment she had frozen in fear, but at the last second she somehow managed to get her feet out so she hit the boulder feet first before sprawling in the snow.

Mark raced down the slope, out of control himself, half-stumbling, half-sliding, feet plunging great holes in the white banks, but then he saw her sit up, snow all over her and a look of childlike awe on her face.

"Phew!" she said.

Mark stood stock-still, gave a short gasp or laugh, he didn't know what it was. "What did you say?"

"I said 'phew!' "

Mark put his hand up to his forehead, his fingers were shaking, and he began to laugh, for all the sweet absurdity of it, and she started to laugh too, laughing at herself, but even as she did she was protesting, "I could have gotten myself killed! Did you see how close I came?"

"I did." He knelt down and wiped the melting snow from her hair, from around her neck.

"I could have broken my leg! We would have had to get a ranger up here . . ." He stood up, took her hands and pulled her up, helped her wipe the snow from her clothes. "I was fantastic, wasn't I?"

He grinned at her. "You were. The most fantastic thing I ever saw in my life."

"I was really going . . ."

"Like a shot," he said.

"Mark, it was wonderful, you've got to try it . . . Honestly, it will be the greatest thing that will ever happen to you."

Everything had changed. It had all happened so fast, that was what made it so outrageous, zooming from silliness to terror to relief in a matter of seconds, in and out of the jaws of death in a flash and on a runaway sled, no less. It made it impossible to be solemn, suddenly, to be tense and inward and hurt, made it impossible for either of them. It had the effect of a great prank.

Mark retrieved the sled and Barbara walked with him, trying to shake the snow out of her sleeve, out of her shoe, going over all the details for him, about how terrified she was, what the rocks looked like, whizzing by, how she thought for a second that she was going to die, and how the next second it was hilarious, telling him how clever and brave she'd been. She was animated, charged up, she couldn't stop talking. They walked back up the slope, side by side, hauling the sled between them.

The second time they went down together, Mark in the front and Barbara in the back, or at least that was the way they started. Again the ungovernable sled veered left about halfway down, spilling both of them. Mark somehow kept a handhold and slid another hundred feet on his belly, side by side with the runaway craft. At the bottom he leaped up and waved at Barbara.

"You creep! You finked out on me! You coward!"

She sat in the snow, waving cheerily back at him.

She stood up as he approached. "Better safe than sorry," she said.

"Well, you're plenty safe all right."

"I hope so," she said. It was with that note of caution that the story came back to him. She had told him about sledding before; it was with Salvatore in Central Park on a snowy day that she had been exposed, found out. Mark wasn't her first sledding partner. Mark tried to put the thought out of his mind. At least up here there would be no photographer from the *Daily News*.

They sledded together for almost an hour. They rode together, one leaning back between the raised knees of the other, holding on tight as the maverick sled sped past boulders and open patches of shale, threading a blithely unpredictable path through a thousand potential disasters. They hauled the sled up the slope again and again, tumbled over one another, threw snowballs, shouting, their voices echoing off the distant rock walls. They blew into their hands, stinging red from the snow. It was a lark, a romp. They trudged together up that field of white, pulling each other over the steepest parts. Even early in the afternoon shadows from the towering walls began to creep across the basin, but there was still sun where they were, and the snow shone with it.

She was a clown, a daredevil, Mark had never seen that so clearly before. They made up new games. She tried to ride down standing up; it was an absurd idea and she immediately went head over heels.

Mark ran down the slope, pulled her up out of the snow. There was suddenly a sharp, echoing crack from the far slopes. They both looked across the wide bowl. There was another crack, louder than before, and then the clear, pinging sound of falling rock.

"What's that?"

"I don't know," he said. He shielded his eyes, scanned the high cliffs. "There," he said. He pointed far up, to a slope just below one of the peaks. A spray of rocks was sailing, bounding down.

"Is it dangerous?" she asked.

"No, not really. It's so warm, everything is loosening up. Even up here. Don't worry. Nothing's going to happen." There was another loud crack and a fresh slide of rocks through a narrow cleft. "Come on." He gave the sled a shove with his foot. "I'll give you a push."

"I should go," she said. The space had suddenly grown too large, too alien.

"Sure," he said. He pushed the ancient sled again with his foot. It slid about ten feet and came to rest in the wet, melting snow. "If you want to come back to my house, I'll make you some tea."

She leaned against his kitchen table, bent her elbow, twisting her arm so she could examine the brown stain, the small frayed tear in her blouse.

"I'm not quite sure how I'll explain this," she said.

"Maybe you can just say you were clawed by a bear," Mark said. He turned up the flame under the teapot.

She didn't smile at his joke. "I don't think I can," she said.

"Don't worry," he said. "Let me see."

She held up her arm and he rubbed the gritty brown stain between his fingers. "There. It's not so bad." Mark wet his fingers with his tongue, rubbed at the stain again. "Mostly just dirt. Take a look. Almost all gone."

Mark cradled her bent arm in his hands. He was suddenly aware of how close she was. He could embrace her or not. He let his hands drop and stepped away. She smiled, ran her hand softly

down his sleeve. The air was suddenly loaded. They both turned at
the same moment and stared at the water, just beginning to boil.

"You want sugar in your tea?" he said.

"You have honey?"

"In the icebox."

"Icebox? Who says 'icebox' anymore? You mean the refrigerator . . ." She opened the refrigerator door. It took her only a second to figure out what she was looking at. She lifted out a wrapped
package, opened it, saw the soft French cheese. "Oh." She turned
back to him, her face flushed. "Our lunch. You bought all this for
our lunch."

"Umm."

"You're sweet," she said. "I'm sorry." She came to him now,
kissed him softly on the lips. He was leaning back against the stove.
She put her arms around his neck, put her forehead against his,
shook her head, smiling. "I'm sorry. I was just so tense . . ." The
smile disappeared. "It's no fun, having to lie."

"You didn't lie to me."

"No, I didn't lie to you. I lied to Rob. About . . . well, you can
guess, can't you? Sometimes I feel as if I'm the world's biggest hyp-
ocrite."

Mark reached past her, closed the refrigerator door. Her arms
never left him. He felt her weight, her warmth against him. Mark
didn't know what to say. He was lost.

"You were so nice. So patient to put up with me. You were perfect," she said. He leaned down and kissed her, felt her tongue
brush his lips. "You're a sly fox, aren't you?" she whispered.

"I don't know."

"You *do* know."

"No," he said.

She looked up, ran her fingertips across his forehead. "You got
some sun."

"You did too," he said.

They kissed again. Mark felt the quick flickerings of desire. They
went on: light kisses, play kisses, it became so easy, so easy to surrender to. When he closed his eyes he could still see, as if the impression had been burned on the inside of his lids, the dazzling
snow, slipping beneath them. That play, that snow, had cleansed
them, washed the dread away, they could go forward again. Her
fingers caressed his face, she kissed his eyes, his cheeks. The point

was that it had become accidental again, it wasn't according to plan, and that made it possible.

Mark had never wanted a woman so much. It was impossible to take his hands off her. It was so clear now that she desired him. She was his. He held her by both arms, trapped her, kissing her hard. She pulled back, holding both his hands. Her face was flushed.

"You're wonderful," she said. "But I can't. I can't stay. I know, it's so stupid. I was so stupid before . . . but I really can't now . . ." She was holding her elbow, covering the torn sleeve. "Mark, I'm sorry."

"I want you so much," he said.

"I want you so much too," she said, but she saw the doubt creeping back into his eyes and she was back in his arms again, kissing his face, again and again. "There will be time," she said. "Don't worry," she whispered. "Don't worry."

CHAPTER THIRTEEN

There was suddenly time. He didn't think to question it, any more than he would have thought to question a miracle.

It was two days later that she saw him again. She called at eight in the morning to say she was dropping the children off at their friends the Harrisons, and she could come over afterwards, if he wanted her to. It didn't take him a second to decide. He called Patrick and said that he wasn't coming in. Patrick sounded annoyed, but it didn't matter. Nothing mattered except that, an hour later, she was there in his arms again, her face radiant, her hair freshly washed. It all seemed very simple and inevitable.

His life was suddenly filled with her. She would come to his house in the afternoons and they would make love, again and again. He couldn't let her go. He wanted each act to take them further. He became aware of a terrible willfulness, a new and unruly hunger.

She was a gentle, tender lover. He realized that he had not known this woman at all before. Their hours together passed dreamlike, afternoon sun passing outside the bedroom window. What moved him was how much she trusted him, how quickly she gave herself to him. She was transfigured, lit up from within, the cutting edge of irony she'd always had had disappeared.

One morning she brought him a packet. She needed to get it out of the house, she said. She was shy about giving it to him. Maybe it will scare you off, she said.

After she left, Mark sat down and spread the contents of the huge manila envelope across the kitchen table. There was a great hodgepodge to be sorted out: sketches, postcards, notes scrawled across yellow legal pads. Some of the papers were held together with pins or paperclips, others floated free.

Mark leafed slowly through them, not knowing where to start until he found a note with 2 A.M. scrawled across the top. The note looked as if it had been written in the dark, the handwriting was unsure, oversized, sprawling.

A rich fantasy life laced, now and then, with a real affair—

Who can wig out every night and keep up the matinee performances of family, etc. every day?

The children are real—carrying me and my fantasy world inside them—and is it crippling them?

My life wants to run and hide—

Sordid secret lives between rooms of responsibility—

Mark set the note down, pushed away his coffee cup. He was sweating. He should open a window. Morning light crept silently down the wall, across the kitchen floor, like a thief. In case he hadn't remembered how deep it all went, this drew him back down into the dark well.

He found a series of drawings, done in panels, with an unruly-looking tree in the process of being whittled and pruned. Dali-esque scissors floated in the air, snipping away, twigs flew. There were voices too, maybe they were intended to be the voices of the scissors, Mark couldn't tell.

"Everyone has to be cut back now and then, it's all part of growing up . . . you can't let yourself branch out every which way, Barbara, it's not healthy, it's too much of a tangle, people get hurt, not to mention that it's very confusing . . . snip . . . you can't have your cake and eat it too . . . No such thing as a free . . . snip . . . lunch . . . Don't be greedy now, dear heart, it happens to all of us . . . Prudent limits, that's the key, loppedy-lop . . . You've made your choices, dear, it's up to you to honor them . . ."

In each successive panel the tree was more and more shorn, and in the last panel there was nothing left but a forlorn stump surrounded by voices.

"Barbara? Are you there? I don't understand why she's gotten so quiet all of a sudden. It's not really like her. Maybe it's a phase. Midlife Passage. Oh, dear, I guess we'll just have to wait and see."

Pinned to the drawing was a tiny card with a note scrawled in green ink. It said, "This is a covering letter. Take the enclosed with all the weight of your varied life experience and then RUN! Away!!"

He set the drawing aside, pulled the paperclip from a sheaf of notes. The phone rang in his bedroom. He ignored it. He read again.

I feel very limited, fragile, boxed, defined. You are free. I want all these lives, these occult, dark, curious ones, ones like yours—

He set the note aside, picked up another.

We have made a house—Boxes of time
Boxes proliferate—appendages everywhere—
THE HOUSE IS FULL
What is left?
We'll make our days into windows for each of us to pass through—
The right frame, the right space can take something and make it into more—
I wonder what it would be like to travel with you?

He stopped, closing his eyes for a second, rubbed them with the palms of his hands, seeing white spiderwebs spinning in the darkness. Desperate was what it was, all of it, and yet he was so linked with her it was as if it wasn't another person writing, it was like discovering a journal he had forgotten that he'd written himself.

He pulled his hands away, leaned back, flicked at the pile of papers with his finger. Out the kitchen window he could see a pair of teen-age girls guiding their horses through a run of barrels on the rodeo grounds. He felt very tired. Then he saw the letter, on the thin blue paper. It was addressed to him.

I feel so full—so expanded and richly warmed by you—I don't know what to do with myself, with these wonderful sensations—you are an amazing force—I would like to sing to you, sew you up with my threads, warm you the way you warm me, take you and lead

*you through my life. I'm in a cosmic spin. The world is sharp, in
the most complex focus, all the extraordinary details of sun on the
window, a dog barking outside and all of this mixed in with the
great unwieldies of why and where and how and what again after
that? You are new—yes—and I'll have you—I'll learn you—and love
you properly—that means a lot, altogether.*

Mark had never done anything even close to this before. He had
never stolen a girlfriend from a buddy, and certainly never slept
with a married woman. People who did either he had always
viewed with contempt and a certain pity. Cheating was not the sort
of thing he liked to think about. The facts damned them both; the
experience was an exaltation.

There were moments of immobilizing guilt, moments when she
would arrive at his house so tense she couldn't speak. He would
hold her there at the door, the muscles in her back rigid with fear.
So much of the necessary ugliness fell on her, the arrangements, the
lies, the covering up. When she was like that, so full of terror, so
caged, he would say, "I don't want to do anything to hurt you, we
don't have to do anything you don't want to do," and he would
mean it, it would be clear in his mind just how much was at stake,
clear that it couldn't go on, and still they would end up together,
together in such a way that it felt like it couldn't be wrong.

She never lied about what limits were there. She would never do
anything to hurt her children, she would never break up her family.
What she and Mark had together had to remain secret. The
thought of being discovered terrified her. "If Rob were to find out
it would be the all-time worst . . ." was a refrain Mark heard more
than once.

Promising nothing, that was their rule, yet everything in him
strained against that rule. He yearned to make promises, even as he
knew that what they had together was based on a premise of despair; that everything vanishes in time, dissolves in the air, all vows
are betrayed.

One night, after having spent the afternoon together, she called
him. She told Mark how he'd stayed with her all through the evening, through the dinner conversation, how she'd kept wanting to
insert his reactions to things, kept thinking of stories he'd told her.
She told him how he was there, even now, in her bedroom, in the
darkness.

"I wish I was there," he said.

"You are here," she said. "You're right here beside me."

"Good," he said. "That's right where I belong."

"It's so dark. I could hide you so easily."

"I'll bet you could," he said. "What will you do tomorrow?"

"I'll work. All day. Like a demon. To make up for this indulgence," she said. He didn't answer; it hurt a little, being referred to as an indulgence, even as a joke. "Can you see the stars where you are?" she asked.

"If I crook my neck," he said.

"I can see the whole sky, just lying here. The stars are so beautiful. Can you see them too?"

"Of course I can," he said. "I'm lying right next to you, aren't I?"

It was one of her favorite conceits, imagining him being there with her when he wasn't. She would call him after a day apart and tell him how he'd spent the day right alongside her, reading to the children or poking fun at a pompous dinner guest. She carried him around inside her, she said. She would collect him, she said. She joked about roosting right behind his eyeballs and making him see everything differently.

In another situation Mark would have found those kinds of metaphors disingenuous or coy, but he didn't now. The force that was creating them was too great, the need that it met in himself too essential. She had to talk about him as if he were there with her because mostly they were apart and yet they had come to inhabit one another with a power that seemed akin to haunting.

One afternoon they drove up to the park, pulled into a small gravel lot overlooking Jenny Lake. She was tense and distracted. They could hear the clear ringing of an axe as someone chopped firewood. The lake sparkled with late-afternoon light. Barbara wouldn't leave the car, she was terrified of someone seeing them together. They stared across at one another like prisoners. She was impossible to deal with. Finally Barbara confessed: Kate had called Rob, she had made her plane reservations, she was coming.

Mark and Barbara went back to his house and made love. It was a long, slow time, Mark hovering above her, holding himself up with his long arms. Afterwards she started to cry. She wept and wept and Mark couldn't seem to comfort her. It frightened him, it seemed a release of such immense sorrow, such inconsolable grief.

He sat on the bed, cradling her. "Hey. Hey. What's wrong? Tell me. Please, Barbara. What's wrong?"

She had stopped crying, but she still struggled for breath, like someone after a long, painful run.

"Nothing, nothing." She turned into him, resting her fingers lightly on his chest. "It's just that sometimes it's like that after sex."

"Not for me," he said.

"No?" She smiled. "That's because you're still a child."

Mark said nothing more, but his fear did not go away. Because he was so happy, he hadn't been able to believe in her unhappiness. But he did now; he would never forget it again.

You're a more peaceful person than I am, she would tell him, you calm me down. She told him that she felt easier and better with her husband and children since she'd been seeing him. It meant a lot, her telling him that. He needed desperately to believe that he was good for her.

We'll find our own form, she would say, and he wanted to believe that too, but he couldn't quite. It wasn't making art they were engaged in. Some forms of art or life end up monstrous. He felt she trusted too much to will, to wit, to ingenuity. There was too much he couldn't know, too much of her life existed in shadow for him, his feelings were in a constant state of anarchy. The one thing he did know was that for the first time in his life he had allowed himself to be sustained by someone else. He had trusted himself to her, abandoned himself with the recklessness of a child. He had never been in a state of such unreasonable hope.

Late one afternoon, after spending most of the day together, they were driving back to Mark's house so Barbara could pick up her car. There were big clouds piling in from the west as they drove, and with the sun setting behind the mountains the effect was spectacular, layer upon layer of color over the peaks, dark purples and blues, brilliant reds and yellows, shafts of light and shafts of mist where it was already raining.

Mark tried to sing "Country Roads" and Barbara joined him, but they couldn't remember all the verses.

"It's weird," he said. "I don't think there's a single song I know all the words to." Sheets of rain filled the far canyons.

"I'll bet there is," she said.

"I'll bet there's not."

She started to sing. "She'll be coming round the mountain when she comes . . ."

"Well, yeah," Mark said.

The curtain of rain moved across the flats, a strong wind blew tumbleweeds across the highway in front of them. The sky was black. Barbara kept singing, "She'll be riding six white horses when she comes . . ." Mark joined lustily. The first heavy drops of rain splatted against the windshield.

Barbara let the song just trail off. She put her hand into Mark's and they both stared out into the rain.

"I always thought that would be the greatest thing," she said.

"What's that?"

"Riding six white horses. All at once."

"I hate to correct you, but I think it's supposed to be *driving* six white horses, not *riding* 'em."

"How would you know? You just admitted yourself that you don't know the words to songs."

"No, but that one I do. It's perfectly clear from the song that she's in a carriage and that she's driving 'em."

"Really?"

They were crossing over a bridge. Mark put on his lights and they flashed off the metal guardrails. Mark listened to the steady beat of the windshield wipers, the hiss of tires on the wet pavement. He felt himself coming down a bit. Ten more minutes and they would be at his house, she would get in her car and leave.

"Riding six white horses," Mark said. "It doesn't make sense. How could a person ride six white horses?"

He heard her stifle a cough. "I don't know. It just always seemed wonderful to me. To ride them all at once, standing up on top, I guess that's how I imagined it, six horses abreast. I suppose it's like being able to live all these different lives and not having to give any of them up."

Chapter Fourteen

Ellen had always talked about something called the real world and Mark had always made fun of her for it. She had a point, though. What she called the real world was no great respecter of privacy, wasn't going to stay politely outside Mark's door forever. When it came in, it came like a hostile intruder, throwing multiple blows.

The first was that Mark walked into work after a three-day absence only to discover that Patrick had fired him.

Their conversation in the yard behind the office was short and unsatisfactory. It wasn't a very easy thing for Patrick to do. Patrick was confused, but he was mad too. Things were not working out. For the last couple weeks Mark hadn't even called when he wasn't coming in. Patrick needed people he could count on. Mark had been acting kind of weird, Patrick said, people had started to notice. Patrick would have listened to any explanation, but Mark wasn't giving any. Patrick would have hired him back in a second, but Mark wasn't letting him. He felt bad for Patrick, trying so hard to be a decent guy, but at the same time Mark felt terrific, almost gleeful. Patrick didn't know what a favor he was doing him, he was setting Mark free. Having no money wasn't going to matter, he'd done without money before, what it meant was that he would have more time for Barbara.

When they said goodbye, Mark, on impulse, grabbed the bewildered Patrick by the head with both hands and kissed him on the cheek.

"Bless you, man, bless you." Patrick's eyes widened in surprise. Mark backed away, moving past the trucks, giving one of them a hollow-sounding thump, sauntering toward the street. Patrick just stood there, abandoned, watching him. Mark put a closed fist up to his chest in final salute.

When Mark arrived home in the middle of the morning, with an unexpectedly free day in front of him, the phone was ringing. It was the pianist who played for Ellen's classes. During the morning session, doing a perfectly ordinary exercise, Ellen had slipped and turned her ankle. It was a bad sprain; by the time she was driven to the doctor she couldn't walk on it at all. The pianist thought Mark should know, in case Ellen hadn't called already. The pianist just assumed that things were the same. How could he know that Mark hadn't talked to Ellen for two weeks? Ellen must not have told him anything.

As soon as he hung up, Mark called Ellen and insisted that he was coming over. She told him not to, that there was nothing he could do, but he rolled right on past her objections, he was coming. It was not a long conversation.

When he knocked on the door there was no answer and he let himself in. He found her sitting on the edge of the bathtub, soaking her foot. She was still in her leotard. He put his hand softly on her shoulder. He did not try to kiss her.

"Wow," Mark said. There was a purple lump the size of a softball protruding from the side of her ankle.

She looked up at him, her eyes red. She'd been crying. "It's awful, isn't it?"

"They always look awful," Mark said. The bathroom was steamy from all the hot water. Mark felt perspiration forming on his face. "You have any Epsom salts in there?" he said.

"No," she said.

"You should. They really take down the swelling. I'll get you some when I go out." He saw her mouth quiver. He was afraid she was going to cry again. "Hey, it's going to be all right."

She lifted her foot tentatively out of the water. "I just don't know how I'm going to do my classes," she said.

"You'll do just fine. We'll get you a big chair and you can just sit up there like a queen on your throne and order them to dance their little tails off. Hell, if Martha Graham can do it, so can you. We'll get you a very elegant-looking cane." He hated the sound of false cheer in his voice.

She ignored his talk, putting her hand against the wall to brace herself as she tried to stand. He reached out to help her. She glanced at him swiftly, but took his hand.

With Mark's hand around her waist Ellen hopped on one foot into her bedroom and lowered herself down on her bed. The biography of Nijinsky, his gift to her, lay on the nightstand. The eyes of the mad Russian dancer stared up at him.

"I'll wrap it for you," he said.

"The bandage is there on the table," she said. He could hear the anger in her voice.

She lay back, her head propped up on a pillow, watching him. He sat on the edge of the bed, her swollen foot across his knees. He felt shy and awkward sitting there. He feared her anger; he braced himself for it.

"Why are you looking so solemn?" he said finally.

"It's been a long time," she said. "Since you've sat on this bed."

Mark winced at her bluntness and said nothing. He let the Ace bandage unfurl through his fingers. "Lift up your foot," he said.

He wrapped the foot slowly, winding the bandage gently in a figure eight over the discolored ankle. He avoided her eyes. He dreaded the conversation they were about to have.

"What are you thinking?" she said.

"What are *you* thinking?" he came back at her.

"I'm thinking about what's happened to you."

He pulled the bandage a little tighter, looked up at her. "That's not hurting too much?"

"What has happened to you, Mark? Maybe it was something I said, I don't really see how, but that stupid business about our lives being small or something, maybe you were insulted . . . I said I was sorry, I said it then. I was upset. But at least I let you know these things . . . I just don't go run away and hide. It's not fair."

"It's nothing you've done, Ellen," Mark said.

"Then what is it?"

He felt curiously lightheaded. "I don't know. Maybe it would be better if . . ."

"If what?"

"I don't know."

"If we don't see each other? But we're not seeing each other now. I assume we're not. Am I right?"

His fingers were trembling. "Are you seeing someone?" she asked.

"Who would I be seeing?"

"I don't know," she said.

"No," he said. He felt his chest tighten. "I'm not. I'm not seeing anyone," he said, repeating, letting the lies build on one another, like notes running up a scale.

"If you've got a girlfriend, just tell me. You owe me that much." Her voice was shaking.

"I'm not seeing anyone," he said, his voice resentful now.

"Then what is it? What have I done?" He said nothing, winding the bandage again and again, under the foot, over the ankle. I will pay for this, he thought, I will pay for hurting her. She fell because I was not there, I was not there to catch her. "Why are you even here?" she said, her voice rising, sharper.

"You hurt your ankle. I'm wrapping it."

"It must be making you miserable," she said. "You don't even want to be here."

"Shut up, Ellen."

"You don't have to be here," she said. "I have friends, you know. If I called them they would be over here in a minute."

"I'm going to wrap your ankle, and after that I'm going to go. You can call them then."

Stung, her eyes filled with tears. "Do you even like me?" she said.

If he could only fix her hurt and then go, it wasn't going to work that way, he had to sit here and watch her suffer. "Of course I do," he said. "We're friends, right?"

"I care for you, Mark. I love you, even if I'm always making you mad."

Mark stared at her. Barbara never said it first, I love you, and here it was. The words suddenly came cascading out. "I care for you too, Ellen, now listen to me, I promise you . . ."

"No, don't. Don't start promising things. Don't start now. It's not your fault, what happened, it's mine. I want too much."

"Stop, Ellen!"

She was relentless. "I don't want you to be miserable being with me, I'd rather be by myself."

She pulled herself up to a sitting position on the bed, pulling away from him. She was in pain and his instinct was to comfort and heal, but he had to be careful, all his consolations would end up as more lies.

"Just hold still," he said. She glared at him. "I said hold still. You want me to fix this or not?" He took her foot again in his hands, his head bowed, looked up at her. What a fool he was. Her decency seemed, at that moment, like the most appealing thing in the world. For a second he thought that he must love her, but, no, that was delusion, the thought frightened him. What he felt was pity, respect, something else . . . What a fool if he loved them both. He could feel the avalanche of feeling coming down on him and nowhere to take shelter.

If he could only tell her, tell her everything, then he might be saved. But it would hurt too much. To tell her about Barbara he would have to be willing to give Barbara up and he wasn't willing.

His fingers trembled as he fastened the bandage with tiny metal clamps.

"I care a hell of a lot more than you think," he said.

"I can't stand your being like this!" she said. "Just tell me this, Mark, if you can't tell me anything else. Tell me that you don't want to see me anymore."

"It would be a lie," he said. He felt sick, feverish. He stared across the bedroom at the hanging plants in front of the windows, at the familiar prints on the wall.

"Go ahead then, lie! Say that you don't want to see me anymore. Please, Mark."

He stared at her as if hypnotized, dazed by a sense of his own evil. "I don't want to see you anymore," he recited.

Mark almost didn't recognize her. Judy sat in the booth at the Wort Hotel coffee shop. She was waiting for him, but her back was to him and she hadn't seen him yet. Judy had chopped off all her hair, her head looked almost shaved.

The effect was jolting. She had always worn her hair long and straight, Mark and Tommy used to tease her about it, about the way she would toss it, Joni Mitchell-style, when she walked. Now it was gone.

Mark stood in the doorway of the coffee shop, just looking at her for a second. The changes in her were eerie. Always thin, she had lost even more weight and seemed all wire and edges, like a deer that had just smelled danger and was ready to take flight.

Mark hesitated for another moment, then strode forward, reached out and touched her lightly on the elbow. He shouldn't have. She whirled around, terrified.

"Hey," Mark said. "It's just me."

"Oh, sorry . . . sorry. . . ." She tried to smile.

"I'm the one that's sorry," Mark said. "I shouldn't have caught you like that."

"You're not the one I was afraid of getting caught by." She gestured for him to sit down. He slid into the booth opposite her.

"I hope you haven't been waiting long."

"Not long at all." She fingered the coffee cup in front of her, then looked up at him. "I was surprised that you called."

"Why should you be surprised? We're friends, aren't we? I wanted to see you." Mark turned away, tried without success to get the attention of the waitress who was busy at the next table with what looked like fishermen from Detroit, middle-aged men with loud voices, windburned faces and vests with a lot of pockets.

Calling Judy had not been easy. Now that Barbara and Rob had taken her in, Judy was in a charged position, a link between two worlds that Mark would just as soon have kept separate. Talking to her felt risky, whether it really was or not. But he had put off coming through on his promise to Tommy long enough. Both Tommy and Judy mattered to him, risk or no risk. He had called her the evening after his blowup with Ellen and arranged for them to meet.

"So how are you doing?" Mark asked.

"I'm doing fine. I know I don't look it."

"You look terrific to me."

"No, I know I don't. How do you like my butch haircut? That's what Michael calls it. He says it's a man-hating act, cutting hair this short, maybe he's right. He says it's the most overtly castrating gesture he's ever seen."

"You know Michael," Mark said. "With him a woman picking up a fork can be a castrating gesture."

"I don't care, really. I was just tired of all that hair. It gets so hot in the summer. I was tired of looking like a little girl. Time to grow up."

Mark saw the lines tighten around her eyes and mouth, new lines. She had never had that bitter set to her face before. She noticed his watching her. He looked away, tried again to flag down the harried waitress.

He looked back at Judy.

"I saw Tommy," Mark said. "He wanted me to talk to you. He made me promise."

"Is that why you wanted to see me?"

"Partly," Mark said. "But I thought I should tell you. He would like you to come back." The fishermen from Detroit rose from the next table, emptying their pockets of coins, spanking down generous tips. "He says he knows it was all his fault. He says he can be different. I'm just telling you what he said. Is that all right?"

"Yes," she said, her voice constricted and careful now.

"He wants one more chance. He says if he can't make this work he'll never be able to make anything work."

She put her fingers to her lips, regarded Mark with the meditative distance of a dreamer. "And what do *you* think?"

"I think he'd try."

"*Try?* But sometimes trying isn't enough. I think he's always tried. But people don't change, not really."

"No?"

"No."

A couple of bearded musicians with monster-sized brass belt buckles and floppy outlaw hats strolled past, sucking on toothpicks.

"But maybe if you hadn't discovered him that day, maybe it would have all just passed, maybe you'd still be together, you don't know."

"Do you believe that?"

"I'm not sure."

"No. You think I didn't know, all along? I knew. There's no such thing as a secret when you're living with somebody. Nothing ever really stays hidden. It would have happened sooner or later." She picked one of the little packets of sugar out of the sugar bowl, stared at the picture of an eagle on it, tossed it back. "We were always best with you guys, you know? With you and Ellen. Those were the best times, the four of us. But things never stay the same, do they?" There were tears in her eyes. The waitress was striding toward them finally, apologetic, shiny menus in hand. "I don't want any more coffee. I don't want anything. I don't think I should stay here any longer. I'd better go."

Mark rose from the table with her. "I'll walk you to your car."

Outside they walked through the jammed streets. They were both silent for a while, the way old friends can be. There was so much that didn't need to be stated between them, and there was a comfort in that. He didn't want to leave her.

Mark wondered if he should tell her anything about his being fired, or about Ellen, or even more. It would be so easy now, their discussion in the restaurant had opened him up. The temptation to confess, to be understood, was powerful.

"Maybe you shouldn't be living out there now," Mark said. "Maybe it isn't the best place. If you had a place of your own . . . I could help you look."

She shook her head. "I don't want to be in town now. I don't want to be anywhere near him. I feel safe out there."

Across the street in the park there were kids from the high school playing basketball, young bodies leaping high again and again, the loose rim rattling. "He's not going to hurt you," Mark said. He held her by the elbow to let a car pass.

"I know," she said. "But I still feel safer out there."

"You can't spend your whole life hiding out from him. You should be around other people. You can't stay out there forever."

"Maybe not," she said. "But Barbara says I can."

They had entered the parking lot. Mark looked around for Judy's car and didn't see it. Judy saw him looking.

"I didn't bring my car," Judy said. "Barbara lent me hers."

"Ah. You told her then, you were seeing me."

"Of course. It's over here." Judy led him to the familiar green Datsun. Mark ran his fingers over the roof of the car. The metal burned with midday sun. It was the same car that had been parked, hidden in the trees in front of his house, so many afternoons. The effect of seeing it now was eerie.

"So you like it out there?"

"It's nice. They make me feel as if I'm part of their family. It's a borrowed life, I suppose, but it's better than the one I had. I would like to be like her."

"Barbara, you mean?"

"Yes. They seem about as close to a perfect couple as I can imagine."

"They probably have their troubles too."

"If they do they don't show it. No one's ever been as kind to me as Barbara's been. She's the best person in the world to talk to. You can say anything to her and she understands. She makes you feel not so bad about yourself."

"She's not too bossy for you?"

Judy gave a smile of recognition. "Not really." She opened the back door of the car and tossed her packages inside. Mark ran his hand over the familiar dent in the front fender.

"You don't find yourself arguing with her?"

"Sometimes, I guess. She says all these outrageous things and she's getting in trouble for it all the time . . . but, really, I think she's wonderful."

"I think she is too," Mark said. "Though it seems to me she doesn't always see herself that way."

"I know," Judy said. She paused for a second, considering Mark. There was a question in her eyes now. "Have you seen her at all recently?"

"No, not really. I just remember that about her."

Judy slammed the back door of the car. "I love her children. I love to spend time with them. They're bright and happy, Rob and Barbara are remarkable parents. That's what hurts the most, I suppose, about knowing that it's really over between Tommy and me. No matter how bad it got, as long as we were together I always thought we would have children, sooner or later. You know Ellen and I always talked about it. And now I guess . . . there's no way . . ."

Suddenly she was weeping.

"Hey," Mark said. He stood bewildered for a second, then held her, letting her cry without interruption. Her hair, short as a boy's, bristled against his cheek, smelled faintly of smoke. She felt so thin, so fragile. He comforted her the way he hadn't been able to comfort Ellen, leaning against the burning car, Barbara's car. It's inevitable, he thought, we will all give ourselves away, sooner or later.

Finally she put her hands against his chest, pushed gently away from him. "I should get back," she said. "A friend of theirs is arriving tonight and I promised that I would cook dinner."

"What friend is that?"

Judy fished in her pocket for her car keys. "I don't know. Some actress from New York."

Chapter Fifteen

The woman was a real knockout. Tommy had come wheeling his van into the parking lot, the raft bouncing behind him, and he had given the passengers the once-over like he always did, and there she was. No way he could have missed her.

She was amazing. She had style, East Coast style, with a kind of confidence that comes from reading a lot of books and riding a lot of National Velvet-type horses. She was tall, with long legs, a strong frame, big beautiful eyes and the kind of cheekbones you could hang yourself on. A classic. No kid, either, she had to be at least in her mid-thirties. A real woman, the kind you almost never get on float trips. She had a real air about her. She was one of those women who made you look at them.

That was the reason why he didn't notice who she was with right off. It wasn't until after he'd swung down out of the van and said hello and the crowd had headed slowly toward him, sheepish like they always were—an older woman with smoky glasses, the kind you wear if you've got cataracts, and with her she had a couple of grandsons it looked like, and there were three college boys with Michigan State t-shirts and cutoffs leaning against a dirty Volkswagen, and a couple of chubby girls, secretaries from Phoenix, Tommy figured—it wasn't till after that that Tommy saw that the knockout of a woman had two men with her and Tommy knew both of them. One of them was Rob Campbell, and the other his tall wise-ass buddy Michael something, Tommy had met him in a bar once, acting like an idiot.

Tommy took a deep breath. He hadn't liked Rob much before

Judy had split, and he had even less reason to like him now. The man probably thought he was a real Good Samaritan, sheltering Judy from God knows what. It probably made him feel real good. It was meddling, the way Tommy read it. Maybe it was unreasonable, but there were times when Tommy believed Judy would have been back with him if the Campbells hadn't taken her in under their cushy wing. She always had wanted to live in the country. Hell, for all he knew, she was having a real ball.

It had been three weeks since Mark had promised to talk to Judy, to tell her that Tommy wanted her back. Three weeks and Tommy hadn't heard a word. Tommy was a little surprised, maybe he shouldn't have been. He had lived long enough not to trust anybody too much. For some reason he'd always thought Mark was different. When a friend didn't come through for you, it hurt, but you couldn't do much about it. When a rich son of a bitch stood between a man and his wife and thought he was a hero for doing it, it was another story. Maybe there wasn't anything you could do about it, but then again, maybe there was. At least you didn't have to be so careful.

"You our guide?" It was one of the towheaded kids.

"That's right," Tommy said.

"And we're going down the river in *that?*" the boy said, pointing to the huge orange raft.

"Right again," Tommy said.

Campbell had pushed himself up from the car he'd been leaning on. He and Michael and the woman came ambling over, taking their time, like people who were used to being waited for. The woman was telling a story. It looked like a good one; her gestures were both big and exact.

Tommy felt the muscles in his stomach tighten up. What the hell was Campbell doing here? What sort of number was he trying to pull?

Tommy's paranoia only lasted a second. When Rob looked up and saw Tommy standing in the open door of the van staring back at him, his eyes opened wide in surprise. Tommy felt a warm flush of pleasure. Good, man, good, he thought, I'll take you down the river if you want, I'll give you your money's worth. The two men exchanged polite nods.

A second van and rubber raft had just pulled into the lot. The other boatman, a bearded biology teacher from Colorado named Brian, leaped out of the van, waved a pair of clipboards at Tommy.

"Here you go," Brian said. "One for you, one for me." He handed one of the clipboards to Tommy.

Tommy scanned his list of passengers. "Hey, hold on," Tommy said. "Let me look at your list for a second. You got somebody named Campbell?"

Brian went down the list with a stubby finger. Tommy spotted the name even before Brian got to it.

"There," Tommy said. "Three of them. Why don't you let me take 'em?"

"Sure. No problem. Friends of yours?"

"In a way," Tommy said.

When Tommy called out Campbell's name, the woman stepped forward, but Rob wasn't so eager. The woman looked back at him, a question in her eyes. Rob had been hoping to get the other guide. Great, Tommy thought, this is going to work out just fine.

Tommy helped his passengers into the van. As he took the woman's elbow, as gallant as anything, she smiled at him and he grinned back. Rob was right behind her.

"This is a pleasant surprise," Tommy said.

"I hope so," Rob said, climbing unaided into the van. Tommy turned and shrugged at Michael, like he didn't get it.

It was a twenty-minute drive to the point where they put the boats in the water. The grandmother with the smoky glasses sat up front with Tommy, her grandsons crowding up between them, intent on listening to everything Tommy had to say. Rob and Michael and the woman sat at the back of the van, but Tommy could keep his eye on them through his rearview mirror.

The woman with the smoky glasses had promised her twin grandsons that she would take them on a whitewater float trip for their birthday and now she was getting a little anxious. She wanted to know exactly how rough it was going to be, if there was any danger. Tommy had to play it a little cagey, to keep her reassured and her grandsons jacked up, all at the same time.

"All I can say, ma'am, is that I haven't lost anybody yet," Tommy said. He winked at the two boys. "Course you are going to get a little bit wet. The rapids this time of year, well, you just never know . . ." He paused, let it sink in, making sure the two boys were still with him.

One of the boys pressed his face to the window, staring down at the river tumbling down through rock cliffs. Tommy smiled. It was almost as if he could see the boy's imagination run.

Tommy glanced in his side mirror. Michael said something that made the woman laugh. She brushed back her hair. Lord, the woman was beautiful. Tommy could see that the other passengers were watching her too.

Rob leaned forward to say something to the two of them, his face shielded from Tommy's view. Tommy wondered if that could have been on purpose, for a second he wondered if Rob could have been talking about him. Tommy felt the giant rubber raft sway behind them as the van went into a curve. One of the assistant boatmen riding back on the raft peered through the back window and waved for Tommy to take it a bit slower.

"You don't think there's any real danger, do you?" the woman with the smoky glasses asked. "For someone of my age?"

"Ma'am, I'm going to take real good care of you," Tommy said. "I'm going to turn you into a real river rat before we're done."

Her grandsons beamed.

Tommy heard the beautiful woman's laughter, rising and falling like little bells, coming from the back of the van. He glanced back again.

Tommy wondered about the three of them. When there were three he always wondered, it was a funny number. Michael and the woman, it wasn't very likely, they were too easy with one another, she kept laughing at him, no . . . But Rob, that was a different story. He seemed a little bummed out, a little surly, maybe he wasn't getting it like he wanted, when he wanted. It was possible. That would be just too damn good. Tommy loved the idea of it, this White Knight who had stepped in to save Judy from her no-account husband having a little something going on the side himself. The idea excited Tommy. Maybe he and Rob weren't so different after all. Hell, he had to have tried. A woman as good-looking as that, you'd have to be a robot not to try.

The passengers stood in a semicircle on the grassy bank, meek as Baptists on the first Sunday of the month, the river roaring past behind them. Tommy stood at the center of the gathering, holding up an orange life preserver. He spoke loudly, to make his voice heard over the roar of the river.

"Now, I've never dumped anybody in the river yet, and I don't intend to start today, but we're not going to take any chances. One thing about rapids, you can't predict 'em. They're not the same one day to the next, not even one minute to the next. This river is wild, folks, and when you come to it, you come humble. So we're all going to wear one of these. They may not be pretty, but they're going to keep you safe. It's perfectly simple to wear one of these, and I can see this is a particularly intelligent group, so if you just listen up for one second, we'll have it. First thing is, I want a volunteer." Tommy looked out at his passengers. Behind him the young tanned assistant boatmen were unlashing the rafts and shoving them down toward the water. "All I need is one volunteer. One brave soul. Come on, now, everybody hasn't turned shy on me, have they?"

He looked at the woman standing next to Rob. She was smiling back at him. No, she hadn't turned shy. Tommy couldn't resist.

"How about you? You come on up here."

She came easily, not embarrassed at all, a woman who was used to being picked out of crowds.

Tommy took her hand. "What's your name?"

"Kate," she said.

"O.K., Kate. Folks, Kate's going to show you how easy it is to wear one of these. Now, you just slip your arms in here . . ."

She followed his instructions perfectly like a pro, Tommy figured she must have been a model. Tommy loved it. He played with her, he played the crowd, he imagined that he saw the uneasiness on Rob's face when he reached back and flicked a strand of Kate's hair that had caught under the collar of the life preserver.

Kate didn't seem to mind at all. Tommy deliberately took his time, fumbling with the orange straps at her waist, standing a little too close, being cute about it, watching Rob out of the corner of his eye. The rest of the passengers didn't mind at all, Tommy had them in the palm of his hand. But Rob minded, Tommy saw that.

Twenty yards away Brian was talking to his passengers, explaining things earnestly, like the high school biology teacher he was.

Tommy pulled Kate's straps up nice and snug, jerking her accidentally toward him, smiling the whole time, suggesting not too much, just enough. He glanced back at Rob. Poor bastard, Tommy thought, I'm going to steal your woman right out in front of a boatload of tourists and you won't be able to do a damn thing about it.

"Isn't she terrific?" Tommy said, appealing to the group. "Doesn't she look great? Who says you can't look like a million dollars in a life preserver? Thank you, Kate." The passengers loved it, laughing and applauding, Kate giving a little curtsy. Tommy caught Kate's hand for just a second as she headed back to Rob. He felt Rob watching him.

The assistant boatmen waited, holding the huge rafts steady in the swift water. The passengers helped each other with their life preservers, got themselves shined up with suntan lotion, rolled up their pant legs, made nervous jokes. The two young boys made a last-minute run up to the wooden outhouses.

Tommy moved in and out, taking care of people, checking everybody. He made a point not to miss Rob.

"Here. Let me fix that for you," Tommy said. "The strap's twisted in the back." Rob said nothing as Tommy undid the buckle and straightened out the twisted strap. Tommy patted Rob on the back. "Gotta take good care of you, man."

Tommy helped the passengers into the raft. As Kate stepped past him she smiled at him, narrowing her eyes. She flirts like a little girl, Tommy thought. He liked it all the same.

Tommy got in last, took the oars, the assistant boatmen shoved them off. Tommy felt the boat pulling beneath his feet. The passengers around him were all staring and smiling, being real still. Tommy worked the oars to move them out into the middle of the river.

They were well away from the banks now and the river began to pull harder. Riffles and curls of water were everywhere around them, gleaming and rocking in the sun.

Tommy talked about the water, about how you read a river, how you negotiate the rock ledges that come down from the banks and make the water foam across them.

Tommy looked downstream and saw Brian's raft a hundred yards or so ahead, bobbing through the first small rapids. He heard their shouts.

Tommy leaned harder on the oars, working for position. "O.K., everybody, first rapids coming up. Hold tight."

Tommy felt the water quicken, heard the rumbling grow louder. The raft was set just right, sliding directly into the tongue of the rapids. The current sucked them, lifted them, plunged them, water sprayed over the whole lot of them, some of the passengers shrieking at the coldness of it, and then suddenly they were through.

The passengers stared wild-eyed at one another, teeth chattering, laughing at each other for being scared. It was fun. It was always fun. Tommy looked down at the grandmother, who looked stunned.

"How you doin', ma'am?"

"Oh, my," she said.

"You came through that just fine, ma'am, just fine," Tommy said.

Her two grandsons stared at Tommy. They thought he was great, no doubt about it.

Rob wiped at his wet trousers and shirt. Well, good, Tommy thought, got him pretty good. And I'll get him a couple more times too, before we're through. Give Mr. Clean a real good rinsing.

Kate was laughing, she had a wonderful laugh, it was like liquid. She was having as good a time as any of the kids. She glanced up at Tommy, approving, narrowing her eyes again, giving her special look. Tommy winked at her.

As they moved down river, Tommy pointed out the sleek, bobbing head of an otter swimming near the shore, the slope where the elk came down to graze late in the day, the eagle's nest high atop a dead tree.

The river always worked for Tommy. Even with the most out-of-it tourist chattering around him, Tommy never totally lost it, the sense of wonder about the river. The sound of these waters churning through rock walls was a refuge for him, he almost felt like he could curl up in that sound and no one would ever be able to hurt him. It got rid of his meanness. He stopped feeling so bad about himself. The river was the one place where he felt something like reverence, where that made sense.

Tommy looked back in surprise when he felt the tremor of some-one moving in the boat. It was Kate, edging forward to take a place nearer him.

"Hey, now," Tommy said. "Remember what I said? Everybody stays put, otherwise it gets dangerous."

She smiled, turning it on, sure that she had done nothing wrong. "I couldn't hear what you were saying where I was sitting."

"I wasn't saying that much," Tommy said. He knew that he should scold her for the sake of the others, but he was secretly pleased. He looked back at Rob, who was still rubbing his jeans, trying to get them dry. Rob glared blackly at Kate.

It wasn't a fair fight and Tommy knew it. Tommy got to stand up in the boat in a tight black rubber vest and show off his muscles, work the oars, give the folks a few bits of lore, everything he did looked good and he knew it. All Rob could do was sit there looking as squat as a toad in his bulky orange life preserver and watch. Tommy didn't care that much whether it was fair or not. It was never fair, one way or the other; usually it was the guys like Rob with the nice money and the nice manners that got the women like this, and it was the guys like him, the ones who pulled the oars for guys like Rob, who ended up with the crazy elementary-school teachers from San Diego. So this once it was different.

Tommy looked down at her and smiled.

"You havin' a good time?" he asked.

"It's exhilarating," she said.

"Good. Glad you're liking it."

"It must be a wonderful way to live," she said.

"How do you mean?"

"Doing just this."

"It's O.K."

"Just to be able to test yourself against something real, that physical . . . to fight against it, every day."

"You talking about the river?"

"Yes."

He regarded her warily. He felt uneasy, putting all these words on it. He wondered if she was for real, or if she was just playing with him. She didn't seem to be.

"You don't really fight the river. It's too strong, you'd have to be an idiot to try. You just learn to go with it, let it work for you."

She pushed her hair back, smiling like an angel. "I stand corrected," she said. "But I think it is wonderful. And can you do it all year round or . . ."

"Around here you can float till the end of September, maybe. Long as the tourists keep paying us, we'll keep floating."

"And then?"

"I pick up work. Whatever there is." Tommy frowned. She was awfully curious for a pretty woman.

"And before this? What did you do? Where did you come from?"

"I took dories down the Colorado. Now, that was what you call wild water . . ." Tommy was not used to people getting so personal, at least not in boats. Trying to ease it out a little, he winked at the two boys. "Now, that's one you guys should take your grandmother down next, the Colorado."

The boys' grandmother looked up through her smoky glasses and smiled weakly. Her hands were knotted around the rope that ran all the way around the boat.

Kate wasn't through yet. "But you really do live for the river," she said.

"I've never said it like that," he said. "But, yeah, I suppose. I like the river a lot."

She was encouraging him, leading him on. He was a little embarrassed, but that didn't mean he didn't like it.

"In a way, you're a real American sort of hero," she said.

"Hey now, come on," he said. The lady was too much. Maybe he did think of himself as a hero, but he'd never admit to anybody that he thought so, not like that, anyway. Too much talk made him suspicious.

"No, I mean it," she said.

He stared down the river, watched Brian heading his boat into the next rapids.

"It must be almost a religion, then, isn't it?" she asked. Religion, my ass, lady, Tommy thought, stop trying to put words in my mouth. He pulled hard on the oars, working against the strong current, moving the boat wide of the water that frothed over jagged teeth of rock.

"Isn't it, though?" she said. "It has its own rituals, rules, even vows, I imagine . . ."

"What kinds of vows?" Tommy said.

"I don't know. Poverty, chastity . . ."

Tommy grinned. "Well, now, lady, it's not as bad as it looks."

"Really?" she said. Tommy heard the pounding of the big rapids ahead, felt its urgency, it was like somebody banging on a drum. "I wouldn't imagine there's much of a place for women in a world like this."

"You'd be amazed," Tommy said.

"No, I'm being quite serious. Isn't it really a modern equivalent of the mountain man or the trapper . . . I'm not being critical at all . . . I'm just observing . . ." Tommy suddenly got uncomfortable, where the hell was she going with this? He looked back at Rob, who was pointing ahead to the rapids, pointing out something to Michael.

"In a life like this," Kate said, "I could see how it would be very hard to be with any one woman for very long . . ."

Suddenly Tommy knew. Rob had told her the whole damn story. The three of them had sat in the back of the van and snickered over it, making fun of him, and Kate had been curious enough, had guts enough, to come check it out, see exactly how big a fool he really was.

Tommy said nothing, leaning on the oars, letting the current take the raft, just staring at Rob until finally Rob had to feel it and look up.

"You should learn to keep your mouth shut," Tommy said softly. The sound of the rapids probably drowned out his voice, but Rob knew anyway. The water was singing around them now, corkscrewing behind giant rocks. Tommy felt the current in his body, felt the big pull starting. The passengers were stirring, twisting around so they could see the churning rapids. Tommy just let the oars lay there.

"You like to talk about people, right?" Tommy said. "Gives you a lot of pleasure?"

The grandmother stared up at Tommy, not getting it.

"No, it doesn't give me pleasure," Rob said.

"Then, why do you do it?" Tommy said, raising his voice to be heard over the rush of water. "You should learn to stop interfering in other people's business."

"Some things are past the point of interference," Rob said. Tommy scarcely heard him, but he heard him.

"Like me and my wife, right?"

All the other passengers were silent now, they knew something wasn't right. Tommy knew he was going to get in trouble for this, one of these people was sure to go back to the office and tell them what a madman they'd got for a guide, but, hell, Tommy wasn't going to back down now, even madmen have their pride.

Rob didn't answer the question, looked out over the water. Tommy couldn't let it drop, it had gone too far.

"Where's your wife, man? You should have brought her."

"She doesn't like the river," Rob said, trying to be steely. "It scares her."

"Oh, yeah? You sure? You'd be surprised, a lot of the time the women are a lot braver about this stuff than their husbands. But, hell, I don't blame you, partner, a man's got to get out, doesn't he? If she wouldn't go with you, get who you can get . . ." He nodded at Kate.

"That's enough, Tommy," Rob said. Michael was looking down into the bottom of the boat, his face all screwed up.

"You just take care of your own damn wife and lay off of mine," Tommy said. He pulled hard on the oars, ready to end it there, but then he saw Rob start to move, lurching to his feet in the raft. Seeing the anger in Rob's eyes, all Tommy felt was pleasure. Tommy was still in control, one quick move and he could sit Rob back down in the boat, but then he saw that Rob was reaching back to take a swing and that was where Tommy lost it. It was too damn perfect. Tommy left the oars and moved on Rob, he heard somebody shout in alarm. Tommy came in under Rob's swing, sticking him like a middle linebacker, his head butting into Rob's cushioned life preserver. He meant to grab on and twist Rob down into the boat, but the raft swung quickly now with the oars trailing free in the quickening whitewater. Tommy slipped and fell across one of the boys, he had lost Rob. The roar of the rapids was like thunder now, but the screams of the passengers were way up high. Scrambling to his knees, Tommy saw Rob bobbing out in the river, the orange life preserver keeping his head high. There was nothing now that Tommy could do. The river had them all. Rob had gotten his feet out in front of him and shot into the chute of water, right down the gullet of rock, disappearing only for a second and then appearing again in the pool below, safe.

Tommy did not look at the other passengers. He quickly regained control of the oars, working furiously to position the raft, and then they tossed and bucked their way through, waves drenching them, making them gasp; they came banging down on stones, then were floating again.

Tommy began to row. He tried not to look at their faces, but he saw them anyway, saw the shock, saw the fear. Many refused to look at him, clinging to the sides of the raft.

Kate was shouting ahead to Rob. She turned back to Michael. "Oh, Michael, he's all right, he's all right." One of the young boys was sobbing and his grandmother was comforting him. It was as if Tommy didn't exist anymore.

Tommy stood by his oars. Up ahead he saw Brian hold up his raft, waiting for Rob to float down to them. Brian held out an oar, Rob caught it and scrambled in, a dozen hands reaching out to help him. Tommy stared down at the sobbing boy. He wanted to reach out to the boy, but he couldn't, his hands were locked on the oars. He felt the waters closing in over his head.

CHAPTER SIXTEEN

Barbara was scared and angry. "Rob could have been killed," she said. "I don't see how you could ever have been friends with someone like that."

"The guy felt like he was in a corner, that he was boxed in," Mark said. "Tommy's never done anything like that before in his life. He's a desperate person."

"A lot of people are desperate," she said. "They don't go around shoving people out of boats."

"I'm not excusing him," Mark said.

"It sounded like you were."

"That's the problem with the phone," he said. It was midmorning and Mark slouched down in his chair, phone cradled in his lap, his hair still wet from the shower. A copy of *Runner's World* lay open on the floor. He had nothing to do, nowhere to go, except to her, if she would let him.

He should have been just going along with her, agreeing, but it was hard. Tommy was wrong, no two ways about it, when you're a hired boatman you don't go pitching passengers out in the river, no matter what they say to you. But the way Mark figured, Tommy had paid for it. He'd been fired on the spot. He would go on paying for it. In the end the humiliation was his, not Rob's. Tommy had lost the only thing he had going for him in the world.

It wasn't just that Mark had an excess of charity, either. Whether he was willing to own up to it or not, the idea of a confrontation, even of Rob bobbing down over the rapids, had its attractions. Fairmindedness had nothing to do with it. It wasn't anything new that Rob had said or done, it was just the way things were. Face to face, Rob was nice enough, even likable, but the point was they weren't face to face. Mark was working Rob up into a rival all on his own.

"That's Kate for you," Barbara said. "What a perfect introduction. It's all so true to form. I almost want to laugh . . ."

She was full of scorn, she was upset, but there was something else in her voice too, something that made Mark even more uneasy. She defended Rob, was protective of him in the way that one expected women to be protective of their husbands. She wanted him safe from lunatic boatmen and ex-lovers, she wanted him back on dry land. No decent person would dare begrudge her those feelings; Mark knew that, and the knowledge made him surly. It was just another bitter reminder of the state of things.

"It was a miracle, really," Barbara said, "that he came out with no more than a few scrapes and bruises . . . It's really criminal, Mark, what Tommy did. I'm serious."

Mark couldn't help himself. "What else do you want them to do to him? He's lost his job, he's not going to get another one, not on this river, probably not on any other, once the word gets around."

"What's wrong with you, Mark?"

"Nothing's wrong with me," he said, but they both knew it was a perfect lie, what was wrong with him was that he'd been sitting around his house for three days going crazy, waiting for Barbara to call, knowing that Kate had come, knowing that that would change everything, but not knowing which way it would go, but afraid it wasn't going his way.

He knew how competitive Barbara was. He knew her well enough to know that, contradictions or not, she would fight to keep her husband and family right where they were. Maybe Mark wasn't out of the picture, but he wasn't exactly sure he was in it, either. Tommy wasn't the only one who felt like he was being backed into a corner.

"This talking on the phone is no good," he said. "I need to see you."

"I know," she said. "I need to see you too. It's just been so hard, with everyone here."

"I'm sure."

"Listen to me," she said. "I know what you're going to say, but just listen for a second. They're showing one of Kate's films this weekend at the Elkhorn. There's a movement afoot for all of us to go tomorrow night. Why don't you come? I'll tell Rob I invited you, it will be all right."

"That's a terrible idea."

"I knew you'd say that. I'm not exactly wild with excitement about going myself, but it would be so much better for me if you were there."

"I'd rather see you alone."

"So would I, but it's really impossible right now with Kate here, and the children are hanging all over me . . . Why don't you come? We can make it be all right. You'll see."

Of course he didn't want to go. It sounded perfectly awful. He didn't see the point of these gatherings, why Barbara kept arranging them. He didn't understand what motivated them, whether it was misguided sentimentality, psychoanalytic curiosity, or just a certain appetite for taking chances. He didn't need to meet Kate, he didn't need to see Rob again, and he didn't want to see the movie, some remake of a Broadway sex comedy that had been out a year anyway. Of course he went.

He told himself he hadn't made up his mind, even as he sat in his car across the street from the theater, watching the people buying tickets. There were elk antlers over the entrance, seven points on one side, six on the other, Mark had plenty of time to count them as he waited.

Finally he saw them, the four of them, arm in arm, taking up the whole sidewalk, Barbara and Rob and Kate and Michael. Mark didn't move, just watched them. Kate, after all the buildup, looked, not like the brilliant monster that Barbara had conveyed to him, but like an attractive woman, someone Mark would have looked at twice, for sure, but not someone you would wreck your life for. Of course this was from across the street. From across the street they looked like nothing more than two good-looking couples on vacation.

Mark waited for them to go in, gave it a couple more minutes, then got out of his car, crossed the street, bought his ticket.

He sat down in the back row of the theater. Barbara, Rob, Kate and Michael sat down near the front. They were absorbed in conversation, whispering back and forth to one another. They hadn't seen Mark come in.

There were only thirty or forty people in the whole place. Mark recognized a couple of kids from the high school, out on a date. The boy waved hello to Mark, then settled back, trying to nonchalantly leave his arm draped around the back of the girl's seat. "Sentimental Journey" throbbed through the loudspeakers. A family was seated off to one side of Mark, the mother running back and forth with orange drinks and candy bars, trying to keep her four-year-old quiet. A couple of rows down a pair of young honchos were laughing, talking loud, acting corny. They hadn't taken off their cowboy hats.

Mark never moved.

As the lights started to come down, Mark got what he wanted. Barbara turned, her gaze searching the audience, betraying her anxiety. Then she saw him. She waved. The others turned then, raising their hands in greeting. Kate smiled brilliantly. Mark could see a little now what Barbara had been talking about. They motioned for him to come down and join them. He gestured with his hand, no, he was staying right where he was.

The theater went dark, the lights came up on the screen. After the ads for the local roofer, a muffler shop and a home for retired actors in L.A., the film began. The opening shot was the skyline of New York. For a second the shadow of one of the ten-gallon hats was magnified at the lower edge of the screen, then disappeared. Two men walked down a crowded, boutique-ridden street. One of the men, the married, self-assured, broad-shouldered one, was advising his lovable but anxiety-wracked friend Lenny on how to score with women. They sized up the women who passed them on the sidewalk. Boob jokes fused with New York insider jokes, cracks about the size of the melons at Zabars.

Mark could hear Michael's drawn-out laugh down front, then the two cowboys joined in. The rest of the theater was quiet, not really getting it. Mark didn't like the movie at all.

He was angry at Barbara. It wasn't normal, a situation like this, and they shouldn't be acting as if it was. It was like being an amputee and going through life pretending you weren't.

The two kids from the high school had settled in comfortably, the boy's arm firmly around his girlfriend's shoulders.

The movie went on, a machine gun of one-liners. The friend knew a woman that Lenny should meet, very, very intelligent, legs that went on for miles, a class act, loved the country because she'd owned a lot of it, loved animals. Animals? Lenny was alarmed. Turned out she lived alone with her dog, a Russian wolfhound that ate five pounds of meat a day. She also kept a horse in the city. Lenny couldn't believe it. All his life he'd dreamed of meeting one of those girls who go around with little whips stuck in their boots.

The movie was getting a few laughs now. Mark sat there, thinking about leaving. He stared down at the silhouettes of Barbara and Rob and Kate and Michael. Suddenly he saw Barbara stand, make her way to the aisle. His heart leaped.

He had no idea what she was up to. She walked up the aisle, smiled blithely at him, gave a tiny wave of the fingers, continued out into the lobby. Mark's mind was racing. He thought of going after her, but he couldn't, she couldn't possibly intend for him to . . .

Barbara was back in a minute, carrying a box of popcorn. This time she stopped at his aisle and leaned in.

"Why don't you come sit with us?"

"I'm fine where I am."

"No, you're not." Something on the screen got a big laugh.

"Yes, I am."

Barbara straightened up, gave Mark a sad, hopeless smile. He could see in her face that she had more to say, but she decided against it.

Mark watched her walk down the aisle. For a second, he wondered if he was doing the right thing, maybe he was being too hard, too unreasonable. As Barbara bent into her row, her shadow flickered along the border of the white screen. She whispered something to Michael, he whispered something back. Michael glanced back toward Mark. Mark wondered what they were discussing and then he knew. Barbara planted the box of popcorn in Michael's lap, turned and came back up the aisle, arms swinging, carefree as a girl after the last day of school. She stopped at Mark's row, waited patiently for the man on the end to stand and let her by.

Mark couldn't believe it. He felt alarm, anger and pleasure all mixed together. Her coming back to sit with him was more than daring, it was foolhardy, outrageous. It was just like her, thinking she was getting away with something when she wasn't. If Rob hadn't suspected before, he had to suspect now.

As she sat down she was smiling, with all the confidence of someone who was sure she was being pleasing.

"Hi," she said.

"What the hell are you doing?" he said.

"What else could I do? You wouldn't come sit with us."

"Christ, Barbara, you're too much."

"You know what they say about people who sit by themselves at the movies."

"No, I don't know. What did you say to them?"

"Everything's all right. They have their popcorn, they're perfectly happy." She patted his arm. "Don't worry." He stared at her. The fact that she was enjoying this made him furious.

"This is pretty dumb, Barbara."

"Why?"

"You know why."

"You're just too cautious."

"You're crazy," he said.

He didn't sound like he was being funny, and that didn't slip past her. She didn't speak for a second.

Up on the screen Lenny was singing in the shower, fumbling with a bar of soap, getting ready for his big date.

"Do you really think I am? Crazy?" Barbara said. "Seriously . . ."

"Oh, God," Mark said. He stared down at Rob and Kate and Michael sitting up front, proud as lords, you would have thought they were sitting in box seats. Their eyes were on the screen, Kate was pointing out something, Michael was munching popcorn. They were talking about the movie. It seemed incredible to Mark. Maybe nobody really cared. Maybe Barbara had told them. Maybe . . .

"You weren't so subtle yourself, you know," Barbara whispered, "sitting in the back in a pout as if you were the young James Dean or something . . ."

"Yeah?" Mark said.

"Yeah." Barbara leaned into him, squeezed his hand for a second. "Just watch the movie. Her scene's coming up soon, our own little femme fatale."

Mark said nothing. He put his elbow on the armrest between them, shifting slightly so their shoulders were touching. He was suddenly very aware of her physical presence; the gentle pressure made him quiet, began to wash away some of his anger.

The screen images flickered past. Mark heard Michael and Rob laughing. The New Yorkers were the only ones laughing in the whole theater. Mark took Barbara's hand. There was no one sitting around them, it was dark, it was safe. She didn't fight him; her hand was warm. Mark felt himself grow hard with desire for her. He began to run a finger slowly up and down the inside of her arm. She stopped his hand.

"Here," she whispered. "Here is where she comes in."

Mark stared up at the screen. Lenny stumbled across the room, nearly knocking over a lamp, finally made it to the door and unlocked all six locks. Joke One was that Kate was six inches taller than he was.

As Lenny buzzed frantically around her there were several close-ups of Kate's bewildered face. The worshipful camera seemed to crawl over her, made her seem a virtual monument of attractiveness. The screen was filled with her.

Mark was holding Barbara's hand again, playing with her fingers, working them. He felt his whole body tense with urgency. The film seemed to be at another remove now, it was like trying to watch television through a neighbor's window when you're standing in the yard, yet the film never entirely went away, he felt his desire for Barbara mediated, mocked by that face on the screen.

His eyes stayed on the screen, but he'd totally lost track of the point of the scene. The character of the woman up there was grotesque, flat as cardboard, a parody.

"Usually," the woman on the screen said, "when men meet me they compare me to America."

Mark didn't really hear Lenny's comeback but it got a big laugh, as it had to. The scene was Lenny's, the jokes were all about sexual terror and class intimidation—Lenny battling to uncork a wine bottle, Lenny trying to get comfortable on a couch. The climax of the scene was the explosion of Lenny's new cappuccino-maker.

The two cowboys sitting down a couple of rows started to get into it. You didn't have to be from New York to understand sexual panic.

The film moved on. Mark found it slipping in and out of focus for him, it was like trying to read when you have a fever, pages keep turning and nothing ever quite registers. He moved his hand down on Barbara's knee. He began to caress the inside of her leg. He wanted her terribly.

The film flowed onward, a stream of deranged, senseless sex jokes. Mark's hand kept moving, first just with the tips of the fingers, then the whole hand stretching out, moving deeper between her legs. Barbara was holding his arm, her grip tightened, yet she shifted toward him, letting him go on.

A girl got up out of her seat, stared toward the back of the theater. Mark stopped his hand. The girl ambled blindly up the aisle, out into the lobby. Mark reached again for the inside of Barbara's leg, but this time she stopped him.

Mark didn't care anymore who knew, who saw. Let Rob come back and look. Let him see and get it over with. Mark was overwhelmed with a sense of his own degradation, with the perversity of what they were doing, yet he had no will to resist. A voice told him that they were just using one another to even the score, to get back. But who were they getting back at? The face on the screen? The dark figures laughing in the front rows of the theater? He was afraid to look at Barbara. All he knew was that he wanted to be allowed to go on.

His hand was high on her thigh. Her fingers closed tightly around his fingers, lifting them off. He looked over at her, even in the darkness he could see her flushed face. He heard Michael's cackle ring through the theater.

"No," she said. "Don't, please."

Mark said nothing, staring back at her as he would have stared at an enemy. He took his hand away, looked out in the aisle, blinking back tears of shame. "I'm sorry," he said.

She reached out, touching his face, the gesture unguarded, consoling. "Don't say that, don't."

The film was coming to an end. The two men were walking down the same boutique-ridden street, eyeing women once again, making the same jokes, the same, except maybe a bit hollower, a bit more acidic than before.

The lights came up in the theater. Mark stood up, defenseless in all that sudden light. He turned to her, trying to shake his trance.

"What are you going to do now? All of you?"

"Drive back, I guess," she said. "I don't know . . . I don't know what else we can do."

He stared blackly at her. Michael and Kate were out in the aisle already. Michael hitched up his pants, smiling. Kate turned back to Rob to explain some point about the film to him. She was gesturing floridly. The two cowboys were staring at Kate, thinking that maybe they had seen her in the film, but not quite ready to believe it. One of them, grinning and sheepish, hat in hand, ambled toward her.

"I have to go," Mark said. "I can't handle meeting anyone like this. I'm sorry. Just make up whatever excuses you need to, O.K.?"

"O.K."

"Try to call me later, all right? Just try to call me," he said. She said nothing, her face was still flushed. He was too agitated to kiss her goodbye, to even touch her. He turned and pushed past people, making his way out of the theater.

Back at home, Mark moved from room to room, restless as an animal, turning on lights, turning them off again. He lay down on the couch, stared up at a pair of moths batting against the overhead light. The night had turned cool, a breeze riffled the curtains. It was impossible to read, to do anything but wait.

There was nothing that could please him now; nothing existed but his own desire. She would find a way to come to him. She had to. She would drive the others back, make some excuse for why she had to come back into town, she could say that she'd lost something in the theater, anything . . .

He expected her to act, yet it never occurred to him that he might be able to, that it might even be easier for him. Passivity wrapped him like a soft blanket. You could only be a cowboy if you were in the right, only then could you go busting down doors, carry off your woman. If you were in the wrong, you had to wait, trust to some chance, some aberration, let it come to you in darkness.

An hour passed and he still waited. He thought of calling and hanging up; he didn't do it. His depression grew as he realized that she would not come, she would not call.

He began to tremble. At first it almost pleased him; the physical sign was a confirmation that he felt this as deeply as he thought he did. He hadn't been fooling himself, the body doesn't lie. His hands and arms were shaking and then his back muscles. He watched his body react the way he would have watched a performer onstage, for marks of sincerity, signs of true feeling.

He covered his face with his hands. The curtains were still blowing in through the window, rustling like small night predators. It was cold, but he couldn't get up to close the window. He was not watching himself react anymore, he was just trembling because he was ashamed. It is happening for real now, he thought, this is what they talk about when they talk about being damned, this isolation, this terror, being so far from help.

He lay exhausted. He tried to think, it was important to think now, he had to make himself do it, the way a person who's just had the breath knocked out of him has to tell himself to breathe, to think now, not to feel.

He yearned to be a good person. Mark had always thought of himself as a good person, and that thought had always been precious to him. He relied on it. A good teacher, a good friend, a kind soul. Now he knew that he wasn't good.

He knew that he could still get away with seeming to be good. He could find people, if he wanted to, who would be sympathetic, even charitable and consoling, about what he had done to himself. Mark had never had any trouble presenting a sympathetic view of himself, or drawing people to his side. But he didn't want that. He didn't want to spare himself anything. There were words to describe what he had become—sneak, a goddamned snake, cheat, adulterer, philanderer, back-door man—and he wanted to use them, to test them, to find what power he could in them.

What he had been doing was toying with evil, treating it experimentally, to see what it would bring, as if he didn't quite believe in its existence.

He knew what Barbara would have said to what he was thinking. That he was blowing everything out of proportion, that his exaggerated severity was just another version of self-importance. It was no help, imagining what Barbara would say. Rob and Barbara and Kate didn't feel guilty in the same way he did, they weren't so fiercely self-condemning, but that changed nothing.

He knew now that there were certain things he couldn't trust them to know. What he had learned over and over, and kept forgetting, was how ignorant these people were—not correctly educated, his father would have said. To trust in their worldliness was like putting your life in the hands of an eight-year-old.

What if they were damning themselves without knowing it? Because they were smart they thought they could get away with things, take chances that ordinary people couldn't take. But what if nobody got away with anything?

Mark sat there, not moving, trying to think. If he followed out all the consequences of what he'd done, he saw that he was potentially hurting a dozen people, making havoc in all kinds of lives.

But if he took things out as far as he could take them, was the only conclusion that he had to give her up? He couldn't do that. He knew it. To even consider it caused instant panic. To give her up was to give up something more precious than his own goodness, was to deny what he most deeply felt. He refused. The price of goodness was too high.

CHAPTER SEVENTEEN

Barbara had cut flowers to put in Kate's room before she arrived.

When Mark heard that it made no sense to him. Wanting to scratch out her eyes would have made sense. To be icily polite, to be wounded and a little catty, or distant and punishing, any of that would have made sense. Cutting flowers to welcome your husband's ex-lover, no, that was just too far out there, beyond Mark's comprehension.

There was so much Mark couldn't know. He wasn't there, he had no chance to observe firsthand, all he really knew was what Barbara would tell him and what he could infer. He felt a little like an Eastern European sitting by his short-wave radio waiting for the reports on Radio Free Europe; even the things he did hear had a slightly unbelievable air about them.

He knew certain things. He knew that Kate brought expensive gifts for the children. He knew that Rob and Kate had gone out riding alone and when they came back they made a point of insisting that the next time Barbara had to come with them. He knew that Barbara was trying to avoid being alone with Kate, but that inevitably it happened that after breakfast one morning everyone else somehow cleared out, leaving just the two of them, and that Kate, too anxious a soul to let things go unsaid, had tried to talk about it, about their old friendship, about what they'd all been through.

It sounded as if Barbara had just sat there and taken it. To Mark it seemed that while any number of astonishing things were allowed, anger was not. To Mark it all sounded too civilized to be believed, tolerance strained beyond the most bizarre limits.

The question was why Kate had been allowed to come in the first place, and the answer Barbara had given before was not one that Mark could really buy—that she couldn't stop Kate from coming, that she didn't really care, anyway, the visit would end the same way the affair had ended, in waste and depression, and that maybe the repetition would teach Rob his lesson once and for all. Mark couldn't buy that answer because he didn't believe Barbara could be that confident.

If it had been Patrick giving some crazed version of sixties laid-back idealism Mark might have bought it, about how we don't own each other, and everybody's got to follow their star, and we can love lots of different people and, hey, sex isn't property. But it wasn't Patrick talking. The group Mark was dealing with, whatever their sympathies with the sixties, were very alert to questions of property.

So Mark had no good answer, though he did have a clue. They had been on the phone when Barbara casually mentioned that she had cut the flowers for Kate's room, and Mark hadn't been able to suppress his irritation.

"Why do you put up with it?" he'd said.

"I don't know," she'd said. "I suppose because I feel as if I owe him."

Mark hadn't pursued it then, he didn't think very much about it, but what she had said came back to him, later, that she felt as if she owed him, as if there was a debt. She had said that she owed him this, as if a line of credit had been established between them, because of the damage she and Rob had inflicted on one another in turn. It was as if they had arrived, after a number of years, at a point where they no longer felt they had the right to make certain claims on one another, all they could do was to make trade-offs, allow one another to pursue certain doomed paths to their doomed ends, and be around when it was over to pick up the pieces.

If that was true, then those cut flowers were all part of a pay-back, the flowers had been cut for Mark, whether he saw it as bizarre or not, they hadn't been cut for Kate. The cutting of those flowers was to cancel a debt, those flowers that sat now in their bedside vase, filling a clean, quiet room with the fragrance of roses, reassuring, no doubt, to a visitor in a strange house.

Mark felt terrific. They had been riding for almost two hours and a lot of it had been riding hard, splashing through streams, galloping through herds of cattle just for the hell of it, sending calves bawling for their mothers. Mark felt terrific the way anyone feels terrific who's just broken through an old fear, and if his fear of horses wasn't gone entirely, he was at least on top of it. He felt like he could fly.

Since Mark was the novice of the group, Rob had supposedly given him the gentlest horse, but it was no nag. It was a mare called Star, a little broad through the middle from having plenty of colts, but she had plenty of life and had been keeping up just fine. It took Mark a while to get the hang of things, how to lay back in the saddle and get into the horse's rhythm, how to move the horse up or down into a more comfortable gait. He also learned not to get too comfortable; galloping up a hill Michael's horse came up from behind and Mark's horse shied, throwing Mark a little to the side, but Mark was able to quickly right himself. It was important not to lose all your fear.

He was among them all again. Rob and Mark rode out in front. Barbara and Michael were just behind them, a little off to the side to avoid the dust raised by the horses' hooves. The dog was barking at some cattle that had found shade in the shelter of one of the old machine sheds and Kate was over there too, riding in and out of the rusting machinery to watch the fun.

How much easier it was than he'd thought it would be. If the fierce bout of self-condemnation he'd suffered after the evening in the theater wasn't enough to keep him away, then nothing, it seemed, was going to keep him away. He'd given in. Whatever the conditions were, he wanted to be with Barbara. Degrading or not, he'd accepted the invitation to come riding without a protest, it almost felt like serenity.

It wasn't as awful as it should have been. The awfulness just somehow dissolved in the racing across the open flats on horseback. It was an incredibly clear day; every time Mark looked at the mountains it was as if they'd just jumped out of the prairie, sharp and clean. The horses were beautiful, Tennessee walking horses, red glossy coats and blond manes and tails, and when they came up a rise together it sounded like thunder. The dog ran in wide circles around them, tireless, chasing up birds and calves.

It was Kate, though, who was turned on by the riding more than anyone else. She was a totally confident rider, she could make her horse do just about anything, and she loved to let it run. She would kick her horse up into a gallop even after Rob had said he thought they were running them too much. Kate was in no mood for moderation, she was having a great time, breaking away from the group to go examine the innards of an old cabin site, a dry creekbed, a cow skull that had to remind her of a Georgia O'Keeffe painting.

Barbara seemed subdued by comparison. She wasn't angry, just a little quiet, didn't seem either tense or excited about seeing Mark. Mark had never seen her that way before, he wasn't used to her being mild. Throughout the ride she seemed happy to just let herself drop into the background, to yield the stage.

The ride was a series of couplings and uncouplings, people riding side by side by one person, then the next, one horse falling back, another catching up, riders exchanging a few words here, pointing out a hawk in a dead tree or a group of calves there. Kate, though, was always ranging out on her own and it seemed to irritate Rob, as if he thought she was showing off, and it wasn't long before she was getting irritated back.

She handled her horse beautifully, moving it over to the fence line, pulling it up to a complete stop so she could bend over and pick some blackberries from a bush. She called to Rob and when he rode up she leaned across, hand raised, intending to pop a fresh blackberry in his mouth, but Rob, less spontaneous, his wife riding up behind him, took the berry with his hand instead, put it in his mouth himself, the less intimate gesture. Mark saw Kate's face when he did it; she looked at Rob as if he'd just committed the un-forgivable.

Michael wanted to turn back, his rear end was getting sore. Kate was having a wonderful time and wanted to go on. The compromise was that they would ride up to see the lake, a half mile away, which Kate led them to, in a gallop.

The lake was lovely, a narrow, winding piece of water with all kinds of snaking inlets, lined by overhanging pines. Cattle grazed along the edge, a few stood in the shallow water, cooling off. A massive bull stood his ground, staring curiously at the riders.

"Just gorgeous," Kate said. "Absolutely gorgeous."

Rob was already turning his horse back. "All right?" he said.

Kate didn't like being rushed. "We don't all have to go back, do we?" she said.

"Well, I do, that's for sure," Michael said, "before my whole backside turns into bacon slabs."

Kate had her eyes on Rob. "But it's so lovely. Why couldn't we just follow the lake around. You and I did it the other day, Rob, it can't be that much longer."

Barbara said nothing, leaning forward to pat the shoulder of her horse. Michael shifted gingerly in his saddle.

"It's longer, Kate," Rob said. "And Michael's sore. We should go back."

"We don't all have to," Kate said. This time it wasn't put as a question. "Doesn't anyone want to go with me?" She looked from Barbara to Mark and then back to Rob, challenging him. "No one?"

"I'm going back, Kate," Rob said.

"Come on, Mark, you'll come with me."

Kate kicked up her horse. Mark was caught, not wanting to say no, not wanting it to seem as if he had to stay with Barbara, and he found himself shouting back, "O.K.," even as his horse was moving, responding to the quick start of Kate's horse. The two animals galloped up the slope, the bull giving way, eyes rolling in alarm, turning and lumbering off into the brush with quick little steps. Mark turned to wave goodbye, saw Rob and Barbara and Michael holding their animals with a tight rein. Mark didn't wave long, ducking down just in time to avoid the oncoming branch of a cottonwood.

The horses slowed to a walk at the top of the slope. Mark followed Kate as they wound around the far edge of the lake, leading their horses in and out of the trees, scaring up some cattle that crashed through the thickets ahead of them, bawling in complaint. The lake moved in and out of view through the trees. Mark leaned way back in the saddle as the horses picked their way down a ravine. At the bottom the horses took off, going all out to get up the other side. Mark held on, one hand on the horn, keeping his head low as the overhanging branches clawed at his legs and shoulders and hair.

At the top of the ridge, Kate looked back and grinned at him; it was fun. Somewhere behind them the stirred-up cattle were still mooing. The horses were blowing hard. Below them was the lake, and a group of mallards rose out of the water, spinning like a funnel for a second, then gliding back down, skating along the surface.

"I'm sorry I didn't have a chance to meet you the other night at the theater," Kate said.

"I'm sorry too," Mark said. He wondered what explanation Barbara had given them for his sudden exit. He patted the neck of his horse. "I had promised to meet someone," he said.

"Oh, you don't need an excuse," she said. "It wasn't a very good movie."

"No, I liked it," Mark said.

Horseflies looped around the ears of the two horses. Mark's horse, impatient, jerked its head up and down. Mark felt the quiver of nerves along the animal's back. Both horses were tired. Mark could see the lather under Kate's saddle blanket, like white suds on the wet, reddish coat.

"You don't have to be polite," Kate said, smiling at him. "I may have my faults, but one thing I can say about myself is that I've always been able to take criticism."

"I thought it was funny," Mark said. "A good New York film." The cove directly below them extended into a marsh. They would have to go around. "Which way should we go?" Mark said, pulling his reins to the left of the horse's neck.

"Oh, it doesn't really matter," she said. She nudged her horse lightly with her heel. "I know what you're saying. Crass." They moved slowly along the ridge, through tall grass and flowering silky thistles. It was going to take them a while to make their way back. "Well, I agree. When I signed up for the film I thought it had a chance. But four writers later, you can imagine . . ." A western tanager flitted in a nearby tree, a tiny ball of yellow and red, a movable Christmas tree ornament. "You have to admit the script was unerring in its way, if there was a cheap laugh there, they found it."

The woman is out of her skull, Mark thought. What the hell were they doing out here in the wilderness, discussing reviews?

"I'm not blaming the script entirely either, I was flat, one-dimensional. I gave in to the film, if you see what I mean. Really, you're not telling me anything I don't know."

It didn't seem to Mark that he was telling her anything, she was going on her own, but he let that pass. They moved down a gentle slope into the head-high willow and alder bushes. They were totally out of sight of the lake now.

"Hey, Kate, do you know where we are?"

"Not exactly. Rob and I were out here the other day. There are supposed to be some meadows up here somewhere. I think we'll find our way out."

"What if we run into a moose down here, Kate, what are we going to do?"

She didn't hear what he'd said. "That's show business," she said. "The great crap shoot. You take whatever you've got and you put it all out there, blood and guts, right on the line, and if people don't like it, well, you just go looking for another show."

"Don't you think we should maybe turn back? They'll be waiting for us."

"No, no. Trust me. Barbara was telling me that you were seeing a dancer."

"She told you that?" Riding behind, Mark slumped in his saddle, watched the tail of Kate's horse swishing back and forth, steady as a pendulum, driving off the flies.

"I was asking. I was curious."

"Well, she's not really a dancer. She teaches dance."

"See? What did I tell you? You should have trusted me."

They came up out of the thickets into a small meadow. There were patches of flowers, balsam root and gentian, a few cotton-woods. Out in the open again, it felt hot. Kate draped her reins over the horn, arched her back, turned her face up to the sun.

"It was her you were going to see the other night?"

Mark saw the trap being set. It was no time to get into lies.

"No," Mark said, "we haven't been seeing that much of each other lately."

Kate looked back over her shoulder, her face suddenly empathetic. Mark felt a bead of sweat form on his upper lip. He wiped it away.

"I'm sorry," she said.

"No reason for you to be sorry," Mark said.

"Do you think that it's over or . . ."

"I don't know." The horses were following the meadow, it felt as if they were moving even further from the lake, but Mark couldn't be sure, he was all turned around.

"Well, I sympathize. I'm a disaster area when it comes to men."

"Maybe you've just had some bad luck," Mark said. As the horses moved together for a second Kate's leg brushed Mark's.

"No, no, I don't blame anyone but myself. I really think we end up getting what we want, don't you? If you or I really wanted a permanent, stable relationship, we'd have one by now. I believe that. Don't you?"

"I'm not sure."

She rolled the sleeves up on her t-shirt, exposing more of her arms to the sun. "I'm sure you wouldn't have any difficulty finding someone new. You're a very attractive man. It all depends on what you want."

"That's comforting to know, I guess," Mark said. He wiped the sweat from the back of his neck. Both horses were dragging along now.

"It's hot, isn't it?" she said. "Do you mind if I take my shirt off? I'd like to get some sun."

The question was put so casually that Mark was left without a reply, and Kate wasn't really waiting for one. She kicked her horse, moved up in front of Mark, her back to him. She pulled her shirt up over her head in one fluid motion, with the assurance only an actress could have had. She kept perfect balance in the saddle, never exposing more than was proper. The sight of her bare back and shoulders was unsettling enough. She folded her t-shirt neatly, reached back and tied the sleeves in a knot, making a nice bathing-suit top out of it. She made it seem perfectly natural, as she made everything perfectly natural.

"I don't know how much Rob and Barbara have told you about me," she said.

"Not so much," he said.

"No?"

"Not really. I guess Michael mentioned something about the play you were in."

"Oh, Michael! Well, don't believe anything you've heard from Michael. Charming as he may be, he can't resist slandering people when he has the chance. Not that I care what Michael says, really. It scarcely matters, does it? There are probably no such things as secrets, anyway, are there? Not *real* secrets."

Mark couldn't answer; he didn't know if she was confessing or probing. His horse jerked his head toward the woods, Mark had to kick him a couple of times to get him to move. "Kate? Do you think we're lost now?"

"It's very irresponsible of us, isn't it? I'm always getting in trouble like this." She waved away some horseflies. "They are very dear people to me, Rob and Barbara. Both of them. They are probably among the half-dozen people I feel closest to in life. Remarkable. I think you'll realize that more and more, the longer you know them. They've been through a lot. A lot more than you'd think."

Mark's horse pulled up again, turning toward the woods. "Kate?" Mark said. "Maybe we should try cutting through here. The horses seem to be pulling this way and they probably know the way back better than we do."

"Fine," Kate said, "whatever you say." Together they turned their horses into the trees. "They're such enthusiastic people, so open, so full of energy. They're always bringing in new people, that's one of the nicest things about them. It's a paradox, in a way."

"What is?"

"Well, that they're rather more conventional than the people they bring in. Don't you agree?"

"About it being a paradox, or that they're conventional?" Mark said.

"That's not a criticism," Kate said.

They were making their way through deadfall timber, the horses picking along on their own, hooves clattering over the downed trees.

"I think that convention is a good thing," Kate said. "But Rob and Barbara, let's face it, like to view themselves as adventurers in a way that isn't quite accurate." A red squirrel chattered angrily at them from a nearby tree. "They like people who take chances even if they don't want to take them themselves. And there's nothing wrong in that."

Mark stared down at the forest floor, at the maze of dead logs, at the narrow channels bored in them by the bark beetles. They looked like they were covered by hieroglyphs. Her tone seemed so weirdly intimate. At moments she seemed to be speaking as if he already knew everything. Certainly she suspected. Mark didn't quite know how to play it, but he hadn't missed the malice in her voice.

"You don't think I'm being unfair, do you?" she said.

"No, no," Mark said.

"It's as if they never want to stray too far from home. You see what I'm saying? I don't think anyone can quite perceive at first just how dependent they are on each other." She looked across at him. Light filtered through the lodgepole pines above them. "You don't agree?"

"I don't know."

"Oh, they're very capable of closing ranks if things get a little threatening. And it's Barbara, really, who's the stronger of the two. You do see that. She really holds Rob together."

"I'm sure she relies on him too," Mark said. He leaned forward and mashed a horsefly caught in the mane, flicked it away.

"You must think I'm such a bitch."

"No," Mark said. "I just think she relies on him too."

Again she didn't bother to listen. "God knows, I love them both," she said. "I admire them. You have to believe me. Anyway, they're probably right and we're probably wrong."

"Why is that?"

"Oh, I don't know. People are always being attracted to one another, but what is it, really? Attraction, after all, is very different from the real business of life."

"And what is the real business of life?"

"Having a family. Raising children. I do believe that."

"Meaning that you and I . . ."

"I don't know about you, but I would be just terrible at it. I know my limitations."

"So what do you do then, knowing your limitations?"

"Who knows? I may go to San Francisco and do a play there. *The Country Wife.* You can really go stale in films. Films aren't really acting, anyway, so much as attitude . . ." Mark saw light through the trees ahead, they were coming back out into the open.

"What theater would you be in?" Mark asked.

"I doubt if you've heard of it. It's not got much of a reputation yet, but they've been doing some first-rate productions. The director is an old friend of mine from Harvard, a really brilliant director, a genius in his own way, and just the chance to work with him again . . ."

They broke out of the woods, back onto the flats. For a second Mark was bewildered, all turned around, until he shifted in his saddle and saw Rob a quarter of a mile off.

"There they are," Mark said.

Kate turned and saw Rob. She cupped her hands to her mouth and gave a shrill Confederate yell. She waved both arms in the air. Rob pulled his horse around, looking, then spied them and waved back. Mark saw Barbara and Michael further on, heading along the fence line toward home. They must not have heard Kate; neither of them turned back.

Rob waited for Kate and Mark, holding his horse in. His horse was impatient, trying to turn toward the barn, but Rob fought him, kept the reins tight, kept turning the champing horse in a circle.

Mark loosened his reins, touched the animal's ribs with his heel. "Maybe we should hustle it up," he said.

"No, it's all right," Kate said. "I think he'll wait for us." The drop in her voice was alarming; she meant what she was saying. She was an actress, after all, who had an instinct for not rushing an entrance, but that wasn't all, there was something more, something that sounded like punishment. Mark took up a couple of quick inches on his reins.

Mark and Kate rode silently, side by side. Kate kept her horse at a walk, Mark did the same. Rob had kicked up his horse a bit and was cantering toward them across the open field. Rob and Kate were like two generals approaching warily under a flag of truce. It was as if they were riding into a showdown, there was nothing very veiled about it. Kate wasn't even trying to hide anything. If I hadn't known before, Mark thought, I'd know now, Kate was making a point of it. She rode straight-backed, her bare shoulders a bit red and as squared as if she was riding in an honor guard, letting Rob hang a bit, letting him make the approach, making him declare his need.

Barbara and Michael rode on slowly, never looking back. They were way off now, and set against the flats and the mountains, with the cattle grazing all around them, they seemed no more than a nice detail in a big canvas.

Kate picked it up, letting her horse go into a running walk and Mark did the same. The two horses' heads bobbed back and forth, steady as clocks.

As they came up, Mark could see that Rob didn't look pleased at all.

"I'm sorry if we kept you waiting," Kate said. "We got lost, it was all my fault. I hope you weren't worried."

"I was. A little," Rob said. His horse was fighting the bit and Rob had the reins tight, wound once around his fist. He gazed at her steadily, his eyes needy as a dog's, lodging a silent appeal.

"You shouldn't have worried, we weren't that lost." She smiled, beautifully, but he didn't smile back. Rob's horse shook his head from side to side, pawed the ground. "Mark and I had a chance for a nice talk. And I got a little tan."

"I'm glad," Rob said.

She cocked her head, gave him a smile of mock distress, kicked her horse up, moved closer. She reached out and touched his face. "Now don't be in a bad mood," she said. "Please. I'm sorry."

Rob's horse didn't like being crowded. He shied away, backing off like a crab. Rob yanked the reins, kicking him in the ribs, but the horse reared back. Kate tried to stay with them, trying to help, reaching out for the bridle of the riled-up animal, but Rob wanted to handle it on his own.

He whipped the horse angrily with the ends of his reins, first on one side of the neck, then the other, whipped him hard, the sound sharp and popping as a small-bore rifle.

Rob's horse came down under control, head pulled up high by the taut reins, but then Kate's horse started, sliding out in a quick sidestep. Kate was fearless, shouting something back to Rob that Mark couldn't hear, but he could see that she was laughing, as if it had been nothing more than a joke for her. She swayed in the saddle, kept her balance, gave her horse a slap along the side of the neck, then gave it the heel, and the startled animal bolted. Instantly Rob's and Mark's horses broke after her, all three in a gallop. The animals knew they were going to the barn, there was no way anyone was going to hold them now. Maybe, Mark thought, that was the difference between people and animals; people will put up with anything, and animals will only put up with so much.

The horses pounded across the flats, Kate and Rob in front, Mark behind. When they came to the creek the horses slowed a bit in a series of stiff-legged jolts, came down the cut bank, then tore through the water, the front horses splattering Mark with water and mud, then thrusting hard up the far bank. Barbara and Michael had turned in their saddles and were watching them come. As the riders bore down on them, Barbara and Michael's horses got restless, sidestepping and ducking at their reins, and just before they were overtaken they broke out, all five horses now going flat out, as if they were being sucked up by some powerful magnet.

Mark felt his horse seem to drop down as if he was going into overdrive. It was a little scary, feeling how much power was in the horse and nothing he could do but lay back in the saddle and go with it. There was no control now, the horses knew they were heading in. Mark heard Michael let out a whoop, and right after that Barbara's horse shied at a log hidden in the grass. She was off-balance for just a second, but she grabbed for the horn, caught it, recovered. It was a race for the gate and Rob got there first. As the horses got close they geared down, like planes touching down on a runway. The riders rose up to take the jolts in their stirrups. Rob was already off his horse by the time the others got there, whipping the reins over the head of his horse, pulling the animal roughly toward the gate, Rob, the responsible one, undoing the chain, lifting the heavy wooden barrier with the horses blowing hard all around him and Michael letting go a series of shouts just for the sheer exhilaration of it.

When Mark arrived home in the middle of the afternoon, his knees and thighs stiff from the ride, there was a letter from his mother waiting for him. The hard news was all there in his mother's careful, girlish hand, on the familiar pink stationery. His father had gone in to see the doctor because of numbness in his legs and they had discovered large blockages in his femoral arteries. They weren't sure yet whether it could be controlled by diet and medicine, but if it wasn't there was the possibility that he might have to have bypass surgery in the fall. She went on to tell him not to worry, they were both feeling just fine otherwise, they sent him lots of love, if he could come home sometime during the summer they would love to see him.

Not to worry, that's what she always said when there was trouble. Odd, but right when he read the letter it didn't worry him, it was just a piece of news, but as the day went on its effect grew, like the muffled rippling from an explosion deep beneath the surface of the water.

He hadn't thought of his parents for weeks, but the idea of his father ill, his father lying in a hospital bed, being cut on, brought Mark close to tears, struck at him with all the force of terrors you thought you'd gotten over. Suddenly he felt such a long way away from them.

They would love to see him if he could get away, his mother had said. Maybe he should go, now. He didn't know what he should do. He was not out free-floating in the world, despite what it felt like sometimes, despite what it had felt like an hour before, hanging on to a runaway horse. The letter was proof. He tried to imagine what his father would think of him if he knew what Mark's life was like, he imagined his father's shame.

His father was not an easy man. His father had been a preacher. Not for very long, for less than a year in a small rural church in Indiana, but that year had branded him more than any of the half-dozen jobs he would hold later. He would always be more of an ex-preacher than he would ever be a present anything.

His father was impatient and intelligent, and when things did not break his way and he had three children to feed he took over the management of a small motel near the Delaware Bridge.

Mark's father did a bad job of running a motel. He didn't seem to care whether people rented rooms or not. When middle-aged couples came in for tawdry afternoon liaisons, his contempt was minimally suppressed. There were not many repeat customers. Mark's father much of the time had the rather unpleasant air of a man who feels that the human race has let him down. He almost took some dark pleasure from the curious inversion of the American dream his life had become, from a midwestern man of God to a renter of cheap rooms, a peddler of transience in an industrial backwater, a world of smoke and highways. One of the few reliefs he had was at night when he would sit down and read the novels of Tolstoy, Balzac and Dostoevsky.

He was a difficult man and yet Mark remembered times with his father, golden times after church on Sunday when he would ask Mark to stay in the car for a second and his mother and two sisters would go inside and he and his father would sit in the carport and talk.

To Mark those times seemed mysterious and solemn, his father's hand resting lightly on his shoulder, the car smelling faintly of cigarette smoke. It was a time to sort things out, to discuss hurts, difficulties, misunderstandings, to talk about school, his sisters, his mother. His father's voice seemed like the most wonderful sound in the world. He knew, at those times, that his father loved him.

Yet there were also moments too painful to bear, moments when his father confessed his own failures. He had been too impatient when he was young, made mistakes, this was not where he'd intended to end up, running a motel, but his life had been taken over by necessity. He knew how hard he had made things for Mark's mother, how difficult his temper had been for her to bear, knew that he should have been a better provider, he had not done well enough by them, she had not been able to buy a dress for herself in almost two years. Mark would say nothing, just listen, thinking a dozen things at once, thinking, he knows, he knows everything, my father is the most intelligent man I know and yet he can't do anything other than what he's done, and Mark would think at the same time, he shouldn't be telling me these things, he wants me to forgive him and of course I forgive him and no, I can't, of course I can't, I'm only his son.

Not everything needed to be told to him. More than once, at night when he was supposed to be asleep, he would hear his parents arguing, voices rising and falling in the darkness, arguing over money, over he didn't know what, his mother crying, "When the children are raised my obligations are over. . . ." Mark would lie awake for a long time after that, watching the bars of light slide over the ceiling of his bedroom, lights from the cars passing endlessly on the highway.

Mark stared at the letter. Obligations are never over, Mark thought, they are endless, without boundaries. He stood up from the table, felt the pains shoot up his legs, the pains from his ride, wondering if his father could ever forgive him.

Chapter Eighteen

Two nights later he called his father from a pay phone at the edge of a campground in Yellowstone Park.

He had fled, fled from the terror of his father's illness, fled Barbara, Kate, Rob, all of them. Flight hadn't worked quite the way he'd hoped. It only intensified his loneliness. He had stayed in a campground at the north end of Yellowstone and he was the only one who was camping alone, the others were all families on vacation. At night there were the shouts of children darting back and forth among the tents, the smell of cooking, the sight of families gathered, sitting on logs, eating off of tin plates. He felt them watching him. They must have wondered who he was and what he was doing, one man alone in a small tent, cooking his meal over a fire down by the stream, talking to no one.

By the second night the isolation was more than he could bear. After dinner Mark walked to the glass booth that sat in a grove of pines near the gravel road and dialed the familiar number. The sun had just disappeared behind the mountains.

"Hello?" His father's voice was gravelly and a little vague. Mark guessed that he had wakened him. It was two hours later in New Jersey, a little after ten o'clock.

"Hey, Dad. It's Mark."

"Mark! How are you?"

"I'm fine, Dad. I got Mom's letter a couple of days ago. She told me. . . ."

"You know what an alarmist your mother is. I'm going to be fine. It's just a little circulation problem in my legs. Don't you worry about me."

Mark turned in the narrow booth, the metal cord twisting around him. He stared out at the glow of campfires. "I could come out, you know," he said.

"No, no, you've got things to do. I'm all right. If anything more happens, we'll let you know." The smoke from all the fires hung in the still night air, gray against the dark woods. High above the trees there was still light in the sky. "I've got to get out there one day and see all this country you're always talking about. This probably isn't the summer to do it, but there will be other summers."

"Sure, Dad, sure." Mark leaned his forehead against the glass of the pitch-black booth.

"I'd put your mother on, but she's already gone to bed."

"O.K., Dad. I just wanted to hear your voice."

"You're doing all right out there?"

"I'm doing just fine, Dad." His father waited for him to say more if he wanted to. Mark said nothing. There were some things sons should never tell their fathers.

"Well, I don't want to eat up all your money. This must be costing you a fortune."

"No, Dad, it doesn't matter. You do what those doctors tell you, all right? You listen to them."

"Bunch of charlatans is what they are. But I will, don't worry. Good night, Mark."

"Good night."

Mark clicked the phone down, stepped out of the booth. Across the campground he could see the luminous tents, the wavering shadows of parents inside, putting their children to sleep. His father was too proud a man to ask for help, and Mark was too proud too.

Mark got up early in the morning to start the drive back to Jackson, a day earlier than he'd planned. Half a mile north of the Jackson airport his car died. He could guess what the problem was. The alternator was what the repair people told him every time it happened.

He was stranded and after a long, dusty walk to the phone at the airport road junction it was Barbara's number he called this time. It was she he had tried to run away from, and now it was she he called for help, almost without thinking.

Barbara was home alone with Sarah and sounded surprised and pleased that he'd called. She would come pick him up, she said. It only took her ten minutes to get there, but ten minutes was enough for the old tension to return. He slid into her car, leaned across and kissed her lightly on the cheek.

She looked fresh and clean, as if she'd just come out of a shower. She was wearing shorts and sandals and a bright-green t-shirt. The soft curve of her tanned, bare thighs gave him a twinge of desire. How foolish it had been for him to go away at all. She had been working all day, she said, and it had gone well. By the end of the week she would be ready to cast her new sculpture. She was in a high, easy mood. She invited him out to the house for a beer. That would be nice, he said, feeling something relax inside him for the first time in days.

Barbara got them a couple of beers and they sat in the back yard while Sarah practiced her piano inside. They could see out across the pasture, see the horses grazing and, at the far edge of the woods, a few cattle bunched up to escape the flies. Mark had sat here before. The other time, the first time he had met Rob, they had sat in these same chairs, looking down on the same scene, except that the fields of snow nestled among the high peaks were smaller now and traced with dirty stripes from rock slides. They both listened as Sarah stumbled over a phrase, stumbled again, then got it right.

Mark stared into his beer. All he could think was that he was going to lose her. He didn't know where they stood and he was too proud to ask. Kate's coming had to change everything. It was Kate and Barbara and Rob's drama being played out now, not his. He was left out in the dark, the dark that he had chosen.

They talked about Mark's phone call to his father and his father's illness. She asked the right questions, letting Mark do most of the talking. He was reminded of how kind she could be, how that was one of the things that had first drawn him to her.

Illness and the terrible things it could do to people were things that Barbara understood. It touched the deepest chords in her, made her angry, she wanted to strike out at it, as if it were a person, when there was nothing to strike out against.

Barbara looked back toward the house. Mark was suddenly aware that the piano had stopped. They both listened. Sarah appeared on the screened-in porch.

"Mom?"

"Yes, Sarah?"

"Do you know where my Tolkien books are?"

"I'm not sure, honey," Barbara said. "Weren't they in the bathroom upstairs? I think I saw them there this morning." There was no answer from the porch. "Why don't you come out here to see us for a second, Sarah?"

Sarah opened the door, dragged down the porch steps. The slow-swinging screen door slammed shut behind her. Mark and Barbara waited, half-turned in their chairs, as Sarah scuffled to them.

Barbara reached out and pulled Sarah to her. "That wasn't too long a practice, was it, sweetheart?"

Sarah tilted her head, gave her mother a crooked, pained look. "I got bored again."

"Sarah, Sarah, Sarah." Barbara spun Sarah around, tumbled her into her lap. The back of Sarah's head rested against her mother's chest. From her mother's embrace she gave Mark an embarrassed smile; she was being a pain, she just couldn't help it.

Mark showed her a trick, showed her how he could sew his lip with an imaginary thread and an imaginary needle. He made a real production out of it, wincing as he pretended to prick the inside of his lip, working the imaginary needle all the way through. He felt the eyes of the child on him, taking everything in, sizing him up, the whole time never letting go of her mother's hand.

"Gross!" she said when he was done. The trick was a success. She was both disgusted and fascinated.

"That's enough, sweetheart," Barbara said. "Mark and I are

going to talk just a bit longer. He has to leave soon. You can finish up your practicing."

Sarah stood up. She tried to curl the corner of her lip the way he had, then skipped off, taking a dancer's turn and an exuberant leap before running up the porch steps and into the house.

Barbara and Mark were both silent for several seconds.

"I should be getting back," Mark said.

"No, no, it's fine," she said. "Here. Why don't you finish my beer? I can't drink all of it." Barbara leaned across and poured beer from her glass into his. "In case you're worried about their coming back, they won't be, not for a while. They're all in town. Rob and Kate wanted to go in, but they couldn't go alone, just the two of them, because they're so considerate of my feelings, you see, and so they said they would take the children so I could work. Sarah didn't want to go, so it was just Rob and Kate and Jeffrey."

"And what about Michael?"

"Oh, Michael's gone. You didn't know? I guess you had already left for Yellowstone. The situation was too weird for Michael, and the morning before last he came down to breakfast with all his bags packed and a story about how he had to get out to California to find out what the money people were doing with his project. He claimed he wasn't coming back until he had a Rolls-Royce, a cocaine habit and monogrammed underwear. That's Michael, I guess, always a little in bad taste when he gets uncomfortable. Michael doesn't like it when things get too tense."

"And have they been? Too tense?"

"They've been pretty tense. Rob keeps thinking he's in control when he's not. And that means mistakes."

"It must hurt."

"Him?"

"No. You. I don't know why you can't admit that it hurts."

"I didn't think I needed to. I thought that some things were self-evident."

"I'm sorry," Mark said.

"All I want is for her to go away and leave us alone." Suddenly she was near to tears. "That was a nice trick. Sewing your lip. Sarah liked it." She felt Mark watching her and it made her uncomfortable. "Rob just needs a little space right now."

"Space? I'd think he'd have all he'd need of that out here."

"You know what I mean. Don't jump on me."

"I always jump on language like that."

Mark stared down at his lap, wiped the beads of water off his beer glass with a single finger. Maybe he was just becoming querulous. Still, it did bother him, soft language that was a disguise, it was like the billyclubs that bad cops wrap in towels before working over a suspect so that the blows will leave no marks on the outside even if the guy is bleeding to death on the inside. He looked back up at her.

"If you don't mind my prying, what is it that they do together?"

"You saw yourself. Some of it at least. They take long, sad walks. They stay up an extra half hour at night to have a final drink together after I've gone to bed. They find new ways to make each other unhappy. They try to behave well. They're ending it, ending it their own way. I leave them to their own devices."

"Do you ever wonder what the kids pick up?"

He saw anger flash across her face. "I wonder all the time." Barbara reached down, picked a bottle top out of the grass. "Kate said you had an interesting conversation."

"It was interesting."

"She thought you were very intelligent, very sensitive."

"I thought she was awful."

"She's not awful. Not any more than the rest of us. Just a little more extreme."

"I still don't like her. I don't trust her."

"Then why are you so interested in what goes on between the two of them? Just casual inquiry?"

"Not casual at all. For two days all I've been able to think is that I was going to lose you, that her coming would mean the end . . ."

"No. You haven't lost me. Not at all."

The music started up again inside the house, still flawed, but surer now and more vigorous than before. Mark and Barbara smiled at one another. They both listened to Sarah work her way faithfully through her lesson.

"It's so nice out here," Mark said. "It's so nice just to sit."

Barbara said nothing, but Mark felt that she was allowing him to go on, that she would accept whatever he had to say. "I like being able to see you like this. I just . . ."

"Say it," Barbara said.

"I was thinking that it would be very nice just to know you. I was trying to imagine what it would be like to be able to come over in the afternoon and just sit with you in your back yard and have nobody disapprove or suspect, not have it threaten anybody . . ."

She smiled, shifted in her chair so she could see him better. "Why isn't that possible?"

He frowned. She didn't understand then, what he meant, just when he really wanted her to. "Maybe it is, maybe it is," he said. He stared at her a second, then pressed on. "Did you ever wonder what it would be like if we were married? You and me?"

"Of course," she said. The matter-of-factness of her answer made him glad, it was like a key opening a new door. It was one of the best things she had ever told him. "It's probably very dangerous to think like that. But I have wondered."

"Me too," Mark said.

"I'll bet we would be terrific," she said.

"That's just what I thought," he said.

He didn't say anything more. There was no need to spell everything out, no need to tell her that he could imagine himself being Sarah's father, no need to tell her how appealing the idea was, the imagining of innocence, solving a child's boredom on a summer afternoon, sitting together after a long day, the basic stuff, simple things, peaceful things available to every fool in the world, except for him. Now he was feeling sorry for himself, but it was true, Barbara would always be this girl's mother and she would not always be Mark's lover. The thought scared the hell out of him, but he was happy all the same, as happy as he ever would be, sitting with her, with the faltering notes of the piano, the birds flying low over the grazing cattle in that golden light, it was that hour of the day when everything was sharp and clear, there was no need to utter a word. She was only a foot away from him, he could reach out and touch her, but he didn't need to, she did understand everything he was thinking, he was sure of it. They were at peace for a second, even if it had taken a series of accidents, a broken-down car, Kate and Rob's trip into town, things all had to break right against long odds, but they had, and out of all that, with the fervency of a gambler who knows he's on a roll, came the conviction that there was nothing debased about his love for Barbara, nothing he need be ashamed of, it was right, despite all the provisions. If it wasn't right, then all that kept it from being right was no more than a pane of glass that would shatter at the lightest tap, the thinnest of tissue to be torn through. If there was something wrong, it was something very small, very adjustable, not major, easy. If he could go on seeing the way he saw now, if he could hold onto it, it could be very easy. He hadn't lost her yet. She'd said it herself and she wouldn't lie to him.

CHAPTER NINETEEN

The effect was ceremonial. Barbara and Mark and Kate were dressed in heavy leather aprons and chaps, leather gloves and masks of clear plastic. The heavy clothing made every movement stiff and slightly clumsy. Mark wasn't quite sure what it was the three of them looked like, whether it was spacemen or hockey goalies or Japanese actors in a Noh play.

The studio was intensely hot, the exhaust fan seemed to have no effect. The plaster molds were buried in the sandpit in the middle of the floor, the airholes covered with pieces of Saran wrap to keep out bits of sand and grit. In the corner sat the welding tanks. Pieces of plaster mold were scattered across the floor like broken crockery, like something to be fitted back together by an infinitely patient anthropologist.

Looking out through the window, Mark could see the lawn where sprinklers rotated slowly, waving their soft spray over the brown grass. Sweat poured off him, his body was drenched. The three of them were sealed in.

He and Kate stood to one side, watchful as interns. Barbara stood at the sunken furnace, looking down to see if the bronze was melted yet. Her head was cocked to one side, like a robin listening for worms.

Barbara stepped back, nodded to them. Kate and Mark moved to the furnace, slipped metal rods through the hoops in the furnace top. Kate looked up at Barbara to be sure. Barbara nodded again, she already had the tongs in her hands. Kate and Mark lifted the furnace top and searing heat rolled up at them.

Barbara reached down into the furnace with the long metal tongs. She fixed the tongs over the graphite crucible, looked past Kate, nodded to Mark. Through her plastic mask her eyes were filled with a sweaty intensity. Mark grabbed the far end of the tongs and he and Barbara lifted the crucible between them. Mark felt his back muscles tighten up with the weight.

Kate stepped back, waiting to be called on, but she was on the wrong side, between them and the sandpit. Barbara glanced quickly at her, lancing the air with anger; she was in the way. Kate backed off. Mark, bending under the weight of the crucible, missed whatever it was that passed over her face.

Barbara and Mark moved with careful, measured steps to the sandpit. Kate was somewhere behind them, drifting on the periphery.

Mark had never been aware of how physically strong Barbara was. Her end of the tongs was forked, like the handlebars of a bike. She began to tilt the crucible. She was very sure, very exact. The molten bronze appeared at the lip of the crucible, moving slowly, like syrup, then began to pour. It ran down the holes, down into the buried molds. The heat was so intense that the Saran wrap covering the airholes burst into flame.

The bronze reappeared at an auxiliary hole. The cast had held. Barbara looked up, smiled curtly at Mark. Out of the corner of his eye Mark was aware of Kate standing, watching them, like a little left-out girl in the schoolyard.

They moved on to the next casting. There were six altogether, hollow plaster molds in the shapes of horses and riders buried beneath the packed sand and they had to be filled quickly, while the molten bronze was still fluid enough to flow into every nook and cranny.

They finished the second casting and went to the third. Kate moved away from them now, then bent down, picked up a broken piece of plaster mold with her heavy leather glove, then pitched it lazily underhand into the huge wastebasket in the corner. It landed with a clatter and at the sound Barbara straightened up, staring at her. Kate gestured with her heavy gloves; she was sorry, she'd slipped up. Barbara nodded to Mark that they would go on.

From the moment Mark had arrived it was evident that something had changed between the two women. All through the preparations for the casting, through the strapping on of the bulky protective garments, they treated one another warily, spoke to one another with a glazed politeness, their voices ever so slightly constricted.

Sweat was running into Mark's eyes, he nudged his plastic mask into place with his shoulder. There were five down now, they were going on to six. Kate stood at the far end of the studio, her back to them, staring through the window, absently removing her heavy mitts, finger by finger, as if they were dainty kid gloves. It wasn't even good acting, there was nothing subtle about it, she was signifying emotions all over the place.

Suddenly they were through. Mark stood up, put his hands in the small of his back and stretched. Barbara scraped the slag out of the inside of the crucible. Mark lifted off his headpiece.

"How did we do?" he said.

"We have to wait and see how we did," Barbara said. "But I think we did just fine."

Mark tried to smile. Kate's presence was like a clamp on them. It was still too hot to catch a breath. Mark felt the sweat trickling down his stomach and back, down the insides of his legs. Kate bent down to undo her chaps. Barbara pulled her gloves off, took an old rag and wiped her hands with it, her eyes on Kate the whole time.

"Why don't we go outside?" Barbara said. "There's no point in our staying in here any longer than we have to." Kate didn't seem to hear. Barbara tossed the rag away. "Kate? Why don't you let me help you with those?"

Kate turned, her face flushed, the corners of her eyes oddly pinched, trying to put a good face on things and not making it. Barbara, not smiling, but relenting all the same, went to her, knelt and silently unbuckled Kate's chaps.

Stepping out into the open air, it felt almost cold. The sprinklers clicked monotonously across the lawn, lines of green hose snaking along the brown grass. The sky was perfectly clear except for the ozone tracing of jets, far up. Mark pulled his wet t-shirt out of his belt, flapped it to get it dry. It was an awkward moment; none of them was quite sure which way they were going to move next. Kate ran her fingers through her wet hair.

"I'll go up and bring us down some beers," Barbara said.

"We'll all go with you," Kate said.

"No, no, that's all right, you just relax. Three beers is something I can handle on my own." Barbara squeezed Kate's arm. "You've earned your reward. I'll be back in a minute."

Kate and Mark watched her walk up the hill. Mark wiped his face with the sleeve of his t-shirt, glancing sidelong at Kate.

"I'll tell you," Mark said. "I thought we were all going to melt in there for a while." Kate didn't seem to hear him, still gazing up the hill at Barbara, mounting the steps of the house now.

"I'm so glad I had a chance to do this before I left," Kate said. "I'm very excited for her." She turned back to Mark, she looked terribly serious. "I know how important this is for her."

"It would be for anybody," Mark said. "She's worked hard."

"Yes, I know, but I think her work is so far ahead of where it was a year ago."

"I wouldn't know," Mark said.

"I'm sure you've seen her earlier things," Kate said. Her remark carried its reproach with it effortlessly, on gossamer wings.

"Yes," Mark said. "But it's hard for me to judge."

She looked at him quizzically. "Really? Well, I find it's developed so much. There's no comparison. Of course there are still derivative ideas, traces of sentimentality here and there . . ."

"Such as?" Mark said.

"I'm not being critical at all. She's been a housewife and mother for so long, running a three-ring circus and being terrific at it, it's wonderful to see her take hold like this. It just pleases me that she would still want me to help."

"Why wouldn't she?"

Kate looked at him darkly, a don't-play-dumb-with-me look. "You don't know?"

"No."

"You can't guess?"

"I suppose I could guess," Mark said. As soon as he said it, he knew it wasn't a good thing to have said. There was no point fooling with this sort of stuff, but she was irritating the hell out of him.

She turned her back to him. Mark's first response was something close to hatred. She was playing this for more than its due, he thought, as she raised her hands to her face. He was sick of her self-dramatizing, but then he saw that she was really crying. He just stood there, too amazed to do anything. They were standing on the lawn just outside the studio, in plain view of the house, a very odd place, Mark thought, to choose to have a scene. The only sound was the clicking of the sprinklers.

"I'm sorry," she said.

"Don't be sorry," he said.

She reached up and touched the corners of her eyes, wiping away tears. Mark stared at her. Her eyelids seemed heavy with weariness. He should comfort her, he thought. He found himself disarmed and stirred.

"Let's not just stand here, all right?" she said.

"All right. Maybe we can go up and sit in the hammocks."

"Fine," she said.

They walked slowly across the lawn toward the hammocks under the grape arbor. Mark looked up at the house. There was no sign of Barbara. As they passed, Mark gave the tire swing a hollow-sounding thump.

Mark tested a hammock with his hand, then sat down. Kate remained standing, resting her hand on one of the rough, rusted poles that supported the arbor. She took a deep breath, her eyes still teary, a little puffy.

"She asked me to leave," Kate said.

"Are you serious?"

"I'm perfectly serious. I'm surprised she didn't tell you." Kate peeled off a flake of rust from the pole, flicked it away with her fingernail. "It was a real attack. Quite vicious. I suppose I can understand her feeling some of those things, but Rob . . . I'm really enraged at Rob." She moved to one of the hammocks, fingered the braided cords that held it up. "Rob is a weak person, I don't know if you knew that. For him to expose me to cruelty from another woman the way he did, he owes me more than that." She fixed her gaze on Mark. "You know we had an affair."

"No, I didn't know," Mark said without much force. He couldn't tell whether she believed him or not. He glanced up at the vine above him; it was half dead, a brittle, brown tangle. Still, the arbor shielded them from the house; they wouldn't see Barbara when she came out.

"Well, I just assumed that you knew, that someone had told you. The thing is with this group, you see, everyone is so intelligent and accomplished and egomaniacal, everybody knows everybody else's secrets, but somehow persist in believing that no one knows theirs . . . the naïveté is almost touching . . ." She reached up and snapped off a piece of dead vine, stripped it with her fingers. Mark could see the terrible weariness in her face.

"Everybody assumes that they're the exception . . . and it might be possible to keep a secret too, if it was just a matter of intelligence, but unfortunately people are also equipped with faces, and untrained faces in most cases, and that gives them away."

Mark sat on the edge of the hammock, holding himself up with his hands, hunched a little forward; it wasn't the most comfortable position. "No one told me," Mark said, lying again, more forcefully this time.

Kate reached up and put her fingers through the cagelike wire mesh that enclosed the top of the arbor, gave it a quick jerk.

"We were involved. It wasn't for very long. But it was something that had been coming, something we both felt. There'd always been an attraction between us, a certain charge. Rob is a very attractive man, don't you think?"

"He is," Mark said. "Sure."

Kate sat down, finally, in one of the lawn chairs. She ran the palms of her hands against one another, back and forth, considering. Then she looked back at Mark, sharply. "He was a great help to me when I'd come through a very difficult relationship. It was an extraordinary situation or it wouldn't have happened at all. I'd never had an affair with a married man before. As a matter of principle. Marriage is too solemn a thing for me, and I know myself, I demand too much to be involved with someone who has other serious involvements . . ."

Mark picked at the twining cords of the hammock, glancing sidelong at her. He was a little afraid of contradicting her. She was too powerful. She went on, speaking quickly, not really giving him room to break in.

"You know how these things begin, you assure one another that you can have a relationship that won't change the structure of each other's lives, but that's exactly what you *do* want, something that will change everything . . ." She smiled at Mark with her large, frank, beautiful eyes. "So then either it changes or doesn't and you're unhappy in either case." Kate looked back up toward the house. "I wonder where Barbara is?"

Kate ran her hand up and down over her elbow, scrutinizing Mark for a second. "It lasted only a few weeks," she said. "I acted very badly, but he wanted it to end as much as I did. He may deny it, but it was a relief to him when it ended." Mark could feel the anger stirring in her like a wind rising before a storm. "Barbara was very hostile and resentful. That was what I felt worst about. I'm probably even closer to Barbara than I am to Rob, that's the funny thing about it, and it hurts me that there's such a distance between us. I'm a much better friend to women, really. And you know what she called me? A predator. A sexual predator. God knows what Rob's told her. It enrages me. She says I was out to destroy her family. For her to attack me like that and Rob just sitting there, letting her do it."

"People say things in fights, Kate."

"I know I've acted badly, I always do, but one of the reasons I wanted to come back here was to get our relationship back on its old basis, to make it all right again."

Mark looked over at her. "Maybe some things you can't make right."

"I don't believe that," she said.

"I do," Mark said. "Maybe there are some things that, even with the best intentions in the world, you aren't going to be able to fix. Maybe some things never had a chance. You said it yourself, a married man, with a family . . . the fact of your wanting it to be nice isn't going to make it nice."

"Nothing's ever that simple," she said.

"No, I think some things *are* that simple," he said. He had spoken with more intensity than he'd intended to. It made her silent. He stared at her, his eyes wide, waiting for her to challenge him. He could win this argument, but only with evidence he didn't dare use.

After a moment she said, "You must think I'm a freak."

"No," he said.

"Sometimes I think I am. Sometimes I think there's something wrong with me, that I'm a Frankenstein."

"That's ridiculous," Mark said. "You didn't understand what I was saying."

"No, I do understand," she said.

"What an awful way to feel about yourself," Mark said.

"It's just the way I feel," she said. She lifted her head, pushed her hair back with her hand.

She looked exhausted. No, she wasn't a freak, or a demon, whatever Mark had worked her up into before, not the ghostly rival on the movie screen or the moral horror show of Barbara's stories. All she was was another person who needed to be comforted, calmed down. It was just that she was more difficult to comfort than the others. Exhausted or not, she still wasn't ready to put her knives away.

"Barbara has her cruel side," Kate said. "All her friends know that, but you forgive that in her because she can be, well, you know yourself. I know my feelings haven't changed toward her. I can understand that their lives have moved on, but there's no need to be so cruel."

A jay was crying somewhere off in the trees. The dog had spied them and was slinking their way, head low, tail wagging, looking for company.

"Rob was never really in love with me. He needed me in a way, for some part of himself, for a certain time. We would have been a disaster together. He knows that." The dog nosed up under the hammock. Mark reached down and scratched the dog's back. Kate picked up on his silence.

"I know that you think I'm a terrible person."

"That's not true," Mark said. He wished that Barbara would hurry up.

"You don't have to deny it. I know you wouldn't say anything. You're a kind person, not an honest one. You seem very open, but you're not, really. Rob noticed that about you."

"Rob did?"

She leaned back in her chair. "Rob may be a little threatened by you." She reached out a hand, the dog turned, came to her, tail thumping the ground. "I hope what he said didn't upset you." Mark didn't say anything. "Married people have such curiosity about how we lead our lives, don't you find that? It seems as if I'm always explaining and explaining and they never seem to get it. Do you really think they can forget so totally what it was like? They make such judgments, I suppose it's inevitable. They somehow assume that they're around the human campfire and we're not. Their lives are not a threat to me, why should my life be a threat to them? I think they secretly believe that we're all out here leading these selfish, self-absorbed, luxurious lives and they envy us. If they only knew, right? I'm about ready to give up on the whole lot of them. You and I have more in common, as little as we know about one another."

Kate's slanders lacked their earlier punch. Mark leaned back in the hammock, put his hands behind his head, stared up through the wire mesh, the tangled branches of the arbor. Mourning doves cooed somewhere nearby. He felt drained suddenly from the heat of the studio, from the talk. He turned back to face her.

"So what are you going to do?" he said.

"I'm going to leave, of course. Tomorrow morning. The earliest flight I could get," she said. "Let me ask you a strange question."

"Sure," Mark said.

"Do you find me attractive?"

"Sure."

"You can be honest. You don't have to say it to be nice."

"I wouldn't lie to you," Mark said.

"It doesn't mean anything, of course, since we'll never see one another again. Do you think you could care for me, even a little?"

Mark squinted at her, feeling the distress welling up in him again. "Of course," he said. The sprinklers were ticking like clocks.

"Thank you," she said. Both of them heard the door bang, far off. It had to be Barbara, Mark thought. "I find you very attractive," Kate said.

Mark made a move to get up. Kate's hand was extended toward him and he took it. They rose together, pulling each other up. The arbor shielded them from Barbara's view, at least for a moment.

She stood close to him, her arms lightly around his waist, her forehead resting against his shoulder. Mark felt himself stiffen in alarm, yet his hands remained lightly on her arms.

"I'm sorry you've had such a hard time," he said.

She looked up at him. "I'm not so bad as they say."

"Of course you're not," Mark said. He took her hands from around his waist. He lifted her hands and kissed them, the gesture odd and slightly courtly. He stepped away from her, but the gesture still stood, the impression that they had been in an intimate scene, that something had been established between them.

Chapter Twenty

Summer colds were the worst kind, she said. The only sound in the empty house was the sound of her coughing. She'd probably picked it up the day they'd done the casting, she said, daubing at her nose with a Kleenex. All that going back and forth between the sweltering studio and the chill outdoors.

Barbara and Mark were alone now, sitting across from one another at the long dining-room table. The blinds had been partially drawn and threw gleaming bars of midday light across the polished wood. The dishes were still there at all the places, but Rob had gone, taken the children off in the pickup for the afternoon.

Barbara rose in her seat and Mark instinctively started to get up with her. "No, you sit right there," she said. "I'm just getting the coffee."

They were still polite and a little awkward with one another, as if someone were still watching them. They had pulled it off. Rob had been distracted but civil, still suffering from Kate's departure. He gave no sign of suspecting Mark of anything. Mark even liked talking to him. Anyone listening to their conversation would have thought they were old friends. Mark found that the temptation was to speak too intimately, too urgently to Rob. The discovery of just how good he was at deception left Mark with the faint, bitter taste of self-disgust in his mouth.

When she came back with the coffee Barbara said, "We didn't tell you. Tommy was here yesterday."

"Tommy? Why?"

"He came to see Judy. He had the idea that he could get her to come back."

"Did you see him?"

"No. But Rob did." She set a cup down in front of Mark. "You take anything in it?"

"No," Mark said. "And what happened?"

"Rob had just come back from seeing Kate off at the airport. I'm sure that didn't help. Tommy and Judy were down at the barn with the children. Rob asked him to leave. It didn't sound like it was very nice. At least no one got hurt."

"What you mean is that no one laid a hand on anyone, right? This time. What about Judy?"

"What about her?"

"It seems to me that she's the one who has the right to decide."

"Decide? To go back to him or not? She never would. Never."

"You know that?"

"I know that." Her gaze faltered. "I'm sorry. I'm sorry for them both."

Mark was silent for a second. The idea of Tommy having been here filled him with some undefinable sense of alarm. Barbara waited for him to say something. He wanted to press her, to know the details, but he knew that pressing would only bring out the differences between them.

"Rob seemed fine. Just now."

"I think he's fine. He's better." She brushed her palm across the smooth wood of the table. "I'm sorry you haven't had a chance to meet Rob at his best." Mark raised his coffee cup, blew across it. He looked over at Barbara, saying nothing. "People do admire him, you know. They look up to him. You really haven't seen any of that."

Mark set down his cup of coffee, considered a second before he answered. "I assumed there was something there."

"Yes." She poured some milk into her coffee, stirred it slowly. "Last night when I came in, I turned on the lights and there were flowers on the table. In the hall there. Everyone was already asleep. He'd made a little sign to go with the flowers."

"What did it say?"

"It said, 'Give Peace a Chance.'"

"And what did you think?"

"Maybe you're too young to get it, there's a joke there, in the old Vietnam protest days there was an antiwar song . . ."

"I know," Mark said. "So what did you think?"

Her voice, deepened by her cold, betrayed more emotion than she intended. "I thought it was very sweet," she said.

Mark leaned back in his chair, his face stony. He thought to himself, so Rob gets another chance, but Tommy doesn't. "It must feel very different. Now that Kate's gone."

"It *is* different. Of course it is."

"Did Rob mind my coming to lunch?"

"No, no, it was just fine. And you were just perfect, by the way. I think he thinks . . . oh, God knows what he thinks . . ."

"Say it."

"He thinks I've got you tied around my little finger. He said he thought I could get you to do whatever I wanted."

Mark stared out through the blinds, then sharply back at her. "Well, I guess that's true, isn't it?"

She brushed the palm of her hand along the tabletop, feeling its sheen. She was in one of her moods, handing out wounds as if they were awards.

"I'm sorry," she said. She stood up. He watched her as she came around to his side of the table. She stood behind him, put her hands on his shoulders. He looked up at her. Nothing could happen here, not in the house, after a lunch with the whole family. He had put it out of his mind. She kissed him lightly on the top of the head.

She started to move away, but he reached up and held her hand there on his shoulder. He bent back and she leaned forward, coming down, kissed him softly on the lips. He felt her hair brushing his face.

He pivoted in the chair, still holding her hands. She looked at him, her eyes pleased, she didn't know what he was going to do, but she didn't seem to be minding. He reached up for her, stood himself, yanked the chair that was between them out of the way, folded her into his arms. She averted her face, coughing again, rested her head against his chest.

"Summer cold," he said.

"The worst kind," she said.

"I know," he said. "They make people say terrible things."

"I said I was sorry."

"I know."

He lifted her face so he could see her, then kissed her once, twice, felt her rise up to him. He began walking her even as he kissed her, walking her away from the table covered with dishes, away from the open window, back toward the kitchen. Desire was there again, she wanted him; whatever she had said a minute ago, she did want him.

Her face was bright, her eyes and hands searching his face. "What can we do?" she said. She was very pleased that he wanted her, she needed him to want her.

"I don't know what we can do," he said.

Her fingers ran down along his neck, pressing his shoulders, moved down over his arms, held tight to his hands. "Let's go upstairs," she said.

He didn't believe her at first. At first he thought it was another kind of joke, but it wasn't. She ruffled his hair, not smiling at all.

"What if someone comes?" he said.

"You're afraid?" she said. The cold had made her voice husky, heavy.

"I don't like the idea of someone coming," he said.

"We'll lock all the doors," she said.

When he didn't respond she stepped back from him, pivoted quickly, crossed the kitchen, set the hook in the door. "See how easy?"

She moved into the hallway, he followed uneasily. Something was balking in him, but he couldn't bring himself to speak. She turned the heavy latch in the front door. "Nothing to it at all," she said. Her chipper voice seemed to echo in the huge empty house. "I'll be right back."

He stayed in the hallway, staring through the window at the green lawn, the trees stirring in a soft breeze. He could hear her quick, purposeful steps and the pulling and closing of one door and then the next. When she came back through the kitchen she surprised him. Her hands were raised and flared outward, like a performer ready to accept applause. "There! All taken care of. O.K.?"

He wasn't sure whether he heard something mocking in her voice or not. "O.K.," he said.

When she came to him she was gentle again. "Does that make
you feel safer?"

"Sure," he said, brushing her cheek with his hand. "Anyway, I
can be with you, I want to be with you."

She smiled. "Even all locked in."

As they walked up the stairs Mark thought, we can't do this, it is
impossible, all these things cannot exist together, a half hour ago
we were a family, a circle around the table. The ordinary world
was being swept away, everything shattered, this would turn him
into something other than he had ever been.

She coughed again. He could see the beads of sweat on her forehead, whether from the sudden exertion or from her cold he didn't
know. She led him to the guest bedroom, the room where Kate had
stayed. An aquarium bubbled in a corner, the walls were a quilt-
work of children's drawings. Together Barbara and Mark unfolded
a blanket, spread it on the floor.

Even as they knelt together on the blanket Mark imagined someone coming back, trying those locked doors, calling out. Unbutton-
ing her blouse he was listening to every sound, every creak and sigh
of the house, every bird call in the trees outside.

After they had finished making love, he looked down at her,
holding himself up on his hands, his lips pressed mum. Everything
was silent again, after her one sharp cry. Her auburn hair was
fanned out on the blue blanket, her eyes stared fearlessly up at him.
He couldn't fully meet her gaze, had to avert his eyes as he wiped
her face gently, wiped the wet hair from her temples.

When she went into the bathroom he walked to the window,
stared down at the trees, at the light shining on the leaves. He
folded up the blanket, then walked into the hallway, stood in the
doorway of Rob and Barbara's bedroom. He had never been in their
bedroom. It was lovely, immaculately done, big windows, an an-
tique dresser, a Robert Motherwell on the wall, a small Shaker table
next to the bed. He stared in, absorbing every detail, but he could
not bring himself to step inside. He hated what they had just done.
He was still standing there when Barbara came out of the bathroom.

"What do you want to do?" she said.

"I don't know," he said. "I just want to get out of here, I'd just
like to get out of this house."

"O.K., we can," she said. She took the folded blanket from him,

folded it again over her arm, looked at him curiously. "Are you
going to be all right? I want you to be all right."

It was only on coming down the stairs that Mark saw the vase of
roses sitting on the table in the hall; he had missed them before.

"Those are the flowers?"

"Yes."

Mark said nothing. It was a nice thing to have done, he thought,
the sort of thing he could imagine a friend of his doing, or himself,
on the right kind of day.

"Where's the sign he made?"

"I put it away," Barbara said. Mark looked at her, noted that she
didn't offer to let him see it.

"I think we'd better get out of here," he said.

"O.K.," she said. "It's going to be O.K. Really." She tripped
down the stairs ahead of him, then looked back up at him. She was
shining with happiness. "You're going to be O.K., aren't you?"

"Sure."

"Just let me unlock the doors. It will only take a minute."

Barbara had wanted him to be all right, but he didn't feel all
right, he felt that things were terribly wrong. He was spooked. That
night he ate alone downtown, took a long walk afterwards, ambling, staring in the windows at the carved wooden bears and the
buckskin jackets that seemed to be the summer's big sellers. He
walked for a couple of hours and then, without having consciously
set himself to it, he left downtown, began to walk the dark back
streets where ordinary people lived. He passed the laundromat and
a couple of the cheaper motels, passed the houses of friends and
people he knew, crossing over to the far side of the street to lessen
the chances of being seen, then crossing back again. He walked
faster, began to make the familiar turns until in the end he found
himself standing in front of Ellen's house.

He had no intention of knocking. He walked around to the side,
just stood there on the sidewalk under the big trees, looking in.
There were lights on in her kitchen, spilling out onto her back yard.
There was a sound of a TV somewhere, and of a child crying.

Mark saw no one up or down the street. He knelt and picked up
a handful of pebbles from the gravel driveway.

The first toss fell short, he heard it rattle in the plants just below
her bedroom window. A real high-school trick, that's what it was,

he knew it, but it didn't stop him. He lofted the second toss higher, heard it skip off the glass with a soft tick.

Headlights turned the corner at the north end of the block. Mark watched the car move slowly down the street. He froze, fingers tight around the handful of pebbles. It was a bunch of kids. One of them stuck his head out the window and shouted something. Mark heard the others laugh. The car slid on down the street.

He looked back up at Ellen's windows. There was no sign that anyone had moved inside the house. It was crazy for him to have come, crazy and a little sappy, and no doubt shot through with bad motives he hadn't even thought of.

With one swooping underhand motion Mark released the whole handful of pebbles, watched them rise and spread like a covey of quail, heard them rain against the glass of the window.

He waited and in three or four seconds he saw the silhouette in the lighted doorway. Ellen switched on the light and he could see her.

She was bewildered, looking all around. She had had her hair done, gotten a permanent, it was something she'd talked about doing for months, something Mark had argued against, but it looked nice. She stared out into the night. Mark was standing under the trees and she couldn't see him. She looked so exposed, standing in the lighted room. Her gestures, the way she brushed her forehead with her hand when she was perplexed, he knew by heart. Mark took a step forward out of the shadows.

Suddenly she turned her head, looking away. He saw her lips moving, she was talking to someone. Mark saw the tall figure fill the doorway behind her, blotting out the light behind him as he stooped to come through the low frame. He straightened up, a beer in one hand. It was Patrick.

Patrick gestured with his free hand, Ellen pointed to the window, Patrick shrugged his loose, marionette-like shoulders and went to the far end of the bedroom, knelt on the couch, shading his eyes with both hands now, looking out.

A dumb show, that's what it was, what Mark was always trying to teach his kids about when they had their unit on Shakespeare, and here it was right on the streets of Jackson.

Patrick pushed himself up from the couch, came back, put his hand on her shoulder. Ellen slipped away from him, came right up to the window, still staring out, still unable to penetrate the darkness. Her fingers played absently with her wind chimes.

Mark moved away, slipping sideways at first, then walking fast, not looking back, staying in the shadows. He had been a fool to come. It was just a possibility, that's all it had been, a possibility that she might be alone, might have seen him, might have been willing to just talk. Mark started to run. He had been a fool to think that possibilities could be kept alive forever.

Chapter Twenty-one

For a week she didn't call him.

Whatever it was possible to imagine, Mark was ready now to imagine. Cheating was a two-way street, if he was the one being betrayed now, there was nothing he could say. It was possible, he saw now, that Barbara may have always loved her husband in a way she had never expressed to Mark. It would have been prudent not to express it. And kind. Even if Mark gave her the benefit of the doubt, say she was telling Mark the truth all along, still it was the truth as she felt it then, at the moment when she was hurt and angry and betrayed. At one moment she had been willing to live out another kind of life, take bigger chances than she'd ever taken before. No one said that moment was going to last forever.

Kate was gone. Mark remembered the flowers Rob had left in the hallway, the sign he had made Barbara. The sign had read GIVE PEACE A CHANCE. Maybe she was giving him his chance. If he had come looking for forgiveness, how could she deny it to him? Not very easily, Mark imagined; the man was the father of her children.

She had said she would never consider leaving her husband. The ground rules all along had been that Mark wasn't going to swoop in and disrupt her life. From the start she had counted on his good manners. All that passion, all that fervor, and still he was not an ultimately serious person to her. He lacked substance, the resources that allowed things to happen. If he had come in and said he was whisking off her and her two children, she would have been a fool to accept. He didn't have enough cash to last them a weekend in a medium-priced hotel. An affair of sentiment, that's all it was set up to be, nothing more.

One desperate thought triggered another. Mark, for the first time, found himself tormented by the thought that he was becoming blurred together with her other lovers, with Salvatore, with others whose names she hadn't given him, men who in the end had become nothing more than obstacles or symptoms of deeper problems. Then, even more bitterly, he wondered if he would be nameless to her future lovers.

It was a perfect time to choose virtue, to save himself, to go back to being the good teacher, good friend, good guy that he had been. All he had to do was separate himself from Barbara, accept the fact that it was impossible, and then act on it.

It was just that Mark was too willful. The problem with love was not that it was fleeting or elusive, but that it persisted like the hardiest week, snaking its roots deeper and deeper into porous soil. Love wore him down, drove him beyond endurance. He did love her and he was not capable of taking it back, he wouldn't take back something that he knew was true. He was ready to insist.

He dreamed of her for the first time. He was at a reception in a garden. There was a huge house with columns and balconies, there were women in long dresses. Set out in front of the garden were tables where white-jacketed bartenders served pink punch in small glasses. It seemed like spring. There was a receiving line, but Mark held himself back from it. There were people that he and Barbara both knew, all around. He didn't see her at first and then he did; she stood in a circle of friends and he came up to her, spoke to her and her friends. Both he and Barbara were very cautious with one another. Mark felt the friends scrutinizing him, but gradually they began to drift away. Others came up, Mark and Barbara greeted them together. Mark held her arm innocently, no one seemed to think anything about it. It seemed perfectly friendly. The scene was suffused with the sweetness of seeing her.

He wanted to take her through the reception line, he was proud to be with her, and yet he wanted to get her to someplace else, someplace where he could acknowledge his feeling for her. He led her down into a grove of tall, dark trees. She was nervous, she didn't want to take any chances, but he felt he had to. He laid his hand on the hollow of her thigh, on the soft, silk dress, just looking her in the face the whole time, perfectly calm. The gesture was all that he needed.

In the morning he remembered the dream and its strange hopefulness. He remembered touching her, the oddness of the gesture, and later that morning, as the dream spread out like ripples on a pond, he remembered his father reading him the story of Jacob, wrestling all night with the angel, Jacob the thief who had stolen his brother's birthright. The angel had touched the hollow of Jacob's thigh and crippled him, thrown his leg out of joint, but Jacob had still held on and the angel had given him a new name for his stubbornness.

Mark didn't understand his dream exactly. He remembered something Ellen's therapist had told him, how you're really all the characters in your dreams. That would make him both Jacob and the angel, both the one touching and the one being touched, but he couldn't take it much further than that. He was hostile to dream analysis anyway.

Still, that dream did change something, because when he went out for his afternoon run on the Elk Refuge Road, he carried with him that aura of hope, he carried the sense that debris had been cleared away, that somehow it was possible for him to be more daring than he had ever been before.

It was early, mist was still rising off Jackson Lake. He waited outside the Colter Bay Indian Museum for almost twenty minutes before he saw their car pull into the parking lot.

Mark moved slowly down the stairs, squinted into the bright morning sun. Jeffrey waved as he slid out of the car and Sarah came running toward him. Her exuberance caught Mark by surprise; at the last second he grabbed her arms, swung her once around. Barbara, locking the car, stood watching them and smiling. She looked tired. Anyone seeing us, Mark thought, would think I was just an uncle, one of those harmless, trusted uncles.

"Sorry we're late," Barbara said. "You know how things happen."

"I do," Mark said. He leaned forward and gave her a light kiss on the cheek.

Sarah tugged on his sleeve. "Look," she said. She held up two fingers, pinched together. For a second Mark didn't understand, but then she aimed her invisible thread through her invisible needle.

"Oh, come on," Mark said, grinning at her. Mark grabbed at her hands.

She pulled away from him. "No! Watch! Watch!" Backing up onto the steps of the museum, Sarah proceeded to sew her lip, ignoring the stares of a pair of muscled climbers passing through the parking lot. Sarah's technique was exquisite, a perfect imitation of Mark's trick. She'd been practicing. Everyone applauded.

Mark took a mock swat at her. "I can't believe it, the only trick I know and a nine-year-old goes and steals it."

"You should be flattered," Barbara said.

"I am flattered. Come on," Mark said. He put his arm around Sarah's shoulders. "Let's go inside."

Everything about the museum was new and artfully done. In the lobby was a picture window that looked out across Jackson Lake to the mountains. They could see a man down in the marina fooling around with his catamaran. Behind the circular reception desk sat a large middle-aged Indian in native dress and a young blond woman in her Park Service uniform. At nine on a Tuesday morning business was slow. A European-looking family stood at the bookstand, leafing through wildlife guides, arguing back and forth in French. There didn't seem to be more than a dozen people in the whole place.

Mark and Barbara trailed the children through the museum. The exhibits were cunningly organized on a succession of levels. There was a slide show on one wall, images of winter teepee encampments, buffalo herds, pueblos and mounted warriors clicking on and off in an endless round. Indian faces had been etched on wood and on the black glass of the display cases so that when you looked through the etching you could just make out the actual objects inside, eagle-wing fans, headdresses of beads and porcupine quills. The effect was eerie, like looking at an x-ray, or trying to look through water.

The innocent curiosity of the children pulled them onward, down a series of white curving staircases. Jeffrey was the thorough one, reading every label and explanation one by one, while Sarah ranged out, exploring, trying to get everyone's attention when she found something she liked.

Mark stood silently in front of a case where a war bonnet of eagle feathers, a painted and feathered shield, and a rusted rifle hung before the etching of the face of a Sioux chief, an icon of male pride. Counting coup, the plaque read, was the bravest act a warrior could accomplish; not killing his enemy, but just touching him, in the midst of battle. The simple act of touching could be the most daring act of all.

He heard the children's bright laughter below him. He looked up slowly, saw his own somber face mirrored in the glass of the case; for the first time he had the feeling that he was dangerous to those children.

Barbara, halfway down the next set of steps, looked back at him, her eyes wide and questioning.

"Coming?" she said.

He nodded. "I had a dream about you last night," he said.

"Did you?" There was a smile on her lips. She didn't understand. She thought he was just flirting.

"It was nice. We were in a garden."

"Mom! Come look!" It was Sarah, come partway up the stairs to get them. "There are all these neat dolls and stuff, all made with beads . . ."

Barbara and Mark joined the children again. Sarah took her mother's hand, pulled her off to look at the display case she had discovered. Mark watched them go. It wasn't the right moment. But there would never be a right moment, he would just have to create one.

A magnified, slightly blurred voice came through the loud-speaker. "There will be a twenty-minute film, *Little Wolf, the Life of a Plains Indian Boy,* beginning in the auditorium in ten minutes. In ten minutes."

Sarah looked up at her mother. "So, are we going?" Barbara asked. Sarah nodded happily that they were. "Of course we're going," Barbara said, smiling at Mark. "What New York City kid have you ever heard of passing up a free movie?"

There were only a handful of people in the small auditorium. Children sat cross-legged on the floor, a pair of grandparents sat in chairs, ducking under their camera straps, getting untangled, happy for the excuse to sit down. The middle-aged Indian who had been behind the main desk gave a soft-spoken introduction to the film, hands held primly before him. Jeffrey and Sarah had found seats in the back row, Mark and Barbara stood leaning against the wall behind them.

The film began with a shot of the open prairie, the sound of hooves. A young Indian boy rode his pony into view, wheeling and turning as the camera moved back farther and farther, taking in more and more until finally, in the distance, it gathered in the patiently working oil rigs, pecking at the earth like mechanical robins. It was going to be a film about the passing of old ways. In the darkness Mark felt the tension between him and Barbara stretch tight as wire.

"I need to talk to you," Mark said.

Barbara glanced over at him, the reflected silver light from the screen flickering across her face. "Now?" she said.

"Now," he said. "If we can. We can go outside."

The Indian boy was watching his father and the other men dance now, they were all in their feathers and beads and paint. There were drums and chanting. Sarah and Jeffrey were rapt with attention. Barbara leaned forward and whispered something to Jeffrey, patted Sarah on the shoulder. Jeffrey turned to stare blindly at Mark for a second, then went back to the movie. Barbara and Mark slipped out of the dark auditorium.

The Indian and the Park Service woman sat on their stools, sipping Cokes. They looked up at Mark and Barbara, the woman smiled a midwestern smile.

In the light, Mark noticed again how drawn and tired Barbara looked. She was wary of him. She knows what I'm going to say, Mark thought, she must know. She stopped and bent over the water fountain, took a long, delaying drink. Mark waited for her, staring at the guide books along the wall, all of them with the same shot of the Tetons.

Together Mark and Barbara moved down the staircase, not having to say where they were going, both moving by unspoken agreement to a place where they wouldn't be heard. A white-haired woman in a serape who looked a little like Margaret Mead passed them on the stairs, holding onto the rail, making her way back to the lobby with frequent stops to catch her breath. There seemed to be no one else on the lower levels of the museum. Barbara and Mark could still hear the recorded dirge-like chants.

"Yes?" she said. They stood in front of a case that held medicine bags and carved wooden masks. Both Mark and Barbara looked in, but not really looking at all.

"I want you to tell Rob," Mark said.

She looked at him, squinting as if it was no more than a bad joke. "You what?"

"I want you to tell Rob about me."

"That's crazy."

"Maybe it's time to be crazy." She turned, moving away, disgusted and upset. He followed her. "We would be better off if everyone knew the truth."

"Whatever that is."

"Yes," he said. "Whatever that is."

They ambled through the maze of glass cases. Barbara stared at the floor ahead of them, weighing her reply. "Better off, you say. How would we be better off?"

It was important to keep his voice down, to stay calm. That was how he had thought it out; the more outrageous the gamble, the calmer he would have to be.

"How could it be worse? He must suspect already. Do you think he even cares?"

She looked darkly back at him, almost with scorn, as if she knew but wasn't telling.

"You do think he cares," Mark said.

"I do."

"I don't," Mark said. "I don't think anybody really gives a damn. The way it is now, we're paralyzed. I can't call you, I can't see you, to make love we have to lock twelve locks. I have to go around pretending I'm the guy you've got wrapped around your little finger. I'll tell you what's driving me crazy, it's walking around, all I can think about is who's going to find out, how I'm going to blow this . . . It's contemptible, having to play roles like this . . ."

"What's more contemptible is hurting people," she said.

"If we don't do something, it's going to die between us, you know it is. You talked once about our finding our own form, remember that? So when are we going to do that?"

"Not now," she said. He stared at her, stung, not knowing what to say, and then she turned away, covering her mouth with her hand, stifling a cough.

"What's the worst thing that could happen?" he said.

"If?"

"If you told him."

"I don't want to think about it."

"No. Think about it. Tell me."

"I have to get back to the children." She moved toward the staircase. He grabbed her wrist. She tried to pull away, glaring at him.

"I want you to tell me," he said.

"It would mean I would lose everything," she said. He let go of her hands. "We've pushed the limits back as far as they could go, Mark. When you think about what we've done, what we've imagined, imagining that we could get married, imagining that we could really make plans to travel together. We've spun out this whole impossible world. Things don't give forever. I'm a coward, Mark, you shouldn't push me. I'll protect myself, I know I will. Don't get me in a corner."

His voice was down to a whisper. "You're not going to ignore me. Whatever's happened between you and whomever . . ." He couldn't even bring himself to speak Rob's name. "I'm still here. You said you loved me. I'm holding you to that."

"I do love you, you know that."

"But you're going to leave. Another month you'll be gone. It will be over."

"Don't be so frightened. That's never the way things end . . ." She stopped as if she had remembered something, and a shadow of distress went across her face. She looked up toward the stairs. "Mark, please, I have to get back to the children."

His own tears caught him unawares, caught her too. She reached up, took his face in both her hands, pulled him to her. He buried his face in her hair, their arms were around each other. Still, he hadn't forgotten where they were, that it was a public place.

He shook his head and pulled back, but she caught his hands. Her eyes were glistening with tears. She wasn't ready to let him go. Her lips parted as if she had something more to say, but then he saw her eyes lift, focusing on something high above him. He saw her eyes change, darken the way water will darken under moving clouds. She let go of his hands. Mark turned and saw Jeffrey standing at the top of the stairs.

Barbara's voice betrayed nothing. "Is the movie over already?"

"No," Jeffrey said. "I thought it was boring, so I left." He stared down at them with the suspicious incomprehension of a child looking down a deep well.

"Where's Sarah?" Barbara said, moving a couple of steps up the stairs.

"She's still watching." The boy hadn't moved, standing above them in small-boned judgment, his hands fixed on the rail. There was no way to know how much he had heard, how much he had understood of what he'd heard, but stubbornness was visible in him. Barbara moved higher, toward her son.

"Jeffrey, there's something Mark and I want to show you, we found these wonderful shields . . ." She turned back to Mark for just a second. "Mark, are you coming?"

From far off they could still hear the soundtrack of the film, the drums, the keening chants. Barbara tripped up the next series of stairs, rising like an angel of deception, rushing to save them all from what her son may have seen.

CHAPTER TWENTY-TWO

Sarah knew it was her fault. She and her friend Brenda stared up the steep slope, the water cascading over the rocks. Far up the light was bright on the high peaks. There was no sign of the two boys.

"Jeff-rey! Kev-vin!" The sound echoed off the rocks. Nighthawks were coming in now, squeaking and darting, catching insects. Sarah could feel the cool air rising off the rushing stream.

"Jeff-rey! Kev-vin!" Sarah climbed easily from one boulder to a higher one. She looked back at Brenda. "This is how you get to the falls, right?"

"Yes. But it's a ways, Sarah. We might as well wait for them. You know they'll be coming down sooner or later."

Sarah wasn't sure. "We can go up a little way. Come on, Brenda, it'll be good for you. They couldn't have gone that far."

Brenda followed, reluctantly. After thirty yards of climbing she was breathing hard. Sarah moved swiftly, looking ahead, listening for voices. There were none. Sarah had a spooky feeling that something had happened to her brother. She had to find him. She started to walk even faster. The water in the rushing stream seemed darker now, the frothy cascades even whiter, almost glowing.

Sarah didn't know exactly what she had done, all she knew was that the afternoon after they came back from the Indian Museum Jeffrey started being mean to her. It all began with a game of naming the capitals of all the states. It was Jeffrey's idea. It was always Jeffrey's idea, it was the kind of game Sarah was terrible at. Jeffrey was the one who always knew the names for things. He badgered her into playing anyway, and every time she guessed wrong he would make fun of her. It started to make her mad.

"I'll bet you don't even know the capital of North Dakota yourself. It's such a stupid game. Besides, there's lots you don't know, you know."

"Like what?" Jeffrey said.

"I forget. But you know you just pretend to know things when you don't."

"I know a lot more than you think."

"Like what?"

He considered her, his eyes newly superior and bitter. "I can't

tell you. Maybe someday I will. When you're big enough. There are
some things you can't understand when you're only nine."

The next day they went to see Brenda and Kevin. They had been
invited for the whole day at the Harrisons' ranch. Jeffrey was quiet
going over in the car, sitting in the back by himself, thumbing
through baseball cards. Sarah could tell that her mother was
worried. She kept glancing at Jeffrey through the rearview mirror,
asking him questions, but Jeffrey didn't want to talk and finally she
just let him be.

In the afternoon the four kids went fishing in the lake and Jeffrey
was no better. The boys wouldn't have anything to do with the girls
and it was all Jeffrey's doing, Kevin just did what he said. Jeffrey
was punishing Sarah for something, but she didn't know for what.
Finally the two boys left, said they were going fishing up by the
falls. They were tired of having girls bother them.

Two hours passed and the boys hadn't come back. Sarah got
scared. She knew there were things she couldn't understand, being
only nine years old, but she could understand hurt without knowing its source and her brother was hurt somehow and she had to
find him.

As the two girls moved higher up the mountain it wasn't long before Brenda began to complain. First she had a side-ache, then she
thought she had a blister. She wanted to turn back. Sarah made a
deal with her; they'd go up to the falls, that was all, they'd come so
far already it couldn't be much farther. The insects were really
coming out now, dancing like bits of asbestos in front of a blower,
luminous against the dark forest.

Finally they heard the water running louder than before. Neither
of them said anything, they didn't have to. It was the falls, it had to
be, the boys would be there. They picked up the pace, pushing
aside briars that caught at their clothing, spruce branches that
swished back after they passed, the supple dark boughs closing
behind them the way water closes finally over a skipped stone, leaving no trace. The two girls broke into the open finally and stopped
short, dumbfounded. There was no falls, just the convergence of
two streams, a field of downed timber and a great jumble of boulders.

"Jeff-rey! Kev-vin!" The calls echoed off the far canyon walls.

"I thought you said the falls were up here," Sarah said.

"They were. I mean, they are. Somewhere. I forget." Brenda
flopped against a boulder, lifted one foot, and tried to pick a small

rock wedged in her tennis shoe. "It's just so ridiculous. We should go back, Sarah. It's getting too dark. What a dumb idea in the first place."

Sarah stared out across the boulder fields. It was the time of day when the light started playing tricks on you. In the dimness the stunted trees began to look like hulking moose or bear, rising up on hind feet to sniff the twilight air. Sarah looked up at the blue sky above the dark ridge line.

"Are you scared?" Sarah asked.

"No, I'm not scared." Brenda rolled over on her side, tore a clump of moss from a fold in the rock, absently picked it apart. "I don't know what you're so worried about, anyway. You know where I bet they are? I'll bet they're sitting down by the boat, just laughing at us, I'll bet it's just a big trick they cooked up."

"What if something happened to them, how would you feel?" Sarah said. She paused, giving it time to sink in. "What if something awful happened, like one of them was swept over the falls or something, and had a broken leg and the other one was afraid to leave them and we could have helped but we didn't because we were just too tired to walk just a little ways further?"

Brenda didn't say anything, but tossed away the last chunk of moss and brushed off her hands. One of the reasons that Sarah was friends with Brenda was that she could always talk Brenda into things.

"I've got one more Pop-Tart," Sarah said. "You want half?"

Brenda nodded.

Sarah took the squished Pop-Tart out of her back pocket. The jam had oozed out and was sticking to the paper, but it didn't matter. Sarah divided it solemnly, Brenda watching the whole time to make sure it was even, and the two girls sat down on the same rock to eat their sticky prize.

"So which way?" Sarah said.

"I don't know." Brenda licked the last remaining jam from between her fingers.

"But you've been here before. You said you had."

Brenda stood up, staring at the rushing silver fork of water. "That way." She pointed up to the left.

"You're sure?"

"Of course I'm sure," Brenda said. "I'm the one who's been here before, aren't I?"

They headed off again, up the left fork of the stream. Brenda was limping a little now. The trail leveled out, wound through a boulder field. They could see the small, dark shapes of coneys and marmots scurrying ahead of them, disappearing into the gray rocks, they could hear the sharp whistles of warning.

The trail meandered away from the stream for a while and then came back to it. The stream seemed shallower and less powerful now, whispering over the rocks. For the first time Sarah was uncertain. It was hard to imagine that there could be a falls at the head of such a small channel. It didn't matter; all that mattered was finding her brother, they had to keep looking until they found him.

They entered a dark grove of alpine fir. Brenda, too tired even to protest, dropped further behind. When they came out into the open again there were clouds floating across the ridge line, pink and harmless in the falling sun, the first clouds they had seen all day.

Dusk was falling faster, everything seemed eerily alive, things seemed to be moving when they weren't moving at all. Sarah imagined her brother hurt somewhere, mauled by a bear. She remembered what her father had told her, how a grizzly bear can run as fast as a horse, run faster going uphill than on the level, how your only chance, if you couldn't get up a tree, was to lie perfectly still and let the bear sniff you and lick you if it wants, even take a nip out of you and you can't let out a sound or move or else it will kill you with one swipe of its paw.

"Jeff-rey! Kev-vin!"

The clouds above them looked darker, massed all of a sudden. The path had petered out to little more than a game trail. The canyon seemed to tighten around them.

Sarah loved her brother. He would tease her sometimes, but mostly it was fun. It wasn't like him to be mean. Usually he let her ride his bike whenever she wanted, and sometimes they'd play catch or soccer, just the two of them, her playing goalie and him practicing his kicks. When his friends came over he'd be nice to her and so his friends would be nice too, and they'd let her tag along, and when Sarah did something that she knew was wrong Jeffrey would never tell on her.

A grouse drummed in the woods, very near them. Startled, both girls stopped in their tracks for a second, then went on again. There was no sign of a falls.

Sarah's legs were tired, she could imagine how Brenda must feel. She knew that Brenda hated to walk anywhere. She thought of how nice it was going to be to go to sleep in her own house, to take a bath and then slip under the crisp sheets of her own bed, to have her mother tuck her in. She thought of how wonderful it was going to be to go to sleep with the soft sound of the grandfather clock downstairs chiming every hour, and the sound of her mother's laughter. Her mother had the most wonderful laugh. Her family had more fun than any other family, Sarah was sure of it. All she wanted was for her family to be all together again.

She felt a drop of rain on her face. Then she felt another. She kept walking, hoping that Brenda hadn't felt anything yet.

"Sar-rah!"

Sarah stopped and looked back. "What?"

"It's raining."

"I know it's raining."

"Sarah, this is stupid! I'm going back."

"You do what you want then."

"Sarah! They're not up here!" Sarah stared up into the darkness, pulled up on the oversized pair of Brenda's blue jeans she was wearing. Clouds blanketed the sky now, making it much darker, and she could hear the rain hitting the trees all around them. "My mother is going to be really mad, Sarah. I knew I shouldn't have come up here, I knew I shouldn't have listened to you."

Sarah looked down at the way they had come up. They had climbed a long way. Below them now it looked like layer on layer of darkness. Even if the boys were up here, Sarah and Brenda would never find them now. The only hope was that they were already down somehow, that they had gone off on another trail, that it had been a trick, a mistake, something.

Brenda stood forlornly in the middle of the trail. She didn't want to go back down alone. "Are you coming with me?"

"I guess so," Sarah said.

Brenda set a fast pace going downhill. Her limp seemed miraculously to have disappeared. They turned once, they turned twice, they were descending in a hurry. Sarah followed, not paying much attention to where they were going, but it seemed much easier than it had before, most of it was that they were going downhill rather than uphill, but there didn't seem to be as many boulders, either. Brenda kept on doggedly. It was very dark and there was a steady drizzle. The temperature was dropping fast.

Sarah began to get an odd feeling. They had been walking for a long time and hadn't come to anything that she recognized. There was no sign of the stream or the forks. Dark as it was, the ridges didn't seem as high. They seemed to be in the middle of a sloping meadow and Sarah couldn't remember having been in a meadow before.

"Brenda, do you know where we are?"

Twenty yards up the trail, Brenda stopped and turned around, her round face shining palely in the darkness. "Sure. Why?"

"Because it doesn't seem the same as the way we came up."

"That's cuz it's dark." Brenda had pulled her hands up inside her sleeves to protect them from the light rain.

They walked on. It didn't seem quite as cold when they were moving. Somewhere down below them came the yipping of coyotes.

"You know we never came back to the fork in the stream," Sarah said.

"So? If you're so smart, why don't you lead?"

"Don't get upset, Brenda."

"I'm not upset. It's just that you're always criticizing me."

There were dark shapes looming on the hillside. Sarah thought she saw one of them move. It was just her imagination playing tricks on her, it had to be, she would just put it out of her mind.

"I'm not criticizing you, Brenda, but what if we made a wrong turnoff?"

"I don't see how you can blame me," Brenda said. "I was the one who wanted to turn around before, you know, you were the one who had to keep going . . ."

Again Sarah thought she saw something moving out of the corner of her eye, but Brenda showed no sign of having seen anything. The two girls walked on silently. Then Sarah heard, very distinctly, the sound of munching.

"Brenda?"

"Yeah?"

"Did you hear anything?"

"What do you mean?"

"I just wondered if you heard anything." It was enough to get Brenda's attention. They both listened for several seconds.

"You know that's not really funny, Sarah! If you think it's a big joke . . ."

"I wasn't making a joke, Brenda. I really thought I heard something." Sarah wiped the cold rain from her face. She was shivering in Brenda's middy blouse. "Let's go."

They started walking again, but more slowly now, both of them alert and listening. When the next sound came, they both heard it. It was the tinkling of a bell. Both girls froze. A hundred yards up on a slope was a large whitish shadow. Sarah stared at it, she couldn't tell if it was a rock or not. She wished for her brother who knew the names for things, the nameless things she was not old enough to know. Then they heard the tinkling bell a second time.

"Sar-rah!"

Sarah didn't breathe, didn't say anything. The whitish ghostly shape had started to move.

"Sar-rah!"

At Brenda's second cry the whitish shape stopped. Further down the slope a second darker shape, large as the first, was moving slowly, curiously, toward them. Sarah saw a third shape move and then a fourth, the whole hillside was alive. There was a soft snort. Sarah knew what it was, they were surrounded by horses. It was a bell mare they had heard, which meant there had to be a camp nearby, if they could catch one of the horses the horse could take them in, they would be all right.

Before Sarah could do anything Brenda started running up the slope toward the horses.

"Brenda, come back here!"

Brenda shouted something back at Sarah that Sarah couldn't make out, then tried to call the horses, clapping her hands. "Here, girl, come on! Here, Horsey!" Brenda was tired and out of control, she was too keyed-up. She stumbled up the slope, waving her arms erratically.

"Brenda, don't, you get back here right now! You'll just scare them! Brenda!"

Brenda wasn't listening. She ran blindly on, her hands outstretched. The half-dozen ghostly white horses moved away from her, slowly at first, like great shadowy underwater creatures sliding along the ocean floor, but Brenda kept darting back and forth, going after one horse and then another, and they started to get riled up. Sarah ran toward Brenda, but Brenda, oblivious to danger, was well out in front of her, calling out. The skittish horses started to run. Sarah shouted to Brenda to get out of their way. An Appaloosa, snorting and plunging, headed right at Sarah. Sarah scrambled into some scrub pines as the animal galloped past. The sound of horses' hooves pounding all around her in the darkness was terrifying. Sarah couldn't see Brenda anymore. The horses swept in a circle, the white bell mare out in front, her bell clanging wildly, gathering the other horses in behind her like a magnet, leading them off into the darkness. They were suddenly gone.

Sarah heard Brenda sobbing further up the slope; Sarah made her way cautiously across the damp, uneven ground. Brenda had slipped on a wet rock and scraped her knee. She was weeping and hysterical.

"It's going to be all right, Brenda."

"No, it's not, no, it's not, you're just saying that. I'm never going to believe anything you tell me ever again. We're lost, you know we are, and I didn't want to come up here anyway, you made me . . . Look at my knee, it's all bloody and everything, I'll probably get an infection and die . . ."

"You shouldn't have chased the horses, Brenda. It wasn't a very good idea."

"Everything's always my fault, isn't it? Well, it's not fair. It's not the boys who need help, we're the ones who need help. Those dumb boys are probably down there now, they probably think we drowned or something. My mom is going to be really mad, Sarah, and I'm going to tell her just what happened, don't think I'm not."

Sarah stood, shivering, looking down on Brenda. "Come on, Brenda. We should get out of the rain."

Sarah led the sobbing Brenda down into a grove of spruce trees where they found a rock big enough for both of them to sleep on, high enough, they figured, to keep them free from bears. Sarah made Brenda get up on it and then Sarah covered her with spruce branches, and when she was done she crawled in under them herself.

It was prickly, but at least it would keep some of the rain off. Sarah felt soaked through already, Brenda's middy blouse was not enough to keep anyone warm. She hugged her arms to her body. Brenda sobbed for a long time and finally she stopped.

"Sarah?"

"Yes?" Sarah raised up on her elbows, saw Brenda's eyes peering through the dark spruce boughs.

"You don't think there could be any weirdos out here, do you?"

"Don't be silly. Just go to sleep." Brenda lay back down under the cover of branches and Sarah did too. Sarah felt the hard, uneven rock against her cheek. "In the morning we'll be fine," Sarah said. "In the morning we'll be able to see just where we are."

Brenda didn't say anything more. Sarah didn't know if it was because she had gone to sleep or not.

The rain kept coming. Sarah felt prickly and dirty all over, she thought how wonderful it would be to have a warm bath, it would be even more wonderful than food. The branches helped some, but she couldn't stop shaking, and it seemed as if every three or four seconds another raindrop would creep through, splash down her back. She shifted from side to side, half asleep, trying to find a perfectly dry place, but it was as if the slow cold tapping was following her, deliberately tormenting her, and then suddenly it came to her that the tapping on her shoulder was not rain at all, but something else. She opened her eyes and saw her father's face above her. He was telling her very calmly that it was time for her to get up and get into the car. Sarah was very glad. She sat up, pushed aside the spruce branches, and shook Brenda. Brenda woke up with a little choked cry.

"Brenda, come on, come on!" Brenda's eyes were wide and bewildered. "Come on," Sarah said. "My dad says we have to get into the car."

"What car? What are you talking about? There's no car!"

Sarah stared out into the rain. Brenda was right. There was no car, no sign of her father. There was only the dark woods, the rain, the smell of wet spruce. Brenda burrowed back down under the branches and was whimpering again. Sarah didn't say anything more. What branches she could reach she pulled back around her, the rest she just left. She felt all cold inside. Shaking, she clung to the rock, as if she might squeeze some warmth from it, and then she fell asleep.

CHAPTER TWENTY-THREE

Mark woke up in the middle of the night, his heart pounding, covered with sweat, and it took a second before he realized that what had wakened him was not a nightmare, but a perfectly real phone. He groped across the bedside table, found the receiver. He knew even before he picked it up that it would be Barbara.

"Hello?"

"Mark?"

"Hi."

"They can't find her, Mark. Sarah. She's gone."

"What? What time is it? What do you mean, gone?"

"I'm just so scared, Mark. I can't think anymore. There's no sign of them. We've been out looking all night. I feel like I'm going crazy, Mark, you've got to help us. You know it's not like her, you know how careful she is. I can't believe she would deliberately . . ."

"You're not making any sense, Barbara. Tell me what's happened. From the start."

"Nobody knows what happened," Barbara said. "Jeffrey and Sarah went to spend the day with their friends Kevin and Brenda, the Harrisons, you remember, you met them . . ."

"Ya."

"They went fishing, the four of them, and for some reason they split up, I have no idea why, apparently Jeffrey had been picking on her all day, now he tells me different things . . . but the boys came back and the girls didn't. There's no sign at all of them. Rob and I and the Harrisons have been out all night, searching the shoreline of the lake."

"Have you called the sheriff?"

"The sheriff is out there now. The Park Service too. There's going to be a search as soon as there's enough light. I've been calling everyone I know . . . Mark, please, you've got to help us."

"Come on, of course I will. You should have called me before. You should have called me right away."

She was silent for a second, weighing what she was going to say. "I didn't know if I should call you at all, Mark. I feel as if we caused this, somehow, Mark, that none of this would have happened if you and I . . ."

"You don't really believe that," Mark said.

"I don't know what I believe," Barbara said. "I'm sorry. I'm just so tired and confused."

"Where are you now?"

"I'm at home. I just got back a few minutes ago. I just put Jeffrey to bed, he's been up all night too."

"You should try to get some sleep," Mark said.

"I can't," she said. "I tried to lay down but all these crazy things keep going through my head. It's too much for me to deal with, Mark. If anything happened to her I don't know what I'd do."

"Barbara, listen to me, I'll do anything you want."

"The only thing I want in the whole world is to have my child back."

Her words were like a spear hurled at his heart.

"You try to sleep," he said. "Lay down at least. I'll go out there now. The Harrisons' ranch, right?"

"They'll all be there," she said.

He hesitated. There was no point in telling her that he loved her, it was neither proper nor a consolation, not now. "You try to sleep," he repeated.

He dressed quickly, slapped some water on his face. It was a little after five o'clock. Outside it was still dark and cold. It had stopped raining, but water still dripped from the wet trees.

Heading north, the only traffic he ran into was three or four slow-moving delivery trucks with their headlights still on. Slowly it began to sink in, what had happened. Sarah was probably fine, Mark thought, probably she had just gotten turned around and was sound asleep under a tree fifty yards from where her parents had been looking, that was how these things always turned out. It would be something they would all laugh about later.

As the first light came in, Mark could see steam rising off the river. Everything looked the way it always looked, nothing had changed.

He was sure Barbara didn't really believe what she'd said. She and Mark hadn't caused it. No way. He didn't even understand what she could mean by it. Then it came back to him, the two of them standing in the Indian museum, looking up, seeing Jeffrey at the top of the stairs. He remembered the look of distrust in Jeffrey's eyes, the way Barbara had gone to him, trying to cover up. If that's what Barbara was thinking, it was absurd, it made him furious, there was no way you could make that kind of connection, that was just hysteria, the kind of nightmare connection that only comes at five in the morning. You couldn't believe in that stuff, or you'd go mad.

So maybe something had happened finally. For a moment he felt almost glad, maybe this was what he had wanted, a move off of stalemate. He would find Sarah and he would be a hero, that would be the final bit of mockery. He thought of Barbara, lying in her bed, he was sure she couldn't be asleep now, she would be staring up at the ceiling, watching morning light slide up the bright walls. No way was it their fault. No way.

He made the turn and headed up into the Gros Ventre. Leaving the paved road and rumbling over gravel, it occurred to him for the first time that he would be seeing Rob.

There were small groups of solemn men standing in the Harrisons' yard. Some of the men were blowing on cups of coffee, others hunched forward, hands in their pockets, trying to keep warm in the chill morning air. Some of the men were local ranchers that Mark had never met, though he'd seen them before, old-timers who'd been pointed out to Mark when they were having breakfast at the counter in the Wort Hotel. The only person in the yard that Mark knew was Ike Watkins leaning against a hitching rail, talking to a couple of the younger men.

Parked haphazardly around the yard were a dozen pickups, a couple of sheriff's cars, some trucks from the Forest Service and the National Park. There were three or four horse trailers and a couple of horses already saddled and tied up to the rail, rifles in the horses' scabbards.

Mark got out of his car, came up to a group of men talking next to one of the horse trailers. "You know where I could find Rob Campbell?"

He felt the men's eyes looking him over, curious and quiet. A lantern-jawed man in a dirty Scotch cap pointed toward a shed set back of the Harrisons' house. "Probably over there in the cabin. Think I saw him go in there a little bit ago."

Mark felt them waiting for him to talk, talk was all they had right now. "Thanks," Mark said.

The shed had been set up as a makeshift headquarters. There were more than a dozen men inside, half of them wardens, rangers or sheriffs, with badges on their chests and walkie-talkies on their belts. The other men could have been hunters the way they looked, lounging back in their chairs in plaid shirts and heavy boots, talking low. There was a pot of coffee on the wood stove. A deputy sheriff with a Butch Cassidy mustache leaned against the wall, phone cradled to his ear, taking notes in a small green notebook.

Rob stood in the middle of the room, his back turned. He hadn't seen Mark come in. He stood with the sheriff, a man of fifty with big cheeks, black-rimmed glasses and a big pistol at his belt. The two men examined a survey map that had been tacked up to the wall. The map had been broken up into sections by different colors of magic marker.

Mark didn't move any closer. Rob squinted at the map, hands on the small of his back, trying to understand what it was he was looking at. He looked pale and cold, his hair was dirty and sticking out in all directions, his boots and the lower third of his trousers were caked in mud from his all-night search. His face seemed haunted; it had a quality of eerie power that Mark had never seen before.

"We're going to use all the men we've got," the sheriff said. "We'll cover as much territory as we can." The sheriff gestured to the map with a thick finger. A walkie-talkie crackled somewhere behind him. "There are a lot of logging roads all through here, some old cabins, it's very possible that the girls found one of them and spent the night up there . . . I'm going to send you up there in a truck with one of the Forest Service people. He knows the roads up there like the back of his hand."

"But what about helicopters?" Rob said. His voice was edgy. He ran his slightly trembling hand over his dirty hair. "It would seem to me that if we could get up in a helicopter so we could see, it would be much faster."

The sheriff crinkled up his nose, pushed his glasses in place, looked at his watch. "The copters should be in the air already," he said. "And there's a man coming up from the Hoback who's got some tracking dogs, and if you could get us some item of the girl's clothing so we could pick up a scent . . . almost anything would do. These are really super animals." The sheriff picked up one of the magic markers lying on the windowsill, began to play with it, glanced sideways at Rob.

Rob must have felt Mark's presence because he turned then, gazed absently at Mark. For a second it was as if Rob hadn't seen him at all. Mark nodded carefully. Rob seemed almost contemplative, and then the muscles in his face pinched, Mark was sure Rob was going to say something, but he didn't, turning abruptly to the map.

"I don't understand what you're telling me," Rob said. "What about these pilots? Are they any good? A good pilot could take us right up these canyons."

The wood stove was burning hot; Mark could see the waves of heat radiating up at him.

"They're good, Mr. Campbell, as good as they come." The sheriff snapped the top back on the magic marker. "One thing, Mr. Campbell, you know it's part of our job in a situation like this to consider everything." He pushed in on the bridge of his black-rimmed glasses again. "Something we always like to know in a situation like this is what the girl was like, what she'd be likely to do. Whether she might have been troubled in any way."

"She was as happy as any little girl could have been," Rob said, his voice suddenly hard as metal.

"We have to consider everything," the sheriff said. "We wouldn't be doing our job if we didn't ask."

Mark suddenly felt dizzy and a little sick. He turned, made his way to the door and then outside.

Ike Watkins still stood at the hitching rail, talking with some of the foremen from the other ranches. Ike saw Mark come out of the shack and he kept his eyes on him. Mark went over to join them.

"Hey, Mark," Ike said. His voice was gentle.

"Hey," Mark said. The other men nodded to Mark. A hawk-faced little man with a two-day growth of black beard offered Mark a Styrofoam cup full of coffee. "No, thanks," Mark said. "I don't suppose anybody's heard anything."

"Not really," Ike said.

"Draggin' the lake, that's what they should be doin'," said one of the men, a strapping young guy with a sour face.

"One thing I heard over the police radio," said the hawk-faced man, "they say there was some guy hanging around down at the schoolyard in town yesterday, some big guy, three hundred pounds, cruising around in a yellow convertible." The hawk-faced man spoke with a high, reedy voice.

Ike spat on the ground, nudged the spot with the toe of his boot. "Now, Tray, you know better than that. Nobody knows that. Rumors like that are always going around."

"Maybe so, maybe so, but they're looking for the car, one of the deputies told me."

"No, that ain't it," Ike said. "They're up there." Ike nodded toward the mountains, where the morning mists still hung below the tops of the ridges. "Somewhere. It's just a question of us getting to them in time."

"You ever been on one of these searches before?" Mark asked.

"Yeah, a few," Ike said.

"And what happened?"

"Some succeed, some don't. You hope you get lucky."

"She'll be all right, won't she?" Mark said. "It's summer, she's probably just sleeping out under some tree."

"Yeah, probably," Ike said. Ike looked at Mark, his eyes still gentle, but wondering a little now. "Only bad thing is the rain. The rain can make it bad."

A door banged shut. They all turned back to look. Ann Harrison had just come out of the house and there were three women with her, staying close. She was distraught, wild-eyed, dressed only in a bathrobe and slippers. The three women held her up, trying to comfort her and a large, red-faced man with a gimpy leg and a ten-gallon hat scuttled across the yard to meet her.

Mark looked back at Ike, blinked his eyes, tried to smile. "There are a lot of people here," Mark said.

"Well, they still do that in this valley. People have been on the phone a lot of the night. Something like this, it changes things. Some of the people you see out here, some of the old-timers, they haven't spoken to each other for a couple of years, cuz some of them fight over a fence line or lost cattle or some damn thing, but somebody loses a child, that other stuff doesn't matter anymore. A lot goes out the window."

The door to the shed opened and four of the rangers came out, hitching up their belts, putting on their hats. Ike looked keenly at Mark.

"You talk to Barbara?"

"Uh-huh."

"Did she say how Jeffrey was?"

"I think she said he'd just gone to bed. This was maybe an hour ago."

"The kid was taking it pretty hard last night. As if he'd caused it somehow. But something like this, it's nobody's fault. But that's a tough thing to get through a kid's head."

Rob and one of the Forest Service men came out of the shed, strode out across the yard toward the trucks. Mark excused himself, moved quickly to catch up, grabbed Rob by the arm. Rob turned back, taken by surprise.

"Would it be all right if I came with you?" Mark said.

The Forest Service man was already up in the driver's seat of the truck. "Sure," Rob said.

The Forest Service man was a short, squat man who drove the rutted back roads with a sullen, one-handed nonchalance. Rob made no effort to speak, conserving what energy he had, drawing into himself. He sat stiffly, hands on his knees, staring blankly ahead like a quarterback staring from the bench in the fourth quarter of a game already out of reach. He didn't seem to question Mark's presence, or even particularly notice.

They bounced along a gravel road for four or five miles, past bald red hills, then turned up a steep grade onto a logging road, up into timber. Rob and Mark were thrown against one another, Rob grabbing Mark's arm to steady himself. Mark's eyes moved restlessly up and down the border of the woods, searching for some sign. Finally the Forest Service man pulled over to the side of the road.

"We'll start here," he said. He opened his door, swung down, waited for them. He offered no further explanation.

The area looked both desolate and unlikely. For the first hundred yards back from the road there were only stumps, low weeds and piles of brush.

The Forest Service man's instructions weren't much.

"What I thought we might do is search all along the road, check the ditches, check those piles out there . . ." He reached up and rubbed the corner of his eye lazily, looking sidelong at Rob, a little afraid of him. "Anywhere somebody might be likely to . . . You just use your judgment." He had let the sentence trail off, not willing to complete it. "Likely to dispose of a body," that's what he had meant to say. Mark didn't like the guy at all. This was the kind of guy who could get on your nerves.

The three men worked on their own, kicking through some brush in a hollow. It was obvious to him that Sarah wasn't here. It was a pointless charade. The Forest Service man had a stick and was poking it lackadaisically into a pile of brush like a man poking a haystack for rats. Rob had gone farther out than the other two and seemed to be wandering in a daze, like the homeless men you see wandering in the parks of large cities early in the morning.

The Forest Service man made a loop and began to meander back toward the truck. Mark watched him for several seconds, then stared down at the brown grass again. A bit of color in the weeds caught his eye, he felt his heart make one wild leap. For a second he was sure it was a girl's sock, but then, no, he saw it was only an empty beer can. He picked it up, drained it of the night's rain, crushed it, stuck it in his back pocket.

Mark wandered farther down along the ditch, scanning the field for more piles of branches, any pile big enough to conceal a child's discarded body. A red squirrel leaped across the open field a hundred yards ahead of him, heading for the safety of the trees.

Mark looked back. The Forest Service man leaned against the front fender of his truck, having a swig from his canteen.

Mark felt a quick clutch of anger. What they were doing wasn't just stupid, it was a nice piece of sadism, forcing them to imagine exactly what they most feared to imagine, that the two girls had been picked up, killed and dumped. It was the only point in searching a place like this; it was not a place where two lost girls would seek shelter from the rain.

The Forest Service man gave a sharp whistle and waved for them to come in. When they came in he had nothing more to say than that they had other places to cover. He wasn't very comfortable looking Rob in the eye.

For two hours they searched, stopping in a dozen different places. They searched through old campsites, grown-over roadbeds, more clear-cut fields, shepherders' shacks, under plank bridges. Twice they heard helicopters whirring overhead. The aimlessness of what they were doing grew more oppressive. The radio in the truck stayed silent.

Even though the three of them scarcely spoke now, it was as if they were all under one spell, all jerked around like puppets on a single string, all subject to the same erratic swings of emotion, moving from despair to hope to boredom. Some of the time it was as if they were floating, just going through the motions, almost as if they had lost track of what it was they were looking for. Mark started to get the eerie feeling that Rob was reading his mind, that he could read Rob's, it was getting rubbed that raw.

Mark began to play games with his mind, games like, "By the time I count to a hundred somebody's going to call on the radio and say that Sarah is safe." He would count the numbers off in his head, feeling as if he could will Sarah being all right, and then when he got to a hundred and there was no call he would say, "By the time I count to two hundred somebody's going to call . . ."

His imaginings became more and more real to him, the vision of a little girl curled up under a bridge, or a body pushed down by the fast current of the river, caught up in some piled debris. Even the absurdity of the three-hundred-pound child molester in the yellow convertible began to take hold. He tried to banish it from his mind, but it kept coming back. He turned over again and again everything Barbara had said, how it was somehow their fault, he found himself arguing with her, trying to convince her.

Two or three times he felt something behind him, turned to find Rob staring at him with a gaze so intense Mark didn't know if he was being looked at or looked through, with a gaze that could have been pure hatred.

After two hours of nothing the strain began to show. Trudging back across an open field, Rob and Mark had to wait as the Forest

Service man chug-a-lugged from his canteen. He paid them no mind, leaning back against the door of his truck, head back, eyes closed against the hot midmorning sun, his big belly moving up and down like a panting dog's. Tiny rivulets of water ran down from the corners of his mouth, wet the front of his shirt. Rob, beads of sweat standing out on his forehead, watched the man drink, never taking his eyes off him. Mark could feel Rob's contempt. When he was done, the Forest Service man held the canteen out to Rob. Rob made no move to take it.

"I know we're not going to find her like this," Rob said. The Forest Service man said nothing, just put the cap back on the canteen. "You know that as well as I do," Rob said.

"I'm not sure I know what you mean, Mr. Campbell."

"It's just damn ridiculous. She's not up here. I know my daughter. My daughter is not going to get in some car with a stranger."

"No one said she did." The Forest Service man wiped his mouth with the back of his hand, eyes guilty as a cat's. His thick face was beginning to color.

"Then why are we looking in all these damn brush piles? Can you tell me that? We were sent up here to look for a body and there is no body because my daughter is alive and she's . . ."

"We have to cover everything, Mr. Campbell. That's why we have a search." The Forest Service man's thick fingers were tight on the canteen, his face down. He was trying not to get riled.

"She's not here! Do you hear me? She is down there in one of those canyons . . ."

The Forest Service man looked up, a pained expression on his broad face. "They sent me up here, Mr. Campbell, to cover this area because I know it. Now, if you don't like it . . ."

Rob's voice began to rise. "I trusted you people, I assumed that you knew what you were doing, but now I see this whole thing is a fiasco, there's no organization, it's too slow, nobody is goddamned thinking and it's my daughter's life that's at stake here . . . I want to talk to your boss. I want you to get him on the radio."

The Forest Service man tossed his canteen lazily up on the seat of the truck. "Listen, my boss is busy, he's trying to find your kid."

Rob spun, slammed his open hand against the side of the truck. He put both hands on the side panel of the truck, his head slumped forward. Mark couldn't see if he was crying or not.

The Forest Service man, face flushed, looked at Rob, wiped his hands down the front of his shirt. "If you want, I can try and get somebody on the radio." His voice was gentle all of a sudden. Rob didn't move. "There's one more place on this road I want to check. It will only take a few minutes." He opened the door of the truck, waited for Rob.

The one last place he wanted to check was some fishing cabins down along the river. They wandered from cabin to cabin, peering into the dark, streaked windows, looking under the rotting porches. A rusting snowmobile sat near the rushing stream. In the dark outhouse there was a pile of blistered, rain-warped three-year-old girlie magazines.

The back door of one of the cabins was ajar and Rob banged it open with his shoulder; what was private property and what wasn't didn't matter anymore. Mark followed Rob in. Mattresses were stacked against the walls. In a bookcase there was a stack of *National Geographics* with rat droppings on them. There were sporting prints and a framed copy of "The Sportsman's Prayer" on the wall.

> And if I kill, dear Lord,
> Let me kill clean.

Over the fireplace was a mounted fish that stared down at them with great glistening plastic eyes.

It didn't look as if anybody had been there for years. Animals had gnawed through the walls in a couple of places. In the middle of one of the bare bedrooms was a pile of feathers where some bird had met its death. The feathers fluttered across the floor as Rob and Mark walked through. There was no sign of anyone. Rob finally sank down in an ancient stuffed chair.

"I'm sorry," Rob said.

"Sorry about what?" Mark said.

"I'm sorry I lost control back there."

"Come on, stop it."

Rob looked up at Mark, his hands gripping the arms of the musty chair. "At times like this I wish I were a better person."

"I don't know what you mean," Mark said.

"Something has happened to her, I know it."

"No, you're just scared, that's all."

"No, it's more than that. She's such a commonsense kid. The kind that always looks both ways before crossing the street, always has her clothes laid out for school the night before. Like a little grown-up. It's as if she thinks she's responsible for taking care of all of us."

Rob picked at the loose threads in the arm of the chair. He was trying hard to be very exact about what he was saying, very rational.
"Jeffrey's the impulsive one, it's Jeffrey we're always having to pull
out of scrapes. You know the things that go through a parent's
mind, you think about if one of your kids ends up in real trouble,
which one will it be . . ."

Rob just stopped talking, staring motionless for several seconds,
and then suddenly lifted his left hand in a fist and brought it down
on the arm of the chair with all his might, letting out a terrible cry.
He covered his face with his hands. Mark felt the tingling of shock
go through his whole body.

"I just can't believe it," Rob said. "I've never felt so goddamned
helpless in my life. As long as you have kids there's this little knot
of feeling you carry around with you, all the time you're wondering, is my kid safe, is my kid all right? The feeling never goes away.
No matter how much you want to break out, no matter how
screwed up or crazy your own life is, you try to protect them, to
give them a sense that this world is an O.K. place to be. Barbara
and I have tried, Christ, we've tried, no matter what it looks like,
and for this to happen . . ."

"You don't know that anything's happened," Mark said. His tone
was almost brutal and it made Rob look up. "She's going to be fine.
We're going to find her."

Rob's eyes shone with emotion. He was soft now, drained of rage.
"I hope you're right," he said.

"I am right," Mark said.

"I want to tell you how much I appreciate your coming out . . ."
Suddenly there was a flicker of trouble in his eyes. "How did you
hear about it?"

It was no time for Mark to tell a lie. "Barbara called me."

"This morning?"

"Yes."

"Ah," Rob said, looking quickly down at the arm of the chair,
smoothing the loose threads with the heel of his hand. The note of
irony in his voice couldn't be perfectly stifled. The way he'd said
"Ah" was the way someone else might have said "Of course." It
took an edge off Rob's gratitude.

Mark stared out the window, saw the Forest Service man pull a
tarp off the back of one of the sheds.

Mark was the one who'd been the keeper of the secrets, the
holder of the trump cards, and he'd even had the ego to believe that

he was the one who understood, yet now he saw that he understood nothing. He had been blind as a mole, blind as Old Pew tapping his way down the road, and not because secrets had been kept from him. All the things he had missed were the simple things, the ABCs, like what parents loving their children was all about. It was as if he'd been living in a tunnel and spinning his theories of the firmament based on tunnel life, curved walls and no sky. It was a classic case of false extrapolation based on partial facts, a fool's game, and now all the walls were crumbling.

All those things Mark had believed about Rob he realized now were just what he had chosen to believe: that Rob was jaded, spoiled, too proud of his cleverness, an upper-middle-class liberal preppie snob, a smoothie. Mark had chosen to believe those things because it made being Barbara's lover a hell of a lot easier. Those things didn't matter anymore. Rob may not have been any better than Mark, but it wasn't clear that he was any worse, and if he had any chances for peace, for reconciliation with his wife, Mark had been doing them in. Everything had to be rethought, it was time to start over from zero.

Things like this were nobody's fault, Ike had said. Mark hoped that Ike was right. If Barbara was right, that she and Mark were somehow the cause of Sarah's disappearance, then everything ended. No woman could love a man she had to sacrifice a child for. Mark could never choose to be that man.

From somewhere outside came the sound of a muffled shot. The two men looked at one another.

"What was that?" Rob said.

"I don't know," Mark said. Mark moved to the window, saw the Forest Service man, the tarp collapsed around his feet, staring off toward the heavily wooded ridges that rose quickly on the far side of the stream. The Forest Service man was perfectly still, alert as a hunter. He waited for several seconds, listening, and then when there was no second shot, he began to jog heavily back to his truck. Rob was out of his chair now, looking over Mark's shoulder.

"What is he doing?"

"I don't know yet," Mark said. Together they went outside. Through the trees they could see the Forest Service man open the door of his truck, lunge across the front seat, wrest the speaker off his radio. Rob and Mark stood side by side on the back steps of the cabin, waiting, suspended. The Forest Service man got off the radio, stood up and looked back down through the trees. He waved for the two of them to come in, the gesture large and impatient, like a lifeguard waving swimmers in from rough water.

He rubbed his cheek, uncomfortable with what he had to say. "Somebody thinks they've found a piece of one of the girls' clothing." He glanced quickly at Rob. "That was what the shot was, someone signaling. You were right. It was up in the canyon. Get in and let's get going."

They headed up a rutted logging road. The Forest Service man drove hard, banging the daylights out of the truck, spruce branches swatting the roof. No one complained. They climbed to the top of a ridge and then headed back down into a canyon. As they came into a long clearing they saw the flash of light reflecting off the windshield of a couple of four-wheel-drive vehicles. Getting closer, bouncing over loose rock, they could see the saddled horses tied up, browsing on the low branches of the trees, and then they could see the circle of men. Someone knelt at the center of the circle.

Rob was out of the truck even before it came to a complete stop. He ran across the uneven ground, Mark right behind him. Mr. Harrison was on his knees in the center of the circle, holding his daughter. Brenda was dirty and sobbing, her hands clutching her father's hair.

One of the men in the circle stepped back to let Rob in. When Brenda saw Rob she shrank back as if expecting to be hit.

"Where is she, Brenda?" Rob's voice was eerily mild.

"It's not very far . . . uh . . . I don't know exactly, but it's not very far. I didn't want to leave her, but . . . uh . . . she slipped and there wasn't anything else I could do . . ." Brenda spoke in short, anxiety-choked gasps. Her father held her, never looking at Rob, just staring vacantly through the circle of men. "I mean, she couldn't walk . . . I had to get someone . . . she was so cold, I gave her my sweater . . ."

One of the rangers, a lanky man with a long Scandinavian face, took Rob by the elbow. "Come on now. We think we know where she is. We've got some men down there now. We're close, we know we are." Rob still stared at Brenda, at her father stroking her hair. It was just unfair. The ranger pulled Rob away. "Come on. She's told us all she can."

They walked together at march step, a phalanx of men, Rob and Mark, four of the rangers leading the way. They heard the frantic thudding of helicopter propellers over the canyon. They came to the dropoff, a steep quarter-of-a-mile bank of willow thickets and rubble that sloped down to a roaring, boulder-choked stream. There were men down there, moving cautiously to keep their balance on the treacherous incline. Dogs thrashed this way and that through the willows, searching for a scent.

Rob stood at the edge, stared down at the river. The other men's eyes were all on him. Mark could see the helicopter now, hanging motionless as a dragonfly over the water.

"The girl couldn't tell us exactly where it was that Sarah fell," the ranger with the long Scandinavian face said. "She did the best she could. You know how it is when kids get frightened, they can't remember things real well . . . It doesn't sound like it was that much of a fall, Sarah was all right, Brenda insisted on that, it sounds like it wasn't anything more than a sprain, but she had trouble moving, that was why the other girl went to get help . . ."

Rob's eyes kept scanning the endless rush of water. They could hear the dogs barking and whining below them.

The ranger kept talking, trying to keep Rob calm with a steady stream of information. "The only way we found her was that she had to cross the river and she didn't want to get her shoes wet. It's incredible after a night like they had, she was worried about getting her shoes wet. It just goes to show you, you never know what's going on in a kid's head. So she took her shoes off and tried to throw them across the water and she didn't make it. That's what we spotted. One shoe in the water."

Suddenly there was a shout off to their right. A young ranger stood at the top of the bank, a hundred yards away, waving for them to come on. As they headed toward him the young ranger ran to meet them.

"I think we've got something," the young ranger said. He took off his hat, wiped the sweat from his forehead. He was a big, strong, tanned, blond kid, looked like a California climber, and he was a little scared now, it showed. He had figured out that Rob was the father. "I think we've found some slide marks."

The young ranger led them back. The slide marks were something only a trained eye would have seen, a few faint scrapings in the gravelly soil, a couple of broken willow branches twenty feet down. The pitch was even steeper here than on the rest of the slope, broken up by a series of rock terraces. From where they stood it was impossible to see the river, though they could hear it roaring below.

Mark stood behind the others. Looking would do him no good.

He felt numbed, invisible. The older ranger knelt, examining the marks, running a handful of the gravel through his fingers. The young ranger watched him, almost bashfully, waiting for some sign that he had been right, that he had found what they'd been looking for.

The older ranger looked up. "Yeah," he said. "That's something."

"Let's go then," Rob said.

"Just hold your horses, Mr. Campbell. We're going to need ropes to go down in there. We don't need anybody else getting hurt." He turned to the young blond ranger. "Bobby, there's gear in my truck, get Emil to help you."

"I'm not waiting for ropes," Rob said. "That's my daughter down there."

"Now, hey, Mr. Campbell, I understand that, but get hold of yourself, if she's down there we're going to get her out."

The ranger tried to take hold of Rob in a comradely fashion, his hands on Rob's forearms, but Rob broke away from him and leaped down the bank, skidding on the gravel incline, grabbing hold of willow branches to keep from falling.

The ranger shouted at him. "Hey, mister, don't be crazy! You're going to get yourself killed!"

Mark went after him. He skied through the loose rock, using the willow branches the way a skier would use poles. A cascade of rubble came with him. Ahead of him Rob fell and got up quickly, stumbling forward. Mark almost caught up, staying with him like a shadow. The two men rushed headlong through a maze of willows, leaped down over the edge of one rock terrace, landed heavily on the next. Mark slipped and rolled over twice before he could stop himself. He felt blood ooze from just below his knee, soak through his pant leg.

He rose slowly to his feet, saw Rob stalking through the thickets ahead of him, intent as a hunter. For Mark everything was taking on the sharp edge of a hallucination, everything was too clear suddenly to be real. Mark heard the shouts of the men above them, irrelevant now as the sounds of flies on the outside of a window.

Rob stood on an outcropping of rock and scanned the thickets below them. Mark came up behind him. Rob never looked around. Mark stared down too, looked right where Rob had been looking and saw a child's white arm sticking out of some low sage. For one frozen moment there was nothing but Mark and that white motionless arm, and in that still moment he was convinced that she was dead, he was sure of it, and Rob hadn't seen her yet. In that moment he thought he was going to go mad, in that one moment he found himself making silent utterances, praying to a God he didn't even know if he believed in, "Make her be alive, God, let her live and I'll do whatever you want, I'll give up anything, I'll give up Barbara, just make her be alive again, show me, God, show me if you can . . ."

Then Rob saw her, gave a cry like an animal attacked suddenly in the night. Rob leaped down off the rock, stumbled forward through the willows, brushing aside branches, crying out words now, but not words that Mark could understand, and then Mark saw the fingers of the white still hand open up, reaching. He saw Sarah sit up, turn toward her father.

Rob bent over her, held her, rocked her. She was shaking all over. She clung to him. Over Rob's shoulder Mark could see the wide, scared look in Sarah's eyes. The scared look didn't go away even with her father rocking her.

Mark took a step forward. He felt a terrible compulsion to comfort this child, this man, he needed to be able to touch them.

"She's going to be all right," Mark said. "I know she's going to be all right." He reached out and put his hand on Rob's shoulder.

Rob jerked around to face Mark, still cradling his daughter. His face was tight with emotion. "Just leave us alone," he said. "For God's sake, can't you just leave me and my family alone?"

Mark never moved. Rob turned his attention back to Sarah, stroking her hair, holding her head to his chest. Mark felt a muscle in his cheek quiver, then quiver again. He heard the sounds of the helicopters, barking dogs, men shouting instructions. Mark looked up the bank and saw the rangers making their way down, a couple of them carrying a stretcher overhead. He looked back at the river. Light danced on the water, but the sound was like thunder. He put his hand on his cheek to still the tiny spasm of muscle.

CHAPTER TWENTY-FOUR

There was no time for pretense now. When a day passed and Mark hadn't heard anything, he called out to the ranch. Judy answered.

Judy didn't seem at all surprised that he'd called. Mark even had a suspicion that she'd been prepared to intercept the call. Sarah was doing fine, Judy said, better than they'd hoped. The doctor had been out to see her and had assured them that she was all right, that there would be no aftereffects. They had been lucky, the doctor said, to find her when they did, another hour and hypothermia would have worked its inevitable course, the body's core slowly freezing, the body's heat dissipating from the rain and exertion and night of falling temperatures. Another hour, the doctor said, and she would have been dead.

"And is Barbara all right?"

"Better." Mark heard the caution in Judy's voice. "It's been very hard over here, Mark," Judy said. "She's tired. I think she'll be a lot better when she's convinced that Sarah is really out of danger."

"But she *is* out of danger. The doctor said so."

"I know. But they want to take her to some other doctors to be sure."

"Other doctors? What kind of doctors?"

"I don't know, Mark, specialists, I guess. People Rob and Barbara know."

"Where are they going to get these specialists?"

Judy paused for a second before she answered. "They're going to take her back to New York."

"When?"

Judy was faltering in her task now. "I'm sure Barbara meant to tell you this herself."

"Judy, when are they going?"

"Sometime tomorrow."

"All of them?"

"All of them."

"That's crazy. The doctor said she was all right. They were going to stay the rest of the summer . . . and now they just pick up and go. . . ." Mark felt himself struggling to keep his voice under control. "I mean that's really nuts." There was nothing that Judy could say. "I'm coming over," Mark said.

"There's no one here now, Mark."

"I'm coming over anyway. I'll wait for them."

"No, don't. It wouldn't be a good time." There was real warning in her voice. Mark had never heard that tone from her before. Judy used to be his friend, now she was Barbara's shield, and she wasn't sure how far she could trust him.

"I'm not looking for a good time," he said. "I just need to see them."

"Mark, please. Don't come now. Give people a chance. If you come, come tomorrow."

"You tell them I'll be there then. So it won't be a surprise. Tell them I'm coming to say goodbye."

He had vowed to give Barbara up if Sarah was saved, but giving someone up wasn't the same as being abandoned. He needed to see her one last time. He wouldn't be able to end it, he told himself, unless he saw her just once more.

He didn't know if it was a miracle that had saved Sarah or if it had just been his own freeze of hysteria that had him convinced that Sarah was dead in the sagebrush in that first moment he saw her. What he did know was that he had vowed to give Barbara up, vowed with the most serious part of himself.

Rob and Barbara weren't leaving just for Sarah's sake. Mark knew that. Barbara had been looking for a way to pull back from Mark for a long time, it was just that Mark had been too blind to see it. She'd had more trouble finding time to see him, even to call him. It had gotten harder to reconcile the competing demands of children, husband and lover. Sarah was just the last straw.

Mark was going to make it easier for everybody. He was going to end it for her. That's what he thought as he drove up to the house.

A station wagon sat in the drive, back door open, and suitcases lined up on the ground. Mark loped across the familiar lawn, up the steps, knocked on the door. There was no answer. The door was open. Mark stepped inside.

Judy stood on a chair in front of the hall closet, a Valpack of clothes on her arm. Startled, she stepped down from the chair, stood erect and silent as a sentry.

"I did knock," Mark said.

"I know. I was just coming to answer," Judy said. The distance between them seemed immense. Boxes were strewn up and down the hallway. There was the sound of steps overhead. Both Mark and Judy looked up to see Barbara standing at the top of the stairs. Barbara came down without a word. Her face seemed puffy, her eyes tired and resigned. She didn't touch Mark.

"I just came to say goodbye," Mark said. Behind them Judy shook out the Valpack and disappeared down the hall.

Barbara regarded him evenly for a second and then said, "I have to take some things out of the dryer. Why don't you come with me?"

"Fine."

Mark followed her through the house. Passing through the kitchen Mark saw paperbags, plastic burger cartons and milkshake containers on the table. It seemed odd to see that kind of stuff in this house, Mark thought, but that's what everybody does on the last day, orders take-out to save a little time, the less bother the better.

The washer and dryer were in a small white room off the kitchen that had the vaguely acrid smell of cleaning fluids. Barbara worked quickly, emptying the dryer, sorting things out, folding them neatly.

"How is Sarah?"

"Sarah's all right. At least that's what this doctor tells us. She's upstairs sleeping now."

"I'm sorry."

"There's nothing you have to be sorry for," Barbara said.

"I'm sorry I didn't see where it would all lead."

"Nothing led to anything. What happened to Sarah was an accident. Here, help me with this."

She handed Mark one end of a sheet. Together they pulled it out, found the matching ends, folded it once, then twice. She took the sheet from him, gave it a last efficient snap.

"We told Sarah a hundred times what to do in case she thought she was lost. Not to move, to stay right where she was, if she had to move to move down, not up. She knew all that. Both our kids know better than that."

Barbara folded a pair of Rob's bright-blue running shorts. All the laundry was stacked in piles—socks, underwear, t-shirts—and all her remarks seemed framed, almost rehearsed. Everything was a little too neat.

"Sarah panicked. It was senseless, but senseless things happen all the time. There's no lesson to be drawn."

A sock had fallen to the floor. Mark bent down to pick it up. "Why are you leaving then?"

Barbara stacked the folded laundry in her arms. "We want to get Sarah back to New York and have some doctors look at her. Rob knows some very good people."

"I thought you said she was fine."

"She is. We still want to have her looked at."

"Whose idea was it? Yours? Or Rob's?" Barbara didn't say anything, her lower lip was trembling. She put the laundry down, turned away from him. Mark didn't know why he was doing what he was doing, he had come to give her up and now he was punishing her.

"If you were a parent maybe you'd understand."

"I understand all the same," Mark said. "Could I see her?"

"Of course. Come on." They left the folded laundry behind and went upstairs. Barbara opened the door to Sarah's room and Mark looked in.

Sarah was still asleep, her face resting in the crook of her arm. She had tossed her blankets half off and Mark could see the soft rising and falling of the sheet as she breathed. Mark watched the gentle, steady movement, as if to reassure himself. A little breeze stirred the white curtain and then died away. Mark felt Barbara watching him. He remembered his vow.

"We're not going away forever," Barbara said. "We'll be back."

"When?"

"You know we always come back. Every fall, I told you that. For the hunt. It's all part of the great Campbell white hunter tradition."

"This is going to be the last time I'll see you," Mark said.

She looked at him sharply. "Don't be ridiculous."

"When I saw Sarah lying there I thought she was dead. I was sure of it."

Barbara looked angrily at him for just a second and then her face softened. "I know. I've thought about that. About what you must have gone through."

"I made a promise then."

She didn't seem to hear him. She walked into the bedroom, pulled the blankets back up over Sarah. Sarah tossed her arm, but didn't wake up. Barbara tiptoed back out of the room. She felt Mark as some sort of threat again.

"What sort of promise?" she said.

"You said yourself that you thought that you and I had caused it."

"That was the middle of the night," Barbara said. "I didn't know what I was saying."

"No?"

"No," she said. She pulled the door to Sarah's room shut behind her.

"I don't understand you," he said. "I don't understand whose side you're on. I came here to end it, to say goodbye, I don't want to hurt anyone anymore, and you, you're going away, you're running out and still you won't let it end . . ."

Barbara leaned back against the door of her daughter's room. She raised her eyes to meet his, her face lit with an ironic, shamed smile. "I suppose that's what they call wanting to have your cake and eat it too." Suddenly her eyes darkened. "I guess I'm not ready to release you yet."

She was suddenly crying, noiselessly, and he held her to him. All the muscles in her back were taut, she would not give in to his embrace, and in that moment Mark would have broken any promise to have her back.

"Let's go out. I can't say goodbye to you here. Let's go out for a walk," Mark said.

"I can't. Rob will be coming back any minute." Her face seemed shattered now.

"Is there anything I can do for you?" he said.

She looked around wildly, like a swimmer struggling for air. "No. I don't know. Mark . . ." She reached out and touched his face and, on the touch, pulled back, forbidding herself. "You see? You see why I have to go?"

The phone rang downstairs, rang twice. Mark heard movement below them. Judy must have heard them, heard at least a part of it.

"Yes, I know what you can do for me," Barbara said, reining her voice in, getting back in control. She picked up a pile of books from a stand in the hall. "These are Sarah's books. If you could take them back to the library for us. They're a day or two overdue, I don't think it's more than that. You know how there's always too much to do when you're leaving."

"Sure."

He took the books from her. There was *Julie of the Wolves,* a Nancy Drew mystery, and *The Mixed-Up Files of Mrs. Basil E. Frankweiler.*

"Barbara?" It was Judy, calling from downstairs.

"Yes?"

"It's for you. It's Rob. He's still in town."

"Tell him I'll be right there."

Together Mark and Barbara walked down the stairs. They stood together at the front door, looked out across the pastures at the sharp, polished pinnacles of the Tetons, the scudding clouds above them.

"They're beautiful, aren't they?" Barbara said. "When something's beautiful, nothing can really change it." It was the kind of remark that, at another time, Mark would have argued with her about. Without looking Mark could tell that Judy was in the hallway, watching them, he could feel her wary, protective presence.

He leaned over and kissed Barbara lightly on the cheek, then moved quickly down the steps. He tossed the books in his car, they bounced across the front seat. Barbara hadn't gone to answer the phone, she was still standing on the front porch. This was not how he'd meant it to end. He drove off in confusion, left without an ending, only with an errand, the chance to save her a few cents' fine.

CHAPTER TWENTY-FIVE

What made it impossible was that there was no one to talk to. He was grieving and yet there was no way he could declare his grief.

He felt as if the breath had been knocked out of him. He found himself swallowing all the time. He had no energy to run, to work, to do anything. He found himself disgusted by his lassitude. He imagined how Barbara would have mocked him for his self-pity. She would have mocked him right out of it.

He still inserted her reactions into things. When he passed a gallery window full of sentimental western paintings he imagined the pleasure she would have taken laughing over them.

He knew what he had to do but he couldn't do it. What he had to do was accept the fact of it being over, come to terms. It was not a very good deal; one fact he had to accept, another he had to abolish, the fact that he still loved her. He was haunted by her. He had no photograph of her, and when he tried to picture her face in his mind he couldn't do it. He tried to call back her mouth, her nose, her eyes, the way she smiled, and there were times he could almost do it, but not quite.

There were good days and there were bad. One of the worst was the day he got a postcard from her in the mail. It didn't say much, just that Sarah was doing fine and she hoped that he was doing well too. Just the sight of the familiar free-flowing hand was enough to break everything open again. Their love was a baited trap, it was never going to get better, he saw that now. He was very angry. She shouldn't have written him at all.

That night Mark wandered the streets of Jackson, city of motels. Everywhere there were the blinking VACANCY–NO VACANCY signs, coin laundries, families out looking for a place to get ice cream. Around ten-thirty the theaters let out and the young actors, flushed from their performance and still in makeup, stood in the doorways singing show tunes. Young, dirty and exhausted climbers clumped along the boardwalk paying no attention. A young woman in Pappagallo pumps sat at a table in Peppermint Park eating a banana split and reading *Creative Divorce*, the title page bent back so the dude ranchers at the next table couldn't see.

Mark wandered for hours, speaking to no one, wandering till the streets were deserted except for a kid he found curled up half-asleep in the back of a pickup. The kid was nineteen and worked at one of the ranches. He was waiting for his buddy to show up and drive him home. His buddy was off with some woman he'd met at the Cowboy. Mark sympathized. Jackson can be a hard town when you're on your own, he said to the kid.

Mark discovered that the worst thing he could do was to lay around the house, wondering where Barbara was right then, what she was thinking, if she was up or down, wondering how she would go on with her marriage, whether she would take another lover. If he stayed in the house his mind inevitably began to turn over every event of the summer like a mad person might finger an amulet. He began to stay away from the house as much as he could.

One day he took the boat across Jenny Lake with all the tourists and hiked up into Cascade Canyon. Starting out, Mark passed people in Chevy hats and GET HIGH ON THE TETONS t-shirts and cameras swinging from their necks. A family of six was strung out along the trail, the white-haired grandmother gamely bringing up the rear, leaning heavily on her stick. Chipmunks darted in and out of the rocks. A pair of heavy middle-aged women with their pant legs rolled up sat together on a rock, eating bananas, faces to the sun, rested and happy.

It didn't take long before Mark was breathing hard. He wasn't in very good shape. The trail followed the stream and its banks of moss and ferns. On the switchbacks Mark could look down and see cowboy hats of other hikers gleaming below him. Everyone he passed on the trail said hello, two or three told him where he could see a moose feeding half a mile on. The rush of water was like an endless wind below him. Mark began to feel the mountains folding around him, he began to get some of the old exhilaration back, the old sense that he was getting to the heart of things.

He knew suddenly that he was going to be all right. Everything that had happened to him didn't matter, it had all been blown massively out of proportion. He broke into a field of yellow flowers. Looking up at the clouds passing over the high peaks, it seemed as if the mountains were moving, were about to fall in on him. Mark walked on for another half hour, scarcely conscious of himself. He was happy for the first time in a long time, he had almost forgotten what it felt like.

When he stopped finally for a drink and a rest he realized he was more tired than he thought he was. He lay on a rock for twenty minutes and then headed back. The clouds were coming in more quickly now over the peaks and it looked like it could rain. He felt the prickly beginnings of blisters on his feet.

Halfway down, a young woman ran past him. She was tanned, attractive, in perfect shape, a hard body, and she was running all the way down. When Mark got to the bottom she was there, lounging on the dock, her eyes on a young man in cutoffs swimming in the shallow water. He was as proud-bodied as she was, showing off for his chubby girlfriend, who sat smiling on the dock with their packs. He dived, came back up, smoothed back his long, black hair. His stomach muscles were tight and perfect. The tanned young woman was doing little things to get his attention, kneeling to splash water on her face, then stretching her tan legs out on a wooden bench, posing while trying to look like she wasn't, her sunglasses set up in her sun-bleached hair. The boy was too absorbed in his own preening to notice her. The two narcissists cancelled each other out. Everybody else, sad-faced and exhausted from their hiking, sat like lumps in the boat, waiting to be driven across.

The sun had come back out and glistened on the blue water. It should have been beautiful, maybe it was, but Mark suddenly felt the beauty mocking him. It felt hollow, this beauty, it was all surface, all fleeting, full of false revelations. There was no answer here, it was all tease. Mark felt incredibly alone. It wasn't mountains that he needed now.

At about noon the next day Mark drove into town. He found a place to park in front of the old stone church. Hands in his pockets, he moved quickly up the cobbled walk.

Mark stepped into the dim hallway. The swinging glass doors to the rehearsal hall were still shut. There were a half-dozen mothers waiting. At least one of the mothers recognized him and gave him a leery and knowing look. Jackson was finally a very small town. People kept up on who'd been mistreating whom. Mark stared through the glass doors at the young dancers and at Ellen. They were still dancing to the same slightly off-key Debussy. Her classes still went overtime.

After about ten minutes the music stopped and the children came pouring out to greet their mothers. Ellen was still inside, answering questions, and when she finally came out into the hallway she was absorbed in a conversation with an animated, spidery, little dark-haired girl. Ellen's short blond hair was damp and curled from per-spiration, her face glowed from her workout. She hadn't seen Mark yet. Something the spidery little girl said made Ellen laugh. Mark stepped forward, drawn in by her unconscious grace, the dignity with which she held herself.

"Ellen?"

Ellen turned and faced him. Mark saw the uncertainty in her face, saw it tighten into anger. She looked away, patted the dark-haired student on the shoulder, cutting her off midsentence, saying goodbye. Ellen grabbed her sweater off a hook behind the bench, her motion precise, defined, and walked through the door into the sunshine, never looking back, never wavering.

Mark didn't go after her. What had happened was only his due.

Two days later Mark got up a little after seven and got into his running clothes. He drove out to South Park and stopped his car in some cottonwoods along the road. It was a long shot but it paid off. He'd been waiting about fifteen minutes when he saw Ellen come jogging around the corner. She didn't seem to notice his car. She was a hundred yards ahead of him before he got up enough nerve to get out of his car and start after her. It was a hundred yards more before she turned back to see who was running after her. She slowed up to wait for him, running in place, even though the look on her face wasn't much more welcoming than it had been two days before.

"Hi."

"Hi."

"I was wondering if you still ran out here," Mark said.

"Well, now you know, don't you?" she said.

They ran side by side. On one side of the road there were cattle grazing, on the other were the small ranch-style homes that Mark disliked so much, with their buck-rail fences, campers and snowmobiles.

"You still see Rey out here in the mornings working on his fence?" Mark said.

"No," Ellen said. "He finished. A month ago." Ellen set a fast pace, Mark had to stretch out a bit to stay at her shoulder. "You shouldn't have come out here, Mark."

"I didn't know how else I could get to see you."

"No? I didn't know you were worried about that. It's a little late, isn't it? Just when I'm almost used to it. Running by myself."

A small black dog came tearing out of one of the driveways, barking ferociously. Mark stopped for a second, pried the biggest rock he could find out of the gravel. The dog seemed to remember Mark and stopped, still surly, keeping up his barking until they were well past.

"I needed to talk to you," Mark said.

"To me? You're sure?"

Without losing stride, Mark flung the rock far out over an open stretch of pasture. "I needed to talk to someone."

Ellen kept looking straight ahead, but Mark could see the flickerings of hurt in her face. "Can't we finish this first?" she said. "I don't like to talk when I run."

When they finished their run they were standing in front of Ellen's house. They were both breathing hard. Mark bent down, touched his toes. Ellen wiped her forehead, watching him warily, then delicately tapped the wooden gate.

"I think it would be best if I just went in now," she said.

"I've got to talk to you, Ellen."

"Mark, you don't have to explain anything to me."

"No, I do have to explain. To somebody."

She opened the wooden gate, then looked back over her shoulder at him. "You'd better come in then," she said. "It's ridiculous to be standing out here in the street."

Everything looked the same. The childish drawing by Ellen's niece was still taped inside the front door, the hanging plants were still arranged in front of the bright windows, the battered milk pitcher with wild flowers in it still sat in the middle of the dining-room table. Somehow Mark had expected that there would have been some sign of change. The impact of all those familiar things made Mark ill-at-ease. Ellen went into the kitchen to make them coffee.

They sat at the dining-room table in their sweaty running clothes, fingering coffee cups.

"So," she said. "You need to talk to me. What about?"

"About the summer. About what happened."

"I hope you don't think you're doing this for my sake."

"No, I don't think that."

"I know what happened. There's nothing to explain. If some-body's not in love with someone, it's too bad, but there's nothing to say, really. You wanted to hang around with a little faster crowd. It flattered your ego . . ."

"Maybe."

"I hope you had fun at least."

"Not particularly."

His answer seemed to soften her tone. "I heard about Sarah get-ting lost," Ellen said. "That must have been awful."

"It was awful. I caused it."

"Caused it? What do you mean, you caused it?"

Mark said nothing. Ellen got up and walked to the window, snipped some dead leaves from one of the plants. She was begin-ning to understand. "I don't like those people," she said. "I never did. I never trusted Barbara Campbell."

"No?"

"No. What about you?"

Mark set down his coffee cup, leaned forward, elbows on the table. "I loved her."

Ellen looked as if she had just been slapped across the face. For a second neither of them moved. Ellen crushed the dead leaves with her fingers, let the pieces drop to the floor.

"You really think you're something, don't you?" she said. "You really know how to make a person feel great. Just terrific." Her face went into a pout, her chin trembling as if she was about to cry. "What sort of thing is that to say? Why are you telling me this?"

Mark stood up from his chair. "Because I feel like I'll go crazy if I can't talk to someone about it and I've got no one else to tell. I know. What's crazy is my coming to you. If you don't want to listen to me, that makes sense. If you want to throw me out, that's fine. Honest to God, Ellen."

"Sit down," she said. She gestured impatiently to him. The morning light pouring in from the window behind her made it hard to read her face. "Go on, sit down. Of course I'll listen to you."

He told her then, as best he could. He got tangled up, inevitably softening things in order not to be hurtful, but he persisted, staying as close to the truth as he dared. He told her about how he had been drawn to Barbara, why he had kept on, what it had called up in him.

He let himself say all kinds of things. Talking about Barbara he was also talking about Ellen, saying more than he had ever said before, about what his feelings had been for Ellen and how things went wrong. A lot of it hurt her, a lot of it made her angry, Mark could tell, but she held her tongue, until out of the blue she said, "You just got tired of me, didn't you?" When she said that Mark's first thought was that she hadn't understood anything he'd been saying.

He was as honest as he dared to be. He told her about Kate and Michael, about the way concealment worked on all of them, about Mark's final demand for openness, about the moment at the Indian museum when Mark and Barbara turned and saw Jeffrey staring down at them from the top of the stairs. The one thing he didn't tell Ellen about was the prayer he had uttered on the side of the mountain. He didn't know if it was because he thought she wouldn't believe him or because he thought, of all the mad things he was telling her, that was the maddest.

He never said a word against Barbara the whole time. He remained loyal, after a fashion, knowing that just the fact of his telling was a kind of betrayal. Barbara had trusted him to protect her and now he was breaking that trust, yet telling was the only way he had of understanding what had happened to him.

When he was finished talking, Ellen said, "Why did you tell me this?"

"Because I couldn't stand going on the way I was. Because I'm ashamed. I don't know."

"You were in love with her."

"Yes."

"Are you still?" Mark couldn't answer. He leaned back in his chair, his long legs stretched out in front of him. His muscles felt stiff and cramped from their run. He reached out and picked up his empty coffee cup. There was no way he could answer her question. She asked another. "What was it about her that you liked?"

He spoke slowly, carefully. "I think that she's smart. And kind.

We disagreed about a lot of things. I think she's a generous person."

"She doesn't sound like a generous person to me," Ellen said. "To have done all the things she's done to her family."

"That's not fair," Mark said.

"Isn't it? You're still trying to protect her."

"I'm trying to tell you what she was like."

"I'm too mean, aren't I? To me she sounds like a desperate woman in a bad marriage, she doesn't have that much to lose. She's out to get what she can . . ."

Mark stared at her. It had been idiotic, telling her anything at all. Suddenly he hated her. The two of them were too different, this was why they could never get along before. She would never understand him.

"Were you that unhappy with me?" Ellen said suddenly, tears welling in her eyes.

"No. It had nothing to do with that," he said.

"You're so intelligent. I don't see how she could fool someone like you. It just makes me angry."

"She didn't fool me. Maybe it was wrong, maybe it was evil, but she didn't fool me."

"You sound so proud of it," she said. "You tell me that you're ashamed, but you're not. You're full of all these contradictions. They sound like disgusting people to me. The way I feel now, it's as if I don't understand you at all. How you could keep it hidden all that time."

"I thought you must have suspected."

"I never did. I had no idea. I don't know how I could be so far off about someone. I don't see how you could say it was good. Maybe it's that I'm not smart enough. Didn't she ever think of her children in all this?"

"She loves her children."

"How can you say that, Mark?" Ellen stood up again and began to pace the room. "I'm sorry. Maybe my imagination is just too limited, but I don't see how cheating can be good, how running around on your husband can be good. What you did, you had a fling. Now you come here to tell me about it and you want me to listen and agree how wonderful and sad it was. How special and doomed. I just don't think you have any right to go around treating yourself as if you're doomed."

"But maybe I am."

"I feel sorry for that little girl. Maybe I just see things too simplistically, but don't people like that ever think about their children? Oh, God, Mark . . ." She was weeping now. "I just feel so sorry for you."

CHAPTER TWENTY-SIX

Mark didn't see Ellen again for two weeks. He had no line on what their talk might have meant or where it could lead. He wasn't even sure that he wanted to see her again. The next time he saw her it was an accident, on the first day of school.

The first day of school was a lot more pleasurable than he thought it would be. He squelched the inevitable wise guy in the senior English class, the kids laughed at his jokes and even seemed to pay attention to some of the other things he had to say. His spirits rose.

He even found himself a little unreasonably happy to see people, as if being with people satisfied some suppressed and unacknowledged craving. He glad-handed old friends in the noisy hallway between classes, even found himself sitting contentedly in the teacher's lounge with Jack Bertram, the school's most notorious bore, listening to Jack's long and exaggerated stories of his summer climbing in Utah. Old patterns reasserted themselves; with no effort he fell back into a pattern of outrageous flirtation with Torrey Peck, the principal's secretary.

At the end of the day Mark was feeling good and a little exhausted, senses blitzed by the sound of banging lockers and hallways echoing with keyed-up adolescent chatter. He wiped his blackboard clean, handed in his class lists at the office. He ambled through the near-empty hallways, past the trophy cases, pushed open the door and stepped out into the autumn sunshine. Ellen was coming out of another door.

"Hey," Mark said. "What are you doing here?"

She had her dance bag over her shoulder. "I'm teaching here." She smiled at him. He could see no trace of anger in her, just a slight awkwardness.

"No kidding?"

"No kidding."

School buses were lined up at the curb and kids hung out the windows shouting to their friends. There was the thud of a football being kicked and then the crash of branches as the ball landed in a tree. Kids stood around, looking a little stiff and self-conscious in their new clothes. Five or six girls stood in a circle, their books pressed to their chests, pretending to ignore the boys tossing the football around in the street. A couple of freshman boys wobbled down the street on their bikes, ignored by everyone. The senior fullback, a big kid named Cork Billington, lounged against his car, holding court.

"I'm just teaching part-time," Ellen said. "Dance for a couple hours a day and then the drama club."

"That's great. I had no idea."

"It came through this summer." The note of reproach in her voice was mild enough.

"Which way you going?" Mark said.

"I'm walking home," she said.

They headed up the sidewalk together. The group of girls separated to let Mark and Ellen pass, smiling shyly.

"I could give you a lift," Mark said. She looked quickly at him, not answering. "A ride home," he said. "A perfectly innocent offer."

She smiled, swung her dance bag off her shoulder. "Sure," she said, "that would be fine."

They crossed the street to his car and he went around and opened the door on her side. As he closed the door after her, a football bounced crazily in the street in front of them. Mark picked it up and threw an underhand spiral back to the waiting kids. When he got into the car Ellen was sitting stiffly with her dance bag on her lap. She was still wary of him. It occurred to Mark that she could be disgusted by him; confessing to somebody was no guarantee they'd like you for it. He was as wary as she was. They rode for a couple of blocks without speaking.

"So how was your first day?" Mark asked.

"All right. Not what you'd call great. These kids are a lot harder to teach than ten-year-olds, I'll tell you."

"Really? Why is that?"

"Oh, I don't know. They just seem so silly and self-conscious. They get it into their minds that they can't do something and all they can do is giggle about it."

"I guess that's what it's like being a teen-ager."

They slid past an old man raking the leaves off his curb. There was a smoldering pile of leaves in the street.

"These kids are so damn skittery, they panic, you know? Sometimes I think what people call stupidity isn't anything more than fear. That if people could just calm down they could understand just about anything."

"How was *your* first day?" she said.

"Fine. First days always seem nice to me. It's always nice to start with a clean slate."

She smiled, then looked away, out the window. Her face, lit up by the afternoon sun, had turned suddenly pensive. Mark thought of her standing on her porch on a summer night, staring out into the dark, Patrick standing behind her.

"You ever see Patrick?" Mark said.

"Patrick? A few times, I guess. What about you?"

"Not at all," Mark said.

She looked over at Mark. "What are you looking so strange for?"

"I know it's none of my business . . ."

Her eyes widened in surprise. "Patrick? I've seen him, but I'm not *seeing* him. Is that what you were asking?"

"I guess it was."

"That's really ridiculous," Ellen said. Mark stopped the car in front of Ellen's house. She opened the door and started to get out. "Thanks for the ride," she said.

"Ellen?"

"Yes?"

"You wouldn't be interested in having dinner, would you? Next week sometime? Tuesday, say?"

Mark saw her face suddenly fall. She wrapped the straps of her dance bag around her fist. "No," she said. "I can't. I'm busy Tuesday." She tried to pull off a polite smile. "Thanks anyway." She stepped out and slammed the car door behind him. Mark watched her walk toward her house, then run the last few steps. Mark cursed himself. He had been clumsy. One of his students could have done better. The whole thing had been strictly high school.

He saw her around school, but he didn't try to seek her out. When they talked everything seemed perfectly friendly, on an even keel. He didn't know if there was something more that he wanted from her, but he was alert to her and she was alert to him too, he was sure of it. He threw himself into his teaching and three nights a week he played basketball in the school gym with some of the other teachers. He left as little extra time in his life as possible.

There were still times when he desired Barbara, times when he dreamed of her and would wake up trembling, dreamed dreams in which he and Barbara would have conversations just like they would have had in real life. Twice he drove out to the ranch and at the last moment was too afraid to go in, just turning his car around and driving all the way back into town, enraged at himself.

Then one day after school Mark ran into Ellen in the hallway. She seemed harried and distraught and there was a smear of white paint on her jeans.

"Hey," Mark said. "How you doing?"

"Pretty terribly, thank you. It's this ridiculous school play. I don't know why I ever agreed to it. For three hundred extra dollars you're supposed to direct, build the sets, make the costumes. . . ." She ran her hand over her hair. "You don't want to hear all this, do you?"

"Tell me anyway."

"The kid who promised me he'd build the set has been out of school for two days to help his father put up hay and we're supposed to have the set up tonight so the actors can have one real rehearsal with it. There's not a kid down there who knows how to cut a board straight, somebody just fell into the birch-bark canoe and broke it, and the janitor is telling us we have to be out by eight o'clock. It's total chaos . . ."

"But you're not nervous," Mark said, trying to tease her out of it.

"Of course I'm nervous."

"You shouldn't be. Hey . . ." Mark said.

"Oh, I know what you're going to say. What do four hundred million starving Chinese care about your silly stage set . . ."

"No, come on, don't be so hard on me. Let's go down and take a look. I'd like to see this."

Mark and Ellen walked to the auditorium. A trio of demoralized kids sat cross-legged on the stage and the janitor was lecturing them. A redheaded techie perched on a ladder, adjusting the stage lights. The busted birch-bark canoe leaned against the back wall. There were piles of fresh lumber, bags of nails and hinges, several cans of paint. The few frames for flats that had been finished lay haphazardly across the stage floor. The kids roused themselves a bit when Mark and Ellen came in.

Mark stared at the scene. "You should have gotten Patrick," he said. "Patrick could have knocked this stuff out in no time."

"I tried Patrick. He wasn't in."

"Ah." Mark grinned. "Well then, I guess you're just stuck with me, aren't you?"

They worked three hours straight, right up until eight o'clock when the janitor came to kick them out. They built frames, braces, doorways, stretched muslin, they sawed and hammered and stapled. Seeing how hard Mark and Ellen worked, the kids revived, managed to patch up the birch-bark canoe and even do some painting. Once they realized that things were actually going to get done, the work became a pleasure, everybody got a little giddy. One of the kids went out and got Cokes and doughnuts and brought them back.

Mark and Ellen worked well together. If there was one thing that Ellen appreciated it was competence and, while Mark wasn't the greatest carpenter in the world, working for Patrick had at least taught him how to drive a nail with authority. There was nothing ineffectual or helpless about Ellen, she could do anything with tools that a man could do, and she was fast. They worked as a team and Mark could feel that he was rising in her estimation. The kids were noticing too. High-school kids were always looking for that kind of stuff, who had a crush on whom, and if it was teachers, it made it just that much better. They picked up on the new warmth between Mark and Ellen, Mark could tell from their sidelong looks.

It was a little after eight when they walked out of the high school. It was dark and a cold wind rattled leaves along the street. Ellen and Mark walked down the sidewalk, neither of them speaking. Mark carried Ellen's toolbox that she had brought from home to use for the set-building. When they got to Mark's car Ellen said, "Would you be up for getting something to eat?"

"Sure," Mark said.

They went to one of the downtown restaurants and ordered hamburgers, set Ellen's toolbox down on a third chair. There were only a half-dozen people in the whole place. The whippet-thin manager and the white-shoed waitress with platinum blond hair sat at a table in the front listening to a baseball game on the radio. Now that it was fall and the tourists were gone, some of the restaurants had a rough time staying open.

Their conversation moved effortlessly. What had seemed like a disaster earlier was just funny now; Ellen told Mark an animated version of the story about the kid tripping and landing right in the middle of the birch-bark canoe, the only gorgeous prop in the whole production. She acted out all the parts, down to the look on the face of the kid who'd built the canoe when he came trudging up from the shop and saw what had happened to his masterpiece. Ellen and Mark both laughed, interrupting each other with details of their afternoon. Talking about the kids made it easy.

Mark could tell that things were changed between them. He had forgotten how funny Ellen could be when she was really relaxed. Certain things began to come back to him. He began to remember why he had been attracted to her.

Afterwards they walked out into the cold night air. They headed back toward her house, neither of them speaking much for the first couple of blocks. Mark shifted the toolbox from his left hand to his right.

"You know what I feel sort of funny about?" Mark said.

"What's that?"

"Talking to you. The way I did. Telling you everything. I'm sorry. I shouldn't have done it. It wasn't very fair."

"No, it was all right. It's always better to know something than to know nothing. Even if I didn't seem too appreciative then." She saw that Mark was about to say something. "We don't have to talk about it anymore," she said.

They walked under a street light, their shadows switching suddenly from behind them to in front of them, swaying a little as the night wind rocked the overhead lamp.

"I was thinking I'd like to be able to see you," Mark said. She was quiet, her hands jammed down in her jacket pockets to keep them warm. "What do you think about that?"

"You *are* seeing me."

"Oh, that word again. You know what I mean." They stood in front of her house. She reached out and took the toolbox from him.

"You know what I think about you?" he said. She suddenly looked alarmed. "I think that the fact that you're the only woman I know with a toolbox is very sexy." She laughed, but he could see that she was still tense. He ran his hand gently along the sleeve of her down jacket. He was filled with yearning for her. "You know what I'd like?" he said. "I'd like to come in for a little while."

"I don't think that would be a good idea," Ellen said.

"O.K." Mark leaned over and gave her a brief, chaste hug. Mark waited at the gate as she walked up to her door. She turned back.

"Mark?" she said.

"Yes?"

"Thank you for your help."

Mark went to the play. It was *Annie Get Your Gun,* and for a high-school production it wasn't bad. The canoe looked great, the sets were all painted and nothing fell down. If a few lines were dropped nobody minded, and at the end the audience of parents and brothers and sisters got up to give the performers a standing ovation. The kids pulled Ellen out onstage to take a bow with them.

Afterwards Mark went backstage. It was a mob scene, about half of Jackson seemed to be back there. Bouquets of flowers were everywhere, there were theatrical squeals of greetings and congratulations. The principal, a heavyset ex-coach in Hushpuppies, gladhanded everybody in sight. A lot of the kids were still in costume and makeup, some were embarrassed and trying to avoid their parents' praise, others were giddy with self-importance. The high-school musicians barged through holding instruments and music stands aloft. In all this Mark found Ellen. He touched her on the elbow.

"Pretty good," he said.

She turned and smiled warmly, instinctively reaching out to touch his arm. "Thanks," she said. The stage manager, a freckle-faced and slightly officious sophomore, ran past them, frantically trying to gather up costumes.

"It all worked out, didn't it?" Mark said.

"It did. With your help."

"Ellen! Oh, my God, Ellen, it was like Broadway!" A gaudy middle-aged woman, a local gallery owner and parent of twins, descended on Mark and Ellen. In tow behind her was her date for the night, an apologetic-looking and tweedy man with a pipe and ruddy Scottish cheeks. "What a job you and your little thespians did! I didn't know you could direct plays too, dear! She's a Renaissance lady, Ames, I tell you!"

Mark stepped out of the way. Mark didn't know why Ellen was always so patient with everybody. In the past it had irritated him, now it seemed like one of the reasons he was drawn to her. He was counting on some of that patience for himself. When things cleared out a bit, Mark found his way back to her.

"You know what I'm thinking of doing?" he said.

"What's that?"

"I'm thinking of having a party."

"That sounds nice." Ellen still had her public face on. Her tone was pleasant but guarded. "When?" she said.

The girl who'd played Annie Oakley stood only a few feet away, letting her little sister admire her costume but keeping her vixen eyes on Mark and Ellen, soaking it all in.

"I don't know," Mark said. "It's all in the planning stages. Next Friday, how does that sound? I'd invite a lot of people from school. What do you think?"

Someone blew on a faulty saxophone. Ellen waved back to someone who was motioning to her from the other side of the stage.

"It might be fun," Ellen said. "A friend of mine might be coming down from Missoula next weekend. You remember me talking about my friend Sally."

"Sure," Mark said. The little Annie Oakley never took her eyes off the two of them. Nothing was more irritating than the knowing looks of high-school juniors. A bunch of the young actors struck up a chorus of "You Can't Get a Man With a Gun."

"She might enjoy a party," Ellen said. "I'd like her to meet some people."

"Great then. Tell her she'll meet all kinds of people."

Ellen stared at the folded program in her hands. She was feeling crowded. "I'm not sure she's coming yet."

"There's no rush," Mark said. "We'll talk about it." He gave her a light kiss on the cheek. The young Annie Oakley's eyes widened. "I'll let you get back to your admirers. The lady was right. It was just like Broadway."

Over the next couple of days Mark started inviting people to his party. He was in an easy, buoyant mood. He waited until Tuesday night to call Ellen. He could tell from just the abrupt way she answered the phone that things were not so good.

"I hope I didn't interrupt anything," Mark said.

"I was watching something," she said. Mark was taken aback. She sounded pretty bitchy and tired.

"I'll let you get back to it then," Mark said. "I just called to let you know that the party's definitely on for Friday. I wanted to make sure you were coming, you and your friend."

"I don't know if Sally's coming or not," Ellen said. "She's supposed to call me tonight. If she comes down, we'll come to the party. If she doesn't, I won't."

"Oh," Mark said. "I guess that's making it pretty clear, isn't it? O.K., I'll let you get back to your program. You have a nice night." His tone had turned icy, offended. It wasn't clear that she picked it up.

"Good night," she said.

After he hung up was when he started to get mad. He wondered what the hell he was doing anyway, why he was pursuing her, if it wasn't love or even honest desire, just need. Maybe he still loved Barbara and maybe Ellen sensed that. The anger he felt toward Ellen also gave him the lowest opinion of himself. Maybe she was right to be so curt to him, maybe she knew he wasn't capable of being any more trustworthy than he'd been before, maybe she knew his motives better than he did. Why did her rudeness bother him so much? The fact that it wasn't like her enraged him even further. She was the person who was never rude to anyone, her politeness was one thing you could always count on. In his rage, he tried not to think of how large a hope he had come to invest in her. All it came down to, he tried to convince himself, was an unforgivable failure of manners.

The next day Mark walked into one of the school bathrooms between classes, and while he was standing at the urinal he looked over and saw carved on the wooden wall of one of the stalls, MR. ERICKSON PUTS THE WOOD TO MISS HARGREAVES.

Mark was furious. He tried to rub it out with the heel of his hand, but someone came in and gave him an odd look. Mark walked out of the bathroom, his face burning. So he and Ellen had become a school joke, it was there for everyone to see. Little did they know how wrong they were. He made a point of avoiding Ellen all that day at school.

There was no point in staying angry, however, if no one was going to notice. When he called her back that night he was going to tell her exactly what he thought. Whatever his intentions, he started out calmly enough.

"Hi," he said. "I just called to see if you'd heard from your friend. I wanted to find out if the two of you were coming to my party."

"Sally's decided not to come down this weekend."

"O.K.," Mark said. "Just one other thing. About the other night.

I'm sorry if I sounded a little cutting or cold or whatever. I'm sorry if I took you away from your program."

"It wasn't very good anyway," Ellen said.

"I guess I was a little angry," Mark said. She was silent, as if she knew what was coming. "I did invite you to a party. Whether your friend can come or not, that's not really the point. You accept or you don't, it's pretty basic stuff. To say you'll only come if your friend comes, that's a little weird."

"What do you mean by 'weird'?"

"I guess what I mean is rude. I just expected better from you."

Ellen was silent for several seconds. "I'm sorry," she said.

"That's all right," he said.

"I have a dance class early that evening. Would it be all right if I came by a little late?"

"Whatever you want," Mark said.

"O.K.," Ellen said. "I would love to come to your party."

It was a big party. There were a lot of teachers and several guys from the climbing school, Patrick came and was perfectly friendly, ready to be buddies again. Torrey Peck, the secretary from the principal's office, showed up in tight jeans and a very low-cut and very sexy blouse, the waitress from the Llama restaurant came, and so did two guys who were in Jackson doing coyote studies on a grant.

The party got rowdy early. Someone had brought a collection of Creedance Clearwater Revival records, and that got the dancing going in a hurry. The music was turned up, somebody knocked over a jug of Almaden and everybody started singing along to "Proud Mary, Keep on Turnin'." The smell of smoke and beer and a lot of people filled the house.

Torrey Peck downed a couple of quick shots of Bourbon and pulled Mark out into the middle of the dance floor. She was very determined, her bare shoulders shimmied and dipped like a disco contest winner. She was younger than most of the other people there, she was twenty-one, maybe twenty-two, she was pretty, her dark hair coming loose as she danced, and she wanted to be treated like something more than the cute girl who worked in the office. It was clear from the hooded looks she was giving Mark that she'd decided that tonight was going to be the night she and Mark were going to go beyond mock flirtation. Mark danced one dance with her and then extricated himself as gracefully as he could.

Mark was a little worried, not because he didn't like rowdy parties, but he wasn't sure that Ellen would. She didn't show up in the first hour and Mark started to get anxious; he found that he was waiting for her more than he was ready to admit.

The party got big enough that it started to spill outside, some of the people wandering off, beers in hand, to look at the horses in the rodeo grounds.

Mark made his way into the kitchen where one of the teachers was holding court in front of the refrigerator. He had been a float-trip guide during the summer and he was entertaining everybody with rambling stories about all the idiot tourists he'd taken down the river. He was on a roll, he had everybody laughing, and what made his stories work was his resentment, his comic outrage, his fantasies about dumping them all in the whitewater, taking them into the biggest rapids and giving them the old Maytag treatment.

The waitress from the Llama restaurant wasn't as into it as the others. "You talk a good game, Boobie, but you know you'd never do it. Now, Tommy O'Donnell, you heard what he did, didn't you? He actually threw somebody out of his boat this summer. Now, that's really incredible."

The teacher got a sour look on his face. He didn't like being one-upped. "Yeah, well, Tommy O'Donnell, he's something else." He looked over at Mark. "Tommy's your friend, isn't he, Mark?"

"Sure, he's my friend," Mark said, feeling his face color.

"I hear he's not doing so great," the teacher said. "Last week up in Lander he apparently got into a fight in a bar and hit a guy with a board, broke his jaw. You hear that, Mark?"

"No," Mark said. "I didn't hear that."

"I know some people used to think the stuff Tommy did was funny. Tommy's not very funny anymore." The teacher was suddenly tired of telling stories. He'd lost his momentum. He yanked open the refrigerator door. "Any more beer in here?"

Mark turned away and when he did he saw the front door open. It was Ellen. She was wearing a rough cream-colored muslin top and her face was shining. Mark made his way through the dancers, gave her a kiss on the cheek. She had brought him a bouquet of flowers. Mark could tell that things were all right, that there wasn't even a question. He took her out in the middle of the floor and they danced. It was terrific, it was like before, only better. It didn't matter that it was too crowded, it didn't matter that there was smoke and noise and that the floor was sticky with spilled wine. She had forgiven him. He could feel the others watching them. He didn't care. This was something he didn't need to hide. She slipped under his raised arm, spun out, he caught her hand at the last second, he knew that she trusted him.

It was more than Torrey Peck could deal with. She'd had too much to drink and now she'd lost out to another woman. She tried briefly to recoup her losses with a brief display of frenzied shake-it-up dancing with Jack Bertram, Patrick and one of the coyote studies men. It didn't last long, she kept bumping into people and finally had to be helped to the bathroom. Fifteen minutes later Mark asked somebody to go in and check on her and they brought Torrey out white-faced and shaky. Torrey asked Mark if she could lie down on his bed. She wasn't feeling too well. A minute after they laid her down she was asleep.

The party seemed to be a roaring success. It was the first big fall party and it had the air of a celebration.

One of the guys from the climbing school got up on one of Mark's couches, a bottle raised in one hand, and whistled for everybody's attention.

"Hey! I'd like to propose a toast. . . ." He teetered on the cushions, hands reached out to steady him. He was pretty drunk. "Hey, shut up over there, I'm proposing a toast." He raised his bottle higher. "Here's to the end of summer!" he shouted. "So long, summer folks, so long, r.v.s, so long, tour buses, so long, rubber tomahawk city . . ." A couple of people started to clap but he shushed them. "The mountains are ours again for nine months, so flaunt it while you got it, happy trails, suckers, until we meet again . . ." A great cheer went up as he tumbled into waiting arms.

Mark and Ellen made their way outside. There was a bunch of guys sitting out on the front porch taking sips from a jar of white lightning and trading elk-hunting stories. They were all counting on getting their elk that fall and they were all trying to top each other with tales of shots at four hundred yards in the inky black, the animal was running, and they knocked the heart right out of it, no piece of heart left any bigger than a dime.

Mark and Ellen stood just outside the group, hand in hand, listening. The night air was chill. The one outside light shone on the leaves of the trees, reflected off the jumble of cars parked in the driveway and lined up out on the road. He knew that Ellen didn't like hunting talk, but this time it didn't seem to matter to her. She pressed closer to him.

One of the guys, a squat, strong-looking man, had worked as a hunting guide for the past three seasons and all the other would-be hunters seemed to defer to him. He told a story about some Texans he'd taken up and how frustrated they got. Every day they'd ride through the Teton wilderness, it had been a dry fall, and they weren't seeing a thing. Then they would glass over the line into Yellowstone and see all those big bulls standing there grazing like they knew they were safe and the Texans were just dying that they couldn't go get them and they offered three-, four-, five-hundred-dollar bribes if the guide would take them across to get one of those big bulls.

"So'd you take it?" said one of his drunken buddies, raising the jar of white lightning. The storyteller looked at him disdainfully. "No, I'm being serious, did you take it?"

"You're talking poaching, man."

"I know what I'm talking about, man," the heckler said.

"Screw them and their money. I'll tell you the truth, these hunters you take up, you work your tail off riding them around for eight, nine days to give them one good shot at a good bull, sometimes you think you'd rather see that bull out there on that ridge again next fall than have him mounted in somebody's den in Pennsylvania."

"I would have taken it," the heckler said. "I would have taken the five hundred."

"Well, you'll have your chance. They'll be back. Those people always come back."

Mark put his arm around Ellen. Mark remembered that Barbara had talked about coming back too, about how they always came back for the hunt in the fall. Ellen looked up and smiled at him. Music throbbed from inside the house. The remembering disturbed Mark. Standing with his arm around Ellen, feeling closer to peacefulness than he had been for a long time, he knew that if Barbara was there he would want to see her. He pulled Ellen a little closer to him.

"You cold?" Mark said.

"A little."

"Why don't we go in then?"

Not many people had left the party and Mark suddenly wanted them to leave. He knew, without having to ask, that Ellen would stay with him if he could just clear these people out. The problem was that people were having too good a time. A couple of lunatics were howling at the moon like reservation dogs, record albums were scattered across the floor.

Jack Bertram kept scuttling in and out of the bedroom, checking on Torrey Peck, and Mark finally went and looked in over Jack's shoulder. Torrey was still sound asleep and didn't look like she was ever going to wake up.

Jack punched Mark lightly on the arm. "Hey, buddy, how you doin'? You having a good time? You look a little tense, pal." He gave Mark a conspiratorial wink. "Look, Mark, I know *exactly* what you're thinkin', Jack Bertram is nobody's fool. You want to get everybody out, right? You and Ellen want to get together, right, but you can't with that mob out there. Well, I can help move everybody out, just leave it to me."

Mark stepped back. Jack's breath smelled strongly of gin. "Jack, I appreciate your concern, but don't you worry about it."

Jack stayed on him, eyes glittering, put his hand on Mark's chest. "I don't think you quite see what I'm saying, Mark. See, Torrey was awake for a little while there, I gave her some tea, tried to take care of her, and we made an agreement if you know what I mean, she promised that we could get together once she woke up." If Mark looked disgusted Jack didn't pick it up. "Don't worry. We could move her, see, you and me, we could carry her out to the couch so you and Ellen could have the bedroom. It's no problem, Mark. The couch would be fine for us."

Mark was suddenly overwhelmed by the absurdity of it all. What had started out as a good-natured party now seemed a nightmare, a farce. One thing in the world he knew he didn't want to be doing right now was scheming with Jack Bertram about how they could both get laid. For a moment everything had seemed so perfect and now it was all ruined because there was a drunken woman asleep on his bed and no one could wake her, because people were having too good a time and had no intention of leaving. It was a weird kind of justice; Mark was being punished, done in by raunch. The most appalling vision Mark could imagine was trying to make love to Ellen while Jack Bertram was in the other room trying to rouse Torrey Peck from her nausea to a state of sexual excitement. It was a fiasco.

Torrey rolled over on her side, still asleep, and Jack went over to check on her.

Ellen was talking to Patrick in the hallway. Mark went to her and said, "Can I talk to you for a minute?"

"Sure."

"Excuse me, Patrick," Mark said.

"No problem, hey," Patrick said.

He pulled Ellen aside. One of the coyote studies men lurched past, his arm draped over the waitress from the Llama restaurant. Mark felt the color rising in his face. "I'd like to spend the night with you," he said. "But there's a problem. Torrey Peck is totally passed out in there, Jack Bertram says he's made some arrangement with her if she ever wakes up, God knows what it is, and this mob shows no sign of breaking up . . ."

"So what would you like to do?"

"I'd like to get the hell out of here."

"Why don't we go to my house then?"

"That would be all right?"

She took his hand. "That would be fine."

He kissed her on the cheek. "Give me five minutes and we'll be out of here."

Mark went and told Jack that he and Ellen were taking off and that he would leave Jack in charge. Jack said that he'd be happy to do it. Jack would take care of everything, make sure everybody left, make sure Torrey was all right, he'd even clean up, he said. Jack's state of lust had put him in an incredibly generous mood.

"And look, Jack," Mark said. "Maybe it's none of my business, but if Torrey wakes up and she doesn't feel like it . . . Well, be a decent guy, all right? She's just a kid."

Jack slapped Mark on the shoulder. "Hey, what kind of a guy do you think I am? Trust me, trust me."

It was no problem slipping out, everybody was too busy acting like maniacs. The only person who noticed at all was a math teacher peeing behind a jeep, who looked up startled when he heard Ellen and Mark open the door to her car.

"Hey, man, what you doing, leaving your own party?"

"That's exactly what I'm doing," Mark said. "You're having enough fun. Nobody needs a host for that."

They were both quiet and a little self-conscious in the car. Their hands touched on the seat between them. Four or five cars passed them on the road from Wilson to Jackson, the headlights flashing over them, lighting them for a second, then plunging them back into darkness, leaving them alone with their thoughts again, and one of the thoughts Mark had was that he was leaving Barbara irrevocably behind.

When they got to Ellen's house they stopped on the doorstep and embraced. Ellen pulled back for a second and scrutinized him.

"You look so sad," she said. "Are you sad?"

"Not at all," he said. "Why would I be sad?" He pressed her head against his chest. "It's just so nice to hold you again. You're so perfect, so perfect."

She looked up at him, troubled. "I'm not perfect. I'm not. If you want me to be your good woman to her bad woman it won't work. You'll get mad at me just like before."

"No," he said. "No, I won't."

"Yes, you will."

"Really? For what?" he said, trying to make light of it.

"I don't know for what."

He kissed her softly on the lips, smiling at her, then kissed her again, more deeply. "Let's go inside," he said.

They made love in the darkness of her bedroom and there was the smell of freshly watered plants. They went slowly, learning how to care for one another again. It was familiar and yet it wasn't; it was as if they were taking a journey to some new place together. He could feel the strength in her body, he felt himself responding to it, matching it, he wanted to surrender to her in a way he had never done before.

Afterwards he wanted to talk about it, about what it meant, but she didn't. She wanted him to stay just like he was, inside her, not to move. Her hand rested on his bare back, she pulled the sheet up to cover both of them.

Finally Ellen got up to open the window a little wider. Mark smiled in the dark. Ellen was a person for whom there was no such thing as too much fresh air. Watching her from the bed, up on his elbows, Mark vowed that he would not hurt her again. The breeze through the opened windows rustled the leaves of the plants, making ghostly sounds. When she came back to bed he held her and, when she reached down and touched him, they made love again.

Mark woke to the familiar sound of the wind chimes. He rolled over. Ellen was still asleep. He pulled up close to her, slipped his hand under her arm, cupped her breast lightly with his fingers, buried his head in her hair. She stirred, opened her eyes and looked at him.

"Hi," Mark said. "Remember me?"

"Sure," she said. She rolled over to face him, still resting her head on the pillow. "What a nice way to wake up."

"I know," he said. Mark heard the yakking of a nuthatch in the trees outside. "You don't know what time it is, do you?"

"I don't," she said. She raised herself up on one arm, stared out at the morning light pouring in through the open windows. "Late, I guess. But it's Saturday. It doesn't matter on Saturday."

"No," he said. "I guess not." He took one of her hands, pressed his lips to her fingers. She fell back against the pillow, smiling, reaching up for him. They kissed once, twice, more urgently. Then Mark said, "Oh Christ!"

"What's wrong?" she said.

"I just remembered. Saturday. I told the principal I'd be a faculty proctor at the football game."

"Oh."

"Oh, my God," Mark said. "It's just ridiculous!" He looked sideways at her. "You don't like football, do you? No, you don't. You're too arty."

"I'm not too arty. I don't understand football exactly, but that doesn't mean I'm so arty."

The wind spun the chimes into a sudden fury of bright sounds. "I'd rather stay here," Mark said. "But I promised the guy." He ran his fingers softly over Ellen's face. "Maybe I can get out of it. I could always call and say I was sick or something."

"But you promised him. You shouldn't try to get out of it."

"No? You wouldn't be interested in going to a football game then, would you?"

"I was wondering when you were going to ask. I'd love to go."

"Really?"

"Really."

Mark grinned at her. "Great. There's just one other thing I need to do. I should go home and see if anything is left of my place and change clothes. I'll be back to pick you up in an hour."

His place was a wreck. Jack was still there, very hung over and abashed, trying feebly to clean the place up. Torrey was gone. The bed had been stripped and the sheets jammed in the laundry hamper. Jack had filled three large plastic garbage bags full of bottles and cans. Still, anywhere Mark wanted to look he could spy another plastic cup with cigarette butts floating in a half inch of stale beer. The whole place reeked of smoke. Someone had poured Gallo chablis down the hi-fi and when Mark punched the buttons the hi-fi made a series of warbling sounds that he had never heard before. There was a giant chip out of the kitchen door where, according to Jack, one of the white-lightning-drinking hunters had flung his Bowie knife in an exhibition of sexually rejected machismo.

"I'm sorry, man," Jack said, following Mark anxiously through the wreckage, a wicker wastebasket in his hand. "I tried to control 'em, but these people just went nuts. I hope I didn't fuck you up, Mark, but I couldn't just leave that girl in the condition she was in, it wouldn't have been right." Jack sat down wearily in one of the stuffed chairs, tossing a potato-chip bag aside, watched Mark pull a clean shirt out of his closet. "You know I took your advice."

"What advice was that?" Mark said.

"I couldn't do it. She really is just a kid, you know. I gave her tea, cleaned her up, sent her home. I acted like a decent guy, after all."

"So how does that make you feel?"

"Not that great." Mark buttoned his shirt, looked back at Jack in the mirror. "Not that she wouldn't have. She would have in a minute. No problem on that account. But the way I figured was, you're going to feel pretty lousy when you know you're just taking advantage of somebody. Not that people don't do it all the time, a lot of the time they do it without even knowing it. But I would have known I was doing it. So I couldn't."

"Good for you, Jack," Mark said.

"It was a great party," Jack said. "You've got to say that."

"That's right."

"That was what you call a wild party," Jack said. "I think people need that every once in a while. People really need to kind of let go."

"They sure do, Jack." Mark took the wastebasket out of Jack's hands and set it down on the floor. "Don't worry about the rest of this, I'll take care of it when I get back. You've helped enough already."

They had a wonderful time at the game. Ellen was radiantly charming and outgoing, laughing and exchanging stories with the other teachers. Jackson rallied to win in the last minute when one of Mark's students, the wise guy in his Senior English class, scooped up a fumble and ran sixty yards with it. The fans went wild. When it was time to sing the school song Ellen held tight to Mark's arm. People noticed. Mark didn't mind at all.

After the game they went out and had drinks with the other teachers. They excused themselves early and Mark walked Ellen home. They made love, then made dinner together. There was not a moment's question whether he was staying the night or not.

In the morning it felt a little different. It was a gray, overcast day. They were both quiet over breakfast, the newly turned-on heat banging in the pipes. They had come a long way in a hurry. Mark felt slightly disoriented and melancholy. He needed more time to assimilate what had happened to them. He guessed that Ellen felt the same way, he couldn't be sure. Neither of them seemed willing to define things yet; both steered clear of starting that conversation. When Mark said that he should probably go back to his place to finish cleaning up Ellen said fine, she had some things to do too. She almost seemed relieved.

Standing at the front door, Mark felt a new awkwardness. He held her by both hands. He couldn't leave without there being some kind of plan. "Maybe what we could do," he said, "would be to have dinner on Tuesday. Over at my place. How does that sound?"

"That sounds great," Ellen said. She leaned into him, pulling his face down to hers. Their kiss was gentle, open-eyed, trusting.

His place was depressing, still smelled of beer and cigarettes. Mark opened all the windows to air it out and did maybe an hour's worth of cleaning up. He thought of Ellen, of the inexplicable tenderness of the weekend, and still he was afraid. He didn't trust himself. He felt as if there were demons of the summer still haunting the empty rooms of this house. Things had changed so fast, he really had no line on what he was doing and there was one insistent small voice in him that kept saying that he had abandoned Barbara, that it was all in bad faith. That voice scared Mark. Now was when he could make some real mistakes.

He thought of going back to Ellen's right then, but she wouldn't have understood. Mark went to the phone and called Barbara's number in New York. When he heard Sarah's voice answer on the other end of the line, he quickly pressed the button, disconnecting them. His heart was pounding. He had to get out, he couldn't stay in this shambles of a house alone.

He went out, got in the car and started driving. For the first ten minutes he didn't realize where he was headed.

By the time he got out to the Campbells' ranch the clouds had broken and there was sporadic sunshine straying across the pastures.

Judy must have heard his car come down the road because when Mark pulled up in front of the house she stood on the steps waiting for him. When she came down to greet him Mark thought she looked different. She looked like a harder kind of country woman, warier, like a person who was growing used to living alone.

They embraced without saying a word.

"What are you doing out here?" she said.

"I don't really know," he said. "I was just driving by. I thought I'd drop in."

"Why don't you come inside?" she said. "I'll make us some coffee."

He followed her in. The house seemed darker than he remembered it and there were many closed doors, sections of the house shut down for the winter. On the hall table was a packet of mail being forwarded to New York. The place felt cold to him; when they went to sit in the kitchen Mark kept his jacket on.

Judy got out a package of cookies, arranged them on a plate. Mark hunched forward, warmed his hands on the familiar cup.

"Gets a little chilly in here, doesn't it?" Mark said.

Judy smiled. "A place like this is so expensive to heat. I try to be careful."

"You don't get lonely out here?"

"Some," she said. "You get used to it. But it's so beautiful. There's a little band of mule deer that come up every evening and feed in the trees behind the barn." She took a cookie, broke it in two. She was avoiding looking him in the eye. "And besides, Ike is around every day. Once in a while I get a visitor. Like you."

Mark sipped on his coffee. Autumn light suddenly swelled, spilled across the kitchen floor. Mark stared out the window. Down in the pasture the horses were galloping, playing, the cold had given them new energy.

"They're going to keep the horses here all winter?" Mark said.

"No. I think the plan is that Ike will take them someplace south of the valley and winter then down there. But not till after Rob and Barbara come back for the hunt. I guess they'll use some of the horses for that." Her voice faltered, gave away the fact that they had stepped onto dangerous ground.

Mark didn't back off. "When will that be, do you know?"

"In her last letter she said that they weren't quite sure yet whether it would be the end of October or sometime in November. It depends on when Rob can get away."

"You do hear from them then?"

"I've gotten a couple of letters."

Mark stirred his coffee slowly with his spoon. "How do they seem to be doing?"

"They seem to be doing fine," Judy said. Judy got up, went to the stove and poured herself a second cup of coffee. "Do you ever hear from Tommy?"

"No," Mark said. He remembered the story he'd heard at his party about Tommy breaking a man's jaw in a Lander bar. He wasn't going to repeat it. It probably wasn't even true. "How about you?"

"He called me once." Judy sat down again. She bit at one of her cuticles.

"How was it?"

"Pretty terrible. You know how he can be. I think he'd been drinking. You know how he paints himself in a corner and then can't get out. He told me I was as boring as ever and not to think that he'd called to talk to me. I asked him if I could have my piano back. He said no, but if I came over we could talk about it. I said I wouldn't do that."

"I'm sorry," he said.

"Don't be sorry," Judy said. "That's really over. I'm much better. I feel so much stronger being out here. I feed the horses in the morning, do my hour of yoga, get the work done around the house here. I have my routines all worked out."

"I would think it would get hard, though," Mark said. "Particularly later, when it starts to get real cold."

Mark saw the anger rise in her, she straightened her back. "I don't think you understand. It's the best thing for me now. I'm so much stronger out here. I really feel as if I'm in charge of my life for the first time. Remember how you and Tommy always used to talk about being self-sufficient? Well, that's what I'm doing, I'm trying to make myself self-sufficient."

Mark looked away, stared at the bulletin board on the wall. All the tacked-up schedules and clippings and pictures from the sum-

mer were still there. He didn't believe what Judy was saying, but
he wasn't going to keep on.

"Did Barbara tell you whether she'd been able to get any work
of her own done lately or not?"

"I think it's been hard for her," Judy said. "It doesn't sound like
they've had much time. One thing, though, she did tell me was that
there was some gallery owner they know who wants to put the
piece she did this summer in an exhibition. One of the things
I've got to do this week is crate it up and get it sent off."

"You mean it's still here? The sculpture?"

"Yes. You know what it was like when they left, there wasn't
time to do anything."

"Where is it?"

"Down in the studio."

Mark didn't even try to hide his eagerness. "Could we go see it?"

"Sure," Judy said. "Just let me go get the key."

Mark stood up as Judy left the room. He was very excited. He
had never seen the completed work, Barbara had never mentioned
it again after the day of casting. Mark had wondered about that, if
something had gone wrong, if she had been disappointed by it. But
Judy had inferred that it was done, complete. Barbara must have
finished it in secret, not telling anyone, or at least not telling him.
Mark set the coffee cups in the sink. Being in the house again was a
disappointment, it had left him feeling flat and cheated. It wasn't
the same at all, the house was a drab shell, a mockery of what he
remembered going on here. The sculpture would be different.

Chattering blackbirds whirled up like a leaf storm as Mark and
Judy crossed the lawn to the studio. The lock on the door was stiff,
it took Judy a second to get it open.

They stepped inside. The studio was chill, yet the real shock was
how much everything was the same, the sandpits in the center of
the floor, the stray pieces of plaster mold, the heavy leather aprons
tossed casually over a sawhorse as if whoever had used them had
just stepped out the moment before. The only difference was the
finished sculpture sitting on the table.

Mark walked up to it without a word. Judy stayed back, not
crowding him. Barbara had always avoided talking much about her
work with him and what she had said hadn't made much sense to
him, but now suddenly all the hints, enigmatic remarks, the obscure
bits of theory she had taunted him with began to cohere. Looking

at the sculpture the first thing he thought was, this is so much like her.

There were six bronze mounted riders in a round and all of the figures, horses and horsemen, were abstracted, relatively featureless, remote, Henry Moore-like. The riders were of different sizes and there were suggestions of masculinity in one, femininity in another, and one of the riders was clearly a child. Though they were placed in a circle, the impression was more of a chase than of a carousel, but a chase with no beginning, no end, of an infinite hunger. The space in the center seemed to define them all, their horses almost seemed to shy from the void. He remembered Barbara trying to talk to him once about negative space and he had thought it was all pretentious crap, but it made sense now, the whole sculpture revolved on hollows, even the riders arched over the necks of their horses seemed to be nursing some emptiness.

It was more like Frederic Remington than she'd want to admit, Mark thought. The idea made him smile. He remembered their old debates. He could have gotten her going with that, accusing her of being a western artist after all.

Sunlight broke through the picture window, lit the inside of the studio. Mark ran his hand over the bronze figures. The metal was cold to the touch, it was a cold autumn day, but still those hard surfaces brought back that summer day and the intense heat when these figures were only molten, liquid, when these forms were nothing but curious cavelike shells buried beneath the sand. Now they were raised, Barbara had secretly dug them out, polished them and there they were, durable and gleaming, they looked like they could last forever. Mark remembered how Barbara had said he and she would find their own form and Mark had finally been irritated by that, but maybe this was what she meant, maybe this was the form, their only refuge, these leaping, plunging figures, the ache of yearning in them, forever frozen in their chase.

Mark finally looked back at Judy, a little embarrassed by his absorption. "I helped with the casting," Mark said.

"I remember."

"Hottest damn work I ever did in my life," Mark said. "We had to wear these things," he said. He held up one of the leather aprons in front of him. "Can you believe it? And these." Mark tried to put on one of the heavy gloves, but there was something stuck in the finger. He took the glove off and shook it. Broken hazelnuts clattered to the floor.

"Mice," Judy said. "They get in everywhere. I'll have to get Ike to put out some more poison."

Mark felt her distance. Mark didn't know if she was embarrassed for him or if she had just gotten out of the habit of being around people.

"You look like you're ready to go," Mark said.

"I'm fine. If you want to stay awhile, that's fine."

"No, that's enough. I'm just glad I had a chance to see it. Thank you."

She opened the studio door, waited for him. Mark slapped one of the bronze horses lightly on the rump, as if he were spurring it on, saying goodbye. He had meant the gesture to be funny. Judy didn't seem to notice.

They walked slowly toward Mark's car.

"I don't think you should live out here," Mark said. "I think it will be too hard, once winter comes. You should come into town. It's no good for you here."

She looked bitterly smug, as if she had known what was coming. "Everyone says that. It's not true. I like being by myself. Besides, I don't have any money right now, I couldn't afford a place in town. It's free rent out here and look what I get."

"But you can't just hide," Mark said. He leaned against the handle of his car door. "You're never going to get over it like this. You're too cut off. I'm sorry I have to talk like this, but you can't just refuse to do anything for yourself." Tears sprang to her eyes. "I'm sorry," he said.

"You just surprised me, that's all."

"I only said it because I'm your friend. It's only my opinion. I worry about you."

"O.K.," she said. "Fine. Everything's fine." She pinched the corners of her eyes with her thumb and forefinger, faced him bravely. "Do you ever see Ellen?" she said.

"I saw her this weekend, as a matter of fact."

"That's nice. I always thought you two were good together."

"Of course you did. You were the one who introduced us, remember?"

"I remember." Judy kissed him goodbye. "Will you see her again?"

"I think I'll see her quite a lot from now on," Mark said.

"I envy you," Judy said. "Both of you."

Mark drove back into town. He felt newly confused and still a little depressed and at loose ends. Something about Judy's passivity made him angry, maybe even angrier than it should have. He wasn't going to trap himself in the past the way she had.

He couldn't bring himself to go back to his house. He stopped at a place along the highway and had a hamburger at the counter. The only other people in the whole place were two wardens from Fish and Game, eating chili, hunched forward with their Scotch caps on, knives sheathed at their belts. There were twenty empty tables, climbing posters of Annapurna on the wall, and a half-dozen pinball machines.

He thought about calling Ellen. Probably it would be better if he waited, he was supposed to be seeing her on Tuesday anyway. It would be better not to press, better not to betray how anxious he really was. The only thing was there was a pay phone sitting right there, next to the jukebox, on the way out.

She answered the phone on the third ring.

"Hello?"

"Surprise," Mark said. "How you doin'?"

"Fine. How about you?"

"I'm doing fine. I'm out here on the highway. Not very far from your place. I was thinking about you. Wishing I was over there, instead of out here."

"That's nice," she said. She paused for a second. "I wish you were here too." The two Fish and Game wardens stood up to pay their bill. They waited at the register, the cashier must have gone to sleep in the back.

"Yeah? What are you doing now?" Mark said. "Anything?"

"Not really."

The taller of the two wardens took a toothpick from the bowl on the counter and went to work with it.

"You tired at all?" Mark said.

"Not really."

"I know we weren't going to see each other till Tuesday, but what the hell, would you be interested in a visitor?"

"If it was you," she said.

"Give me ten minutes then," Mark said. "I'll pick up a bottle of wine on the way."

Ellen met him at the door. It all seemed so uncomplicated suddenly, it almost frightened him. He was safe with her. However obscure the causes, he felt as if he had been released, as if the reins had been cut. They sat at the kitchen table and drank the bottle of wine. Mark listened to a detailed description of her day. Mark didn't tell her about his afternoon and she didn't think to ask.

They were together every night from then on.

CHAPTER TWENTY-SEVEN

Fall was the best time in Jackson. The aspens were gold, the willows gold and then silver as it turned colder. The clear light made everything stand out so intensely that distances were almost impossible to gauge. The mountains took on an unreal edge, it looked as if you could climb to the top of the Grand in a half hour. The pristine beauty of the fall had a lulling effect to it, made perfection, any perfection, seem almost within reach.

Things went easily for Mark and Ellen. Ellen still had fears and anxieties, but most of the time they didn't stand in the way of the trust that was growing between them. Once or twice she had tried to talk to Mark about what his relationship had been like with Barbara, but the conversations were not a success. It upset her too much. She would start to get angry and then Mark would change the subject.

Mark held on to Ellen for dear life. At times he didn't know if it was need or love, but he wasn't letting go. Things seemed so changed from before, the things that used to irritate him, like her finickiness, her exactitude about her responsibilities, didn't bother him now. She was hardheaded and that quality seemed like a prize to him now.

He wanted to believe that she was right about the world, that there didn't have to be tragic divisions, that life didn't always have to be lived under insane strains. She believed in happiness. In some things she was almost totally predictable; if she liked a place she would always say how quiet it was. Mark was beginning to see what she meant. Though there were still times, especially when he was alone, that he thought of Barbara, that he got down and wondered if he was just talking himself into something, Mark was beginning to believe in the possibility of a new kind of peacefulness. He was discovering that life could be more temperate than he had ever thought possible, that there were things that could be reached only through the simple acts of faithfulness, of steadfastness.

It was not that Ellen's life was that tranquil. It seemed to Mark that she was fretting constantly over not having answered her sister's letters quickly enough, not having someone over they didn't like that much but who'd had them over. She took the idea of obligation more seriously than anyone Mark had ever met. She never could do less than her share. It was hopeless trying to change her. Mark would tell her, "Look, if you want to see somebody, you see them, otherwise don't; you see people you don't like, it can wreck your life." She never bought that for a minute.

Mark got a letter from his mother saying that they had decided to go ahead with the bypass operation on his father's clogged arteries. The operation was scheduled in two weeks. There was no pressure in the note, Mark's mother was always very careful, but she said that it would be nice if Mark could come out, anytime, really, she said, she knew how busy he was.

Mark showed Ellen the note. He watched her read it.

"What do you think?" he asked.

"It would mean a lot to your father if you went."

"I know," he said. He took the note from Ellen's hand, tucked it in his shirt pocket. "I'll have to think about it."

She looked at him, wondering. "I mean, you do love your father."

"Of course, I do," he said. "It just scares me. Anything being wrong with him."

One afternoon Ellen went over to Mark's right after school. They were having friends over for dinner and, since Mark was tied up with the first day of tryouts for the freshman basketball team, Ellen had said she would come over and clean the place up some, at least get a roast in the oven.

When Mark showed up at six-thirty he could tell that something was wrong. Ellen seemed tense and withdrawn. Mark wanted to know why. If it was that Ellen had had to do all the preparations for the meal by herself, he was sorry. No, Ellen said, that wasn't it. It was nothing, she was just a little tired.

Their friends arrived and everything seemed perfectly fine, they had a good evening together. The friends left about eleven. When they were gone Ellen suddenly became quiet again, but Mark didn't think much about it, not until she started to get on him about doing the dishes. At one point she took the wet plate out of his hand and proceeded to illustrate how Mark should put more soap on his pad. Mark was at least as amazed as he was irritated.

"Hey, what's wrong with you?" he said. "Jesus!"

She looked attacked. "Nothing's wrong with me at all. I just don't know why I have to tell you these things over and over again and you always agree with me, but you never change. I feel like it's aimed at me somehow."

"It's not aimed at you. I'm just a naturally sloppy guy. O.K.? Look," he said, "why don't you let me do this, you've done plenty already. Just let me finish. All right?"

She left the kitchen without a word. For the next hour Mark worked in the kitchen, scrubbing everything with a vengeful attentiveness. Ellen read in the bedroom, but it wasn't over, Mark could feel the tension between them three rooms away. He found himself getting angrier and angrier. This is why it couldn't work before, he thought, this is why it's impossible. Nothing's changed at all, that was just wishful thinking.

When he finished with the dishes he walked into the bedroom. She sat on the bed, knees drawn up, pillow propped up behind her, a copy of *Mansfield Park* open on her lap. She looked up at him. As if she hadn't heard him coming, he thought. Mark's tone was softer than he felt.

"What's going on with you?" he said. "I know it's something."

"When I was cleaning this afternoon," she said, "I found an envelope full of her letters."

"Oh," Mark said.

"You don't hide things very well," Ellen said.

"No, I guess not."

"I read one. One was enough. Enough to convince me of what kind of woman she was. It gave me a better picture."

"Did it make you angry?"

"I don't know if it made me angry. I just saw how manipulative she was."

"You did." Mark stood beside the bed, looking down on her. He felt himself freezing up.

"I don't see how you could have gotten involved with her."

"I don't expect you to see that."

"What do you mean by that?"

"Nothing. I'm sorry you found the letters. I know how I'd feel, I'd feel lousy." He reached out, touched her hair.

"It just makes me mad that she fooled you like that, that you didn't see . . ."

"There's no point in discussing this," Mark said. "I said I was sorry."

"What are you sorry about? Are you sorry that you're not with her?"

"Of course not," Mark said.

He was angry that she had made him say that. He was afraid suddenly that he had made a terrible mistake. Ellen seemed so angry, so fierce, maybe he should have thrown himself at Barbara and just damned the consequences.

"You'd rather be with her, I know you would."

"That's not true. But if you want me to repudiate her, I won't do it."

"Repudiate? What sort of word is that? You make me sound like some kind of inquisitor." She sprang off the bed, flinging her book aside, and walked out of the room. Mark caught up with her, caught her arm.

"I love you," he said. "I want to be right here, with you. I just don't want to be put in the position of having to attack her . . ."

"But you defend her."

"No," he said.

"You do!" Her arms were folded tight to her body and she was trembling. "I'm supposed to believe that she was so kind and intelligent and that what went on was so sophisticated and complicated, so open-minded . . . I think it's just sick."

"Come on."

"I do. I think they're all just a bunch of spoiled brats!" She was getting real scared now, she was afraid she was going to lose him and that only made it worse, it made her push him away.

"Christ, Ellen."

"I know what you're thinking now. What a simpleminded idiot I am."

"I'm not thinking that. You've got to stop telling me what I'm thinking. It's a lousy trick."

"Why did you keep those letters, anyway?" she said. "You're trying to hang on to her. I know you, Mark. I do."

That night they lay in bed, saying nothing. They were both hurt. Before Ellen fell asleep she rolled over to him and touched his face in the darkness.

"I'm sorry," she said. "I love you."

"I love you too," he said, but it wasn't quite the same. She was the one able to forgive more quickly. Ellen was asleep in a couple of minutes.

It was not over for Mark. He lay awake and in turmoil. Lying next to Ellen was no comfort, no refuge at all. He wondered which of Barbara's letters Ellen had found. He thought of Barbara, he wanted her back. All the anguish he had felt before was there again, breaking down everything he and Ellen had built up together, scattering it as if it were no more than a house of cards. Perhaps all he'd been doing for the last month was making an attempt at saving himself from Barbara, at holding himself back, but now he saw that he wouldn't be able to.

Ellen moved in her sleep and was still again. Lying there in the darkness, watching the shadows of the tree branches sway and mesh on the ceiling of the bedroom, Mark did not love her. It would have been better if he did. He had been trying to talk himself into it, he saw that now. Barbara had understood him at least. He had been too timid, he should have gone after her with all his might.

No line of thought could be followed out very far. He thought of Sarah's white arm, reaching up from the willow bushes just below the ledge, Rob didn't see it yet . . . He thought of his vow. He couldn't abandon Ellen again. He imagined himself out of control, creating havoc in everyone's lives. It was a nightmare.

Why was it so hard to be a decent, civilized person? Why did the costs seem so high? Mark didn't understand. Other people seemed to be able to do it, make rational choices and then live with them. Other people seemed to be able to choose the good, to live with the consequences of their acts, to accept those things that couldn't be changed, things like Barbara being married and having children. But where were those other people now that Mark needed them? He had some questions to ask them, like, What if virtue meant separating yourself from what you loved, from yourself? What if it meant you had to lead a false life? It was too much to ask that he change his dreams, that he say he wanted something when he didn't. Mark felt like an utter sham. He didn't remember falling asleep, but somehow he must have.

It was no better in the morning. Mark was in a state of barely concealed despair, he could tell that Ellen was tense and depressed. Somehow the routines of the morning got them through. Mark snapped on the *Today* show and made breakfast. Ellen did the bed.

Over coffee, toast and eggs they watched Phil Donahue interview wives who'd murdered their husbands, and that rendered further conversation unnecessary. Driving to school together they seemed to have arrived at some unspoken truce, an agreement to stick to safe subjects, to steer clear of anything that might inflict further pain.

Mark spent the day in a daze, just going through the motions. It was noticeable. Several teachers asked Mark if anything was wrong. A couple of the kids who'd tried out for the basketball team came up and asked if the cut list had been posted yet. Mark was not as gentle dealing with their anxieties as he should have been. What he craved was to be alone, to have time to think things through.

After school Mark went on a long run out on the Elk Refuge Road, plodding below the bare hills, gray as bones.

What Mark felt and what he thought he should feel didn't match up. In arguments at parties he could be counted on to represent a fairly consistent point of view. Some people even said he had a line and it was a more conservative line than a lot of his friends.

Terms like *radical freedom, personal growth, life-style, self-expression* were just so many red flags for Mark. He was on the other side. According to Mark's line, radical expressions of self led toward cruelty rather than kindness, toward self-absorption rather than freedom. We'd all be better off, Mark would joke, if some selves had let themselves go unexpressed. Friends who grew irritated with Mark's arguments claimed he was a closet bourgeois. Mark never bothered to deny it. Following out Mark's line, Rob and Barbara were perfect targets, the best examples around of what he thought he opposed. Mark remembered how irritating he had found Barbara the first time he met her.

Pressed in an argument to name some alternative, Mark would always come up with someone like Ike Watkins. Ike worked, knew the country, knew how to fix things, could deliver a calf in the dead of winter, repair a truck, break a horse. Ike was a western man. He still lived by a code, he was loyal to the people he cared about, he was strong. Knowledge, competence, awareness of limits, humility, that was the direction to go, Mark would argue. When people objected that Mark was sentimentalizing, Mark insisted that he wasn't. Ike existed. He wasn't a Hollywood invention, he wasn't John Wayne, he was right there. If you don't believe me, Mark would say, get in the car and I'll take you out to meet him.

What Mark never said in an argument was that he knew he couldn't be Ike Watkins. If you were an ambivalence-racked modern man it did no good pretending that you weren't. If Mark had tried to be like Ike he would have gone nuts with frustration. What little Mark knew of Ike's politics they seemed to be somewhere way off the map to the right. Mark wouldn't have been able to handle Ike's evenings at home, with the color pictures of the grandchildren sitting up over the TV set. Ike really liked figuring out how a piece of machinery worked; it bored Mark.

He couldn't be what he admired, what he argued for. He was in the enemy camp. With Rob, Barbara, Kate. He was one of them, one of those he had tried to run away from. He probably had more in common with Kate than anyone else, Kate who could never fully turn anyone away and never fully take anyone on.

He had come West to escape all prior claims on him, claims of parents, teachers, lovers. He had come West in search of a freedom more radical than any of his opponents in party arguments would have dared to suggest, a freedom from ambiguity, from ego hungers, from compromised desires. He had come West looking for innocence, for simplicity, for purity. He had come West, like all those before him, like Owen Wister, Teddy Roosevelt, for his health, and whatever it was he'd found, it sure didn't feel like health.

He wanted the approval of men like Ike. He could imagine what Ike would think if he knew the stuff that went through Mark's mind. Mark admired the Westerners for their openness, their sweetness, their being straight on, but he wasn't one of them, he saw that now, and he wasn't going to be able to turn himself into one of them.

What choices did he have then? To suck it up and go, be a good man, play-act goodness until the lines come without your having to think about it. Practice. The will not to win, but the will to prepare. Play with pain, one of his old coaches had told him, that was what separated the men from the boys.

The other choice, Mark thought, arguing with himself, was to be honest, to let everything hang out, to admit, at least to himself, every sexual thought, every possible betrayal, to reject nothing out of hand. It seemed to Mark to be the way to turn yourself into a monster. To be a pariah or a whiner, to court evil, maybe that was the only variation of heroism available to him. Let himself make a fool out of himself, follow Barbara anywhere, even knowing where it would lead, be half a man, a hanger-on and a beggar, let people scorn him, trust in God to forgive him, the God he didn't even have guts enough to believe in.

He had run too far. He slowed to a stop. His sweatshirt was soaking wet. He felt the beginning of a charley horse in one of his calves. He turned and looked back. The town was out of sight now, he was surrounded by brown barren hills, there wasn't much light left in the sky at all. He started to walk back down the gravel road. He hadn't been paying attention. How had this gotten started anyway? With Ellen's discovery of an old love letter, something that happened to everybody. Mark went into a slow jog. He would have to run some if he wanted to get back before dark.

The fierceness couldn't last. He had exhausted himself. That was part of the problem, that certain extremes of conviction can't maintain themselves, that they disappear like vapor.

When he got back to his house the phone was ringing. It was Ellen, worried about him. She'd already called three or four times, she wondered where he'd been.

"I just went for a run," Mark said. "Out on the refuge."

"You were gone a long time," she said.

"Yeah," he said. "I went further than I should have gone."

"Would it be all right if I came over?" she said.

"Of course. You know you don't have to ask."

"Do I know that?"

"Of course you do," he said.

When she came over she had a present for him, a copy of a book he'd been wanting, *Appaloosa Rising* by Gino Sky. When he unwrapped it and saw what it was, he softened. When he softened, she eased up too.

"I'm sorry about last night," she said.

"So am I," Mark said. He had just gotten out of the shower and his hair was still wet, he rubbed at it with a small blue towel.

"I just felt so cut off," she said. "As if I didn't have a chance." She looked past him anxiously, as if afraid she would discover something more. All that was there was Mark's running clothes piled in a heap outside the bathroom. "I felt you were expecting me to say how wonderful and talented she was, I felt as if I was supposed to applaud her."

"I never said that."

They still stood in the hallway. She was still not feeling comfortable in his house. She was still not sure that she was welcome.

"Maybe not. But I felt it. I just wanted you to sympathize with my position."

"I think I do, Ellen." So this was the way arguments end, Mark thought, I'll have to remember this. They were going over all the same ground, but it wasn't the same, all the rhythms were going their way now.

"Maybe she did give you something," Ellen said. "I just have trouble believing that she was nice."

"She wasn't always," Mark said. "Can I get you something to drink?"

"Not right now," Ellen said. She picked up the wrapping paper the book had come in and began to fold it neatly. "She has a lot of qualities I can admire. Her energy, she's obviously bright. She has a nice home, she keeps things going . . . but she just seems so manipulative to me."

"I suppose that she was," Mark said.

"I can understand, in her position, why she'd be that way. Why she'd be so desperate . . ."

"Yes," Mark said, not looking her in the eye, not believing that he was saying it all the same, because there was something more important at stake now, being reconciled to her. He picked up the book she had given him, thumbed absently through it. One gift deserved another, it was no time for cruel truth. He had hurt Ellen, he wasn't going to hurt her again.

Ellen moved into the room for the first time, passing Mark, going to the window, testing the dryness of the soil in one of the potted plants with her fingers. She turned back to Mark.

"Would you rather be with her?"

Mark set the book down on the table, looking right at her. It was the same question she'd asked the day before, the same question that had started their fight. Some things you couldn't lie about, some things you don't discover until you say them out loud.

"No, I'd rather be with you," he said.

She snipped off a bit of dried, shriveled leaf from one of the plants. "Sometimes I still have the feeling that you don't want to be with me. I can understand that. I don't know how you put up with me, I'm angry all the time and anxious and I gripe at you."

"Yeah," he said. "That's right. And not only that, you're the kindest person I know and the most honest even when you can't help it and you're always right there for people. Hell, I'm not talking about for people, you're always right there for me, and I guess that's what they call a package deal."

Ellen stood by the window, not quite sure what to do. "I'll never tell you how to do the dishes again, you can do them any way you want," she said.

Mark went to her and held her. Their fight was over.

On Saturday they went picking weeds. Ellen was the only person Mark knew who picked weeds, but the arrangements she made with them were beautiful. Ordinarily, picking weeds wouldn't have been Mark's idea of a great day, but today it was just fine. They were together again, anything would have been fine.

It had been a cold night, there was a dusting of snow up in the mountains, then the day warmed up quickly. As they rode north, Mark put on a cassette of Copland's *The Tender Land* and they listened without speaking, letting the music envelop them. Ellen moved over on the seat to be close to him.

They were heading to a marshy section of a shallow river where Mark knew they could find a lot of cattails. They walked through meadows, meeting no one. They saw a coyote trotting warily on a far hillside, stopping to watch them and then melting into the timber. They felt as if they were surrounded by immense spaces, as if all of this was theirs. Every few minutes they heard the sound of geese, sometimes they could see the V-shaped flights, other times the sound was just carried on the wind.

They came to the broad, shallow river. Ellen worked much harder than he did, cutting the stalks of cattails and milkweed with her Swiss Army knife, getting her feet wet along the marshy shore. Mark worked more sporadically. A lot of the weeds were past their time, the pods already exploded, the stalks so dry they shattered when you tried to pick them.

Ellen moved further down into the marshy thicket. Mark wandered along the bank by himself. Things were better now, but he still felt a little foolish. Less than twenty-four hours before, he'd been thinking that he was wretched and doomed, that the only course available to him was to heroically pursue evil, whatever the hell that meant. Now all of that was just gone, vanished. The common wisdom was that people get over things, but Mark was suspicious of getting over things so completely. The flux of life kept cheating him out of his resolutions, however ridiculous.

The wind carried to him the sound of more honking and crying of birds, it sounded real close. Mark climbed to the top of the next rise. He looked down on a wide bend of the river where there must have been a hundred Canadian geese swimming, feeding, parading in the shallow, slow-moving water. The distortions of the low afternoon light made some of the birds appear huge and strange, like some prehistoric fowl, a mysterious glimpse from another world. Some fought, rising up in the water, spread wings beating, then settled down again, gliding quickly away.

He looked back at Ellen. She was bending down, snapping off cattails, tossing the excess stalks in the water. Her arms were full. He wanted to call to her, to have her come see this, but he knew that he couldn't really, if he tried the birds would scatter, certainly take flight before Ellen could reach him.

A light breeze ruffled his hair. Mark pulled up the zipper on his lightweight jacket. From the small rise where he stood he felt as if he could see everything, understand everything. From where he stood he could look down on one side and see Ellen, cutting weeds, look down on the other and see the geese, wild and querulous. It was all on the same river, no more than a hundred yards apart, separated only by a bend, a small rise, and it seemed to Mark then that there was no such thing as real separation, separation was only a trick of perspective. Then Mark thought, his mind leaping forward, spurred by the beauty of what he was seeing, things can be taken together, he could praise two women, out of one love had come another, out of an impossible love had come a possible one. There would be no sharing of what he was thinking now, he wasn't that crazy, he knew what he could discuss with Ellen and what he couldn't, but he felt as if he had come to a new peacefulness. It was a secret that he could keep in a different way than he had kept secrets before.

The gleaming river that looked still wasn't still. The broken stalks that Ellen tossed into the water moved slowly downstream, the geese drifted on the surface, worked their way back. A cold gust of wind came up, rippled Mark's jacket, the geese turned, facing the same wind, resting their bills on their full breasts, eyes shut. They were all poised on the edge of winter. What is beautiful, Mark thought, is only beautiful for a minute, and after that it is all in the act of remembering. He thought of his father going into the hospital.

Ellen was walking up from the shore. She raised her hand to wave at Mark and Mark waved back. The geese must have seen the motion, because they rose in alarm, flew off, organizing themselves in the long, familiar V. Both Mark and Ellen watched them go.

Mark walked down the slope to Ellen. She was cradling a great bundle of weeds in her arms. Mark took half of them from her.

"I'm sorry," she said. "You must be getting bored."

"No, no," he said. "There were all these geese over there, on the other side of the rise. It was about the most beautiful thing I ever saw."

"Really?" she said. "You should have called me."

"I know," he said. "You know what I decided?"

"What?"

"I decided that you were right. I'm going to go out and see my parents. I think it would be a nice thing to do."

Chapter Twenty-eight

His mother was very excited that he was coming. His father didn't come to the phone. He was in the den watching TV, his mother said. His father's not coming to the phone irritated Mark in an old, familiar way. Mark may have been doing the right thing, but there were some things that even doing the right thing wasn't going to change.

Ellen drove Mark out to the airport. They got a cup of coffee and a doughnut, sat at a tiny table, looking out the windows at the men loading up the plane. Mark's briefcase sat on the table between them, a corner of a brightly wrapped box sticking out of it. It was the present that Ellen had given him to give to his father. She had bought him a puzzle because Mark had said once that his father liked puzzles. One thing about Ellen, she never forgot anything you told her.

At the next table one of the security guards talked to the local cab driver, a ruddy-faced man with his boots propped up on a chair. There was a German family, all in cowboy hats, examining the postcard rack. They all had handles of squash racquets protruding from their luggage. Ellen sipped her coffee, watching them. She was being awfully quiet. Though it may have been her idea, she seemed a little disturbed now by his going.

"Maybe you'll see some of your friends," she said.

"I don't have any friends in New Jersey," he said.

"Well, then," she said, "you give your parents my love."

"I will."

The announcement of the flight came over the loudspeaker. The German family rushed to pay for their postcards, gathered up their bags. Mark reached across and picked up Ellen's paper coffee cup and stacked it with his own. He saw the alarm in Ellen's eyes. He started to get up.

"Yes?" he said.

"Will you see her?"

"See who?" Mark said, even though he knew perfectly well who she meant. "No, I don't think so." He picked up his briefcase. Then, more firmly, he said, "No, of course not."

"The worst thing of all would be if you saw her and didn't tell me."

"I wouldn't do that. Not now." Ellen rose slowly from the table. Mark could feel the appeal coming from her, an appeal for some reassurance not so clipped, not so automatic.

Mark reached into his briefcase, made sure he had his ticket, then looked back at her and smiled. "Hey, come on," he said. He put his arm around her. They walked down toward the gate together.

"Do you think we'll be happy?" she said.

"I think we've got a real good chance," he said.

There were three or four people waiting in line to get through the security check. Mark pulled Ellen up short of the line. "I love you, you know," he said. He smoothed her hair with his hand. "I think you're just perfect."

"I don't know why you always say that," she said. "You know it's not true. But it's a package deal, right?"

The uniformed woman at the security check glowered at them, waiting for Mark. Mark stepped to the desk, offered up his briefcase for examination. The woman shook the wrapped present, Mark could hear the pieces of the puzzle rattle inside. The German family was lined up behind Mark and Ellen now, waiting their turn. The uniformed woman held out Mark's briefcase for him to take. Mark turned to Ellen, kissed her on the cheek.

"Time to go," he said.

"You be careful," she said.

"I'll be real careful," he said. He squeezed her hand. He could feel the German family, the security woman rushing them. He walked through the metal detector, stared out the glass doors at the small prop plane, the passengers climbing cautiously up the narrow metal stairs. He looked back at Ellen. At that moment he wished he wasn't going. He didn't know if he picked it up from her or not, but he felt a new sense of dread, a sense that something was about to happen.

His parents were there at Newark Airport to meet him. It was a freakishly cold and windy night, colder than it had been in Wyoming. His mother stayed with Mark while they waited for his suitcase. His father, more edgy than ever, paced up and down outside the luggage area, his hands clasped behind his back, porkpie hat at a tilt, jaw set, giving people the once-over.

On the hour-long drive home Mark's mother was the one to turn around and ask Mark questions. His father was quiet, distant. He drove in the same proudly casual way that Mark remembered from childhood, one-handed, two fingers hooked at the bottom of the steering wheel, weaving the car from lane to lane with no more than a glance. Mark tried a couple of times to get him to talk but got nowhere.

The New Jersey Turnpike seemed like some operatic version of hell, colored flames shooting up from metal towers, snakelike lines of car lights weaving in and out endlessly, heading into the city for Saturday night. The smell of chemicals, oil, sulphur came, disappeared for a time, came back again. Mark wondered how he could have come home to this place.

The lights of the oncoming cars flashed across his father's angular face. Mark could see the muscles working in his father's jaw. It was an old tic he had, but it made his father seem angry even when he wasn't. Hunched forward in the back seat Mark talked on, answering his mother's questions, but aiming his answers at his father. He couldn't tell if his father heard him or not. His father seemed lost somewhere in his own thoughts.

The wind was very strong, boxes flew across the highway and on the bridges the car shuddered. One strong gust nearly sent them out of their lane, Mark's father had to grab hold of the steering wheel with both hands to pull them back on course.

They pulled into the motel. There were a half-dozen cars parked in front of the rooms, gleaming in the dim light. Across the highway there was a Gino's going up, otherwise things looked very much the same.

Their house sat just behind the motel. Mark's father fumbled with his keys for a second, then opened the door. As soon as he did he cursed.

The house was ice-cold. It was the pilot light on the boiler, Mark's father said, the wind must have blown it out.

Mark's father got a box of kitchen matches and marched down the basement stairs. Mark followed him. The basement had the same musty smell it had always had. The Ping-Pong table was folded up against the wall and the old board games Mark and his sister had played with as kids were stacked in the bookcase. They went into the back room. Mark's father groped in the dark for the string to the light, found it, snapped it on. Mark's father bent over the boiler, examining it, the box of matches still in his hand, then got down on his hands and knees.

"You shouldn't be doing that, Dad," Mark said. "Let me do it."

"No, I've got it," his father said.

Rising abruptly to his knees, Mark's father lit a kitchen match, then got down again. He tried to slip the match in under the boiler, work it in toward the pilot light, but his hand wasn't steady and the match dropped to the floor.

"Damn!"

"Dad, come on, let me do it. I've got longer arms."

"I've got it, I've got it. Just hold your horses."

His voice was impatient now, he didn't want any argument. Mark's father straightened up, got another match.

Wind rattled the window at the far end of the basement. Mark stared across the drafty, dimly lit room. There were the bags of salt to soften the water, the old set of weights Mark had worked with his sophomore year in high school.

This was the room where he and his father had played Ping-Pong, where his father had taught him how to box. Mark remembered running upstairs in tears when, at the end of a close game of Ping-Pong, his father had picked on a weak lob return and put it away with an adult slam for the winning point.

Mark remembered another time when his father was teaching him to box and Mark was improving, hitting his father harder and more often. Mark remembered the elation of it, the release of anger, this dark, damp room turned into an arena. He remembered throwing one wild punch after the other and how his father had stopped him with one swing to the midsection, hitting him squarely as Mark lunged forward. Mark fell, the wind knocked out of him.

He gasped for breath, crawled along this same cement floor on his soft leather boxing gloves. He cried in pain, in anger.

He would never know if his father had hit him really hard or not, just that he had hit him on purpose, had hurt him, and Mark, then and now, wasn't totally convinced it had been just to teach him a lesson.

It was his father now who was down on all fours, groping with a match, trying to light the pilot light.

The second match went out and Mark's father cursed again. This time Mark didn't offer to help.

His father was ill. Mark had a lot of trouble watching. All his life Mark had prepared to do battle with this man. It was his father's furies and angers and scorn that had inspired Mark, that he had tried to match in his own way. His father had always been strong and the signs of weakness disturbed Mark. The anger, the rage, had turned to mere unsteadiness. The hand that had been so quick, putting the top spin on a slam, blocking his son's eager lunge, that hand now shook, couldn't hold a match still enough to keep the flame alive. Now that Mark was strong enough, his father wasn't. Things were never even.

On the third try Mark's father lit the boiler. Mark gave his father a hand up. His father kicked at the burned-out matches on the floor.

"Damn boiler. Happens all the time. Mean to have somebody come out and look at it, but I never do, you know how that goes." His father clapped the back of one of his legs.

"How you doing there?" Mark said.

"Fine. These legs, though. Sometimes they just seem to go to sleep on me. But maybe this operation will fix them all up. Hope so, anyway." He grabbed his son by the back of the neck. "Come on upstairs, I think your mother's got a snack fixed for us."

That night Mark had trouble sleeping. There was the constant sound of sirens and trucks outside his window, the flickering of passing lights across the ceiling of his bedroom. Everything seemed magnified. He thought how much he hated the East, its noise, its dirt, how he could never live here.

He was in his old room, his mother had fixed it up again for his visit. His parents were in the next room and the walls were thin enough that he could hear the murmur of their voices, the creak of the bed and, after a time, the sound of his father's snoring.

They know nothing about me, Mark thought. There was no way to ask or tell about the real stuff of his life, about Ellen or Barbara. It has no reality for them, he thought, my other life, but then in some odd way it didn't have much reality for him either right now, sleeping in the same narrow bed he'd slept in as a boy.

In the morning his father's mood was no better. He was silent over breakfast until, after his second cup of coffee, he got going on a detailed explanation of his operation, continuing on about doctors and how their opinions never agreed, how they were out to screw you, what a racket they had going.

Mark left the table and came back with Ellen's present, presented it to his father. "This is from Ellen," Mark said. "I told you about her. The woman friend I've been seeing."

His father stared at the wrapped present. He apparently didn't remember being told.

Mark's mother hovered over the table with the coffee pot. "Oh, yes," she said. "Ellen. I remember. That's really nice of her."

Mark's father shook the package, heard the pieces rattle around inside. "I wonder what it is," he deadpanned and then looked up at Mark and grinned.

He opened the package quickly, pulled out the large circular puzzle of Brueghel's *The Return of the Hunters*. His father examined it for several seconds and then said, "Fancy." He lifted it up abruptly for his wife to see. "Look at all those pieces. A lot of work there." Mark reached across the table, picked off the last piece of toast. Mark's mother was smiling at him. His father said, "It was real nice of her, this . . ."

"Ellen, Dad," Mark said.

An hour later, Mark's sister arrived with her three children. Betsy was in a good mood, she was easier and more tolerant with their father than Mark was. She'd been dealing with him all along while Mark hadn't. The kids were primed to cheer up their grandfather, but he wasn't having any part of it, retreating behind his morning paper and finally escaping downstairs to work on his new puzzle. It gave Mark a chance to visit with his sister.

"So how does he seem to you?" Betsy said. She was sitting on the couch in the living room. Mark sat cross-legged on the floor tussling with his three-year-old nephew Jamie.

"He seems very abrupt," Mark said. "It's tough. He still makes me angry. He doesn't seem to focus or pay attention to people. You just handle it so much better than I do."

"I don't know if that's true," Betsy said. "I think he's really frightened. That's what you have to remember."

"I suppose so. I should make allowances. I don't know why it is I can't." He lifted his nephew over his head, rubbed his face in the little boy's belly till he started to laugh. "It's old, old stuff, right?"

A little bit later Mark walked downstairs to see how his father was doing. His father had already sorted out a lot of the pieces, separate piles for snow, sky, town, tree branches, hunters and dogs laid across the card table.

On the walls of his father's den were awards from one of the motel management associations, his shell collection, a picture of his mother and father standing on a California dock during one of their vacations. In the picture they huddled together against what must have been a fierce wind off the ocean, and they were beaming, happy.

Mark stood over his seated father, looked down at the jumble of pieces. "So how's it going here, Dad?" he said.

"Better than I thought. Usually I don't like these round puzzles. This one's pretty good."

Mark suddenly spied a fit, two pieces of a bird perched on a limb. He reached down, snapped the two pieces together. His father looked up at him, mildly irritated.

"Pull up a seat," he said. "Make yourself useful."

Mark grabbed a chair and sat down. Mark's father explained his principles of organization. The box with the picture on it sat in front of them so they knew what it was they were shooting for. They settled down to work. Mark could hear the children thumping around upstairs.

"This Ellen," his father said finally. "This is the one you were seeing last year?"

"I saw her some at the end of last year," Mark said.

Mark's father picked up the box with the painting on it, scrutinized it.

"Is it serious?" his father said.

"Pretty serious."

"What are you hiding there?" His father brushed Mark's hand away and took the five-piece section that Mark had been working on, slid it across and fit it in with something of his own. "That's just what I was looking for," he said. "You living with her?"

Mark looked at his father in surprise. "Not exactly, Dad. We still have our own places."

"You're not stammering, are you? You think your mother and me are such fuddy-duddies? Look, we know things are different than they were when we were growing up. There's nothing to be embarrassed about. You got any more pieces of dogs over there?"

"No," Mark said.

"Your mother and I have tried to call you a number of times and we never got you in, so I figured that something was up. Seems like she's a nice girl." He looked at the box again, then back at the pieces, lifting his hands so he could be sure he was seeing them all. "If that's what you want you should stand up for it." Suddenly he spied something, then fit two, then three sections together with evident satisfaction. "Do you love her?"

"Yeah, I think so." Mark looked away. His father's golf bag leaned against the wall. His father had had to give up golf when he started having trouble with his legs.

"You know when you and Kendra broke up, I felt kinda bad. I hope the things I said then didn't have anything to do with it." Kendra, Mark thought, Jesus Christ, he hadn't thought about Kendra for years. "I felt bad. I didn't know if you wanted to talk about it or not. When you're a parent there are times when you wish you could say something, but you're never sure that you can. I felt sorry that I couldn't help you more when you were going through all that."

"It was nothing you did," Mark said. "You didn't do anything wrong. That was such a long time ago. You don't have to say anything, really."

This was just like his father, Mark thought, just when you were maddest at him he would turn around and be like this. This was like all the best times. Just when you thought he wasn't absorbing anything it turned out there was nothing he'd missed.

"No," his father said. "I want to say something. You shouldn't be afraid. You've had one bad experience, that shouldn't mean anything. You have a lot to give a woman. I don't know what your plans are, you and this woman . . ."

"Ellen," Mark said.

"You would be a wonderful husband, a wonderful father. To see a child grow up, I don't think anybody should miss that." His father was holding two pieces of the puzzle in his fingers, two cardboard pieces of dull winter ice. He stared at them the way a person might stare at a cracker that he'd unexpectedly broken. "You never know what's going to happen in this life. There's never that much time. You shouldn't hold back, it goes so fast . . . If you could be as happy as your mother and I have been, a person couldn't ask for anything more. Anyway . . ." He tossed the two pieces back on the board.

Mark tried to concentrate again on their common task but couldn't. Mark's father's theory was all wrong, Mark hadn't been mortally scarred by Kendra leaving him, Kendra was so much a part of the past, Mark could scarcely conjure up what that had really felt like. But the theory didn't matter. What mattered was that his father had remembered, what mattered was that Mark's father had, in his way, blessed him, that the two of them were together like this.

Mark stared at the painting, trying to recapture a sense of what they were after. He stared at the returning hunters and their weary dogs, at the tiny skaters on the frozen ponds in the village below, all of them, hunters and skaters alike, dwarfed by the power of winter itself, by the magnificence of a new season.

They drove to the hospital that afternoon. The operation was scheduled for the next morning, the arteriogram had already been done. There was nothing to do. All that mattered, from the hospital's point of view, was that Mark's father was checked in.

Mark and his mother and father sat in the small room, talked, caught the fourth quarter of Giants football on TV, played a game of three-handed hearts. From time to time a nurse would poke her head in to cheerily inquire how they were. One hour stretched into two, evening came. There was nothing to be said or done now, what was hard was separating. Mark went downstairs, to get coffee he said. Really it was to give his mother and father a chance to be alone.

Mark walked the halls, browsed through the magazines in the gift shop, watched people buying plants with big yellow ribbons on them. He watched a mother get off the elevator with her newborn baby, saw the woman's other children rush to greet her, saw her carefully pull back the blanket so they could see their new sister.

Mark grew more and more tense. Against the wall was a line of phone booths, between the booths was a rack with all the directories for all the New York boroughs. Mark went to the phone books, flipped open the one for Manhattan. He looked under C, found Campbell, Robert. He looked it up just to see, he wasn't intending to call, not at first. He stared at the familiar name. A doctor was being paged over the public address system. He remembered his promise to Ellen. He had promised not to see Barbara. He hadn't said anything about calling. There couldn't be anything wrong with calling. He was alone, in a hospital, hospitals were enough to freak anyone out, no one could blame him for wanting to speak to a familiar voice.

Even as he dialed he could feel the old confusions coming back, the old tightness waiting to see who would pick up the phone. He lucked out; it was Barbara. If it had been anyone else he would have hung up.

She was startled to hear his voice and then, quickly, delighted. He explained why he was in New York, about his father and the operation. The tightness never quite left his voice. She was more relaxed than he was, both sympathetic and curious, she was perfectly willing to let it be a chat. That gradually began to loosen him up. They talked a little about Jackson and what the fall had been like, about how Jeffrey and Sarah were handling school. Barbara was even helpful. A friend of Rob's was a surgeon at Columbia Presbyterian, she would give him a call and make sure he looked in on Mark's father, make sure things went well. It was a nice conversation, it went over to the third and last of Mark's dimes. A worried-looking businessman-type paced up and down the booths waiting for a free phone. Both Mark and Barbara were aware that the conversation was coming to an end.

Mark said finally that he should get off and go check on his parents. Barbara waited just one beat. "When are you leaving?"

"I have plane reservations for Tuesday. I'm assuming that all will go well."

Mark could feel the businessman-type peering in at him, putting on the pressure for him to get off. Mark glanced at him. The guy was in a blue peacoat, had chains across his shoes, had gone a little to fat at the age of forty. There was anxiety all over his slightly puffy face. He probably has a parent in the hospital too, Mark thought.

"It's going to go well," Barbara said. "I know it will. Are you flying out of New York?"

"La Guardia," he said.

"I know this must be a hectic time for you," she said. "But if you

had any time at all, it would be lovely to see you. Even for a
minute."

It was what he had wanted her to say, what he had been afraid
to say himself. Quickly he said, "I'd like to see you too. Maybe
Tuesday morning. I'll call you from Penn Station."

As he left the phone booth the businessman brushed past him.
Mark avoided looking him in the eye.

He tried to tell himself that what had happened was nothing,
that he'd tell Ellen when he got back, even if it did cause trouble,
that there was nothing that he needed to hide. Waiting for the elevator, he closed the tips of his fingers to his palms. His hands had
gone cold with anticipation.

He and his mother drove home together. That night, after she
had gone to bed, Mark called Ellen.

"My dad thinks you're great," Mark said. He sat at the kitchen
table. The only light was the eerie fluorescent light above the stove.
The rest of the house was dark. "He loves your present. We worked
on it for a couple of hours this morning and he was quizzing me
about you."

"How is it there?"

"It's O.K. A little disorienting. Good, sad, a bit of everything. My
mother's been great. When things are toughest she always comes
through. I had a nice talk with my dad. He's scared. I don't know if
he should be or not."

"I wish I could be there," she said. "I wish I could be more
help."

"You're doing just fine," he said.

"I love you," she said.

"I love you too," he said.

"You seem so quiet. There's nothing wrong, is there? Nothing
else?"

"No. It's just that the phone's in the kitchen. You're never quite
sure if you're having a private conversation or not."

"But you're really all right?"

"I'm just fine," he said. Even long distance, Ellen could pick up
the fact that something had changed. He felt subdued, diminished,
and he couldn't be sure where it was coming from, how much of it
was his father in the hospital, how much the fact that he had broken his promise, called Barbara.

Early the next morning he and his mother drove back to the hospital, got there in time to see the nurses prepare Mark's father, wheel him off to surgery. He and his mother sat in the empty room. Ellen's puzzle sat completed on the bedside table; Mark's father must have waked up and finished it sometime during the night. For the first time Mark could see the anxiety showing on his mother. She got up, stared out the window, started at any sound from the hallway. She gave Mark a crooked, nervous smile, trying to be brave.

After about an hour the surgeon breezed in to tell them that the operation had been a complete success. The doctor was a tall, confident man, happy to answer questions, keyed up the way an athlete is keyed up after a good game. After the doctor left, the nurse asked them if they would wait outside while the aides brought Mark's father up and got him settled in the room.

Mark and his mother waited in the hallway on benches, listening to two other worried couples talking about their families' operations. Mark leafed through a *People* magazine, pretending to read. Finally the nurse leaned around the corner and said it would be all right for them to come in.

His father looked so small and pale, the bed seemed to engulf him. A success, the doctor said. That wasn't what it looked like to Mark. It looked like an outrage, his father's body shocked, insulted. The sheets were pulled up to cover the bandages on his upper legs and the lower part of his abdomen. He was still a little glassy-eyed and groggy from the drugs. When he tried to speak his voice was raspy, froglike. The nurse explained that they had given him a tracheotomy, inserted an airtube in his throat for the duration of the operation. The airtube sometimes scrapes the larynx, that was what created the odd-sounding voice. It was just temporary, perfectly normal.

His father's attention wasn't really there. His eyes wandered around the room, taking in things the way a little kid would. Mark's mother was undismayed, hanging on to the idea that all had gone well. She sat by the bed, playing with her husband's fingers. After a few minutes he went to sleep.

Mark paced the room. He found himself full of anger. They were supposed to be meek and appreciative, but he felt as if his father had just been beaten up, as if someone should be clubbed for this, but there was no one to go after, no witnesses, nothing, you were just stuck with it.

After a half hour Mark's father woke up again. Mark went over and sat down next to him.

"Dad, this is probably the last time I'm going to see you. I'm going to be flying back."

His father turned his head on the pillow and stared at Mark. His eyes seemed liquid and dark.

"When do you go?" Mark's father said. His voice was gravelly, like someone else's voice in his father's body.

"Early tomorrow. It's all the time they would give me."

Mark's father reached out and took Mark's arm, squeezed his bicep. It was something his dad had always done when Mark was a little kid, a testing, affectionate gesture.

"You're strong."

"No, not really," Mark said. Mark stood up, leaned over and kissed his father on the cheek. "I see you finished that puzzle. Didn't take you any time at all, did it? I think you're going to be just fine, Dad. I'll call you as soon as I get back."

"You tell that girl we'd like to meet her."

"I will, Dad." Mark moved to the door. His father's eyes followed him.

"Be strong now," his father said.

"You too, Dad, you be strong. I'll call as soon as I get back."

The next morning Mark took the train into Penn Station, checked his bags in one of the lockers. He moved edgily through the crowded waiting room, found a bank of phones. He called Barbara, who picked up on the second ring. She would meet him in a half hour in front of the Metropolitan Museum of Art.

Mark took a cab up and he was there in no time at all. He stationed himself at the top of the steps, watched the people coming and going. There was a brass ensemble on the sidewalk, the young musicians playing in light jackets and sweaters. People sat on the steps listening. Sitting on the ledge near the entrance were a number of older people in nicely tailored wool coats, faces turned up to the sun. Several thin, blond women who could have been models were there, and an Italian man with a long scarf, high boots, stylish dark glasses. Buses roared past, drowning out fountains and brass ensemble alike, the giant banner proclaiming the Viking exhibit snapped in the breeze. The scene was one of constant force, of moneyed optimism, of undeclared holiday.

Mark looked down on all of it, on edge, perfectly alert. A police car had pulled up and one of the cops was talking to the musicians. A crowd gathered around them. Twice Mark saw women with auburn hair, started toward them, then realized it wasn't her.

So this is where she lives, Mark thought. It was something he hadn't really considered. This was where her real life was.

The police had asked the musicians to leave, one or two of the musicians were already packing up their instruments, angry people were arguing with the cops. There was such a constant flow of people Mark didn't see how he was going to spot her. He didn't have to. There was a tap on his shoulder, he turned around and there she was, smiling at him, her head cocked to one side, sizing him up. Her hair was brushed back and gleaming. She looked very much the same.

She kissed him lightly on the cheek. He took her hand, just looking at her. A class from one of the private schools ran up the steps, surged around them, for a second Barbara and Mark were afloat in a sea of blue blazers. Barbara's face was alive, bemused, almost laughing, laughing at him, and then Mark laughed too, at some agreed-upon but not quite understood absurdity.

"So," he said. "So you want to go someplace and get coffee?"

"Not really," she said. "Why don't we just walk?"

They made their way down the long steps and headed into the park. The cold snap had broken and there were older people on the benches, reading newspapers, unwrapping sandwiches, holding sun shields firmly under their chins. Black maids pushed white babies in navy-blue strollers.

Mark and Barbara walked side by side, not touching, not speaking, content to watch. As they entered a tunnel she took his arm, then reached up and covered her mouth, stifling a cough. He looked quickly at her.

"That's not the same cough, is it?"

"Not really. Whatever I had this summer got a lot worse right after we came back. I was actually a little scared, but I saw a doctor finally and he treated it with antibiotics. These things are all in your mind, anyway. It really is better."

"You're sure." Their voices echoed in the damp tunnel.

"I wouldn't lie to you. Some things just linger longer than others. Don't look so serious."

"I'm sorry, I can't help it. A couple of days hanging around a hospital makes anyone a little spooky. I don't like the idea of your being sick."

"That's nice of you," she said. They came out of the tunnel and a few steps later she squeezed his arm a little tighter, then let go of it, bent down to pick up a brilliantly red oak leaf.

They talked about his father, the operation, what Mark's days at home had been like. She asked good questions, she always did. She knew a lot about what happened to people when they were ill. She was smart and she was intuitive and she could be so delicate with feelings when it really mattered. Mark had forgotten how much fun it could be to talk to her, how things could be serious and playful at the same time. He remembered it now, what it had been like in the beginning before everything got so loaded.

They walked past empty baseball diamonds. A pair of old women eating their lunch on the bench eyed them suspiciously. There was a physical-education class playing touch football, the sound of the instructor's whistle was carried intermittently on the wind. Dust blew across the dry playing fields. Off to the north a kite flew above the trees. Mark and Barbara walked toward the pond and the stone castle beyond.

"It sounds as if your family did pretty well," Barbara said. "Families either pull together or pull apart at times like that. It sounds like yours has pulled together. That's nice."

"Yes, it is nice," Mark said.

They passed the pond, moved up the sloping walk into a shelter of trees.

"I talked to Judy on the phone," Barbara said. "She said you were out to see her."

"I was. I always was a sucker for the sentimental gesture, right? I saw the finished sculpture. I thought it was wonderful. It was great to finally see what you were up to all that time."

"Are you making fun of me?"

"No."

They stood under a blue-gray sculpture. A small bird hopped across the walk in front of them, oblivious to danger, looking for food.

"Judy said you've been seeing Ellen again."

"You know all about me then."

"Not all about you, no."

"I've been seeing her."

"Quite a bit?"

"Quite a bit," Mark said.

Barbara smiled. "Good," she said. "I'm glad for you." They had come to a rise and could see the buildings on both sides of the park again, sharply etched by autumn sunlight. "I've got news for you too. Rather less likely than yours. Guess who Kate's been seeing."

"I have no idea."

"Michael."

"You're kidding me."

"I'm not kidding you. She flew out to Hollywood and Michael was there, he finally has a deal on his movie, everything's finally going his way, suddenly he's a genius . . ."

"Michael?"

"Michael. He helped her get a part. I know it all sounds pretty tawdry, but she called and talked to us about it and assured us that it's all much more complex than it sounds."

"But I thought Michael hated her."

"He did."

"I sure never heard him do anything but badmouth her."

"It's what you call a change of heart. He's a new man now, you see, he's not just a supporting character anymore, it's time to test his new wings. If his best friend's done it, why shouldn't he? I suppose he feels as if he's in the Great Game at last. I wish him luck."

"And what does Rob say about this?"

"I'm sure Rob hates it, but he doesn't talk about it."

"It's incredible."

"It's incredibly childish. I'm sick of it. I don't care anymore. Or at least I don't want to care anymore. It's descended to the level of farce, which I suppose is what we all deserve."

Mark could hear the self-hatred in her voice. He wanted to argue with her, to say, You have to make distinctions, I don't think you and I deserve that. He said nothing. They walked on in silence for a while. Mark put his arm around her, but she was unyielding, and he took his arm away again, afraid of being misinterpreted.

They sat down on a bench together. They were near the castle, looking down on the pond. A woman ran her dog along the water's edge. Two Puerto Rican kids were walking furiously, giant radios under their arms.

I still care about you," he said.

"I know. I still care about you too."

"You know what I don't like?" he said. "I don't like the idea of forgetting."

"We won't forget. Either of us," she said. "We were just so outnumbered." He reached out to take her hand, but she pulled it away, not wanting to be touched. She stared up at the stone castle. "I hope you and Ellen do just great. I do. People have the power to do evil. I never believed in that before. We could never get back what we had then, you and I. We could never reconstruct it. The bottom line for me is those children. If I ever did anything to hurt them, I don't see how I could go on . . . You want to hear something strange? I feel as if I have an investment in you and Ellen, I want you to do well. You shouldn't hold back. You should go after it for all your worth. No backward glances . . ."

"Sometimes it's pretty hard not to have any," Mark said.

"I know. But I don't want to undermine you and Ellen the way I undermined my own marriage for years . . . and I don't want to undermine what I have with Rob now. We have something, Rob and I do. We've been half-assed about it and careless, yet it has survived somehow, it even survived this summer." She looked at Mark, swallowing, he thought she was going to cough again. "Rob and I, we're growing old together."

"Yes," Mark said.

He leaned forward on the bench, pressed his hands together, stared down at the cracked sidewalk. He realized how unexpectedly happy he was that she was saying what she was saying. It wasn't what he thought he'd come for, he hadn't known what he'd come for, but she was setting them both free. The terror he'd felt about coming to see her was gone now, the weights had been lifted. He looked up at her.

"I feel if I could just talk to you a couple hours a week, it would be so wonderful, I wouldn't have to see you . . ."

"I know," she said. "Why don't we walk?"

They got up and headed back toward the east side of the park, neither of them speaking, both lost in their own thoughts. At the road Mark pulled Barbara back as a cab came careening around the curve, tires squealing.

"I feel so terrific," he said.

"Me too," she said. They crossed the road, passed a playground where mothers pushed their children in swings, where a three-year-old batted his plastic pail with a stick. "It's funny, isn't it?" she said. "That part of us still wonders if we wouldn't have made the all-time most fantastic couple."

"I know," he said.

They walked on through the sheltering trees. Mark felt exalted. Bless her, he thought, bless her a million times. He wanted her life to be all right, for her family to be all right. He thought of his father in the hospital only a couple of miles away, of Ellen coming to the airport to meet him just hours from now, even though it was three quarters of the way across the continent, it was all intersecting lines. If he did it right, they would all be safe from harm.

Suddenly Mark saw the slate-gray of city buses through the trees, they were coming to the edge of the park.

"How are you?" Mark said.

"I don't know," she said. "Part of me feels very relaxed and part feels very tense."

Mark took her hand. From where they stood they could see across Fifth Avenue now. A uniformed doorman was out in the street, trying to whistle-down a cab. A dark-haired model with her portfolio under her arm stood on the curb.

"I should go back," Barbara said. They were still protected by the trees.

"O.K.," Mark said.

He leaned forward to kiss her and she met his lips quickly. They parted. Pulling back, he saw the distress in her eyes and he reached for her face. They kissed again and again and then he was holding her close, it was happening too rapidly to even think about what it meant, but it was as if everything they had just said so carefully could dissolve into nothingness and neither of them would be able to stop it. Suddenly she pulled back, holding her hands up.

"No, no," she said. She was shaking her head. "I can't, I can't." She swung away from him, holding one of his hands, holding him at arm's length.

"I'm sorry," he said, his voice low, discouraged. She turned back to him, smiling. She reached up and cupped his face with her hands.

"Again you're sorry, you're always sorry. You don't have to be," she said, smiling the whole time.

They walked down to Fifth Avenue.

"I'll walk you home," he said.

"It would be better, I think, if you left me here."

Mark looked at her, bewildered. Across the street the uniformed doorman had gotten the model a cab, he fussed over her, slammed the door behind her and the cab sped away.

"Did you tell Rob you were meeting me?"

"No," she said. "I thought it would be easier if I didn't."

He looked at her, understanding suddenly. He knew enough of

how her mind worked. Maybe it was just that it was easier, not telling Rob, but maybe it was more than that, maybe it was that she hadn't been sure what it was she wanted to do. Maybe when she came to meet him that morning she hadn't known yet that she was coming to renounce her claim on him. The boundaries didn't seem so clear-cut anymore, things were not as closed as they seemed.

"Would you rather I'd told him?" she said.

"I don't know. Whatever you've done is all right. I love you," he said.

"I love you too," she said.

He kissed her on the cheek. He watched her cross the street. When she got to the other side she looked back and saw him still watching her. She waved and he waved back. She did not look again.

As he watched her go he realized how much they hadn't said. There had been none of the usual assurances that people give one another when they say goodbye, nothing about whether she and Rob were coming out to Jackson for the fall hunt.

She was a block away now, on the far side of the street. Mark began to walk in her direction, passing the people gathered at the bus stop, then began to walk faster, trying to catch up. The stream of traffic separated them, a slow-moving river of cabs and buses. He had one more thing to say to her, he didn't want it to end like this. She hadn't looked back. Mark skipped out into the street but a cab suddenly accelerated around a slower-moving car, forcing Mark back to the curb. Barbara had turned down a side street. Mark didn't try to cross again. He watched her disappear down the narrow tree-lined street, all the cars neatly double-parked. Mark hailed a cab and headed downtown to pick up his bags.

Chapter Twenty-nine

A month passed and a new watchfulness came over Mark.

The elk season had opened and Mark began to see the hunters around town in their clumpy boots, red jackets and orange fluorescent hats. There were a lot more four-wheel-drive Scouts around with horse trailers in the back. Every so often Mark would see a gutted-out elk in the back of a pickup, the frozen legs sticking up

toward the autumn sky. Now and then there was the distant booming of guns. Ellen didn't like it at all; it scared her.

The talk was that it was a hard fall for the hunters, warm and
dry. Everyone was waiting for some snow to drive the elk down
from the high country. The Fish and Game people were predicting
a late migration. It felt as if the whole town was waiting. Along the
roads outside of town Mark would see pickups pulled over and
hunters glassing the empty flats.

Mark wanted not to be looking for Barbara, but it was impossible
not to be. They were coming out for the hunt, the Campbells and
their friends, that's what she'd said. When was anybody's guess.
As the days passed, Mark became surer that he would run into her
on the street.

He and Ellen were fine, all the same. It wasn't as if he was thinking of Barbara all the time. On his return he hadn't said anything
about seeing Barbara in New York, but that omission didn't really
feel like a lie. Day by day Mark realized how much he was coming
to count on Ellen. As things loosened up between them, he realized
how funny, how droll she was. They were working out a new kind
of lighthearted style together and a new kind of hope. Waking in
the night, he would call out her name, reaching for her. He was not
going to betray her. It was just that a part of him was watching. A
person could be faithful, Mark thought, and still find himself scrutinizing the face in a passing car just a second too long.

Then in the first week in November it began to snow. There
were flurries for a couple of days, then two inches on the third day
and the temperatures began to drop. When Mark drove into town
to shop on Saturday morning cars were sliding all over the roads.

He had just finished his list when he saw Judy standing at the
meat counter. Her cart was piled high with steaks, several six-packs
of soda, Haagen-Dazs ice cream, fresh California fruit. Mark knew
that they were back. It wasn't the kind of food that Judy would buy
for herself.

Judy smiled as she saw Mark wheeling his cart toward her. She
didn't look surprised. She was smiling almost as if they had arranged to meet here.

"Well, look at you," he said. "Looks like you're getting ready to
feed an army."

"Not quite," Judy said. The butcher banged his way through the
swinging doors, his apron splattered with dull red spots. "They've
all come back, you see. For the hunt."

"Ah," Mark said. He saw the shopping list in Judy's hand. He recognized Barbara's handwriting. "When did they get in?"

"Three or four nights ago. It's a bit of a zoo. Michael flew back and Kate with him. You remember Kate."

"Of course."

An old woman maneuvered her cart past them, muttering, irritated at their blocking the aisle.

"There's her and Michael and some business friend of Rob's from New York who fancies himself quite a sportsman and he's brought his seventeen-year-old son with him. Rob and Ike have taken the lot of them up to the hunting camp for a few days. I don't think Ike was too enthusiastic about it." Judy was looking past him, as if she wasn't quite comfortable talking with him.

"And Barbara?"

Judy hesitated for just a second. A heavyset man in a parka stomped into the store, batting his jacket to get the snow off. He shouted something to one of the checkout clerks. Judy stared absently at the diversion.

"Are you about ready to check out?" she said.

"Sure."

"Me too. Why don't we get in line?" They rattled their carts down the narrow aisle.

"She's here, isn't she?" Mark asked.

"Oh, sure," Judy said, trying to be nonchalant. "She's out at the ranch now with the kids. She's fine. Over here, Mark, there's a checkout spot open."

Mark followed her. A husky-looking climber was leaving just ahead of them, sticking his half-dozen energy snacks in the pockets of his down jacket. He didn't need a bag. Judy stacked her groceries onto the counter. Mark could tell she was holding out on him.

When all her groceries were checked through and packed Mark said, "Hold on a minute and I'll help you with those."

They walked outside together, each of them pushing a cart. There was just a light snow coming down now and kids were running and sliding in the street, packing snowballs.

"I suppose the hunters will be glad to see this snow, won't they?" Mark said.

"The station wagon's over here," Judy said. Mark followed her. She fumbled with her car keys, finally opened the rear door. Mark lifted one of the grocery bags and set it inside.

"Why didn't Barbara go up with them?"

"She never goes up with them. She doesn't like hunting." Judy's tone was sharp, defensive.

"But is she all right?"

Judy suddenly faced him. She closed her hand quickly over her car keys. For a second Mark thought she was about to lash out at him. "No, I wouldn't say that she's all right."

"What do you mean?"

The two of them stood at the back of the station wagon. Flakes of snow settled lightly in the bags of groceries.

"You know that cough she had all summer and couldn't get rid of? The one she thought was all in her mind?"

"Yes."

"Well, they finally decided to take some x-rays, just to be safe. On the first set they didn't find anything. On the second set they did. A spot, a shadow, I don't know what they call it."

Mark frowned, wiped some snow off the roof of the station wagon. "Where is it, this shadow?"

"Somewhere on her lung. She wouldn't really explain. You know how she doesn't really explain things sometimes."

Mark looked away. The kids in the street threw a battery of snowballs at a passing bread truck. The snowballs thudded emptily against the brightly painted panel.

"So what does that mean?"

"I don't know what it means. I don't think she does, either. When they go back to New York she has to see another doctor. They'll decide then whether they need to do a biopsy."

"A biopsy? For what?" His voice was rising now. One of the kids throwing snowballs in the street looked over at him.

"To see if it's . . . whatever."

"To see if it's what?" He was grilling her now and she resented it. She picked up a bag and tossed it in the back. She hadn't been careful enough, the bag toppled over and cans rolled into the corners.

"I'm not the doctor, Mark," she said.

More gently, Mark said, "When do they leave?"

"Sunday's their last day. They leave early Monday morning."

Mark picked the last bag out of the metal cart and Judy took it from him without a word. She set it in the back, slammed the door hard.

"I don't know what you're so angry at me for," Mark said.

"She's my friend too, you know," Judy said. "She's been a better friend to me than to any of the rest of you."

Ellen noticed how quiet Mark was when he came in. She mentioned it several times, but he kept saying that nothing was wrong, so she finally just let it drop.

It snowed all that day. Ellen was gone part of the afternoon because she had a dance rehearsal. Ellen had let herself get talked into agreeing to give a performance with a group of women from town and the rehearsals were now taking up most weekend afternoons. Mark stayed home and tried to read.

That night they went out to an Italian restaurant with friends. One of the guys had worked on an Indian reservation for two years and after a couple of bottles of chianti they got into a freewheeling argument about the American Indian Movement, intertribal politics and Francis Parkman. Nobody won, but it was a wonderful conversation. It felt warm inside that circle of people. Ellen was glad to see that Mark was out of his moodiness. She took his hand under the table and squeezed it now that she saw that he was all right.

It was fierce getting home that night, almost a blizzard, with high winds and driving snow. They crawled along at thirty miles an hour, Mark bending over the steering wheel, trying to see out into the blowing snow. They passed a couple of cars that had ended up in the ditch. Mark was silent again, concentrating on staying in the middle of the road. Gale winds buffeted the car. In the dark the wind seemed to gain some new dimension, an invisible force against which there seemed to be no protection.

That night in bed Mark curled up close behind Ellen, his lips against her shoulder. Wind rattled the windows. He thought again of what Judy had told him. Cancer. Cancer was the word she'd been afraid to say. He thought about the possibility of Barbara dying, of losing her in a way different and more final than he had lost her already. He felt himself beginning to panic. No one that age was supposed to die. Death was something that happened to somebody you didn't know, a long time from now.

Judy hadn't told him enough, it wasn't fair. He should have quizzed her, the only reason he hadn't was because of caution, the old habit that didn't apply now.

Ellen moved in her sleep, rolling onto her back, and Mark moved too, taking her hand. Twice already he had brushed against death,

once with his father, once with Sarah. With Sarah he had been sure
that she was dead, sure that he had won her back by the promise
that he would give Barbara up. He couldn't keep expecting miracles.

Gusts of wind battered the windows. The mobile of brass whales
in the corner spun, clanged together, there was no way to keep the
wind totally out. He considered how he might see Barbara. She
would be here one more day, Judy had said. Ellen rolled back onto
her side, restless in her sleep. You have to stop fooling with this
stuff, Mark thought, you fool with it too many times and it will get
you by the throat. Maybe that was what he wanted. Maybe he
hadn't learned anything at all.

He slid up next to Ellen again, nuzzling his face in the hair at the
back of her neck. The brass whales chimed in the dark corner. He
had one more day to see Barbara, maybe just one more day till forever.

Mark tried to sleep, but couldn't. His mind kept drifting, drifting
to Barbara, to those hunters up in the mountains, they were going
to have one hell of a night up there. This kind of weather would
get the elk moving. In his mind he saw the lines of dark animals
moving against the snow, saw the hunters on their horses, hunters
with guns in their hands, impossible dreamlike figures maneuvering
the high snowy ridges, men and animals slowly converging, fitting
together like pieces in a puzzle. Mark wondered if the hunters were
happy now, if this snow was making them glad.

Chapter Thirty

Ike woke before dawn and rolled out of his bag, lifted the flap of
his tent. There had been a good inch and a half of snow during the
night and it was still coming down. Birds hopped silently in the
snow, searching for food. The horses stood, heads together in the
corral, stomping and snorting in the dark.

The snow pleased Ike. Maybe the snow would get the elk moving, because it sure had been a bust of a hunt so far.

Ike hopped quickly into his clothes in the chill tent, jammed his
Stetson on his head, pulled on his jean jacket and went out and got
some wood to start the fire again.

Ike worked silently, stoking up the fire, put on the coffee, got the bacon frying. This was the moment he liked, the moment before the others got up.

Ike had set up hunting camps for forty years, done it for Mr. Campbell and his friends, and now he was doing it for Rob and his friends. It was work, no doubt about it, a couple of weeks of setting up tents, repairing the corral, cutting the firewood, moving saws and axes and grain for the horses fifteen miles back up into the mountains. It had always been a first-class hunting operation. This was hunting the right way, the old way, not like the road hunters you saw down in the valley sitting in their r.v.s with the TV sets on waiting for an elk to run up their bumper.

Not that it could ever be like it was. This was a different bunch, Rob's bunch. Mr. Campbell was a different sort of man than Rob was. Rob's father was what they used to call a dude and there was no disrespect intended, a man who wanted to learn how to do things the right way, how to ride, how to hunt, how to handle a gun, how to handle cattle, the kind of man who listened to you when there was something he didn't know.

Rob knew how to do things, he'd been riding and hunting since he was a kid, but the rest of them treated it like it was some kind of joke. Ike always had the feeling that they were laughing at him behind his back. This Michael character had been complaining from the first day. The ride up had been too much for him, rubbed his thighs a little raw, and he made sure everybody knew about it.

Then there was the woman. Ike didn't like having women around hunting camps. In the old days they didn't allow it. When there was an exception, when Mr. Campbell had one or two women come up, wives of his hunting buddies, they could shoot just as good as the men. But this one, she wasn't even there to hunt, she was there with her camera, to take pictures she said. Ike wasn't that much of a dummy.

Certain things Ike was supposed to see, like the matted grass where elk had bedded down, their rubbing on the trees, and certain things he wasn't supposed to see.

Kate slept in Michael's tent. When they went out on the hunt she rode behind Michael. They'd come in on the flight from L.A. together, Ike had picked them up at the airport. It just didn't feel like they were together. They sure hadn't been together in the summer, Ike had been around enough to hear some of the terrible things Michael had to say about her. Ike had also been around enough to see how jumpy Rob was with her, to see the guilt in his eyes.

Now in the evenings Kate's hands were all over Michael, but even that didn't seem quite real. It was as if it was all for show, all for Rob's benefit. If that was what it was, it worked. Rob would lean back, pretending not to notice, elbows resting on the long wooden table, looking real uncomfortable.

Michael did a lot of talking, especially the first couple of nights when they played poker after dinner. He rambled on about his movie, how he'd like to put Ike in it, how he'd love to put them all in it, and when he said that, Rob said, looking steadily at him over the top of his cards, "I thought we already were in it." Ike didn't quite know what that meant, but he could feel the friction between the two men. Michael, full of himself, went on about deals and grosses and percentages and who was sleeping with whom and how much money there was out there just for the taking, all this while they sat in front of their stacks of nickels and dimes, waiting for Rob to make his discard, the long tent lit by kerosene lamps. Michael wanted to let everybody know that he wasn't a loser anymore. He had a movie now, he had Kate, he was ready to play with the big boys.

He was a little nervous about it still. He slapped Rob on the back more than he needed to. He wanted to be approved. Rob kept quiet, but Ike knew Rob well enough to read what that kind of quietness meant.

One thing that success hadn't done for Michael was turn him into a hunter. Though he talked like he'd hunted before, it was pretty clear that he hadn't. For three days Ike had gone out with Michael, Kate riding behind with her cameras draped over her neck. They'd had a couple of opportunities, but on the first one Michael had trouble getting off his horse and getting his rifle out of his scabbard, and on the second he'd fired high. He complained afterwards that his scope had fogged up. Kate got pictures of it all.

Rob stayed out of the way, guiding his friend Murphy and Murphy's son. They didn't have much luck either, Murphy missed a half-dozen wild shots on a big bull at dusk on the second day, but it was clear that wasn't Rob's fault.

Ike could see Kate starting to change. Her hands weren't all over Michael quite as often. The morning after Michael missed his shots he came back into camp complaining about his rifle, and Rob finally took him out by the corrals to sight in the scope. Michael stood by as Rob knelt by a hitching post, using it as a rest, targeted in on a rock three hundred yards across the meadow. The first shot wasn't more than two feet high. The horses and mules in the corral spooked at the sound of the blast, milling around, banging against the rails. Kate came out of her tent to watch. Rob checked the rifle; he didn't do much, maybe he didn't do anything at all. The second shot was on target and so was the third. Ike sat on a stump, working on one of the saddles and watching; Rob always could shoot. Rob went on shooting, longer than he needed to, not missing. It was a real fine performance and Ike figured any actress like Kate could tell a real fine performance when she saw one.

When he was through, Rob got up off his knees and handed the gun to Michael without a word, as if to say, it's fixed, now you do what you can. Afterwards Murphy was grumbling to Ike how he didn't approve of shooting around camp, but he didn't say it loud enough for Rob to hear.

It was the screwiest elk hunt Ike had ever been on. The snow couldn't help but improve it. Signs of elk were all around, tracks, beds, rubbings, bugling at night when the hunters were heading back into camp after dark. The snow would push those animals down, the high country was becoming impossible to live in now, the grass too far down under the snow for their pawing hooves. Real hunger made any animal stupid. Ike had seen it happen so fast, one big blizzard and they would all be in motion. Ike remembered one year looking out and seeing five hundred elk all over Big Game Ridge, the place crawling with animals.

Ike looked up when he saw the tent flap open. It was Kate and that didn't please Ike much. She carried her camera equipment and she came in talking.

She was wound up, even more than usual. There was something a little off, Ike could tell, she was like one of those little toy gyroscopes when they start to wobble. She got talking about movies, asking Ike questions but not waiting for answers. She put a pan of water on the stove to boil, paced up and down the tent, once nearly knocking over a kerosene lamp with a gesturing hand.

She talked about cowboy movies, about *Shane* and how much it meant to her. Ike had seen it once but he didn't remember much about it. She had some theory about it and heroes. She wanted to know what Ike thought a hero was. Was he the guy who ran into a burning building and pulled one person out, letting the rest burn?

Or was he the one who saw the fire, called the Fire Department and everybody lived? It didn't seem like much of a choice to Ike.

She washed her face in the pan of water, scrubbing her hands hard with the rough soap. She asked Ike who his favorite cowboy movie star was. He said, Ben Johnson. She said, Why? He said, Because Ben Johnson wears his own hat in every movie he makes. You could tell the sweat was really worked right into the band, Ike said, that was something you couldn't fake. Ben Johnson seemed to him to be a real regular guy.

She stood up suddenly from the bowl of soapy water, her arms dripping wet. She stared across the dim tent lit by kerosene lamps. Ike stood at the grill, doing the eggs.

"We're all freaks, you know," Kate said. "All of us actors. The thing is to know you're one, that you can't be anything else. And not to be ashamed. Even freaks should be able to demand some respect, don't you think?"

Ike didn't know what to say. He didn't like the idea of a beautiful woman thinking she was a freak, and he didn't like anybody implying that Ben Johnson was a freak either, but he held his tongue.

The men came crawling in, Michael and Murphy and Murphy's son. Rob had gone off to get the horses saddled. Ike could hear the horses whinnying down in the corral. Ike poured everybody a cup of coffee.

It was their last day, Murphy was saying, what kind of luck did Ike think they'd have? Murphy's son heated up another pan of water, steam rising in the cold air. He was shy around Kate, a little in awe of her, and when he washed he kept his t-shirt on, running a washcloth over his face and long arms, glancing sideways at her.

Michael didn't talk at all. He sat down at the table, ignoring Kate, and began to methodically lace up his boots.

When Rob came in, Ike threw eggs and bacon down in front of them all. They were going to have to move, Ike said, if they wanted to get into position by daylight.

Kate began stuffing rolls of film in the pockets of her jacket. She stared right at Rob. There was nothing subtle about the way she was looking at him, and she didn't seem to care who noticed. Michael bent over his plate of eggs, pretending to be absorbed in an old copy of *Sports Afield*.

"I thought I'd go out with you today," Kate said. Rob gazed at her calmly, took another sip of his coffee. Murphy's son watched both of them, trying to learn. "If you don't mind."

"I don't mind," Rob said.

"All my pictures are of Michael. I don't have any of you."

Rob glanced over at Michael. Michael looked up from his eggs, smiling. "It's perfectly all right with me," Michael said. "Like she said, she's got all the pictures of me she needs." He tossed the copy of *Sports Afield* back onto the stack of old magazines.

Even Murphy realized that something wasn't quite right. "So what are we going to do then?"

Ike tried to cover up. "Why don't I go with the Murphys here and Michael? Maybe it will change our luck."

"No, you go with us, Ike," Rob said. He stood up from the table, stacking three or four of the plates. "I haven't hunted with you yet. It'll be like old times, Ike." Wind fluttered the canvas walls of the tent. "Michael and the Murphys can go up to the ledges. They've been up there before. They'll probably do better without us."

No one said anything. Everyone in the tent knew it was wrong. Michael and the Murphys didn't have a chance in hell of finding an elk by themselves and Rob knew it. Rob just didn't give a damn. It wasn't like him, Ike thought, not like him at all. The only thing that made sense was that Rob didn't want to be alone with this woman.

Rob helped Michael up into the saddle, spent a minute making sure the girth was tight. Michael, betrayed, pulled the hood up on his yellow raingear. Rob pretended not to notice, went over to Murphy to give him some last-minute tips. When Michael and the Murphys rode off they didn't look back once.

Ike and Rob and Kate mounted their horses. Ike led them out. Everyone was quiet. They rode in the dark, but after twenty minutes it started to lighten up, they could make out the shapes of the trees on the hillsides. They could hear coyotes calling somewhere below them, cries ringing the valley as the animals gathered themselves into a pack.

Ike led them up the ridge, the horses picking their way over deadfall timber and shale, loose rock crumbling under their hooves. The last forty yards to the top were tough, the horses scrambling and heaving, grunting like boxers. They rode out to the point, then dismounted and tied the horses to some scrub pine.

They crouched, moved slowly out toward the point. Kate wasn't making a sound, staying back, behaving all of a sudden. Rob curled up behind a burned-out shell of a tree, gazed down on the meadow a couple of hundred yards below them. Ike lay in the snow, a few yards off. Kate was ten yards back of both of them, holding herself up on her elbows, her camera in her hands.

It was a spot Ike had taken Rob up to for years. Ambush Point it was called. The wind was in their favor. The light started to come up, hitting some of the high peaks of the Tetons. The lakes below the peaks were still slate-gray. Ike glassed the meadow, binoculars clutched in his wool mittens. It was still a gray soup down there. The only sound was the horses scraping their foreheads against the low branches of the pine tree. Ike looked back. Kate had never taken her eyes off the two of them.

The wind blew up on the point and Rob scrunched down a little more. Ike glanced back at the meadow. The light wasn't what it had been before, but there was something else that had changed too. Ike wondered if it was only a trick of the light, maybe it was only a stump or a rock, but where before there was nothing there was now something, out on the snowy meadow were dark-brown figures, set like tiny carved wooden toys on a white table.

Ike stared at them and then one of the figures moved. It was cow elk and calves, a half dozen of them. Ike gave a low hiss and Rob looked back at him. Ike nodded down to the grazing animals and handed the glasses to Rob. Rob stared through the glasses for a second, then pointed to some cows that Ike hadn't seen. Ike saw that the meadow was crawling with elk, but none of them bulls.

Even without the glasses Ike could see the cows jerking their heads up and looking back into the timber, as if there was something in there making them look, something big.

Rob put his glasses down and, moving real slow, reached for his rifle, careful not to knock anything. The gun went up, snug to his cheek. The barrel moved back and forth across the meadow. Behind them Kate was up on one knee, the camera to her eye. Rob was trying to see back into the timber, and the rifle scope let in more light than the human eye could.

Then the bull came out. His head was up, alert and uneasy. He had a big rack, six, seven points, and he was sniffing the air. He trotted a few feet and then stopped, confused. Rob had his gun ready. He used the burned-out stump as a gunrest.

It was a cinch shot, two hundred yards, a still target. Kate slid along the snow, trying to get another angle with her camera. Ike looked over at Rob. Rob was taking too long. Maybe Kate's moving rattled him, maybe it was just some odd self-consciousness about

being photographed. Ike would have waved for her to be still, but
there wasn't even that much time.

The wind shifted, or it could have been the bull sensed something. The bull started running toward the far end of the meadow,
and the cows ran with him. Ike could hear their guts bouncing,
they sounded the way horses sound when they run, the way any
large animal sounds. Rob had to hold for a second more, there was
a cow between him and the bull and then the bull was in the open
again. Rob fired and the bull made a complete three-sixty flip and
was down. The cows and calves went crashing into the timber, they
sounded like an airplane crashing down the mountain, and then
were gone.

Rob and Ike both stood up. The bull wasn't dead yet. It raised its
head but couldn't get to its feet, the head flopped down again. Kate
came up to Rob, put her hand on the back of his jacket. Her eyes
were bright with excitement.

"That was incredible," she said. He moved away from her touch.

"It's not done yet," Rob said. Ike saw the look of self-disgust on
Rob's face, Kate may not have. There was no excuse for not having
taken that first shot when the bull had been standing; if Rob had, it
would have been all over. Waiting that extra second made for a
messy finish. The animal thrashed on the snow below them. "Let's
get our horses and get down there," Rob said.

They took their horses down the steep slope. Rob dismounted
and walked toward the downed bull. As Rob got closer the animal
grew more frantic, the long brown neck arching up and then flopping back down again like a fish flopping in the bottom of a boat.

Kate stood beside her horse, watching, then dropped the reins.
She moved forward several steps, snapping pictures, not a lot of
them, but some, and Ike knew Rob well enough to know that he
didn't want pictures of this one.

Rob was wary for the last dozen steps. He put his gun to the animal's head and fired. There was no more movement. Ike pulled his
axe out of its scabbard. It was time to clean the animal.

Rob and Ike worked together, Rob holding the legs wide as Ike
slit the belly with his axe. The steam from the warm animal rose in
the winter air. Organs glistened, untouched and perfect, tan and
pink and outsized. The intestines were full from grazing during the
night, just hours before.

They turned the animal on its side. Kate stood back. She'd put
her camera away, her hands were in her jacket pockets. There was

blood on both Ike's and Rob's hands now. The trick was not to cut into the guts, then it got real messy. Ike cut the windpipe free, made a tiny hole in it with his knife.

"Here," he said. "Take hold of this. There's a finger hole."

Rob took hold of the windpipe, slipped his finger in the narrow slit and began to pull the huge sac of organs. Kate was scratching the ears of her horse. Ike worked quickly to cut away the last bits of connective tissue. The two men strained and finally the mass of organs was out. Rob wiped his hands on the numbing snow, cleaning them of blood. Ike rested on his axe for a second before starting the quartering. The mountains were a brilliant gold now in the morning light. Already the ravens were croaking overhead, waiting for them to leave so they could begin their feed.

When Rob stepped back Kate tried to take his hand, ready to forgive him for his bad humor. Rob didn't let her, wiping his cold hands again on his jeans. Maybe he was embarrassed in front of Ike, maybe he was mad at her, upset because it had been such a bloody finish. Ike didn't give two nickels what it was, he'd gotten them their elk, that's all any guide was supposed to do.

Chapter Thirty-one

From the front window Barbara watched the children sledding down the slope in front of the house. She snapped up the front of her down jacket, patted the pocket of her jeans to be sure that she had the keys to the jeep.

The kids were having fun out there. It was nice to see them playing together like this, it was something they did rarely now that they were a little older and each had their own friends. Watching them trudge back up the hill with the sled behind them, it could have been a scene from two or three years before.

It was a mild enough slope, but Jeffrey had tried to make it more exciting by setting their course so they had to angle between two trees and then shoot out onto the now icy driveway where the sled would slither and fishtail from low bank to low bank.

Barbara winced each time the sled sailed out into the driveway. The old protective habits were hard to break. She thought of how much her life had been like this, watching them to be sure they were safe. Barbara remembered when Sarah was small, letting her crawl around on the bed. Sarah would always perch right at the edge and look over, exploring the boundaries of everything, and Barbara's hands were always there, ready to catch her, to save her from a fall.

The two kids were at the top of the slope. Jeffrey got on the sled first and Sarah behind. They shoved off, weaving between the two trees, the dog plowed through the snow behind them. They flew out onto the icy driveway, skidded against the far bank, Sarah fell off and Jeffrey kept going. The excited dog tried to lick Sarah's face as she rose slowly from the snowbank, but Sarah fended him off. Jeff got off the sled fifty yards down the driveway, waved to her and they shouted back and forth to one another. They were O.K. Everything was still play.

Watching them climb back up the hill side by side, Barbara felt a sadness come over her and it took a minute to figure out where it was coming from, to remember the summer, to remember Mark and the time they had sledded together in the shadowed bowl of the mountains. That was before it had really started, that was when it had all been new.

The only sound in the house was the ticking of the grandfather clock, then the soft striking of the hour. It was ten o'clock. Judy should have been back from the grocery store by now.

Four days and Barbara hadn't called him. She had been tempted, but she hadn't done it. She and Mark had a pact now and they were holding to it. She had pacts all around, pacts with her children, her husband, with herself. She was trying to hold the ground she had gained. Maybe that was what it meant to be a grown-up, to know when to hold tight and when to give way. One of the things adults were for was the protection of the innocent pleasures of children.

She left the house, walked down toward the jeep. The children waved from the top of the slope. She shouted to the children that she was going to meet the hunters, Judy should be back any minute.

Barbara backed the jeep around, headed slowly down the icy road. The dog chased her for a while, but gave up after a hundred yards and trotted back toward the sledders.

Barbara turned out onto the highway and headed north. She felt the mild pricklings of anxiety. Most people, Barbara knew, would have thought it a bad idea to allow Kate to go up to the hunting camp with Rob. Barbara was starting to think it was a very bad idea too.

She still wasn't sure why she'd agreed to it. Maybe it was the way it had been presented to her. Kate was an old friend, she was deeply involved with Michael, the old stinger was out, there were going to be all kinds of other people around, all she wanted to do was go up and take a few pictures. All summer they'd gotten notes of reassurance and friendship from Kate, notes aimed more at Barbara than at Rob. No matter how terribly she acted, Kate always could write a graceful note.

Barbara had gone along, even though she hadn't been totally convinced of the innocence of the enterprise. Part of the reason for her going along was just style. Neither Rob nor Barbara were in the habit of putting their foot down, they both took some delight in playing against expectation, in being deliberately cavalier about conventions. Besides, Barbara felt very sure of Rob now, she trusted him.

Still, four days was a long time. Barbara hadn't realized it was going to be quite that long. Barbara's casualness was beginning to falter. She knew Kate well enough to know it was almost impossible for her to resist playing one man against another. Barbara was increasingly resentful. Whether she was as ill as the doctors said she was or not, she shouldn't have been left alone. Barbara had never been very good at seeing the consequences of things. Letting Kate go up there now seemed like a very bad idea.

She turned off the highway onto the snowed-in gravel road, making the first tracks. When she came to the lower corrals she saw the empty horse trailers and the pickups right where Rob and Ike had left them. So they weren't even down yet.

Barbara got out and walked through the empty corrals. Maybe she was a little early. Maybe the snow had slowed them down. If they'd gotten anything on the last day, that would delay things while they packed the meat. Barbara just hoped they weren't having any trouble. A raven perched on top of the grain shed took off, flopping heavily through the dark woods.

Barbara got back into her jeep and started it up. She was going to do something Rob didn't approve of, but she didn't care. She suddenly needed very much to see him. Barbara had had too many scares in the last six months. She headed the jeep up the horse trail. The trail was wide at first and easy to drive, but then it started to narrow as it headed up.

Rob didn't like her driving the jeep like this, but Barbara was enjoying herself, it pleased the daredevil in her. Branches slashed at
the windshield. The jeep bounced and lurched through a creekbed,
wheezed up the other side. Partway up, the wheels started to spin
on wet ground. Barbara let the jeep roll back a little, started again,
lurched forward to the top of the ridge. The steering wheel spun
out of her hands as she hit a rock, she grabbed hold again.

It was a beautiful morning, the mountains in snow for the first
time. Great clumps of snow dropped from the trees onto the hood
of the whining jeep. Barbara felt a kind of exhilaration, the daring
of what she was doing driving off the spooky feelings she'd been
having.

Barbara did great until she came to the last hill, three quarters of
a mile from camp. There was a tree down across the trail, and
when she tried to angle around it through the woods she got stuck.
She tried to rock the jeep out, alternating forward and reverse, but
it was hopeless. She got out of the jeep. She could walk the rest of
the way. Ike would be able to get the jeep out in a second, she was
sure of it.

The snow created a cathedral-like hush as she walked up through
the rocks. The great dark wet trunks of the trees stretched up high
above her. All around her she saw the network of delicate tracks in
the snow, tracks of mice and rabbits and birds. She'd been up to
the camp before, she knew it wasn't that far.

It was a hard climb, all the same. She began to feel the prickly
flashes through her body, tiny stabs of fever, the same things she'd
been having for months, one thing she hadn't told the doctor. She
stopped for a second to catch her breath. One of the terrible things
about a doctor telling you that you're ill is that you become too
alert, anything can become a sign of weakness.

It had warmed up some. Melting snow thudded down from the
trees, spraying around her. Barbara opened the top button of her
jacket. As she headed up she half-expected to meet them on the
trail with their horses and mules. She would take them by surprise,
she thought, what a laugh it would be. Barbara stopped to cough,
wiping her mouth with her glove, checking it to be sure there was
no trace of blood.

The distance seemed longer than before. For a moment nothing
seemed familiar, she wasn't even sure she was on the trail, the snow
obscured all the landmarks. She kept on, all the same, the worst
that could happen was that she would have to follow her tracks

back. She labored up the slope for another ten minutes and finally came out on the meadow and could see the tents across on the other side. She felt a flood of relief.

She walked quickly across the meadow, leaping the same meandering stream a half-dozen times on her way. She heard one of the horses whinny.

The camp was silent. There were a couple of the mules in the corral and four or five horses. Barbara was puzzled. It must have been after eleven, they should all be back by now, something must have gone wrong. Rob's horse Charlie trotted over to the rail to be petted.

Then Barbara saw the elk quarters wrapped in cheesecloth hanging from the cooling pole, looking like huge hams. A set of antlers sat on the woodpile. Someone had made a kill. They must be here somewhere, Barbara thought. Then she heard Kate's voice, high and insistent, coming from one of the tents.

"I don't know why we have to be enemies, Rob. Tell me why. Why did you even want me to come here then?"

Then Barbara heard her husband's voice. "Because you're a friend of ours. Of mine and Barbara's."

The canvas tent rippled with a light gust of wind, and then Barbara heard Kate's hoarse, mocking laugh.

"So it's over, is that it? You've changed that much. You're a different person now. So you never desire other women now."

"I never try."

"You tried this summer. It was over this summer too, wasn't it? Or that was what you told me. Explain it to me, Rob. Or wasn't that what you call a real try?"

Rob's reply was muffled, Barbara couldn't make out his words, he must have gone to the other end of the tent. Kate laughed again, mocking him.

"Rob, you are one of the most dishonest people I know. At least Michael admits he's screwed up sexually. You've always been too easy on yourself. Monster that I am, at least I'm not easy on myself."

Barbara shifted her weight from one foot to the other in the snow. Finches darted and pecked at the hanging slabs of meat, pecked relentlessly through the cheesecloth. Again she heard Rob's muffled reply, and then she heard Kate's voice higher and clearer.

"In other words, you're ashamed of me, aren't you? Admit it. The only reason you got involved with me at all was that you were afraid of being left alone on the main stage with her. I'm the only one who really understood you, remember that, Rob?"

"Don't you throw things up to me." Rob's voice was suddenly distinct and angry, he must have come back toward her. The small birds fluttered and fought over the fresh hanging meat, the sun on the snow was dazzling. Barbara felt faint. She shouldn't have come here. She was terrified that they would come out and discover her, but it was impossible for her to move.

"I thought you said you were with Michael. I thought you and he were doing fine."

"Is that what you thought, Rob? That would take you quite off the hook, wouldn't it? A wonderful relief. Am I such a burden to you?"

"I'm a married man. I have two children."

"And I thought you were an adventurer. I see now that I was wrong. You're just a man of habit, and some very bad habits too. Somewhere along the line you've picked up the habit of desire and that's a hard one to break, Rob, it's a lot tougher than stopping smoking . . ."

There was the sound of a slap and then crying. Barbara stood in the snow, amazed. She could never imagine Rob hitting anyone.

She was horrified. Wasn't it ever going to end? It was such perfect Kate. One of the things that made it so horrible was that it wasn't even surprising. It was perfectly simple figuring out what had led up to all this: Kate had gotten bored with Michael, come on to Rob, Rob had turned her down, Kate had started accusing him of cruelty. Maybe Barbara should have been glad; after all, she'd caught her husband in the act of being faithful. But she wasn't glad at all.

Standing outside the tent in the snow, listening to them fight, she realized how much of her husband was closed to her. She wondered if she knew him at all. She wondered if she loved him.

Hearing Rob tell her about his relationship with Kate was one thing, it was a painful story, but this was like walking into someone else's nightmare. It was the details that made it so terrible. Kate had said something about his trying this summer. Not that they had slept together, just that he had tried. What made that so awful was that it meant it hadn't been over when Rob had told her it was over, a small deceit maybe, compared with some of the others, but a deadly one. Barbara suddenly couldn't trust her judgment about anything now. She was no better than Rob, she knew that, she had it coming. That didn't help.

She could even feel sorry for her husband stuck in there with Kate at her most merciless. Kate was crazy, but no one had ever said she was dumb. She was right about them all, again and again, like a skeet shooter on a tear, blowing one clay disk after the other out of the air. Poor Rob, Barbara thought, Rob is an innocent in comparison with me.

When Rob spoke again Barbara was startled by how close his voice sounded. "I'm sorry," he said.

"No," Kate said. "Don't. Please. It doesn't matter. You're very important to me. All I'm asking is that you still care for me a little . . ."

"Of course I care for you," Rob said.

Barbara walked away. All that was left was the inevitable kindness, the necessary concessions. She didn't need to hear any of it. She tramped through the snow, not looking where she was going. If she got lost now it scarcely mattered, she was ready for that. She was maybe a hundred yards from camp when she heard voices, the whinnying of horses ahead of her. Out of the trees came Ike on horseback, pulling a mule behind him. The mule had the quarters of an elk strapped to its sides, the antlers arched over its back like an enormous thorny crown. Riding behind came Michael and then Murphy and his son. When the mule saw Barbara on the trail ahead of them he tried to pull off to the side, but Ike yanked on the rope, cursing him.

"Barbara!" Michael shouted. "My God, what are you doing up here?"

"So who's the hunter in this group?" Barbara said.

"The kid here," Michael said. "Can you believe it? First time hunting, dumb beginner's luck, it really isn't fair. Thank God Ike came up to find us, though, we were lost as hell up there . . . Rob just went and abandoned us." Michael kicked his horse up, rode to Barbara's side, offered her a hand. "Hop up here, Barbara, I'll give you a ride back into camp."

"No, I'm fine," Barbara said. "It's not that long a walk."

Chapter Thirty-two

That night Mark had a dream. In his dream he and Ellen were sitting in the balcony of a theater. They had a baby and the baby was downstairs with the woman in the cloakroom. Barbara was downstairs too. Mark knew she was there even though he couldn't see her. In the middle of the performance the baby started crying and Mark got up to care for it, but when he got downstairs Barbara already had his baby in her arms and was comforting it. Then, somehow, the baby wasn't there, maybe the woman in the cloakroom had taken the baby back. He and Barbara were outside. Barbara was very beautiful, there was an aura around her. There were bleachers and Barbara was leading him toward them, toward the darkness, toward a place where they could be alone.

When he woke in the morning he felt very disturbed. He remembered the dream perfectly and it threw a cast over everything. He was strangely out of touch; making breakfast he put some English muffins with cheese down in the broiler and then forgot about it until the smoke started to roll up out of the stove.

Mark and Ellen sat silently over their coffee, watching the birds flutter in the birdfeeder outside the window.

"Is there anything wrong?" Ellen asked.

Mark smiled at her. "No," he said. "I'm just waking up."

Ellen pushed her chair back from the table. "I should get going," she said.

Mark frowned. "Seriously? I thought you didn't rehearse till the afternoon."

"They want us to come early so we have a chance to listen to the music all the way through. And then we rehearse for a couple more hours this afternoon. Don't worry," she said. "This will be the last weekend. It will all be over and everything will get back to normal."

Ellen gathered up her stuff, put on her jacket. Mark found himself following her around the house, wanting to stay as close to her as he could for as long as he could.

When he walked her out to the car he didn't put his coat on and it was cold. As they stood by the open car door he was shivering. She tossed her dance bag onto the front seat.

"Are you sure nothing's wrong?" she said.

"I'm sure."

"So what are you going to do today?"

"Correct papers. I don't know. I'll have to see." Suddenly he reached out and pressed her close to him for a second. "I love you more than anything," he said. "Do you believe that?"

She smiled at his earnestness. "Do I believe it?" she said, mimicking his seriousness. "Of course I do." She pulled his collar together, buttoned the top button. "I love you too. You make me feel so lucky. I don't know what I'd do without you." She kissed him lightly on the cheek. "You'd better get inside before you catch your death of pneumonia," she said. "I'll see you tonight, right? At my place."

Mark went back inside, not even watching her drive off. He knew what he was going to do. It was all just a matter of time. He cleaned up the dishes, went to his desk and tried to work, finally shoved the student papers aside. He yanked open the bottom drawer of his desk, lifted out the large manila envelope, secured more securely now than before, ripped at the layers of tape. He lifted out one of the letters, read the familiar, flowing hand.

"I feel so full, so expanded and richly warmed by you, I want to take your hand and lead you through my life." He pushed back abruptly from the desk, stood up, knocking the envelope to the floor. Papers slithered out. Mark bent down and gathered them up.

He went to the window. Everything was covered by snow. He knew that he was going to see her. It was her last day, her last day in Jackson, Judy had said. She wasn't going to lead him anywhere, anymore. He had to see her. He felt himself plunging headlong back into the world of deceit, it made him feel distant from the world you could touch. But how deceitful could it be to see a person you might never see again?

He put on his coat, went out to his car. Out on the highway he snapped the cassette of Copland's *The Tender Land* into place. The music filled the car, soothed for a moment the terrible panic.

It was Sunday morning and Michael had decided that he needed a piano. He and Rob stood just outside the house in the snow. Rob was splitting firewood for the fireplace. Michael kept him company, hands jammed down in his pockets, collar turned up against the cold. They were just below the kitchen window and every so often Barbara or Kate would appear, heads bending over the kitchen sink or stove, getting ready for the party. Neither of the women showed any signs of noticing them. It was that kind of morning. Everybody's nose was out of joint.

"What kind of place is this, anyway, that doesn't have a piano?" Michael said. "I thought you said it was civilized out here. When you want to make music, what do you do, bang two stones together?"

"We had a piano this summer," Rob said, "but the sounding board was way out of whack and we had to take it in. I don't know what's happened to it." Rob lifted the axe over his head, brought it down hard, split the log perfectly. "So what is it that you need a piano for, anyway?"

"I want you to hear these songs I had written for my movie. Believe me, they're just terrific. I thought you could be my test audience. Everybody would enjoy them, really. The composer I got to do them is the hottest thing in Hollywood, the young Cole Porter, the young Sondheim, honest to God."

Rob picked up one half of the split log, brushing the snow off it, set it back on end on the chopping block. Ike had taken Sarah and Jeff and Murphy's son down to the barn to feed the horses. Ike banged the pail against the gate and far down in the pasture the horses perked up their ears, then began to run for the barn, galloping, racing across the snowy field.

"Sometimes I get the feeling that people don't really believe that this movie of mine really exists, that everybody thinks, 'Oh, that's just good old Michael bullshitting again . . .'"

"That's not true, Michael, come on."

The horses poured into the barn, banging into the gate. Rob swung the axe again, the wood split with a loud crack, cartwheeled across the snow. Michael bent down to retrieve the pieces, finally taking his hands out of his pockets.

"I don't know where I get the feeling then. Maybe I'm just making it up."

"You're too sensitive, Michael."

"Am I?"

"Christ, Michael, what's wrong with you?"

"Who knows? I don't know. It's all too crazy for me, man, it's all over my head."

"What's too crazy?"

"What do you think? Kate. Kate's out of her fucking mind."

Rob leaned against the handle of his axe, staring at Michael. "What do you mean?"

"You know how crazy she is," Michael said, calming down, not facing Rob. Clouds drifted against the dark mountains.

"No, you tell me."

"You know how she tries to set you against me."

"Tell me how she does it."

Michael bent down, gathered up a handful of snow, packed it into a snowball. He still couldn't look at Rob. "Last night she said that you agreed with her about how fucked-up I was about women."

"She said that?"

Michael arched the snowball high into the air, it thudded harmlessly in the driveway. "That's what she said." He looked at Rob now. "It's not true?"

"Of course it's not true. You think she and I go around discussing things like that?"

"People discuss just about everything."

"Come on. How can a person even answer something like that? No, Michael, no, I don't agree with her."

"It makes me feel so small even to say something about it . . . she does that to you . . ."

"We let her do it, Michael," Rob said.

"She still wants you, you know. Last night she told me that what she had with you was one of the three or four most important affairs of her life. Isn't that something? God knows if I even made the Top Twenty. And she treated you like crap. Crazy. You wouldn't want her back, would you? You wouldn't."

Rob said nothing, wiping the snow off the axe blade. Ike and the children and Murphy's son had come out of the barn. The pickup was down there and Ike pulled the elk antlers out of the back, letting Murphy's son show off his prize to Sarah and Jeff. It was a beautiful rack. They set it on the snowy ground and the distance from tip to tip was about as far as Murphy's son could reach.

"You know what I'm going to do?" Michael said. "I'm going back out to L.A. and I'm going to make one hell of a movie, I'm going to knock those people on their asses, and all this crap isn't going to be any more important than summer camp. These songs, Rob, you'd love 'em. These songs would cheer up Oswald Spengler. I can't believe you don't have a piano, man. Here you got Judy living out here, a piano *teacher*, and no piano."

"She's got a piano," Rob said.

"She does? Where is it?"

"She's got it, but she doesn't."

"What do you mean?"

"Her husband won't let her have it. You remember Tommy."

"Who can forget Tommy? The psychopath who dumped you in the river."

"Tommy's got the piano."

"That's too bad."

"Isn't that the way it always goes? Everything's always too bad." With one hand Rob suddenly windmilled the axe, set it deep into the chopping block.

"We're done?" Michael asked.

"Yes, we're done." Michael began to collect the pieces of wood, but Rob hadn't moved. He stared down toward the barn, at Murphy's son showing off his trophy. "Put that stuff down," Rob said.

"I thought we were going inside," Michael said.

"No, we're not going inside. Not yet."

"Where are we going then?"

"We're going to go get you a piano."

They were going to get Judy's piano back. Rob was talking like it was a prank, a neat little caper, but that wasn't the way he was acting. Rob was taking it real serious, Michael could tell, there wasn't a lot of humor there, and that scared him. Rob talked like they'd waltz in, have a little discussion, all very reasonable but firm, and waltz out with a piano on their backs. Michael didn't believe him. Michael smoked a joint in the pickup on the way in, hoping it would calm him down. It didn't. This was real vigilante stuff, the kind of thing where people start throwing tire irons at each other, Rob knew it just as well as Michael did. It was a lunatic scheme. Maybe Rob was as nuts as Kate was, but at least they were buddies again.

It took only about twenty minutes to get into town, even with the snowy roads. Rob drove hard. They drove the back streets of Jackson, Rob hunched forward, looking for house numbers. Two kids on skis labored across the street in front of them. Rob pulled the pickup to a stop outside a row of small crackerbox houses and turned off the motor.

"This is it?" Michael said.

"This is it."

"Now this piano is actually hers, right? She bought it and everything?"

"Right."

"You don't think this guy is violent-violent, do you?" Michael asked.

"Your guess is as good as mine," Rob said.

Michael grinned at him, rubbing his cold hands together. "Asshole," he said.

The two men stepped out of the truck, slammed the doors shut. Both of them looked up and down the street. There was a teen-age boy walking his horse in circles in the front yard of one of the houses. Rob and Michael could see television sets flickering in the living rooms across the street, all turned on to Sunday football.

"We'll just go to the door and knock and ask him in a perfectly civilized way, assuming he's there of course, we'll say that Judy asked us to pick up her piano for her," Michael said. "Maybe we'll say we just came to borrow it. We're all men of reason and goodwill, right? I don't see any lights on, Rob."

Rob was already halfway up the walk. "Come on," Rob said.

"Oh, shit," Michael said. He kicked once at the snow, then did what Rob said. Rob was in charge now.

They stood together at the back door. A pair of muddy hunting boots sat on a worn mat. Rob knocked. They waited and then Rob knocked again, louder. There was no answer.

"No one here," Michael said. "Just our luck."

Rob stepped down into the snow, peered into one of the windows.

"Hey, don't do that," Michael said.

"It's right there," Rob said.

"What do you mean, right there?"

"It's sitting right there, right inside the door."

"Hey, Rob, you're not suggesting that we actually go in there? It's not like this guy is an old prep school friend or something." Michael saw the hard light in Rob's eyes. "Rob! Christ! I don't need a piano that bad."

"No?"

"No!"

"I don't think you quite understand, Michael, how much this matters to me."

"How much it matters to you? Why should it matter at all?"

"It matters very much to me that something ends up in its proper place. With the person it belongs to. Things have been getting very, very sloppy lately, Michael. Nobody plays by the rules anymore. You know what I'm talking about, don't you, Michael?"

"I guess so." Michael knocked the snow off his boots. "Rob, what if he's asleep in there? The door's probably locked anyway."

"People never lock their doors in this town," Rob said. "It's not that kind of a place. Not yet." Rob twisted the knob and pushed open the door. "You see what I mean?"

Michael wiped his face nervously. "You're a madman, you know that? O.K., Robin Hood, let's go and get it over with."

They stepped inside the house. The place was dark and smelled of cigarettes. An empty carton of a Swanson's TV dinner sat on the arm of an overstuffed chair. Michael and Rob were both still for a second, listening for any sound. Newspapers were piled up on the piano, no one had used it for a long time.

Rob nodded to Michael, who moved quickly to the far end of the piano. It was heavier than it looked. The first try took Michael's breath away.

"Hey, hold on a second," Michael said. "What do you say we call in movers?"

Rob waited until Michael was ready to try again. The tiny wheels squealed, the two men rolled the piano toward the kitchen. As they struggled to angle the piano through the kitchen door, Michael backed up for a second, afraid he was losing his grip, and knocked into a floor lamp. As the lamp hit the rug there was a hollow pop of a bulb exploding.

"Oh, damn!" Michael said.

"Just leave it," Rob said. "Lift up your end, Michael, just an inch and we'll have it."

They rolled the piano quickly across the linoleum kitchen floor. As Rob opened the door to the outside, a swirl of snow blew in. Michael pressed his palms into the small of his back, grimacing. The two men maneuvered the piano down two steps onto the snowy walk.

Bent low, they wheeled the piano down the walk, taking fast little beetle steps. Twice they nearly tipped it, working in too much of a hurry. The horse in the far yard, tied up to a clothesline now, watched placidly.

Rob opened the back of the pickup, slid the two planks down, and they wheeled the piano up into the truck. Rob threw a heavy blanket over the piano and roped it securely. He jumped down and slammed the tailgate shut.

The two men grinned at one another.

"O.K., Butch Cassidy, let's get the hell out of here," Rob said.

They jumped into the truck. As Rob pulled the truck away from the curb Michael started pounding on the dashboard. "Broad daylight! Can you believe that? Broad daylight and we got away with it! Oo-oo-ee!"

Tommy was just sitting there, watching the game, sipping his beer, having a good time. Wiley had invited him over to watch the Broncos.

Wiley was an old-timer, had outlived two wives and divorced a third, ran the worst souvenir shop in town. Wiley drank too much, lived alone, except for a nasty little Chihuahua named Ricky, and he groused about everything. Wiley was the kind of man who didn't give a damn about anybody's opinions and right now that was the only kind of friend Tommy was likely to have. They didn't see a lot of each other, but since they were both batching it, as Wiley put it, and since they lived right across the street from one another, they'd usually get together on Sunday afternoon to watch the Broncos.

Wiley was p.o.ed because the Broncos couldn't get their offense going and he finally couldn't take it anymore, flinging a crumpled-up Coors can at the yipping Chihuahua and stomping off to the kitchen for more beer. Then Tommy heard Wiley call in a queer kind of voice.

"Hey, Tommy, come here."

Ricky cowered in the corner behind the TV. "What do you want? Get back here, Wiley, Morton just ran for a first down, you wouldn't believe it."

"No, I'm serious, Tommy, come here. I want you to look at something."

"Man, I know it's snowing, I saw that already. Get in here, Wiley, the Broncos got a drive going."

"I'm not talking about snow. Just come here."

Tommy reluctantly pushed himself up out of his chair and walked into the kitchen. Wiley stared out the window, looking across the street toward Tommy's house.

"Take a look," Wiley said. "Two guys just walked into your house."

"You're kidding me."

"No, I'm not kidding. You recognize that pickup?"

"No," Tommy said. The Chihuahua snuck up behind Tommy, ready to take a nip. Tommy shook his boot at him and the little dog scampered away.

"Holy Moses, here they come again!"

As Tommy and Wiley watched, the back door to Tommy's house swung open and they saw Michael's rear end sticking out and then they saw the teetering piano and then they saw Rob.

"Jesus, Tommy, they're stealing your piano!"

"Damn," Tommy said softly. "I didn't think they had the guts."

"They're burglars, jackass! Don't just sit there on your butt! Let me get my shotgun!" Tommy held him by the arm.

"Just hold it, Wiley. You don't know what's involved."

Wiley looked at him sideways. "What do I need to know that for? You mean it's not paid for or something?"

"No, it's paid for all right."

Tommy watched, his hands braced on the sink, stretching forward like a swimmer just before the start of a race. Michael and Rob worked the piano down the walk. From the living room came the steady drone of the football announcer. Tommy was suddenly in a very good mood.

"That's great, man, that's really great!" Tommy was almost laughing. Wiley didn't get it.

"What do you mean? You know those guys?"

"Sure, I know 'em."

"Weirdest damn thing I ever saw. If they're such good friends of yours, why don't we go over and give them a hand?" Wiley said crossly.

"I didn't say they were friends, I just said I knew them." Rob and Michael nearly tipped the piano over. They were rushing, Tommy could see that, it was pretty funny.

"I don't get it," Wiley said. "Two guys come walking into your house like that and you're being so calm about it. I guess things are just a lot different these days. There was a time when you could get shot for a lot less than that."

"It's nothing, Wiley. It's just a kind of practical joke, that's all."

Rob and Michael shoved the piano up the planks into the back of the pickup. Wiley popped the top off his beer, sucked off the foam. Wiley was steaming. The pickup pulled slowly away from the curb.

"I'll take care of it my way, Wiley," Tommy said. "Don't you worry about a thing. You drink your beer, go back in and watch the Broncos. I got this covered."

Tommy felt perfectly resigned as he walked across the street. He was in a very good mood, he couldn't quite figure it out. The piano was Judy's anyway. She should have come and got it herself maybe, but it was no big deal. Just that it made him wonder a little, wonder just what the relationship was between them and her. The thought did cross his mind.

He went into his house. He knelt like a hunter looking for signs, fingered the yellow wheel marks on the rug where the piano had stood. He reached out, crumpled up the newspapers that had fallen on the floor. The living room looked bigger with the piano gone.

Then he saw the fallen lamp. Tommy picked it up, saw the pieces of the broken bulb. Very careless, these people. They couldn't even take the time to pick up after themselves. The piano was hers, but the lamp was his, the rest was his, they could have shown some respect.

Tommy still felt pretty happy. Tommy had been in the wrong for so long. Anytime he did anything now people distrusted him. No one would go near him, it was like he was a leper. People wrote him off as a crazy person, it was getting so Tommy was almost ready to believe it himself. Any fears he had about Judy out there on that ranch, fears that they were taking advantage of her, using her in one way or another, he didn't dare mention to anyone. They would have laughed in his face. "After all you did to her and you're worried about *that?*" The way things were, it had been pointless even trying to contact her.

But now it was different. They'd come into his house, they'd broken his lamp. It was pretty clear what had happened. It was nice to feel like he was in the right for once. Watching those guys pushing that piano down the walk Tommy felt alive for the first time in a long time.

Tommy went to the closet, got out his heavy coat, strode out of the house and, letting the door bang shut behind him, headed for his truck.

Mark's heart dropped for a second when he saw all the cars parked in the snowy driveway in front of the house. He should have known that they would be having a party. A crowd was something he hadn't counted on. It would make things a little awkward, but a little awkwardness wasn't enough to turn him back now.

Sarah and Jeffrey and two children that Mark didn't recognize were having a snowball fight in the front yard. When Mark got out of the car they stopped their playing and stared. Mark waved to them and Sarah waved tentatively back. Jeffrey gave no sign of recognition, looking away, packing another snowball. Mark wondered what the children had been told about him, if it ever came up.

Mark walked to the porch. He heard the sounds of a piano and of people's voices. He knocked once, twice, no one came to the door. They weren't expecting anyone else, he thought. Mark let himself in.

He stepped inside and there was a moment before anyone saw him. Michael was at the piano in the middle of the room, playing and singing some pattery twenties number that Mark didn't recognize. There were a dozen people there altogether. The ones who'd been on the hunt Mark could pick out by their ruddy, windburned faces and the expensive Pendleton shirts. Rob stood by the grandfather clock, his back turned to Mark, and he was explaining something to a huddle of earnest people.

There was a long table set with food, there were greenery and candles and a big fire. The place was beautiful but there was something wrong, Mark could sense it, something wasn't working. A woman in a red pants suit was draped across Michael's piano, but her gaze drifted across toward Rob. One of the hunters stood alone at the fire, guzzling his drink. Mark didn't see Barbara or Kate. It had the feel of a party at which something terrible had just happened.

Then Mark saw Judy. She knelt next to the table of food. She had a broom and dustpan and was cleaning up after someone's accident, picking up the pieces of glass by hand.

Mark moved away from the door and Judy looked up. She was the first to see him. Mark saw the shock on her face and, with it, the warning. The others turned toward him, looking up from their plates, their conversation.

Rob came toward him. He didn't seem at all surprised. His smile was more ironic than friendly.

"Well, how are you?" Rob spoke loudly, jauntily, as if it was an announcement.

"I'm sorry to bust into your party like this," Mark said. Over Rob's shoulder he saw one of the guests whispering to another, asking questions. "I heard that you'd come back. I ran into Judy in town."

Rob kept smiling steadily at him, as if he hadn't heard a word.

"Would you like a drink?" Rob said.

"I'm fine," Mark said. "Thanks. Judy told me that Barbara was ill. That you didn't know yet what it was. I'm sorry." He looked Rob directly in the eye, there was no advantage now in clumsy deceits. "I wonder if I could see her."

"She can't see anyone right now," Rob said abruptly. "She's busy." The smile came back. "Why don't you have a drink? There's lots of food. I'll introduce you to some people."

Rob took Mark by the arm, led him into the room. Judy had disappeared. Michael kept playing, rolling his shoulders like some slick old-time bar entertainer, never missing a note. He nodded slyly at Mark, gave him a wink. The woman in the bright red pants suit smiled brilliantly.

Rob took Mark to the long table, ladled out a cup of mulled wine and handed it to him. Mark took a sip of the wine, he could feel the rest of the room watching them.

"You're teaching again this fall?"

"That's right."

"And how is that going?"

"Fine."

"Have you been able to keep up with your running? It must be a little harder . . ."

"Barbara is here, isn't she?" Mark said.

"Yes. She's upstairs."

"I'd like to see her."

"I told you. She's busy." Rob moved to the fireplace and Mark moved with him. Rob picked up a poker and began to stir the fire.

"I don't want to cause any difficulty."

"No, no, you're not," Rob said. He expertly rolled one of the logs onto its side. Some of the coals sifted down and then the flames licked upward again. Rob set the poker back in its stand. "She'd probably be very glad to see you, actually. Sure. Why not?" Rob gestured toward the staircase. "After you."

A ruddy-faced seventeen-year-old boy sitting at the bottom of the stairs with a plate of food on his lap moved to one side to let them pass. Mark walked up the stairs, one hand sliding along the banister, Rob was right behind him. Michael's playing faltered for just a second and then picked up again. Mark moved cautiously, it felt like a trick. At the top of the stairs Mark stopped. Rob gestured again, toward the guest room. When Michael's playing stopped altogether Mark heard the two women's voices arguing. Rob nodded for Mark to go in. Mark didn't move, not trusting him. Rob knocked on the door, the women were suddenly silent.

"It's me, Rob."

Rob opened the door. Barbara sat on the bed, her eyes were red, she had clearly been crying. Kate stood by the toy chest, her hand resting on her neck, perplexed, theatrical. The only sound in the room was the bubbling of the small aquarium. The children's drawings were still on the wall. Mark had made love to Barbara in this room. Now he had walked into a trap.

Barbara stared wildly at Mark, then at Rob. She cried out angrily, "What are you doing to me? Why are you punishing me?"

"I'm not," Rob said. He shut the door behind them. "He came on his own. He heard a rumor that you were ill. He was worried about you. No conspiracies here."

"I don't understand," Mark said.

"It's not so complicated," Rob said. "It's just that you walked in at a rather inopportune time. Barbara's feeling very betrayed right now. She seems to feel that Kate and I have been carrying on behind her back, that we haven't been quite honest with her. Maybe you already know some of this, Mark, I don't know how much Barbara has told you. That's one of the problems, people not being very open with one another, it gets more complicated than it needs to."

"I don't know what you're talking about," Mark said.

"We're talking about betrayal. Maybe you have something you'd like to contribute."

"No," Mark said.

"Barbara?" Rob said. Barbara said nothing.

"Oh, Christ, Rob, let's not have a quiz," Kate said. "You sound so stuffy, Jesus."

"I can't help how I sound," Rob said.

Mark stared at Barbara. She was in gray slacks and a white ski sweater. The sweater made her appear smaller somehow, coiled up like a hurt animal. She seemed to be trying to regain her breath. She looked older, worn, Mark thought. Her face was averted now, she played absently with one of the tassels of the bedspread. Mark searched her for some sign of her illness. Barbara must have felt Mark's eyes on her because she looked up at him suddenly, her gaze steady, without shame.

Rob saw it. He turned away, slapped the globe that sat on the child's desk in the corner, spun it into whirring, teetering motion.

"I just want to get to the bottom of things," Rob said.

"No one's going to get to the bottom of anything, Rob," Kate said. "There is no bottom. You think he's been sleeping with your wife? Then ask him. Or even better, just beat him up on the spot, get it over with," Kate said. "Are you that angry, Rob? Just how angry are you?"

Rob turned to stare at Kate. "Don't try to make me look ridiculous, Kate. Haven't you done enough of that already?"

Kate shrugged sarcastically, hopelessly. She dipped down into the toy chest and picked out a raggedy-looking doll. She began to smooth the doll's hair. Behind Kate on the wall was a quilt with bright, interlocking rings of color.

Barbara's eyes were still on Mark. "How are you?" she said softly, ignoring the others.

"Fine," Mark said.

Rob moved to the door, leaned back against it, facing the three of them.

"We're four intelligent people," Rob said. "I'd like to figure out how we got into this mess. Barbara and I are no saints. But we've had a life together, somehow, we enjoy certain things together, we still laugh at each other's jokes. You know how families get little jokes among themselves, don't you, Mark? Things that wouldn't be funny to anybody else?" Kate was looking bored, as if she'd been through all this. She explored the back of the doll with her fingers, trying to find the voice box. "We love our children," Rob said. "We're not such bad people that it should hurt so much all the time . . . It simply isn't fair . . ." Rob's voice was trembling.

Mark saw Barbara look up at Rob, open her mouth as if she was going to speak, but she didn't.

Mark walked to the window, looked out at the children down in the yard. They were playing Fox and Geese in the snow. The wide circle had spokes in it, pathways that cut it up like a pie, and the children ran back and forth in their puffed-up winter jackets and heavy boots. Mark could hear their cries of excitement. Sarah fell for a second, outside the boundaries, losing her hat, but she righted herself quickly and ran off just before she was caught. The chase went back and forth, innocent, pointless, Mark couldn't even tell who was It and who was not.

Rob pushed himself away from the door, paced the room. "It's clear that we can't go on like this, simply overlooking things. It would be nice to know, when the accounts are balanced, what it is we've got left. If this pain is not going to end, I would like to know what we should do." He stopped suddenly, looking at Kate and then at Barbara. "I can say this. I can say that I still love my wife." He pulled his fingers through his hair, staring at Barbara, waiting for an answer. "Why don't you say something?"

"I don't have anything to say right now," Barbara said.

"Would it be all right for us to go now, Rob?" Kate said. "If you want to know what's going on, talk to your wife. She'll tell you what you need to know. You don't need us."

Mark felt Barbara's gaze again. He turned to her. Her eyes shone now with tears, with some desperate expectancy. Her fingers were closed tight on handfuls of bedspread.

Kate's voice rose higher. "I don't know why we're here at all. He and I, we get the least of anyone. The short end of the stick. We're the ones who get used." Kate squeezed the doll hard several times, forced out of it a feeble, mechanical cry. "We're the ones who get left out in the cold." Kate flung the doll back into the toybox, turned on Barbara. "I don't know what you're attacking me for. You don't have anything to worry about. You heard him. He loves you. Nothing's changed. It didn't end between us quite when he told you it did. So what? So he's less than perfectly honest. You always knew that about him, it was one of the first things you and I talked about. I was never anything to him, I was just a functionary. I haven't done a thing to you. It's up to you two to make up your minds what you want."

Barbara suddenly stood up from the bed. She was looking only at Mark. "I can't stand it anymore. Take me out of here."

"Barbara," Rob said, warning her. Barbara walked across to Mark, took his hand. "Barbara, don't be ridiculous," Rob said. "This is not the point." He reached out and tried to take her arm. She pulled away.

"Don't you touch me!" Barbara shouted.

"Barbara, think about what you're doing!"

"I've thought about it much too much already." She moved to the door, threw it open, she still had Mark by the hand. Moving out of the room, Mark banged against the banister, not looking where he was going.

They went down the stairs together fast, half-running, Barbara just a step ahead of Mark. The people gathered at the piano gawked up at them, the girl in the red pants suit froze, a silver fondue top in her hand. The boy at the bottom of the stairs shot to his feet, Mark and Barbara moved past him.

All Mark could think about was how much like a movie this was. It was a scene only actors could do, it was the scene he had wanted all summer, and now that it was actually thrust upon him it seemed false, impossible, a parody of what he'd dreamed about. It was the wrong time. Barbara led him by the hand, it made him feel slightly foolish, like a child being pulled through a dangerous intersection.

Michael swung around on the piano bench and got up, came to intercept them. Barbara ignored him, pulled Mark into the kitchen. The swinging door banged shut behind them.

"Where are we going?" Mark said.

"I don't know, I don't care," Barbara said. She fumbled through the pile of coats on the table. The kitchen was warm, smelled of baking and spices. Barbara yanked a blue-and-green down jacket out of the pile and pulled into it.

The door swung half open and Michael poked his head in. "There's no problem here, is there?" he said.

"No, everybody's fine," Barbara said. Mark stared at the pegboard on the wall with its lists, schedules, pictures, family reminders.

"O.K. I was just checking." Michael gave them a bright, false, helpless smile and the door shut again.

"Let's go," Barbara said. Mark turned to her. There was something hard, demanding, unpleasant in her voice.

She went to the door, opened it. She was waiting for him. Mark stared at her, the ability to act at all clamped tight for a second, and then he followed her.

They walked out of the house, down into the snow. The children stopped their play. Sarah started to run toward them, but then halted, confused. Barbara moved quickly, head down, walking, then running, to Mark's car. Mark loped to catch up with her.

They got into the car. Four or five people had come out on the porch to watch.

Mark looked across the car at Barbara. She was looking down, concentrating on buttoning her jacket.

"Just go, go, please," she said.

Mark put the key in the ignition, started the car. The tires crunched on the new snow as he turned the car around. Mark saw that Rob was on the porch now. Rob came down into the yard, waving at them.

"Just go, now," Barbara said.

Mark headed the car slowly down the road. They were both silent. Mark could feel the anger building inside him. What was she thinking? Was this for real or was she just infected by Kate's theatricality, was she just trying to upstage the rest of them? Did she think she could have Mark back, just like that, just for the asking? Did she think she could have him back, after all that had gone before, after Sarah's rescue, after Ellen, after the renunciation of all this that day in New York? It made him angry if she could think that.

He looked across at her. Her arms were folded tight across her chest. He remembered why he had come. She could be dying, he thought. His heart went out to her again.

He pressed slowly on the brake, pumping it lightly so they wouldn't skid on the new snow. The car came to a stop. When Mark turned off the ignition, she glanced sideways at him. At the top of the rise, where the dirt road met the highway, there was a pickup parked on the shoulder. A red-jacketed hunter stood like a sentinel, his rifle at his side.

"Why are we stopping?" she said.

"We're stopping because I don't know what we're doing." Mark pulled the keys out of the ignition, closed them in his fist. Barbara stared at him full-faced now, alarmed. "Do *you* know?"

She turned away suddenly, pressed her forehead to the glass, said nothing for several seconds.

"It's just that nothing ever ends, Mark," she said finally. "It goes on and on. How many times do we have to repeat all this? I don't know if anything more has really happened between them, but I'm so tired of it. Nothing is ever over. I feel like such a fool. I thought it could all be reversed, stop, begin again, a virtuous life, innocence reestablished . . . I thought we were all going to get away with it, sneak in under the bell. Now I see that no one gets away with anything. I thought we were all going to get off cheaply."

"What do you mean, 'cheaply'?" Mark said. The snow was gathering on the windshield, shutting them in. Mark could feel the cold rising through the floorboards.

"This summer when Sarah was lost," Barbara said, "I knew that only one thing mattered, and that was that my child was safe. For that one thing I was ready to sacrifice anything, sacrifice you, Mark . . . sacrifice the love I had for you . . . but that was still getting off cheaply. To have your face rubbed again and again in the mess that you've made . . . She wanted me to forgive her, Mark, can you believe that? As if being forgiven was no more than being excused from the table. I don't have the energy, Mark, I'm a sick person . . ."

"I know," Mark said. "That was why I came."

"I'll be all right. You can't believe in doctors anyway." She shifted in her seat, jammed her hands in her pockets against the cold. After a second she pulled a set of keys out of the left pocket and examined them. "Look at that. It's not even my coat."

"Whose is it then?"

"It must be Judy's. They look like her keys. Can you believe it? Here I am running off and I can't even find my own coat. I guess that just goes to show how interchangeable we all are, doesn't it?" She dropped the keys back into her pocket and smiled at Mark. "You know, it's funny. I always had the fantasy that you would deliver me. And now that we have our chance we can't figure out where to go."

"I suppose because there is nowhere," Mark said. Snow blew across the pastures, building into drifts. The windshield was almost covered with snow, all that was left was an oval of clear glass. Mark braced himself against the steering wheel, the plastic cold to the touch. "I'm not going to run off with you. I care for you, I do, I want you to be well . . ." He pounded the steering wheel with the palm of his hand. "It's hard to say these things right. I'm not going to leave Ellen. I'm not giving that up. Can you understand that?" She said nothing. "Remember what you told me? When we were in New York. I did what you told me. Full speed ahead, you said, no backward glances."

"Of course I remember," she said.

"When I heard that you were sick I got panicky, but I didn't know if I should come see you or not."

She smiled at him, he could see her breath in the air. "You haven't done anything wrong. You did what your heart told you, coming to see me, it's not so terrible. And your heart tells you not to leave her, that's not so terrible either. It makes a lot of sense to me."

The hunter still stood at the top of the road, next to his pickup. He had scarcely moved, his hat down over his face, hands in his pockets, gun hanging under one arm, a dark, hunched figure. Barbara stared at him.

"Another trespasser," she said. "I suppose I'll have to tell Ike. The place is posted, but we always have trouble this time of year.

People just don't pay attention to signs anymore. I wonder why that is. I guess the fines aren't high enough to discourage anybody." She reached across, ran the back of her hand along his cheek. "I'm glad you said what you said. I have a lot of affection for you."

"And I have a lot of affection for you," he said.

"Oh, God," she said. "It's a bit embarrassing, isn't it? Now I know why I've always avoided making scenes. God knows what the kids are thinking right now. I've got my work cut out for me. I'll have to pacify Kate, shore up Rob, put on a little song and dance for the guests. I don't know what's wrong with me. For one moment in that room I just felt so trapped, like there was no hope. I felt so doomed, as if everything was just collapsing around me. That's why I always liked being around you. I never felt doomed when I was around you."

The windows on her side were solid with snow, framing her auburn hair. White enclosed them like a cave.

"I'm going to be all right," she said. "Don't worry about me." Barbara rolled down her window. For a second there was a fragile wall of snow free-standing above the lowered pane of glass, but Barbara brushed it away. Together they looked out across the pastures at the massive slopes of the mountains, their tops hidden in cloud and blowing snow.

"I should go back now," she said.

"I'll drive you," he said.

"No, you go on. It will be easier this way. I'd rather have a moment by myself."

"Sure," he said.

She opened the door and stepped outside without looking back at him. She slammed the door shut and began walking away. It was too abrupt. Mark opened his door quickly and stood, panicking again.

"Hey," he said. "Barbara Campbell." She stopped and looked over her shoulder. She was red-faced, crying. Mark could see the house behind her, all lit up, lights blazing through the falling snow.

He walked slowly to her, took her in his arms. She let him hold her only for a second. She pulled away, looking down at the brilliantly lit-up house. "It's just so hard," she said.

"I know."

"Can you understand why I chose this?"

"Of course."

She was standing free of him now. Mark could feel the whipping snow sting his face. "When I first saw that house I thought it was the most beautiful spot in the world. I thought of putting children in that house and all our friends, filling it to the rafters. We have had wonderful times, we have."

"I know. Come here," he said. "You've got snow in your hair." She came to him again and he brushed the snow away. He wanted to hold her now, shelter her. She embraced him, holding tight, resting for a second, her face hidden by his coat. When she pulled back Mark raised the hood of her jacket, Judy's jacket. He pulled the drawstrings tight.

"I have to go back now," she said.

"I know," Mark said. He made a bow with the strings, pulled it tight. She turned and started walking.

It was time for Mark to go now too, just go, not to think anymore about it. Barbara was twenty yards down the road. How could he tell Ellen any of this? He would go see her, stop by at the end of her class and watch them all work, that's what he would do. Ellen would be glad to see him, he would go and watch her dance.

He kicked at the snow with his boot, and turned toward the car.

The mountains had disappeared, obliterated by cloud and driving snow. It was coming down so hard now Tommy could barely see fifty yards down the highway, all the boundaries were gone. He drove slowly, concentrating on keeping the pickup in the middle of the road. He was in no hurry. His rifle rested in the rack behind his head, the gun metal and dark wood straight as a rule against the white window.

He imagined what it would be like walking in, he imagined the look of surprise on Rob's face. Tommy knew what they'd think, but they'd be wrong. He didn't want Judy back, no matter what they thought. He knew he'd lost whatever claim he'd had.

But when he got out there he could see from the road that there were all kinds of cars around the house. It looked like a convention. It was more than Tommy had bargained for. He pulled his pickup off to the side of the road. He'd have to think about this.

A truck drove by with an elk draped across the hood, dried blood black around the gaping mouth, snow caked and matted on the brown coat. Tommy waved to the hunters and they waved back, victorious. For hunters, at least, it was a good day. The first good day they had had.

The snow was driving the animals down out of the high country,

and if it kept up the elk would be coming like a hungry river. The
hunters had been waiting all fall for this. Tommy stared down at
the house set back a half mile from the road. It looked like they
had every light in the whole place on.

He wondered what it was like in there. There was probably a big
fire in the fireplace. People with houses like that always had roaring
fires. Tommy had a picture of it in his mind. He realized he probably got it from some scotch ad. He imagined the piano there, newly
set down in front of the blazing fireplace, the scotch drinkers with
their elbows up on it. Maybe Judy was playing for them. He remembered how she looked when she was playing, how concen-
trated, how absorbed, how beautiful it made her. He could imagine
how beautiful it could make her to a guy warmed by a couple of
scotches and a blazing fire.

One of those guys, Tommy could just see how it would happen, a
lawyer or a land developer, a smooth-talking guy in a ski sweater
and red plaid pants, would ask Rob or Michael who she was and
was she available. The story would come back. Probably Rob
would tell it, about the crazy husband, the lunatic riverboat guide,
and how Judy had been lucky to get out of there alive, and then
the story of how Rob and Michael had lifted the piano would come
up and they'd all have a good laugh. The guy in the ski sweater
and the red plaid pants would get perked up after that, watching
her face softened by the glow from the fireplace, and when she
finished playing he'd go over and compliment her on her music,
flirt a little, take a little chance, hell, she was an attractive woman
and she wasn't with anybody.

A couple more pickups whizzed by, chains clinking in the snow.
Hunters, Tommy could tell by their orange fluorescent hats. Only
hunters would be crazy enough to be out on a day like this. Tommy
turned on his engine to get the heater going, but it really didn't
help much. His feet were numb with the cold. Tommy got out his
flask, opened it with one strong twist, and took a swig. The Bourbon burned for a second and then he hunched forward, staring out
at the distant house, his hands pressed between his thighs. Then
suddenly he pushed the door open and swung down into the snow,
slamming the door shut behind him.

He knew why he'd come. It wasn't because of any broken lamp
or stolen piano. Those people had interfered in the holiest thing in
a man's life, his marriage. If it hadn't been for them, he'd still be
with Judy. It was a simple fact. He'd come real close to getting her

back that afternoon in the summer, she'd been ready to come with him, and then Rob stopped her. A simple fact. These people didn't know what honoring a marriage meant. They didn't know how things were done out here, but he'd show them. The West had changed a lot, but not as much as they thought. There was still a code, whether they knew it or not.

If she was messing with someone down there, Tommy wanted to know who. The thought of it sickened him. If only he could see.

Tommy reached back up into the truck and yanked his rifle off the rack. He raised it to his shoulder, sighted down the telescope. The lens magnified everything, it brought him up real close. He could make out the slats on the house, the lights inside seemed even brighter. The delicate crosshairs floated from window to window. He could see the shadows of people moving inside the curtains, but he still could not see enough.

It occurred to him how simple it would be to put a light out in one of the upstairs windows. Nobody would get hurt, it wouldn't be anything but a calling card. He could be in his truck and out of there in seconds. Only those people who needed to know would understand what had happened. Then Tommy thought, No, that's too crazy, that would be acting just the way they expect me to act. He lowered the rifle, rested it on his hip. His face was stiffening from the cold.

Then he saw two people run out of the house and get into a car. There was some commotion on the porch and then the car pulled down the road, coming toward Tommy. It stopped a hundred yards away.

It looked like Mark's car, but Tommy wasn't quite sure. He shifted his weight from one foot to the other, trying to stay warm. The rifle stayed down at his side.

Tommy was puzzled. He didn't understand why the car had stopped. If it was Mark, maybe Mark had recognized him. But why should Mark stop? Unless he was afraid of Tommy for some reason.

A woman got out of the car. Even at a football-field distance away Tommy could recognize Judy's blue-and-green jacket. He felt his chest tighten in pain. Part of him refused to believe what he was seeing.

Judy walked back toward the house. When the tall man got out of the car Tommy saw that it was Mark, there was no mistake.

The snow whipping across the flats made Tommy turn his back for a second, stung tears to his eyes. Even through the curtains of blowing snow there could be no mistake. Judy stopped on the road, turned and came back to Mark, embraced him. Mark tied the strings on Judy's hood.

Mark. Why not? Why should he be better than any of the others? Tommy didn't want to believe it, but anyone was capable of anything, that was one thing Tommy had learned.

Standing motionless in the snow, staring down at the two figures embracing next to the car, Tommy began to remember things from way back, memory worked like poison in the blood, quickening everything. He remembered how they had always liked one another, how Mark and Judy would sit up and talk after Tommy had gone to bed. Judy said she just felt motherly toward Mark, felt as if he needed someone to take care of him. Motherly, hell, Judy had introduced Mark to Ellen because she said he needed to meet some nice women, that was no accident, that was just part of the smokescreen. It wasn't any scotch drinker in red plaid pants you needed to worry about, it was your best friend.

There was nothing hidden now. He had to give them credit, it took a lot of balls to stand there next to the car, knowing that he was watching them, a lot of balls to embrace like that, a hundred yards away, like they were high-school sweethearts, saying goodbye after the prom. What they didn't have the guts for was facing him.

The wind picked up swirls of snow off the flats, sent giant white ghost columns fifty feet high chasing across the highway. Judy walked back toward the house again. She gave no sign of even recognizing Tommy. She knew he was there. It wasn't right. It was more than anyone could take. There had to be some kind of justice, somehow.

Tommy raised his rifle. Mark was in his scope, the crosshairs fixed in the middle of Mark's dirty blue jacket. Tommy meant to wait until Mark turned completely around, till they were face to face, so Mark would know what it was for, but his hands were clumsy with the cold, he had no feel, his finger was tightening on its own, the shot went off before he meant it to.

The blast knocked Mark spinning into a snowdrift.

Judy was fifty yards down the road when she heard the shot. She ran back toward him. Mark rolled over, pushed up with one arm, then fell again. Tommy stood watching for a second, a statue of ice, then slowly lowered his rifle. Judy didn't acknowledge him; it was as if he didn't exist for her, and then Tommy saw that it wasn't

Judy at all, it was some other woman, some stranger, standing over Mark and screaming at Tommy.

Tommy turned and ran for his pickup. One person and then another came out on the porch of the house. Tommy tried to gun the pickup out onto the highway, but he was in too much of a hurry and the truck fishtailed in the snow, angled into a steep embankment. The tires whined, spinning uselessly as Tommy tried to rock the pickup free.

Tommy gave up, leaped from the truck and began to run across the open fields, heading for the distant trees and the river. The guests lined the porch of the blazing house like people lined up on the deck of a ship, pointed out toward the road and the man plunging through the white crust of snow, making great holes as he lunged forward, falling and rising again, like a wild animal racing for refuge.

CHAPTER THIRTY-THREE

When Mark awakened there was a plastic cup over his mouth and there was a low roaring sound, like something moving under the sea, coming and going. He realized that it was the sound of his own breathing, magnified. Above him there were bottles hanging from slender metal poles. He tried to move, but he couldn't. He was strapped down and there were plastic tubes in his arms and there was a sharp pain across his chest like a runner's pain you get when you're out of shape. But this pain wouldn't go away. There were masked faces above him, faces wrapped in tight white cloth like bandits. He didn't recognize any of them. They were asking him questions or themselves questions, he couldn't tell which. He felt himself slipping down again, disappearing under the sea.

The second time he woke, the respirator was still over his nose and mouth and a doctor was explaining all that had happened. The doctor moved a lot when he explained things, he had a springy, athletic step, a skier's tan. Mark tried to listen, nodding even at the things he didn't understand. He was still scared and woozy, but it felt good just to be talked to.

Mark had been very lucky, the doctor said. The bullet had collapsed a lung and ruptured his spleen. With a bullet that size, you had to consider that lucky, minimal damage.

The lung had been pumped up and was functioning. They'd had to operate to remove the spleen. It wasn't as serious as it sounded, the doctor said; it wasn't as serious as a bypass, say. The spleen filters poisons out of the blood, the doctor went on, but adults can function perfectly well without it. "Blood's tough," the doctor said. Mark didn't know what he meant. "I'll tell you," the doctor said, "if I were you, I'd feel like I came out of this with flying colors."

Mark turned his head to one side, saw that he was rigged up to a machine. A tiny green light fuzzed and jumped as it moved across the screen. Mark didn't know what the green light meant, but he was too tired to ask. The doctor smiled reassuringly. The doctor looked like he was in very good shape.

"I'll be back," the doctor said.

Mark slept and woke briefly and slept again. He had no idea what day it was. He knew that the painkillers were keeping him down under. He wanted desperately to get his mind clear. Everything was strange, there was no one here he knew. He had been shot, but he didn't know why or by whom. He remembered the hunter standing beside the pickup, he remembered saying goodbye to Barbara, he remembered the snow. The doctor said they had removed some part of his body, he couldn't remember which. He wondered if he would be able to feel it, the void, the absence, the rearrangement of his insides. There were bandages wrapped tightly around his chest.

The first face he recognized was the nurse who came to wheel him out of the Intensive Care Unit up to a regular room. She was the mother of one of Mark's students, Mark had met her once at a Parents' Night. Her son had the bad habit of forging excuses from home. She and Mark had had a good talk about it. When they got up to Mark's room and she got Mark propped up in his new bed Mark said, "I don't know what happened to me. I haven't had the chance to talk to anyone. Can you tell me?"

The nurse was fluffing up a pillow for him. She set the pillow down. She looked a little frightened and confused. "You'll have to talk to the doctor," she said. "The doctor will be in this afternoon."

Mark slept again until the nurses woke him up to feed him, and after that the doctor came back. The doctor seemed to be in an even better mood. He looked at Mark's stitches, asked a series of

questions, asked if Mark was feeling comfortable with his breathing. Pretty much, Mark said, though there were still pains across his
chest. Like runners' pains, he said.

The doctor smiled. "That's perfectly normal," he said. "Actually, the pain's not really coming from where it seems to be coming
from. It's what they call referred pain."

"Never heard of it," Mark said.

The doctor scribbled something on Mark's chart. "It's just that
your inner organs aren't used to feeling pain, so when they do your
brain gets the signals all mixed up, misinterprets . . . I think you're
doing reasonably well, though." The doctor looked at his watch.
"This will be the last time I'll be seeing you. No cause to worry,
though. There will be another doctor coming in, I've told him
everything there is to tell."

"What's happening to you?"

"I'm flying back to Denver this afternoon."

"You're not from here?"

"No, I just came in as a favor. I thought you knew that."

"I don't know anything."

"It doesn't matter. You're doing fine."

The medication kept sending him back to sleep and he dreamed
constantly, furiously. The sounds of the hospital, meal carts rolling
past, announcements booming over the public-address system,
wove in and out of his dreams.

He dreamed that his father and Barbara and Ellen were all in a
car and it was snowing and Mark knew it was too dangerous to be
going anywhere, the pass was closed, he wanted to warn them, but
he couldn't get their attention, he was scratching at the windows of
the car. He dreamed that someone had put a watch under his pillow, it was his birthday and he could turn the stem and get any
part of his life, it would appear in the face of the watch, he could
turn it to Ellen, to Barbara, turn it back to his childhood. That
dream turned into another. He dreamed he was home, in New Jersey, on the street where he'd grown up, only the light was like the
light of the Tetons, it made everything beautiful and there were all
these houses to explore, it was endless, and Mark knew that the
only condition was that he would have to explore them alone.

He woke at the sound of a doctor being paged and he was sweating all over. He was angry too. Where was Ellen? She was supposed to be here by now, she was late. He wondered if she'd been
held up, maybe her rehearsal had run over, that was just like her

. . . Then he remembered where he was and why she wasn't there. Then he heard someone cough softly.

"I hope I didn't wake you," Rob said.

"No," Mark said. Rob stood up, came to the foot of the bed. Mark couldn't tell what Rob was going to do. Rob scrutinized Mark, not saying anything, Rob lifted the edge of the blanket, pulled it up a little on Mark, let it fall.

"I understand that you're doing well."

"How do you understand that?"

"I talked to the doctor. He's an old friend of mine. I wanted him to make sure that you were in the best hands available."

"Ah." Mark saw that there was a bouquet of slightly withered flowers on the windowsill. He didn't remember them being there before.

Rob poured a glass of ice water. "Do you want some water?"

"No, thanks."

Rob drank slowly, deliberately. Mark watched his every move. Rob set the glass back down on the bedside table.

"I'm going to be picking up the bills for this, so don't you worry about it."

"I've got insurance."

"Not this kind of insurance," Rob said. Rob went to the window. "Is it warm in here? You want me to open this for you?"

"No, I'm fine." Two nurses walked past the open door, laughing. Rob went to the door, shut it gently, turned back to Mark, his face clouded, somber.

"It was our fault, you see," Rob said. "When you get right down to it. If we hadn't acted like children this wouldn't have happened. Things just got out of control. Barbara was upset, we were all upset. It's one of those freak things. You never figure it's going to happen to you. We knew Tommy was dangerous, but we had no idea he was *that* dangerous."

"Tommy? What do you mean, Tommy?"

"Tommy was the one who shot you." Mark just stared at Rob. "You didn't know that? How could you not know? Good God, yes, Tommy. Who did you think it was?"

"I don't know. I thought it might have been some hunter. I thought it might have been you."

Rob looked at Mark for a second, contemplating, then snorted, turned away, rubbed a clear spot on the frosted window and peered out. "No, Tommy."

"But why?"

"I don't know. Maybe he doesn't know. You know how jealous he was of Judy. You can imagine what jealousy could do to a guy like that." Rob sat back down in the chair in the corner. He sighed wearily, rubbed the cheap covering on the arms of the chair. "Michael and I did a stupid thing, it was intended as a prank. We went out and took Judy's piano out of Tommy's house when he wasn't there. That was provocation enough, I suppose."

"You're sure it was him?"

"There's no question." Mark felt as if he was sliding down into a deep hole. They had all come down together, he and Tommy and all the others. Why hadn't Ellen come to see him? Damn her. "They had to track him down, it was pretty easy with all that new snow. They found him on one of those little islands out there in the river. He didn't fight them at all, he didn't deny anything."

"What will they do to him?"

"I don't know. That's for the lawyers and you to decide."

Mark tried to push himself up in the bed, pain stabbed across his chest. "Are you here by yourself?"

Rob knew perfectly well what Mark was asking. He stood up and wrapped his hands around the metal end of the bed.

"Barbara and the children flew back this morning. The children have school. Barbara said to give you her best." Rob straightened up, his face tightened. "We had a long talk last night, Barbara and I. There's nothing about the two of you I don't know now." Mark said nothing. He couldn't tell if Rob was lying or not. "If you weren't in a hospital bed, I'd beat the shit out of you." Rob turned away. "We're going to be all right. You may think you understand her needs better than I do, but you don't . . . I've lived with her for thirteen years. I love her very much and she loves me. I don't think we're going to be coming back here. Jeff was talking about wanting to go to Europe next summer. I think that might be a real good idea. This place is such a monstrosity to keep up and nobody really wants us here anyway. The National Park keeps pressuring us to get out. Who knows? Maybe we might just oblige them. Is there a piece of paper around here?"

"Sure. In the drawer there, under the table."

Rob yanked open the drawer, took out the pad of paper, quickly scrawled something across it, tore off the top sheet and handed it to Mark.

"I'm going to leave you this number to call in case you have any

problems. I don't think you will have. I've taken care of everything
I could." Mark folded the piece of paper in half, not looking at
Rob. "You've diminished us," Rob said. "I want you to know that,
that you've diminished our lives. I want you to get well. More
suffering isn't going to solve anything. Some people see value in it,
I don't. I don't want you to suffer, I don't want Barbara to suffer. I
just want it all to end."

After Rob had gone, Mark crumpled the piece of paper and
threw it against the wall.

Three times he tried to call Ellen and three times there was no
answer. First he was angry and then he was worried. He imagined
her just taking off, doing something crazy. He wouldn't be able to
blame her.

They wanted him on his feet as fast as possible. In the after-
noon a nurse came in with a walker. As she helped him out of bed
Mark felt the blood rush to his head. It was scary to feel so weak.
The nurse was very firm with him, there would be no turning back.
The sooner he was on his feet, the sooner he'd be getting well.

They made their way together up the hallway, the nurse with a
supporting hand on Mark's back. Mark felt slightly ridiculous, like
a kid on his first bicycle, needing to be held up. It wasn't as ridiculous as it looked. Even the tiny shuffling steps he took sent prickly
pains shooting across his back. They stood for a second so Mark
could tighten his bathrobe around him. Mark saw the nurses behind the desk turn and smile, their eyes alert with curiosity. He was
a celebrity. They'd all heard the story, Mark was sure of it.

Mark's nurse stayed patiently behind him. She was a stern, out-
doorsy woman. Mark felt she didn't approve of him. He could guess
the reasons. In silence they moved up the broad, glistening hallway.
There was the smell of antiseptic.

"Let me ask you a question," Mark said. He picked up his
walker, set it six inches forward, shuffled to meet it. "There wasn't
a woman that came by here anytime, was there? Late twenties,
short haircut, looks like a dancer. Very straight-backed."

"There may have been somebody yesterday," the nurse said.
"There was somebody yesterday. But you were asleep."

"Ah-hah," Mark said.

They stood in front of the windows to the maternity ward. "I'm
sure she'll be back," the nurse said.

"I'm not so sure," Mark said. He leaned forward on the walker, stared in the window at the cribs, at the newborn infants wrapped in their blankets.

"This is about long enough," the nurse said. "We can turn back now."

"If it's all right with you," Mark said, "I'll stay here for just a minute." The nurse regarded him dubiously. "Look, I've got the hang of it, clank and shuffle, I've conquered the thing."

"You're ready to go on your own?"

"I think I'd better learn."

"I'll be at the nurses' station if you need me," she said. She patted his walker twice, as if wishing him good luck, and strode off.

There were a half-dozen newborns in the maternity ward. One was all red and screaming, its fists clenched tight. Another, next to it, with a little shriveled monkey face, was just blinking and looking around.

At the far end of the window were a couple of new parents. They stared down at their daughter on the other side of the glass, a peacefully sleeping baby with a pink bow taped to her hair. The mother was young, in her early twenties, in a robe and slippers. The father was tall and goofy-looking, his tie pulled loose, he was pale from fatigue. They both looked shyly over at Mark at the same time.

"That's your baby?" Mark asked.

They nodded.

"She's the most beautiful one in there," Mark said. They smiled gratefully at him, then looked back at their child, mesmerized by her, as the baby moved slightly in its sleep.

Mark turned away, headed up the hallway, thinking that he might weep right there, but not wanting to, not wanting to be weak and a spectacle, a monster weeping at the sight of innocence.

He didn't care if Ellen came or not. He'd been alone before, he'd done all right. He would learn to live alone. A wilderness freak, that's what he was meant to be all along. People like him should be alone. He'd made an unholy mess out of things, but he wasn't sorry, not at all. At least he'd acted on what he'd felt, that was more than most people could say.

He clanked his way past the nurses' station. One of the nurses smiled at him, clutching a clipboard to her chest. Mark didn't smile back, just looked down, banging the walker along the tiles. He could feel the pain begin again.

It would be a lot easier if she didn't come. He didn't want people feeling sorry for him. Make a nice, clean break, they'd never had a chance anyway, that had all been an illusion.

Talking to himself in this way, a second voice crept in to challenge the first: you're ashamed, admit it, ashamed and embarrassed, just like a little kid. You snuck out on her, never told her where you were going. You call that bravery? Think what she must feel right now. She leaves you for a day and the next thing she knows you've been shot in some tangle with your supposedly ex-lover.

Then the unrepentant voice came back in: O.K., I'm a fool, I'm not denying it, I'm no good for anybody up close. Even if she comes, I don't want to see her. I'll learn how to walk again and then I'll learn how to get on by myself, how to avoid idiocy. The back country, here I come.

Mark looked up. Ellen stood in the doorway of his room. She must have watched him come all the way down the hall. Her face was tight with emotion. In her hand she carried flowers, wrapped in a long cone of bright paper. It was what she would do, even now, Mark thought, her sense of what was right carrying her through. She always brought flowers to people in the hospital, you could count on it.

For several seconds neither of them moved, withholding and wary as animals. Mark lurched the walker forward to meet her. She did not reach out to touch him.

"I'm glad you came," he said. "I tried to call you. I was worried."

"I was here before," she said. Her voice was tired and distant. "The evening they operated on you I was here all night."

He reached out to touch her, but she pushed his hand away. He stared at her for a second.

"Why don't we walk?" he said.

They moved up the hallway side by side, not looking at one another. They passed half-open doorways; inside, figures gathered around a bed, consoling shadows bent forward.

"She was here that night too," Ellen said.

"Did you speak to her?"

"Yes." Ellen put her hand on the back of her neck, her head bowed. Mark could see her struggling. "When someone came into the rehearsal hall and said that you'd been shot I thought it was some horrible joke. I knew it was impossible, I'd just left you, I knew that you were home, correcting papers . . ." She shook her head, fighting off tears, looked quickly at him. "I don't know how I'm supposed to understand this."

"I'll tell you whatever you want to know," Mark said. She said nothing. The hallways were wide and gleaming, they looked freshly waxed. "I had no idea the Campbells were even out here," Mark said. "And then I ran into Judy in the store. She was the one who told me. She was the one who told me that Barbara had been ill, no one was sure how ill. I thought I might never see her again. And I wanted to see her."

"Why couldn't you have told me that?"

"Because I thought it would hurt you. Because I thought there were things I couldn't tell you . . ."

"Not till now."

"Not till now. Ellen, I'm sorry."

"And what is going to happen now?"

"I don't know. Nothing, unless we want it to."

Mark could see the color rising in her face. She still clutched the flowers, too angry to give them to him. "Nothing, except that I've been forced to swallow it all one more time. This is very painful, Mark. I feel as if I've had no choices in any of this. It's all in your ballpark. How do I know you're not going back to her, or to someone like her? I feel as if this is going to be part of us for a long time."

They had come to the end of the hallway. Mark felt darkness welling up within him. He wanted to say a thousand things at once: that he was sorry, that he knew he'd failed not just one person, but many, that what he'd done was not acceptable, and yet beneath all that, running like a chill, fast stream, was the fear that he couldn't have acted any differently, that he wasn't even able to repudiate what he had done and even with all that fear in him he knew he had to change, he wanted to change. All that he could bring himself to say was, "I need you, you know that." She said nothing, turning away from him. "I know I'm in a lousy position to convince you of anything right now, but I'm going to work to get you back, I'm going to earn it. You watch me."

She said nothing for several seconds, unyielding. She set the wrapped flowers down on the ledge of the window. "If anyone like that ever comes into our lives again, I will know who she is," Ellen said.

Mark stared out the window, looking out across the elk refuge. A light snow was falling again. Mark saw small dark clumps out on the white flats. For a moment he was confused, he didn't understand what he was looking at, and then he saw one of the clumps move.

"Come here," he said. Ellen didn't hear him. "Come here," he repeated. Ellen raised her head. He pointed out at the refuge. "They've come through. They made it. The odds can't be any worse for us."

Ellen stood with her arms still folded close to her body. Together they watched the small bands of elk moving across the snow-covered flats, the animals that had come through the gauntlet, come to safety. Mark picked up the wrapped flowers from the ledge.

"Let's see what you've brought," he said.

He unwrapped the paper and lifted out a pair of red roses. He fingered the flowers for a second, stared at her. "I love you, Ellen," he said. He set the roses down on the ledge. "I'm sorry." New snow danced and swirled outside the window. "Jesus, Ellen, please come here."

He reached out for her then, took her hand and pulled her to him. Her head was still turned away from him, but he held her to him, burying his face in her hair. The two flowers sat on the ledge, a brilliant red against the cold glass and the white of the endlessly streaming snow.

She reached up finally, holding him back, her hands tracing slow circles over the tightly wound bandages, over the wound. When she began to cry it was silently, the only way he knew she was weeping at all was by the convulsions of her body against his own.